I opened the shi.. her hit-you-over-the-head-jasmine and patchouli-laced perfume with my name scrawled across in red Sharpie, and took out the matching equally noxious notecard:

Sarah,

I'm sure even you will have to agree that you've become insufferable to live with. These last several months with you have been an unrelenting nightmare. I can no longer tolerate your selfishness, total lack of consideration, and socially unacceptable behavior. Both my parents and therapist agree living with you is toxic to my mental, physical, and emotional well-being. So, at great personal emotional expense, I have devoted considerable time and energy to pack up all your things—except your leather jacket, which has always looked better on me. I am sure you will agree that giving it to me is the least that you can do given that I will have to pay the full month's rent until I can find another roommate since you are leaving without notice.

You can come up for your furniture only when your movers are here. I do not feel safe having you back in the apartment given your inclinations to vengeful outbursts. I hope you will take this as a wake-up call to get the help you need. I am worried about you—Desiree.

The Rise, Fall, and Return of Sarah Mandelbaum

by

Cara Kagan

The Rise, Fall, and Return of Sarah Mandelbaum

COPYRIGHT © 2023 by Cara Kagan

Cover Art by *Lea Schizas*

The Wild Rose Press, Inc.
PO Box 708
Adams Basin, NY 14410-0708
Visit us at www.thewildrosepress.com

Publishing History
First Edition, 2023
Trade Paperback ISBN 978-1-5092-4890-2
Digital ISBN 978-1-5092-4891-9

Published in the United States of America

Dedication

For my amazing husband, Andrew Kagan, my friends and family who never stopped believing that Sarah could sing, and all those fabulous souls out there who let their natural hair fly free.

Acknowledgments

I'd like to thank The Wild Rose Press and its editor-in-chief, Rhonda Penders, for taking a chance on this first-time author and expertly guiding me through this process. I also can't say enough about my amazingly talented and supportive editor, Lea Schizas, for her brilliance and cheerleading. A big thank you also to NYC's Gotham Writers Workshop and Catapult for helping me to create and refine my first drafts, to my buddy Susan Elman for reading every one of them, author Elias Lindert for painstakingly editing initial versions, Matthew Bialer for his expert insight, and my teacher, author Lucy Chan for helping to realize Sarah's full potential. And I would especially like to thank my wonderful husband Andrew Kagan for giving me the time, support, and freedom to embark on this amazing journey.

Chapter 1

"OhmyGod. OhmyGod. You are so good. *So good.* You are amazing!"

Even with the covers pulled over my head, it was like my roommate, Desiree Dershowitz (her real name) was in bed with me rather than in the next room. Des was going at it full force for the sixth or seventh night in a row with something like the sixth or seventh different guy this week. And aspiring actor that she was, tonight Des seemed to be putting on an even bigger show than usual, which to me meant the sex probably wasn't all that great. And I knew I was correct in my assumption when the wheedling started, a sure sign she wanted more gratification.

"Aren't we gorgeous together?" she coaxed, her voice somehow dripping persuasive honey and cautionary poison at the same time. "Don't you think we're a perfect fit?"

I almost felt sorry for the poor bastard in bed with her. He had no idea that at any minute, Des might send her CD player flying in his general direction or start shrieking at him for not worshiping her enough. Thankfully, the VCR was across the room and safe from her outbursts. Last night, it'd been her bedside lamp that had shorted out as the force of her fury had smashed it. I felt lucky this bit of her pique hadn't set the apartment on fire. But it *was* likely that one day

Desiree Dershowitz would spontaneously erupt into flames and take me down with her.

I rolled over to turn on my bedside lamp (thankfully still in one piece) to scan the clock and grab my Camel Lights. Damn her. It was 3 a.m. and mysteriously there were only two cigarettes in the half a pack I had left before I went to work this morning. Desiree strikes again. I was mostly a social smoker, but there was no denying my life sucked right now, and I deserved a cigarette. I was twenty-five-years old and sharing a one-bedroom apartment with a sex-crazed lunatic because there was no way my pathetic salary as the beauty products/features editor at the Fashion Daily Gazette (FDG) could pay for me to have my own place in NYC and cover my student loans. Even splitting a place with Des was a struggle, and I was barely on time with my half of the rent. Luckily, Desiree's parents held the lease, paid in full every month, and didn't seem to mind if I got them my check late. In fact, they'd pleaded with me to move in with her the last summer I worked as a receptionist at our dads' law firm.

Throughout the five winter breaks and summers I worked there, Des would kind of breeze in and out of the office and pretend to do some of her assigned projects before leaving for an "audition," which seemed really cool to me even if I was stuck picking up her slack. At least she was pursuing her art—something I didn't have the stones to do. And she was fun and funny—charismatic in her wild way. And since I was living at the time with my mother, Anna Elias Mandelbaum, in our small apartment in New Jersey, I agreed. Sadly, I didn't know, and no one cared to bring it to my attention, that Des, who had been living in that apartment since she was an undergrad at NYU drama school, hadn't kept a roommate for more than three months. Her parents were likely ecstatic they'd suckered me into signing a three-year contract with them to foot half the bill on this obscenely expensive apartment with their deranged daughter. At the time, it seemed like insurance to me that I'd have a place to live in the East Village where all the music was for the foreseeable future.

And if I started to think about how I ended up at FDG in the first place and why I was no longer a reporter at *40 Days & 40 Nights* magazine or playing music instead of writing about it, I might fling a clock radio across the room myself. I took a drag and was about to reach for my George Harrison *All Things Must Pass* tape to pop into my Walkman to drown out what I assumed would be more sex theatrics—gorgeous George was the only man who could get me through a night like this—but Desiree had other ideas.

"What are you, an animal? You should be on your knees thanking me for letting you in my bed." She was screaming now. I heard a few masculine pleadings in response. It was late and this guy likely was drunk and didn't want to get out of a nice, warm bed to shuffle on home—wherever that was. But I knew his response wasn't going to be enough to placate her. If I were going to get any sleep at all, I had to act fast. I threw off the yellow butterfly quilt that I'd been sleeping with since the sixth grade, strode across the floor, and knocked on the wall our rooms shared—just like I'd done practically every night for months on end.

"Des, come on. It's three in the morning. We've been through this before, repeatedly." I heard her mattress springs squeak and then the clicking of her high-heeled, hot pink marabou mules down the hall to my room. She half-shimmied, half-slithered in through the door without knocking, naked as usual and waxed within an inch of her life, her shoulder-length ash blonde hair artfully disheveled, and her face, including the perfectly pert nose her parents had bought her in junior high school, rosy, glistening from sex.

"Oh, honey. I'm so sorry," she cajoled, as if realizing at least for the moment that it was unlikely she'd ever find another roommate to split a two thousand dollars-a-month one-bedroom apartment with her nymphomaniac, sociopathic self.

"Seriously, Des, this has to stop." God help me but I felt myself channeling my mother, Anna Elias Mandelbaum, as I reprimanded her in the sternest voice I could muster. Stern was not my thing. And it clearly wasn't hers since instead of responding, Des and her five feet six inches curvy self—complete with her newly purchased 36DDs—reached past me to my night table to swipe my last cigarette and scoop up my Bic. She lit up without permission and looked as if she was about to sit down on my futon. I tossed her my robe. It was too small for her but at least it would run some interference between her nude body and my blanket. Thankfully, she slipped it on.

"Honey, do you think he's into me?"

"What?"

"Tell me the truth. Do you think he's into me?" Somehow, she seemed completely unaware that my contact with the dude she'd just been banging was limited to overhearing a few of his grunts and groans, so I couldn't possibly know his true feelings for her.

Hell, I didn't even know what his name was. But if I were going to avoid a temper tantrum and get any sleep at all that night, I had to tread carefully. As if on cue, Mr. X. called out from her room, "Desiree doll, come back to bed."

"There you go. Of course, he's into you," I soothed. "See how eagerly he's awaiting your return?" God, I hoped that'd do the trick.

"Well, I guess you're right. I mean, look at me. I am pretty perfect, aren't I?" She was standing up now, peeling off my robe with one hand as she held my cigarette with the other. I had to admit she looked spectacular.

"You're sensational," I enthused. "But listen, Des, whoever this guy is, no matter how much he's into you and how stunning you are, he can't be in the shower in the morning when I get up. I've been late to work every day this week because of your men."

"Oh, honey. Of course, you can't. I'm going to tell him right now he'll have to wait till you're done or go home in the morning and shower there. It won't happen again. I promise." And then, as if we hadn't been through this every night this week, she continued, "Honey, you actually sleep in that?" She wrinkled her nose and twisted the side of the XL Keith Richards T-shirt from last year's '97 Stones tour that engulfed my four feet eleven and a half frame.

"Des, you know I do. Besides, it's not as if anyone sees me in it but you." There was nothing wrong with my T.

"Well, that rag's likely the reason no one sees you at night *but* me." She released Keith and wagged a perfectly manicured crimson talon at me, which if she were standing any closer might have been considered assault with a deadly weapon. "I know. Let's go to The Inside Story sometime this week and pick you up a few things. Some killer lingerie will change your life." She bent down to hug me. But given that she was naked, sweaty, and insane, I did my best to wriggle out of her grasp. She contented herself by blowing me a kiss and cooing "sweet dreams," instead. As I climbed back into bed, I envisioned her slinking behind the red curtain that divided our "living room" from her "bedroom" and finally fell asleep.

When my alarm went off at 6:30, I felt like an 18-wheeler had hit me, and my ears were ringing from exhaustion. I barely knew where I was until I heard the frigging shower running, which meant, despite her assurances to the contrary, Desiree's latest boy toy was hogging the bathroom. This meant war.

"Come on, Desiree, you promised," I called out, even though I knew she was probably unconscious from the sleeping pills she took every night. Since her only employment was looking for acting engagements, "working" at Dershowitz, Mandelbaum, Katz & Kahan, and some c-level modeling gigs for showrooms and special events like the Auto Show, it didn't matter what time she emerged from her coffin. But I had to get to the paper before my boss, Nils Petersen, did today. Desiree's late-night sex shows and her kept men holding a hostile takeover of my shower in the mornings were seriously interfering with my professional standing. Nils had hinted that I might be up for a promotion, but that it was pretty tenuous since I couldn't seem to get into the office by 8 a.m.—when all the real, hard-boiled, pit-bull journalists showed up.

"You're a great writer and one of the best reporters on staff. I see a real future for you at FDG, but you need to be here when the early breaking news comes in," Nils had cautioned me just yesterday.

I was as big a newshound as anybody and lived to get a "scoop" but for the life of me, I couldn't figure out what kind of earth-shattering fashion, beauty, and retail news broke at 8 a.m. Still, if I wanted to make more money and get better assignments, I would have to show up when all those eager beavers did, regardless of Desiree and her harem. Besides, I didn't like letting Nils down.

Without fully mapping out a game plan, I decided to check the bathroom door. Magically, Prince Charming hadn't locked it. Flinging it open, I thundered, "Hey, Porn Star, get out of my shower." Either he couldn't hear me above the din of the running water or chose not to. So, I tore back the shower curtain and repeated my order. Nicely endowed and muscly, in that beefy, frat boy hedge fund manager way that Desiree favored, Mr. Latest Conquest's hands instantly flew to cover his privates as he tried to squeeze past me to obey my command.

"And by the way, you might want to get an STD panel," I shouted at his retreating figure with my newfound courage for the final *coup de grâce*. "Des has pretty much boned half of Wall Street."

"You girls are nuts," he called out over his shoulder, racing around the apartment searching for his clothes, dripping water all over our already buckling living room parquet tiles. I noticed he had deep red scratches across his back.

When the front door finally banged shut it was

already 7:00, which meant that I would barely have time for a quick rinse in my newly liberated shower. While toweling off, I searched for a suit and blouse that weren't ridiculously wrinkled. Waverly Dry Cleaners was still holding most of my work clothes hostage as I couldn't afford to pay the ransom it charged to free them. And frankly, I wasn't in any kind of hurry to get them back. I still couldn't believe that my life had been reduced to shopping for baggy polyester and rayon pants suits with aspirations for a salary increase that would let me afford better-fitting wool and linen numbers. But if I wanted to be taken seriously by the middle-aged, mostly male presidents and CEOs of the cosmetic companies I covered, I had to wear serious clothes.

I flipped the bird at the navy pants suit and new white blouse I unearthed amidst my ripped jeans, baby doll dresses, concert T's, Doc Martens, motorcycle boots, and leather jacket that comprised my uniform first when I played gigs and then later when I worked at *40 Days* covering up-and-coming bands. Before I put it on, I tore off the little faux-jeweled bow pin that came with the blouse and tossed it into the trash. I will never understand why petite designers believe adult women need to be treated like five-year-olds just because they stand less than five feet four inches tall.

Christ. It was 7:20. I finished getting dressed, tried to subdue my overly exuberant black curls into a scalp-scraping ponytail, grabbed my guitar, and slid the Allman Brothers' *Eat a Peach* into my Walkman. "Ain't Wasting Time No More" seemed a fitting soundtrack for this morning's commute. As I dashed over to Astor Place from our Mercer Street apartment with Dickie Betts' and Duane's hypnotic guitars and Gregg's sultry voice washing over me, I prayed the 6 train was running.

When I got to our office, Nils was already in his cubicle typing away with his usual two-fingered ferocity and speed. He'd never quite figured out that keyboards were much more touch-sensitive than the newsroom typewriters he grew up on, so he went through them like most people go through potato chips. He looked up at me, his face beaming approval as he stroked his white bushy mustache that matched his thick shock of tousled hair.

"Look who's here and nearly on time?" I handed him his coffee. This was my idea, never his. Even when I was late, we started the morning off by sitting in his cubicle, drinking coffee (hot until May, iced until October), chatting about news, music, industry gossip, and why, even though Keith Richards was one of our guitar heroes, we thought the Stones albums that Mick Taylor played on were the best.

Back in the '70s, Nils had been a rock 'n roll reporter in L.A. and partied with most of the greats. Rumor had it he'd even driven cross-country in an orange Lincoln with leopard upholstery accompanied by Lance Boom, the legendary rock critic and editor of *Hammer* magazine. How he ended up here I'll never know, and he kept quiet on the subject.

"Hey, what's with the hair?" He gestured to the skintight ponytail that was already giving me a headache.

"Roommate trouble," I grumbled, gathering up all the press kits and news releases that littered his extra chair, trying to figure out where I could put them so I

9

could sit down.

"You're still with that crazy roommate?"

"Sadly, yes."

"Why don't you move out?" Nils was always so helpful.

"I can't exactly afford to scrape together the first and last month's rent plus the security deposit I'll need to move," I replied, straining not to sound snarky about my pittance of a salary. "And I have another year to go on this stupid contract I signed, and everyone's been pretty clear about how I can't break it without legal actions taken against me. Besides, it's the only way I can afford to live in the East Village."

"Why do you need to live in the Village?" He raised an eyebrow.

"For the music and the open mics."

"You're finally doing open mics?" he asked, nodding over to my guitar that I'd propped up outside his cubicle.

"Well, I mean, I will."

He ducked his head over some papers on his desk and I could tell he was trying not to smile since I'd been talking about playing open mics for a year. And at the one I'd shown up for, I hadn't even performed. I could hear Traffic's "Light Up or Leave Me Alone" playing from the headphones he'd taken off when I arrived.

"Great tune," I said.

"Oh yeah, the drumming is amazing. Funny how most people think it's Ginger Baker. But he wasn't ever in Traffic."

"It was Jim Capaldi," we said at the same time.

"Oh my God," I said. "We are such rock 'n roll geeks."

"We sure are," he agreed, and we laughed. "Your rock 'n roll geekdom must've gone over really big at *40 Days*."

"Not as big as I'd hoped." I sighed.

"Really? That's surprising," he continued. "I still can't understand why you at *40 Days* weren't a slam dunk."

And it was—at least in the beginning. I'd finally figured out a career I could get behind and took a gig as a fact-checker there. It seemed like an amazing way to be in the music world with none of the soul-crushing criticism and politicking of music school, which had pretty much murdered my dream of being a pro. In the beginning, I was just over the moon to be on staff at *40 Days*—I'd been obsessed with the magazine since I'd been eleven or twelve when I first started reading it. But as soon as they promoted me to reporter, things took a turn for the creepy. At first, it was just a lot of talk and innuendo around the office, but once I started going on the road to cover the newbie bands, it became obvious that my job description entailed a lot more than I was initially led to believe.

Things came to a head, so to speak, when I was assigned an interview with Astro Jensen, the lead singer of an up-and-coming grunge band that had been playing to packed clubs and selling a staggering number of CDs. My first clue that this meeting was going to go south should've been when he answered the door of his Pittsburgh motel room in a barely closed robe. But hell, this was par for the course for most rockers. Even his shot of Jim Beam at 10 a.m. didn't faze me because what grunge guy didn't do that? A few alarm bells rang when he sat next to me on the couch vs. across from me, but it wasn't until he grabbed my left breast with one hand, then my hand with his other one, and slid it under his robe that the full extent of his intentions hit me. Luckily, I was able to push him off and storm out before he could stop me.

As soon as my plane landed at JFK, I sprung for a cab to get back to the office as quickly as possible and tell my editor. I figured he'd be outraged and Astro Jensen would, at the very least, be banished from our pages. But that's not exactly the way things turned out. When I told my editor Jensen was more interested in getting off than getting interviewed, omitting some of the more embarrassing details, he seemed astounded that I didn't follow through.

"Well, sweetheart, that's rock 'n roll. Did you get the story?" he asked with a smile and a wink.

When I pressed the issue once I heard he was considering putting the little rat bastard on the cover, the powers that be decided it would be better for me to go elsewhere. So, he "found" me another job within our parent publishing company, which is how I ended up wearing Liz Claiborne and covering the business of beauty at FDG. I, of course, didn't have the cash to sue *40 Days* or that weasel prick who was now charting something like 4 or 5 on *Today's Music's Top 100*, so I was just grateful to have a job. But since Nils changed the subject every time I asked him how he ended up at FDG, I certainly wasn't going to reveal *my* secret. The worst part of the whole sorry mess was that I'd started playing in a really cool band with some of the other reporters there, and when I was "relocated" to FDG, they kicked me out.

"Sorry, Sarah. But you know how it is. Can't piss

off the boss man," Tanner James, Joint Effort's unofficial leader and bass player, explained as he gave me the ax.

"Hey, just toss that on the floor," Nils said, breaking through my reverie, finally seeming to realize that I was juggling piles of his papers and my coffee cup at the same time. "Can you believe all of this crap we get?" I could—since the same mounds of it were littering my cubicle. Once I sat, Nils handed me the morning edition of the *Gotham Sentinel*—NYC's current "it" tabloid. He pointed to a headline:

Sophistiquée Beauty Babe Latest to Defect in Dot.com Craze.

"That's like the third or fourth high fashion magazine beauty director to jump ship to one of those new beauty.coms," I said. "They must be paying *beaucoup* bucks. We should write a trend piece. Why don't I start by interviewing the magazine editors to see where they're getting their new directors from and if they're concerned about the editorial competition or loss of talent?"

"My thoughts exactly. Hey, which one is this? Do you know her?"

"It's Peach Chandler, one of the Fashion Flamingos," I replied, wondering if my album choice this morning had been some kind of weird premonition.

"Fashion Flamingos?"

"You know, those high-fashion magazine beauty girls who half-starve themselves to fit into sample sizes. And since their feet hurt all the time from their ludicrously expensive torturous shoes, they keep shifting from one spindly leg to the other," I explained.

"Ha!" he snorted. "That's both funny and accurate.

And her name is actually Peach? Someone's parents named their daughter Peach?"

"Well, hers did." But personally, I couldn't say she lived up to her sunny name or that any of the Flamingos did, for that matter.

I'd always been terrified of those super-popular beauty editors whom I inevitably ran into at beauty press events because they were exactly like the mean girls at school who terrorized me for wearing Danskin stretch pants, oxford lace-ups, and polyester button-downs with the enormous collars in the era of straight-leg Lee Rider jeans, work boots, and plaid flannel shirts. Since my mother, Anna Elias Mandelbaum, associated the decline of Western civilization with the abolishment of the dress code from the public school system, she was going to do her civic duty by ensuring her progeny didn't further contribute to its demise by looking "sloppy and disrespectful" at school.

Then there was my total lack of coordination and all-around nerdiness, complete with braces and reading glasses. By the seventh grade, the physical bullying had stopped, but the emotional torture began—especially in the gym locker room. And that was far worse than being pelted with snowballs outside. Being part of the fashion industry, especially at a glossy high-fashion mag, was like being in middle school gym class every day for the rest of your life.

Honestly, if it weren't for the dowdy suits and ridiculously low salary, I'd be perfectly happy to stay safely tucked away at FDG rather than venturing out into the fashion or music jungle. At least here you were evaluated based on the news you broke and not on your body type, clothes, or connections.

But not these beauty magazine girls. These were tall, thin, wealthy, well-bred smooth-haired blondes. And if they hadn't been born that way, it was nothing that private sessions with a ruthless personal trainer, the latest cleanse, bone-crushing heels, and a triple process from a celebrity colorist—not to mention hours wrestling with a blow dryer and round brush—couldn't fix. No wonder they were so mean. They were hungry, headachy, and hobbled all the time. And because they spent most of their lives grooming, they had little use for my frizzy hair, frumpy pants suits, and "sensible" shoes, since, to top it all off, I had terrible feet. And they weren't shy about letting me know I was hopeless.

Once I was seated next to Keeley McPheters from *Fashion Chic* magazine at a Dior luncheon to celebrate a new product launch—and after lecturing me about the weight loss benefits of juice fasts and asking to borrow a pen and a piece of paper to take notes—she turned her back on me and started whispering to Peach about "that disaster of an FDG girl." And Keeley was one of the nicer ones; Peach, who was essentially Queen Bee of the Flamingos—if you'll excuse the mixed metaphor—was even nastier.

Legend had it that one time Peach launched a bagel at her assistant because the poor, non-native New Yorker had grabbed it off the top of the counter rather than requesting a fresh one, in her fear of leaving Peach's phones unanswered for longer than the 10-minute break she was allowed for picking up her boss' breakfast. How was she supposed to know that the bagels on the counter are pre-buttered or smeared with cream cheese, and if you want a plain one, you need to ask for it specifically? They didn't even have bagels in

Duluth.

"Do I look like I eat butter?" Peach had screamed after she spat her first bite out into the trash and hurled the remaining bagel at the hapless Minnesotan. Nice girl.

As Nils and I conferred about the best way to cover the story, we overheard the paper's editorial director, Michael Gallagher, on the phone. Amazingly, he sat out on the newsroom floor just like us mere mortals rather than behind the closed door of a private office. And that kicked up the excitement level of the whole place because he was a consummate reporter and a brilliant people-person. Even completely unfashion-forward-me loved the buzz and the hum of the newsroom floor when he broke a story.

"Oscar," Michael boomed. "I love you. We love you. But we will love you even more when you give us the exclusive on your new house in Santa Domingo. So just say the word and I'll send our top home décor writer down to you on the very next plane. Or if you prefer, I'll come down myself." After the call ended, Michael leaped to his feet (shod in Bruno Magli loafers) and addressed the rows and rows of cubicles facing his desk. "Friends, Romans, and Countrymen, we got Oscar," he crowed. We all burst into applause. How could you not?

"Hey, by the way, Dana is getting really good at that Ricki Lee Jones tune you've been working on together. You're pulling great things out of her," Nils said, referring to the guitar lessons I'd been giving to his 14-year-old daughter every Saturday morning for the last few months. The Petersen's lived just a couple of blocks away from me on 11th street so it was super easy and fun. Dana and I had a blast together.

"Yeah, she's a hoot and super talented." Dana was a great kid and was starting to shred on guitar. It was exciting to see her progress. Nils, already moving on to the next thing, nodded and handed me the *Sentinel,* signaling that our daily bonding experience had run its course.

"Okay, Brainiac, time to make the donuts."

I turned to go pick up my guitar but realized I still hadn't gotten reimbursed for my last month's expenses. And I needed that check—today, preferably, so that I could not only pay my guitar teacher that night but also buy lunch and a few subway tokens.

"Hey, Nils, any word from accounting about my expenses?"

"I've been meaning to talk to you about that. You're going to have to resubmit your report without that unauthorized cab you took. You know how strict FDG is about getting prior consent for cabs." His voice became authoritative, which meant he was uncomfortable.

"Nils, it was raining, and the 1 train wasn't running," I tried to plead my case.

"I totally get it, Sarah, but it's company policy." And because he was a really good guy, he pulled out his beaten-up brown wallet from the back pocket of his khakis and handed me a twenty-dollar bill. "It's not a loan. Consider it a bonus for how great you are with Dana."

"Nils, I can't take this," I said, knowing full well I had to, which I found beyond demoralizing.

"Sure, you can." And with that, he started punching numbers into his phone with the same intensity he usually reserved for his keyboard.

As soon as I got back to my desk, my phone rang.

"Mandelbaum," I answered newsroom style.

"Honey, did you say something to Peter?" It was Desiree, and the high pitch of her voice made it clear she was about to throw some craze my way. I had to shut it down fast.

"Des, I keep telling you I can't talk at work."

"Did you say something to Peter?" she insisted, nearly shrieking.

"Who's Peter?"

"Peter, my boyfriend, who you met last night."

"Des, I can't deal with this right now. You kept me up all night and this guy you call your boyfriend was in the shower this morning and almost made me late for work, again. You're going to have to get this under control. And please stop calling me at work. We've talked about this before."

"Well, Sarah, whatever you said to him, you ended our relationship. When I called him this morning to see if he wanted to hang out tonight, he said, 'You and your whack job of a roommate can go fuck yourselves.' Once again, you've ruined my life."

I ruined her life? I would've laughed if I weren't so broke and exhausted. But I knew that when she called me Sarah instead of honey, it was bad, really bad — especially when she was having delusions that her meaningless sex was meaningful. So, I did what any coward would do.

"Gotta go," I whispered into the phone, and hung up as quickly as I could. I had barely taken my hand off the receiver when it rang again. Fucking Des. "Do not call me at work again," I hissed into the phone without waiting to hear the voice on the other line and slammed down the receiver as quietly as I could so Michael and Nils wouldn't hear me. It rang again two seconds later. Before I could admonish Des again, someone else started speaking rapidly.

"Hello? Is this Sarah? Sarah Mandelbaum? I just tried to reach you. I hope I have the right person." Oh great. I'd likely just yelled at someone important. This was turning into the mother of all days.

"Yes. Hello. It's Sarah. What can I do for you?"

"Will you hold for Fiona Doyle?" Fiona Doyle was the new editor-in-chief of *Sophistiquée* magazine and was fabulous. *Sophistiquée*'s publishing company had imported her from England just a few months ago and put her above famed *Sophistiquée* creative director Henri-François Bernard to turn around the magazine's sagging sales. It was the first time in ages Henri-François was second on the masthead and, by all accounts, he wasn't happy about it. But Fiona was fantastic. Not only was she responsible for the miraculous comeback of British *Glam Queen,* but she also had a Masters in English literature from Oxford. I'd heard her speak at a few industry events and she was smart, approachable, and really stylish in a non-scary way. She didn't limp around famished playing the fashion victim. And she had brown hair. Funny, how she was calling me just as I needed to speak to her about Peach leaving for a dot.com.

"Hello, Sarah," she lilted. "I've been admiring you from afar." What? I started wondering if she was calling the right Sarah. But I decided to launch ahead with the interview I needed to write the article.

"Fiona. I'm so glad you called. I wanted to get a

few quotes from you about Peach moving over to beautyhyperspace.com."

"Now that *is* a coincidence because Peach's leaving is exactly why I'm calling you. Would you meet me for lunch or coffee to chat about the possibility of taking her place here?" Now I knew she had the wrong Sarah.

"Fiona, I'm flattered but I just don't think I'm the girl for the job. I'm not all that into fashion, but let's talk about Peach going over to *beauty hyperspace* and what that means for *Sophistiquée*."

"What it means for *Sophistiquée* is that we have an opportunity to try something new and do things differently. To take a friendlier, less I'm-more-fabulous-than-you-approach and make our readers feel included rather than they're on the outside looking in."

"That's a great quote. I love that idea." And I did. It seemed like she was speaking directly to me and why I never could read any of those magazines without feeling terrible about myself. I put my reporter hat back on and asked, "How are you going to implement that strategy?"

"I'm going to implement it by hiring someone smart, witty, and real with proven writing and researching skills. I've been enjoying your pieces in FDG. That's why I'd like to set up some time to talk with you."

"Are you sure you have the right Sarah?" Des notwithstanding, this was maybe the weirdest conversation I'd had all week. I mean, me at *Sophistiquée*? That was crazy. It was like expecting those mean middle school girls to let me sit with them at lunch.

"I absolutely am talking to the Sarah I want to be talking to." She laughed. It was so warm and infectious that I found myself smiling too. "Listen, I must sign off now, but how about you think about this, and I'll have my assistant call back again tomorrow to set up a meeting? Bye for now," she sang before hanging up.

The phone rang again almost instantly. It was Dana.

"Sarah?" she whispered, so I knew she was likely calling from a hallway payphone at school when she wasn't supposed to be. I checked the clock. It was ten.

'What's up, Cheese Danish? What are you doing calling me in the middle of second period? Are you cutting class?"

"It's just gym. Don't tell my dad." I would never tell her dad, my dad, or anyone's dad if someone cut gym. I think school would be a much safer, happier place if everyone skipped gym or if they didn't offer it at all.

"Sarah, I just heard the greatest new band. I mean, they're totally smoking hot. You would love them."

"Really? That's so cool. Who are they?"

"I can't believe how mind-blowing they are. Have you ever heard of Led Zeppelin?"

"Why yes, Cheese Danish, yes I have," I said, trying to keep the smile out of my voice. "And you're right. They're awesome." I didn't have the heart to tell her yet that her discovery wasn't new. When I was twelve, I had a similar conversation with my older sister, Morrisa, after I heard Blondie playing in Igor's record store for the first time. She, of course, told me I was a doofus since Blondie had been around for years. But Dana and I were pals, so why make her feel bad?

"Did you tell your dad about them?"

"No way, he's so old. He'd never be into music like that." If she only knew. "Hey, so are we on for Saturday morning? I've been working on that Ricki Lee Jones song. My dad says I'm getting really good."

"I know. He told me too. You're a total rock star. But listen, I have to get to work, and you don't want to get caught cutting gym. It's beyond humiliating." This I knew from personal experience. "And tell your dad about Led Zep."

We hung up and then I finally got started reporting that dot.com story, all thoughts of my call with Fiona leaving my brain except for her quotes that I could use for the piece. At six, I started packing up my stuff to get to my guitar lesson in Gramercy Park. As I rounded Nils' cubicle, I called out goodnight, but he stopped me.

"Hey, Sarah, I've been meaning to tell you something for weeks. Lancôme invited us to sit with them at the Gotham Gala and I said we'd go." He started searching through those absurd piles of papers he somehow worked around for what I gathered was the invitation.

I was not happy about this—these fabulous industry black ties were worrisome for me. Sure, they were glamorous, wonderful places to people watch and get good quotes for trend stories, but these events inevitably took me back to my prom, which I wasn't asked to and attended with my best friend against my will. And once again, my hair and my older sister's cast-off, several-seasons-past-its-prime Laura Ashley ruffled prairie dress provided hours of amusement to the queen bees of the mean girls Bevin Feldshuh, Ariel Connor, and Jamie Baron, aka the Terror Trio. I was comforted in the knowledge, though, that I had a purpose at these industry events since I was covering them for the paper and could hide out behind my notebook and "journalistic" requests for comments. I had no such protection at the prom.

"Is it for a story?"

"You betcha. We're gonna tear it up." Nils gave me the thumbs up.

"Okay." I sighed. "When is it?"

"Tomorrow night." This was not good. The Gotham Gala was about as dazzling as it got. And my go-to black lace Ann Taylor cocktail dress that I wore to every industry black tie, wasn't going to cut it.

"Nils, really? You couldn't have given me a little notice? I don't have anything to wear." I couldn't even borrow anything from any of my friends since most of them were well over five feet four inches tall. I thought about calling my mother, who was about my height and quite the glamour puss in her way. But somehow that always made me feel worse instead of better.

"Sorry, Sarah. It slipped my mind. I'm not a man of leisure as you can see from all of this." He waved at those precarious stacks of papers, nearly knocking a few down. "You'll look fine."

"Nils, that's easy for you to say. You can just rent a tux and expense it." I searched my brain for a solution to my fashion dilemma and came up empty.

"Sarah, remember you're there to work and we're not these people. We just write about them." He had put on his "boss" voice again. So, I knew he felt bad about the oversight but not nearly as bad as I did. What the hell was I going to wear to the Gotham Gala? I prayed the stupid dress wasn't at Waverly Dry Cleaners, and then wondered if I had enough change in my jar for bail, in case it was.

Chapter 2

When I got to my guitar teacher's apartment building on Lexington Ave and 22nd, I was not in a good mood. This Gotham Gala thing was really stressing me out, and I was so exhausted from Des' after-hour escapades that I felt my eyes closing even as I climbed the four flights of stairs to his apartment. And then there was the fact that I couldn't pay him—again—which made me insane even if he was low-key about it. But when Ollie opened the door and flashed me his supersonic smile, I couldn't help but be happy to see his totally bald, punked-out self. Small and slight, he sported a hoop in his right eyebrow, a dangling cross in his left ear, and full-body ink, including letters spelling out "Iggy" across one set of knuckles and "Sex P" across the other.

We met when I covered a few of his band's shows around the city for *40 Days*. One-Eyed Snake was about to hit it big with a release on a major label when the record company went bust and sold all its works in progress to a major conglomerate. The new company focused on other projects and put One-Eyed Snake on ice—indefinitely. And since it legally owned the band's masters, they were screwed. I hadn't played much since my traumatic five years at the conservatory, except for my ill-fated stint in Joint Effort.

But Ollie was about as laid back and supportive as

anyone could be—not to mention a total rock star. I'd
mainly studied jazz and classical at school since to
avoid being disowned by my parents I'd had to pass
(kicking and screaming) on the free ride I was given to
the College of Contemporary Music (CCM), the top
contemporary music conservatory in the country, which
let you study both jazz and rock. Instead, I finished a
five-year joint academic/music degree (taking out loans
to cover the music part) at Robert Lowell University
and the East Coast Conservatory of Music (ECC),
where at the time rock was considered a four-letter
word. I love jazz and always will, but really wanted to
play both and always regretted trading one for the other.

"Hey, Cobain," he greeted me. "Ready to shred?"

I loved it when he called me that. Not just because
I adored Kurt, but because it gave me hope. Kurt
Cobain was one of the few famous musicians who
played left-handed like me. He also had small hands
like me and sometimes played smaller guitars, like
me—something I was beyond embarrassed about
because like those damn designers and their idiotic
petite women-child clothes, most guitar companies
didn't make any kick-ass "petite" guitars. Except for a
handful of them, that real rockers used for travel or
quick compositions, most short-scale guitars looked and
sounded like they were for kids, and a lot of them were
even pink, which just about killed me. And it had been
the biggest problem for me in my Contemporary Jazz
and Performance classes at school where my teachers
constantly told me I could never be a legit musician
playing a "baby" guitar. I had to fight like hell to be
evaluated on my playing instead of on my instrument. I
figured Kurt must've had some of his smaller guitars

custom-made because they looked and sounded totally rock-star. Hendrix played lefty, too, but he had gorgeous hands with slim, lovely fingers that were longer than my legs. Even Ollie, as compact as he was, had fantastic hands.

As Ollie walked into the kitchen to get me the Diet Coke he always had for me, I admired the rows and rows of guitars hanging on the walls from floor to ceiling in his closet of a studio apartment. It didn't matter that I saw them every week. They were breathtaking. Some of them were his, some of them were his students, and some were ones he was working on for clients. Ollie was also one of the top luthiers in New York City.

"Nice threads!" he said, breaking into my fantasies of playing every one of those guitars as he handed me the Diet Coke. Crap. Typically, I brought jeans and a T-shirt to the office on lesson days so I could change beforehand, but I'd been such a frantic mess in the morning thanks to Des and Peter, I'd forgotten.

"Tell me about it," I sighed. "Hey, so listen. I can't pay you tonight. I still didn't get that expense check. I'm so sorry. I feel like such a jerk."

"It's okay; you can work it off selling CDs at one of my shows—just not the one tonight. That navy blue polyester will scare off any customers." He pulled my ponytail playfully.

"They call it crepe—not polyester," I said, pretending to be offended. "But why didn't you tell me you were playing tonight? I totally would've planned on being there."

"It's just an open mic. Hey, why don't you come? We could do that new song of yours together. Let's leave right after the lesson and sign up. I can give you a T-shirt and you can lose that ridiculous jacket." Ollie's unbelievable patience and support for me made me squirm. I was terrified of going back up there, even if he was playing with me.

"Hey, thanks. But I'm just too fried tonight. Des hasn't let me sleep in weeks."

"You're still living with that lunachick?"

"I know. I know. But it's the only way I can afford to stay in the Village." I was starting to sound lame even to myself.

"You know, Sarah, you're going to have to get back out there if you want to move forward with this. I don't understand what the big deal is. You're really good. Great even. I mean, you got a free ride to CCM even if your parents didn't let you go, and then got into ECC, which is like the top conservatory in the country. And I know you played with some killer bands—both jazz and rock in Boston. And what about Joint Effort? You guys were fierce."

Ollie was really working it. "And besides, what happened at the open mic wasn't even so bad," he continued when I failed to respond with a resounding yes. "So, what if that guy yelled out something uncool when the MC read out your name to come up? He was a total d-bag."

I winced inwardly, thinking about my humiliating aborted attempt there. Ollie and I'd gotten to The Sidewalk Café early for one of its famed open mic nights and picked pretty low numbers. He was supposed to perform tenth and I got twelfth, which meant we should've finished by eleven at the latest. But because I was an unknown, and the host had his own friends to promote, he kept pushing me back further and further. Finally, around one a.m., he called out "Sarah, Sarah Mandelbaum" and that d-bag, as Ollie called him, sneered, "Sarah Mandelbaum? I bet she really rocks. And what's that?" he continued, pointing to the mini-guitar I was about to bring up to the stage. "A ukulele? Look, folks, it's Tiny Tim."

Tired and mortified, I grabbed my "baby" guitar and slunk out. So, between the douche bag incident, the Astro Jensen thing that precipitated my FDG exile, and five years of soul-crushing criticism about the size of my guitars and my moral failings for not being able to play "real" guitars from my teachers, I just didn't feel all that confident anymore and didn't see myself getting back out there any time soon. Since I certainly wasn't going to explain all of that to Ollie, I let him think my stage fright was just because of the Sidewalk episode. Great guy that he was, he continued trying to think up ways to get me on stage.

"Just because you don't have a rock star name or Jimmy Page-sized guitar, doesn't mean you can't be and aren't a total rock star," Ollie continued. "First off, you probably *can* play a full-scale guitar, but it totally doesn't matter if you don't and secondly, you can call yourself anything you want. You know my name is Oliver Lednicer, but I don't go by that in the music world because as Bowie would say, that'd be 'Rock n Roll Suicide.' So, I'm Ollie Led. You can call yourself anything you want." He paused for a minute, thinking. "I know, how about Saffron, Saffron Meadows, like that chick from the Sixties? Legend has it that she inspired all three Jims—Paige, Hendrix, *and* Morrison. She's the one who turned the top hat into a rock accessory even before Marc Bolan, Alice Cooper, Slash and Stevie Nicks made it cool." And Donovan wrote that I'm just Mad about Saffron/*Mellow Yellow* song about her.

"You want me to name myself after a groupie?"

"Oh no, she wasn't a groupie like Pennie Lane or Pamela Des Barres. Saffie shredded on guitar—and it was short scale if I'm not mistaken. And she sang for Janis in the studio when The Pearl was, you know, indisposed. She just never got the credit she deserved."

"How is it I've never heard of her? I mean, I wrote about music professionally. And whatever happened to her? I don't want to name myself after someone who OD'd." Wow, I was cranky.

"She just vanished one day, and no one could find her. Maybe she just got tired of the scene and went to some island," he said, picking up his sublime vintage Guild Starfire electric and starting to tune it. "The disappearance of Saffron Meadows continues to be one of rock 'n' roll's greatest mysteries."

Hmm, this could work. I was starting to like this whole Saffron Meadows thing. I mean, why not? Sarah Mandelbaum certainly wasn't doing me any favors. And it was beyond comforting to know that someone kind of famous played a smaller guitar. This could be just the change in mojo I needed. But while I was wrapping my brain around the concept, I spied Ollie's signature can of Mello Yello on the kitchen counter. I don't even know how he still found that swill, but he was never without it. And now he was using it to goof on me.

"Bastard!" I yelled, punching him in the scrawny arm that sported the Rolling Stones lips logo, the Clash

Combat Rock insignia, and a Halley's Comet tattoo. "I can't believe parents trust you to teach their children."

"They love me." He laughed. "And so do you, Saffron."

I picked up my guitar, plugged in, and hit the opening riff of Alice Cooper's "School's Out." Ollie joined in on rhythm and sang the lead.

Next up, was "Welcome to the Jungle", which was giving me a hard time. I mean, Slash was a genius guitar player; his leads were incredibly complicated and his sound beyond pure.

"You're getting pretty badass," Ollie said as we were wrapping up for the night. I wasn't so convinced. Thanks to Desiree Dershowitz and my navy polyester, um, crepe suits, badass was about the last thing I was feeling these days. But I was glad if he thought so. "How's Dana doing on the Ricki Lee Jones?" he continued.

"She's fantastic. She gets better and better every week."

"She's got a great teacher. You learned from the best." He grinned. "You know, you could take her to Otto's Shrunken Head and do that Ricki Lee Jones song together on Covers Night." Ollie was not going to let this die tonight or probably ever until I got up somewhere—anywhere.

"Okay. Okay. Dude, I get it. I'll think about it."

"Why don't you do it first and think about it after?" he asked, making the serene Zen master face he always did when he spoke his words of wisdom.

"All right already. I read you loud and clear. Tonight was awesome, thank you. Now go kick some ass at Sidewalk."

"I'm not going unless you come with me," Ollie insisted.

"Seriously, I'm just too dragged tonight. But I promise I'll play another time."

"There's no time like the present," he continued, rummaging through the dresser under his loft bed and then handing me a pair of wrecked jeans and a Ramones T-shirt. "Here, try these on. There's no way I'm getting up there with you in that sad and sorry costume."

"You wore these?" I asked, more incredulous that these tiny articles of clothing could fit a full-grown man—even if Ollie was on the small side—than the drastic step Ollie seemed hell-bent on pushing me to take.

"Cocaine diet," he replied with a wink. "But that was many moons ago. Nothing but clean living these days. Now get moving and get dressed. If we don't get to Sidewalk soon, we'll have to play at the crack of dawn."

Amazingly enough, Ollie's sex, drugs, and rock 'n' roll clothes fit, and the best part was that the pants were even long enough to trail a bit on the ground to cover my frumpy work shoes.

"Good. You look good. Very rock star," he said, giving me the once over more approvingly than the Terror Trio or any Fashion Flamingo ever had.

As we headed out, we passed Glenn, the giant stuffed gorilla who stood guard at Ollie's front door. He just happened to be wearing a top hat.

"Here, Saffron Meadows would be proud," he said with a wink as he tossed it to me. But given that my hands were shaking so badly that I didn't see how I could possibly play guitar that night, and that Saffron Meadows clearly was just Ollie's made-up goof, it seemed highly unlikely she could save me. So, I shook my head, and gave Glenn his hat back.

"Okay, then. Maybe another time," he said. "Now grab your guitar, Saffie, and let's go give 'em hell."

When we got to Sidewalk, it was mobbed as usual. But since he was a regular and loved by pretty much everyone who'd ever met or heard of him, Ollie managed to work his way through the crowd and not only sign us up but secure a Mello Yello for him and a vodka grapefruit for me.

"They keep that moose pee here for you?" I asked, gratefully accepting the cocktail, hoping it would work its magic. My heart was beating faster than it had in my whole twenty-five years on the planet and I was starting to sweat enough that it was entirely possible I'd soak the T-shirt Ollie had lent me. How in the world did I let him talk me into this?

"Moose pee? I'll have you know that Ringo Starr, *the* coolest drummer ever, drinks this. That's why they have it here."

"Oh, yeah, sure. Ringo Starr drinks Mello Yello and does open mics at the Sidewalk Café," I said, thankfully feeling just the tiniest bit calm within my panic storm.

"So, what tune do you want to do?" he asked, raising his voice loud enough so I could hear him over the crowd but not so loud that he'd disturb the guy on stage playing. Ollie had excellent music etiquette. "I'm thinking of that new one you wrote last month. It's really good and I have it down."

"You memorized one of my songs?" I couldn't

quite fathom how or why a kickass musician like him would waste his time on anything I wrote, much less memorize it.

"Sarah, it's a great tune. I was even thinking of recording it with you." He took one last swig of Mello Yello and put the empty can on a nearby table. "Okay, we're up next. So, you better down that puppy stat," he said, squeezing my arm.

All right, Sarah Mandelbaum, Saffron Meadows, whoever you are, I chided myself. *Ollie is twisting himself sideways to make this happen for you. So just get your ass up to the stage and make him proud. You can do this.*

I threw back the rest of my cocktail, put the empty cup down, and grabbed my guitar to follow him up to the stage in front of the bar. People actually moved out of the way for us and were, of course, thrilled Ollie was getting up there. There were just a few more steps for me to take when suddenly the heel of my shoe caught in the hem of Ollie's hand-me-down jeans and I went flying headfirst into the crowd and pretty much face-planted on the sticky, filthy floor.

"Oh snap," some helpful patron called out. "Did you see that? She just fell flat on her face." Instantly, Ollie was down on his heels at my side, trying to assess the damage.

"Oh my God, are you okay? Did you hit your head? How many fingers am I holding up?"

It took me a minute or two to catch my breath and feel the complete and utter mortification flooding through my veins along with the jackhammer pounding of my head. Ollie helped me sit up and started scrutinizing me.

"Your lip is bleeding a little, and I'm pretty sure you're going to have a bump on your forehead and quite possibly a shiner. But I think you're mostly okay. At least you didn't knock your teeth out. But I think the important thing here is that you're willing to get up and play again. So, I don't think this evening was a total disaster."

"That's easy for you to say," I replied, trying to keep my voice light and not curse his and my very existence. Along with the crushing humiliation I was now experiencing, it only took me a matter of minutes to realize that now I not only didn't have a suitable dress for the Gotham Gala but I'd have to attend it looking like I'd gone five rounds with Mike Tyson. Those hits just kept coming.

"Come on, rock star, let's get you home," Ollie said, helping me to my feet and grabbing my guitar. He maneuvered me through the crowd out of the bar onto the sidewalk and then went out into the street to hail a cab, which he carefully deposited me in and started to get in himself.

While I was beyond grateful for his care and support. I just couldn't bear any of it one second longer. I just needed to get home, look for our first-aid kit, if we had one, and gather my thoughts. Something had to change. And that was me. There's no way this ever would have happened to Saffron Meadows.

"Hey, thank you so much," I said as quickly as I could before he shut the car door. "I'm fine. I just want to get home and lick my wounds. You don't need to come with me."

"No. No. I really want to see you home and make sure you're all right. If you have a concussion, someone has to wake you up every hour or so."

"It's okay, really. I'm pretty sure I don't have a concussion. But I'll set my alarm, just in case," I said.

"Are you sure?"

"Yes. One hundred percent. Now get back in there and play your butt off."

"Okay, if that's what you want. But call me tonight if you need anything and definitely tomorrow as soon as you get up."

I nodded a yes, thanked him again as he paid the cab driver, and finally allowed myself to exhale as the cab pulled away.

As we made our way to my apartment, all I could think about was taking a bubble bath—something I hadn't done in years. It would require a good scouring of the tub, as God only knows what Des had been doing in it, but it seemed worth it. Every muscle and bone in my body were screaming at me.

Nils' wife Ursula had given me some fantastic-smelling lotions and potions for Christmas, and if Des hadn't used them up when I wasn't home, they might be exactly what I needed. I found myself praying that she would "punish" me and sleep at her grandmother's typically empty *pied-à-terre* on 10th street so I could have the place to myself and relax a little for a change. When I got to my lobby, though, I quickly discovered Des had made other plans for me. My suitcase, duffle bag, amp, and acoustic guitars, along with some boxes that likely held my books and music, plus, my stereo were all piled up in the corner behind the doorman's kiosk and Dennis, the doorman on duty, stopped me en route to the elevator, barely looking up from his *Sports Illustrated*.

"Sorry, Sarah, but I can't let you up. The Dershowitz's called this morning and said they were evicting you."

"What? Dennis, are you serious? You're not going to let me up to my own apartment?' This had to be some kind of crazy Des-teaching-me-a-lesson-scheme.

"I'm afraid I can't. The Dershowitz's were very clear and said I should call the police if you make any trouble." Dennis finally looked up at me. "Wow. What happened to you?" he asked, clearly not caring what my response was.

"I fell," I said simply, trying to keep the mounting panic from my voice as I realized the enormity of my situation, and that Dennis had hardened his heart against me. We used to be pals. Just the other day we'd hung out behind the building smoking and talking about the Aerosmith concert we'd attended separately over the weekend. I assumed this change in attitude was due to a recent cash infusion from Des' parents, even though they had to know how insane their daughter was, though I was certain they had no idea of the depth and breadth of her sexcapades. She must've had a galactic explosion or lied through her teeth to have persuaded them that she not only required yet another new roommate, but that the one she had currently needed to be ejected by force. I knew my dad was going to hear all about this and I'd have to jump through hoops to defend myself. Seymour Mandelbaum was never quick to take my side.

"Des left you this note. I'm going to need you to clear your things out of the lobby as quickly as possible." He was all business despite my obvious injuries and our former friendship. My throbbing head now had a pile driver on top of the jackhammer already inside of it.

I opened the shiny, hot pink envelope doused with her hit-you-over-the-head-jasmine and patchouli-laced perfume with my name scrawled across in red Sharpie, and took out the matching equally noxious notecard:

Sarah,

I'm sure even you will have to agree that you've become insufferable to live with. These last several months with you have been an unrelenting nightmare. I can no longer tolerate your selfishness, total lack of consideration, and socially unacceptable behavior. Both my parents and therapist agree living with you is toxic to my mental, physical, and emotional well-being. So, at great personal emotional expense, I have devoted considerable time and energy to pack up all your things—except your leather jacket, which has always looked better on me. I am sure you will agree that giving it to me is the least that you can do given that I will have to pay the full month's rent until I can find another roommate since you are leaving without notice.

You can come up for your furniture only when your movers are here. I do not feel safe having you back in the apartment given your inclinations to vengeful outbursts. I hope you will take this as a wake-up call to get the help you need. I am worried about you—Desiree.

I was dizzy with rage and fear, not to mention my possible concussion. It was ten at night. Where was I going to go with no money, no notice, and a head wound? I could walk over to Nils' and Ursula's place or go back to Sidewalk to meet up with Ollie and crash on his couch, but both options felt too exhausting and humiliating. So, I did what I always did when things got bad. I asked Dennis to borrow his phone and called my best friend Penny, the pastry chef, at her restaurant, The Rustic Root. The restaurant's notoriously snobby hostess answered only to inform me that Penny was busy in the pastry kitchen, but she would transfer the call, making it seem like I'd asked her to slice open a vein and fill a wine glass with her blood rather than just requesting she connect me with my friend.

"Hey," Penny whispered when she came to the phone, so I knew that her executive chef Tyrone Tannenholz was in the room with her, which was never a good thing.

"Des just kicked me out." I sniffed.

"What? Really?"

"I just got home to find all of my stuff in the lobby and this *Twilight Zone* note from her telling me that my behavior was socially unacceptable, and I couldn't come back up to the apartment to get my furniture without movers because she felt unsafe around me."

"She feels unsafe around you? Kitten, that's crazy. She's the sociopath." Penny was from Savannah, a place where they call you kitten.

"And she stole my leather jacket." I was about to full-on sob.

"What a bitch," Penny commiserated. I envisioned all 5 feet 11 inches tall, 160 lbs. of her, stooping to talk into the wall phone in the kitchen, pushing her large, round tortoise-shell glasses back up on her nose as she spoke and was momentarily comforted.

"She said it looked better on her."

"Oh, for fuck's sake. Now that tramp is getting on my last nerve." I knew it was true. Unlike me, Penny never dropped the F-bomb unless she was really peeved. "Listen, Off-her-Meds Barbie couldn't fit one arm into your jacket much less those ginormous fake boobs of hers."

I actually smiled briefly.

"But, Pen, what am I going to do? I'm totally broke, and it's like ten. Plus, I have to go to the damn Gotham Gala tomorrow night for work and I don't have anything to wear, and well, something else happened that I don't want to get into right now, but I'll tell you when I see you."

"What? Are you all right?"

"Other than being evicted and suffering humiliations galore and likely even more tomorrow night, I'm just fine," I sniffed, swallowing another sob.

"Okay, if you're sure, then let's take things one at a time. We can start with your living situation. Believe it or not, I have some good news for you. And you may not like what I have to say, but I hope you'll keep an open mind about it.'' Penny's Southern accent intensified, so I knew she was about to get serious.

"You've been living with that psycho way too long because of finances and this quixotic idea you have about needing to be in the Village for the open mics you never do, and please don't interrupt. Tyrone is giving me the hairy eyeball and is about thirty seconds away from hanging up this phone."

Penny's boss, Tyrone Tannenholz, whom I called Tyronnosaurus Rex or Rex for short, was a dick. Somehow, it eluded him that Penny Abernathy was extraordinary. At just twenty-five, she was head pastry chef at NYC's hottest "New American" eatery by its movie star-turned-magnate owner, written up in foodie magazines and frequently guested on Cuisine Channel TV shows. Recently, Tyrone had taken to calling her Henny Penny and started sniping that if she sampled fewer of her pastries and moved faster, she would not only be more attractive but would concoct dreamier confections. He might've even said something about her getting laid more often, too. She was hazy about that, and I didn't press the issue. So, I felt doubly bad about interrupting her at work and then giving her a hard time on top of it.

"Sorry, Pen. Go on."

"Here goes. This morning a one-bedroom in the building next door to me opened up, and I put down a small deposit to hold it for you. Seems like fate to me. You can come up to my place tonight and Holt and I can handle the move-in details tomorrow while you're at work. It looks exactly like mine, so it's pretty big and pretty nice." She was speaking faster and faster, so I knew Tyrone was about to erupt into one of his horrendous tirades and we'd have to hang up in a matter of minutes if not seconds.

But my heart had pretty much dropped to my ankles. It was so great of her to do this for me, but despite her generosity and thoughtfulness, I wasn't crazy about moving up to the West Bronx, even if it meant being near my best friend and her dreamy twin brother, Holt, who lived in the apartment next door. I mean, me, in the Bronx? That was just South of Alaska as far as I was concerned and nowhere near the music scene, though I had to admit that seemed less important to me after tonight's fiasco. And what the hell was I going to do for furniture? I only had a futon, dresser, and desk. The Dershowitz's had furnished the rest of our place.

"Rent is only four hundred dollars a month for your own one-bedroom, which means you'll not only have some privacy, but you can also make some headway on those crazy student loans of yours," she continued. "And if you haven't already paid that witch for this month, you can give first and last month's rent for your new place up front." I stayed quiet trying to reconcile myself to this bizarre turn of events. Penny kept right on going, trying her hardest to sell me.

"You can always just jump on the subway if you end up doing one of those open mic things. And Holt's even got some furniture for you since he just redecorated." As usual, Penny had read my thoughts as though I'd printed them out in boldface.

"Henny Penny! Are you going to see to those apple tarts, or are you going to giggle on the phone all day like you're back at your Southern sorority?" Rex thundered across the kitchen.

"I attended the Epicurean Institute and Les Trois Étoiles," Penny replied without raising her voice even half a decibel. Man, she was cool.

"Okay, kitten, gotta go. Holt's cruising around town with some of the guys from the team, likely in somebody's Bronco, and he has a cell phone now. I'll call him and ask him to come get you."

"Pen, I really can't thank you enough," I tried to say as quickly as I could before she hung up; "And fuck Tyronnosaurus Rex. You're the most talented pastry chef in NYC—probably in the country—and just an all-around amazing girl."

"Not in the world?" Penny did giggle this time, Tyrone Tannenholz be dammed. "Love you. Try not to stress. The apartment's great even if it's in the Bronx, and it's just one building over from me and Holt."

Holt Abernathy, a second-string defensive tackle for the New York Missiles, must've been driving around nearby or broken every speed limit on record because in about fifteen minutes he and two of his teammates showed up wearing jackets and ties, which meant they'd also been on the prowl for some action. Ordinarily, I would've been dazzled by this group's height and handsomeness, but I was pretty overwrought about being evicted and all on top of everything else.

Holt was at least six feet four inches tall, and if I had to guess, at least 300 pounds. Like Penny, he had blue eyes you could drown in and smooth, wavy chestnut hair. But unlike Penny, he had a sprinkling of pale ginger freckles across his nose and cheeks. Holt Abernathy was adorable. I didn't know the two guys he brought with him, but they were every bit as gorgeous, though leaner and less towering, which meant they were likely running backs, safeties, or wide receivers. I didn't know or care that much about football, but I did my best given how ridiculously cute and sweet Holt was—he even continued to live in the Bronx so he could watch over his twin after he'd achieved some fame and fortune. I did notice that one of his friends was particularly stunning, with dark skin and extraordinarily even white teeth. He wore his hair in short black braids all over his head. The other guy was "as blonde as the day is long," as Penny would say, with a supermodel-worthy jawline and stormy gray eyes. But we had far more important business than my standing there admiring three amazing-looking guys.

Now that Holt and co. were on the scene, I started

to relax into the idea that in just an hour or so I could say goodbye to Des forever. No doubt these genetic superiors would make short work of hauling my stuff out of the apartment, and since they had women falling all over them all the time, they likely wouldn't be impressed by her "charms." I had proof that this phenomenon was possible since Holt had met Des once or twice when he and Penny picked me up at the apartment to go out downtown and had pronounced her "crazier than a shithouse rat." I even was confident these fine gentlemen could get my leather jacket back.

"Oh my God, darlin', what on God's green earth happened to you?" Holt asked as he covered the length of the lobby in two long strides and enfolded me in his enormous arms, causing me to wince slightly. "You look like you went four rounds with Holyfield."

"I thought it was more like five with Tyson," I replied, enjoying his arms around me even if it hurt like mad.

"That's sweet, sugar. But if someone did this to you, just say the word and I can guarantee you it will be their last day above ground."

"It's okay, Holt. Really, it is. I did this to myself."

"You what?"

"It's a long story, Holt. But I can't thank you enough for coming."

"Well, if you're sure, let's get you out of here, then. Seems like Miss Thing lost her mind entirely this time," he said, eying me dubiously before quickly kissing me on the top of my aching head. Crap. That was definitely a sister kiss. "But it's clearly for the best because now you'll be closer to me and Pen. Course it shouldn't have gone down this way but she's a total freak, no matter how hot she is." Holt thought Des was hot? Since when? I felt a little sick inside.

"I'm James and this is Richie," said the beautiful guy with braids shaking my hand and gesturing over to his blonde buddy.

"Thank you so much for coming. You guys are saving my butt. I owe you big time."

"Sarah, you're family, that's what we do, like what you did for Penny in Paris. Consider yourself an Abernathy. Holt looped a big arm around my shoulder and gave me another quick yet bone-crushing hug.

Penny and I had met at a subtitled showing of Woody Allen's *Shadow & Fog* in Paris during our junior year. I was there on a work/study grant at the Sorbonne and Paris Conservatory, and Penny was at Les Trois Étoiles as a pastry exchange student from the Epicurean Institute. We recognized each other as fellow Americans on sight and became pals. Turns out she was having a bear of a time at Les Trois Étoiles. She barely knew any French and what little of it she did, she spoke with a heavy accent. Her teachers were not understanding in the least, and she was considering just going back to the Epicurean Institute before finishing the term. So, I embarked on intensive tutoring sessions with her, and she finished at the top of her class.

I walked back over to Dennis and asked him to call Des so we could get up there and get out.

"You know, Sarah, this building only allows moving in and out from ten to four," he said, without looking up from his blasted magazine.

"Dennis, are you kidding me? What the hell?"

"Hang on, darlin'. Let me take care of this." Holt reached into the back pocket of his beautifully fitting black Polo Ralph Lauren trousers, pulled out his black wallet, and withdrew a fifty-dollar bill. It was the second time that day that someone was offering up money on my account, not to mention the free pass Ollie had thrown me. Man, I had to get my act together. Holt approached the still-reading Dennis and said with all the charm he had to offer, which was considerable, "Dennis? Is that your name? We'd be much obliged if you could bend the rules a little. This lady is in a jam and we're all here to help her. If you could see your way clear to letting us up, we'll be out of your hair before you know it."

At the scent of the currency, Dennis finally looked up and saw my posse.

"Hey, don't you all play for the Missiles?"

"That we do, sir."

"You guys are having a great season so far. And that was some ten minutes you had in the last game. You're a shoo-in for first-string as soon as Darius retires. It's fantastic to meet you. Go on up." And for perhaps the first time in his career, Dennis waved away the proffered cash.

Des answered the door wearing those damn mules and her microscopic cherry red satin kimono, which she clutched loosely over her naked body. I wondered if she'd been wearing that all evening or quickly stripped when she heard we were coming up. Except for her raising an eyebrow at the sight of my wounds, she ignored me completely though perked up visibly when she saw Holt and his two handsome teammates.

"Hi, sexy," she purred, planting a lingering kiss as close to Holt's lips as he allowed. I was happy to see him shift his face as soon as he saw her moving in, so it landed mostly on his cheek. Des was undeterred. She slackened the already precarious hold she had on her robe and stretched up on tiptoe to try and gaze into his eyes. "I'm sorry we're meeting again under these circumstances, but it's good to see you. I feel so bad that I've been so crazed that I haven't been able to hang out with you since the last time. I've been auditioning like mad, and I joined an improv group." She assumed the breathy banter that was typically effective at entrapping her prey. Without waiting for a reply, she continued, moving in closer for the kill as she whispered, "You're an angel for rescuing me. I just can't have Sarah staying here another minute. She's way too toxic."

My skin prickled with anger and embarrassment. And what was this about her hanging out with Holt? It seemed from the way they were looking at each other, they knew each other a lot better than I thought.

I led James and Richie into my former bedroom to show them the few pieces of furniture I had and the bookshelves on the wall that needed to come down. As they busied themselves stacking things on the dollies Dennis had supplied, I took Holt aside. I could hear Des cooing and flirting with them, and almost see the mental gymnastics she was performing to figure out which guy she could get most easily.

"Really, Holt?" I hissed.

"Don't get mad, darlin'. It was just that one time when you were at that drugstore convention in New Orleans. She called me at two in the morning and invited me over." Perfect. I was trudging through the convention center in New Orleans for the annual meeting of the National Association of Chain

Drugstores, while Des was nailing Holt.

"Holt, how the hell did she get your number?"

"She must have taken it from your address book."

"And you came down from the Bronx at two in the morning?

"Sarah, sugar." He had the good grace to flush slightly. "Do you really want me to explain this to you?"

"No. No, I'd prefer you didn't. Thank you for coming and helping me. Let's just do this."

True to my prediction, the Missiles had packed everything up and moved it all down to Richie's Bronco in under an hour. As we were leaving the apartment for the last time while Des was fawning over the boys, I spied my leather jacket peeking out of her stuffed-to-the-brink-of-exploding closet. Surreptitiously I slid open the door, eased it out, and slipped it into my work tote. For good measure, I also nicked her black nylon and lace chemise that I'd always coveted. On her, it was obscenely short and tight, which I guess was the point. But on me, it just might look like one of the slip-dresses Emporio Armani had been showing that season. In fact, there were some in the store window right now. Maybe after getting Des' version sterilized, I could make it work for the Gotham Gala.

As we walked to Richie's Bronco parked around back, Holt excused himself and jogged up the street. He returned just a few minutes later with a paper bag. We all piled into the car—James and Richie upfront and me and Holt in the back. As I reached for my seat belt, Holt pulled out two bags of frozen peas from his shopping bag.

"Sugar, we're still friends, aren't we?" he asked,

gently placing one bag over my swollen eye and bumped forehead and the other over my now fat lip. There was no resisting that sheepish smile, that accent, those damn blue eyes and freckles, and the fact that he was now touching my face even if it was with two bags of frozen peas.

"Sure, Holt. Always," I said, patting his enormous arm.

It turned out to be a great night with Penny bringing home leftovers from the restaurant and the guys making a beer run. And after an evening of three breathtaking guys and my best friend tending to my wounds and doing their damndest to convince me to move into the apartment, I agreed. I mean, in the end, I had nowhere else to go. So even though it meant being late for work, I left Nils an apologetic, explanatory message as soon as I woke up, and with Penny's help, I applied enough of her foundation and cover-up to camouflage the scars left from my fall from grace the night before. Mercifully, they were either far less serious than they appeared last night, or Holt's frozen peas had worked their magic, so I wasn't too worried about facing the building manager to hand over a check and sign a one-year lease. Besides, this was the Bronx. I figured he'd seen far worse.

It felt good to write a check to someone else besides Des' parents for my living space, even if it meant I now had a balance of only twelve dollars in my checking account. Holt promised he'd move me in that day and said he even had a TV for me since he had just upgraded from a big-screen model to a supersized one. Penny would leave my key in her apartment afterward, which I had the key to.

Things seemed to be going well for a change. Until I started opening my suitcases looking for work clothes, my makeup, and any accessories I had that would work for the Gotham Gala. I found the small, beaded bag my grandmother used to wear for fancy occasions and my lone pair of costume chandelier earrings that Des had had the decency to toss into a sandwich baggie before throwing them into my suitcase. But she'd neglected to pack any of my nice shoes, and had only flung in my motorcycle boots, Doc Martens, and sneakers. Where the hell had she hidden my shoes when we were up there? And now I couldn't seem to locate yesterday's work flats in the mess that had become my life and was strewn about Penny's apartment.

I had no choice but to slip on my Doc Martens, rather than my sneakers or motorcycle boots with my charcoal gray pants suit and maroon blouse. They seemed the lesser of three corporate evils.

Then I gathered up my leather jacket and Des' slip for the Gala, feeling doubly happy now that I'd relieved her of it. I headed down Penny's five flights of stairs onto Bailey Avenue and walked over to Broadway to take the 1/9 train from 238 Street to 34th street. It was going to be a long ride. I hoped Nils would understand.

Chapter 3

Between all the delays on the 1/9 and making a pit stop at the cleaners to get Des' slip disinfected, plus my usual coffee run, I didn't get to work until eleven. As usual, Nils was hunched over his keyboard, his two fingers pounding away for all he was worth when I handed him his coffee. He looked up, smiled, and gestured with his head to the open *Gotham Sentinel* on his desk. The headline and subhead read:

Sophistiquée CD Locks Horns with new EIC. Could Fi be on her way out? I quickly scanned the article which detailed all the issues *Sophistiquée's* prototypically sixty-five-year-old French creative director Henri-François Bernard was having with the younger and more modern Fiona Doyle. It didn't look good for her—at least according to the *Sentinel*.

"Didn't you just talk to her yesterday?" Nils asked before gulping down some of the coffee I offered him.

"I did. She's super cool." I didn't tell him that Fiona had wanted me to interview for the magazine's beauty director vacancy because I was pretty sure she was over that idea by now. And if she were going to get pushed out by Henri-François, there was no point, anyway. Why upset him needlessly?

"Well, since you're buddies now, why don't you give her a call and get her statement about this for our Media Page?" Nils wiped coffee off his mustache with a sleeve and grinned. "That world is pretty crazy. She's barely been there for a minute. Hey, how did your move go?"

"Surprisingly okay."

"Did something happen to you yesterday?" he continued, staring intently at my made-up face. Guess Penny and I didn't do as good a job with the cover-up as we thought. Maybe I could go to a makeup counter at Macy's for a professional touch-up before tonight.

"It's a long and crazy story but I'm all right. Thank you for asking."

"Well, we're all glad you're done with that crazy girl once and for all, even if you're further away from us in the Bronx. You're still going to come Saturday mornings to jam with Dana, right?"

"Of course, that was never even a question. And sadly, I am not quite done with Des as she seems to have kept all of my shoes." I wiggled my foot to show him a Doc Marten.

"Nice." He nodded his approval, rocker that he was. "That's good about Dana. Not so good about Des. By the way, both Ursula and Dana ripped me a new one for not giving you more notice about the Gotham Gala tonight. Sorry about that." Ah, that explained why he was being such a pussycat about my lateness.

"I'll let you slide this once," I deadpanned, picking up the *Sentinel* and heading back to my cubicle.

"Let's plan on leaving here tonight at six. It'll be faster to ride the subway up, but I did get approval for you to take a cab home and I'll get you some petty cash for it."

"And who said we don't lead glamorous lives?" I tossed over my shoulder.

As soon as I got back to my desk, I picked up the phone to call Des. I figured if she left my shoes downstairs with Dennis, I could somehow run down to the Village and get them before we needed to leave tonight. Nils being contrite and all about springing the Gala news on me at the last minute gave me a little breathing room. I got her machine.

"You've reached…" Des' phone number rolled out. "You know what to do. Just do it after the beep." Her voice was so husky she sounded like she would hyperventilate at any second.

"Hey, Des, it's Sarah. Somehow, all my shoes seem to be missing from my stuff. I'm hoping you can put them in a bag and leave them downstairs for me ASAP so I can pick them up from Dennis. I have to cover the Gotham Gala for the paper tonight, and I need my sandals. Can you call me back to let me know you got this message and will take care of this for me?" And even though I knew she had it based on the thousands of times she pestered me at work, I left her my number.

Next, I called Fiona's office to get a comment. Her assistant connected me almost immediately.

"Hello, Sarah, good morning. How are you?" Fiona's voice was warm.

"Good. Good, Fiona. How are you?"

"Splendid. Did you want to set up some time to chat?"

"This is kind of awkward but I'm not calling you about that. We wanted to get your comment on that article in the *Sentinel* this morning about you and Henri-François."

"Oh. That drivel?" She laughed. "There is absolutely nothing even remotely true about that piece.

It's just unfounded gossip to sell papers."

"Do you want to give me a formal statement?"

"Of course. You can write that Henri-François and I are a united front working as a team to uphold *Sophistiquée's* high standards of journalism, photography, and design while evolving our content for the modern audience."

"That's great. Thank you."

"After you and I are done. I'll connect you to his office and I'm sure he'll say the very same thing."

"Hey, that'd be great. Thanks, Fiona."

"So, listen, I don't want to beat a dead horse. But I still think you're a strong candidate for our beauty director spot."

"Thank you, Fiona, but I think it's best for me to stay where I am right now."

"Well, if you're sure. I certainly won't press the issue. Are you going to the Gotham Gala tonight? Perhaps we can at least say a proper hello there."

"Sure. That'd be nice."

"Great. Let's look for each other then. Hold and I'll connect you to Henri-François' line. Bye for now."

After two rings, a machine picked up with a lovely West Indian female voice announcing that Henri-François was unable to take my call but would return it "*Avec plaisir*" when time permitted. From what I'd heard about Henri-François, this recording was true to form. Henri-François was reputed to favor young Caribbean women as his assistants. In fact, he favored them so much the *Sentinel* had recently reported that several of these women had filed a class-action suit against him. And from what I could gather, it wasn't the first time. Henri-François was also legendary for his tight crotch-straining white Levi 501 button-fly jeans and his perpetual pelvis-thrust-forward-hands-on-hips stance. His favorite topic of conversation was the nickname he had given himself.

"Do you know that they call me the trripod?" He supposedly would croon in his heavily accented English, as though mesmerized by himself. "Eet ees not because I am a photographerrr." Then, as legend would have it, he would briefly wrench his eyes away from the breasts of the poor woman he had cornered to glance down at his privates and then back up at her face, daring her to guess the true meaning of his self-selected sobriquet. I'm assuming no one ever did. I mean, I wouldn't.

Given his reputation, I wasn't particularly sorry Henri-François didn't pick up and left a message that I would appreciate his calling me back to give me a comment on today's *Sentinel* piece. I then got down to the business of creating the questions we would ask the beauty executives at the Gala that night on "the state of the industry" and continuing to report on our story about beauty editors leaving magazines for digital ventures. Before I knew it, it was four and I still hadn't heard back from Des. So, I called again.

"Des," —I did my best not to yell into the phone— "I know you check your messages obsessively. So please don't pretend you didn't get my first one. I need you to get back to me about my shoes. Let's end things as nicely as possible between us. You certainly haven't been an angel in any of this. Please call me back." Damn it. She was really going to hold my shoes hostage to teach me the lesson she decided I needed to be taught. It was looking like I would have to wear my

Doc Martens with the slip. This was going to be a disaster. That reminded me, I needed to go pick up the slip at the cleaners. It made perfect sense to me that celebrities had personal stylists. Who could keep track of this stuff?

I ran out to get the slip and iced teas for me and Nils, praying my message light would be on when I got back. It was. "Allo, Sarraah? Sarraah Mandelbaum?" A male voice intoned dragging out my name as slowly and Frenchly as possible. "Theese ees Henri-François Bernard. I am calling to say that I love Feeona, and we work *très bien* ensemble. We are a team. *Merci, au revoir*."

At five-thirty, I realized I was doomed to wearing my Doc Martens to the Gala. Des totally had me this time. So, I hit the ladies' room, put on the newly cleaned slip with my leather jacket, and tried to do what I could with my hair, which seemed to be growing wider by the minute, and my makeup, which I wasn't particularly skilled at applying despite my affiliation with the beauty industry. In the end, though, I thought I looked all right, and you could barely see my Sidewalk injuries. Still, somehow my childhood nemeses—the Terror Trio—joined my reflection in the mirror jeering at my "Brillo-Pad" hair and "Bozo the Clown" makeup job. "I look fine," I said out loud to all four of us. "Good, even."

I went back to my desk to get my bag and reporter's notebook and was about to meet Nils at the elevator when I heard someone boom, "Mandelbaum!" from across the floor. It was Michael. He motioned me over to him. He was wearing the most gorgeous Dior tux and black Stemar dress shoes. "Reporting for us on the Gala tonight?" he asked, discreetly looking me up and down.

"Yes. Nils and I are going to tear it up," I repeated Nils' words from the other day. I always felt shy around Michael. I mean, he was an actual fashion legend.

"I have complete confidence in you, Mandelbaum. You always do great work."

"Thank you, Michael. That means a lot to me."

"Listen, Mandelbaum, this industry gets kind of crazy, and I want you to remember, especially tonight, that it's people like you who make the clothes and not the other way around—the clothes don't make the people. Of course, if you tell anyone I said that I'll call you a liar to your face. Now go have fun storming the castle." And with that, he swept out of the newsroom and then likely into the limo waiting for him downstairs.

Of course, the 6 train uptown was not only crammed to the point of sticky suffocation—we were having one hell of a hot fall—but also running with major delays. We were stalled at nearly every station for what seemed like ten minutes at a time. Nils was in a panic since being late to meet a beauty executive with a potential story was his eighth deadly sin, so once we finally got off the train, I had to run to keep up with him for several blocks to the Metropolitan Museum of Art where the Gala was being held. By the time we got there, I was sweaty and knew without even looking that my hair had assumed epic proportions. As we reached the entrance, we ran into our staff photographer and Nils wanted to strategize with him on the night's plan of attack.

"Sarah, go inside and find our table to let Lancôme

know we're here and happy they invited us. It's getting late," Nils said in his industry-event voice.

I certainly wouldn't go as far as saying I was happy Lancôme invited us, but I understood Nils' point—one had to show one's appreciation to the president of a major corporation who included you at his three hundred-thousand-dollar table. But I had to time my entrance precisely.

The huge marble staircase leading up to the second floor was covered in a red carpet with photographers, paparazzi, and reporters flanking the sides. There was a blur of flashbulbs detonating, cameras clicking and sycophantic voices calling out, "You look beautiful, Jennifer. Over here." "Meryl. Gorgeous haircut. On your right." "Brad, Brad, whose tux is that?" Snap, snap, flash, flash, kiss, kiss, flatter, flatter. As a new group of luminaries proceeded to mount the staircase, I attached myself to the tail end of the procession. Snap, snap, flash, flash, kiss, kiss, flatter, flatter. Keeping my head down and concentrating on not falling, I ascended as quickly as possible praying for invisibility. Snap, snap, flash... But all of a sudden, the lights, cameras, and cajoling voices curled up and died. There was nothing but an earsplitting silence.

Finally, a lone photographer called out, "Who's that one with the hair and Doc Martens?" His disdain reverberated off the museum's soaring ceilings, alerting the entire guest list to my fashion faux pas. Okay. *Steady on*, I thought. *Just keep going. You're almost there.* But in reality, I had a long way to go.

"Oh, her? She's nobody," some helpful colleague or other replied.

After I finally made it up those damn stairs, my

face now as hot as the rest of me, I approached the place card table that appeared to be staffed by two femme-bots in matching strapless black mini-dresses. As I got closer, I realized that one of those creatures was Des. I had totally forgotten that her "C-list" modeling agency often staffed events like these with "hostesses."

"Well, Sarah, I can see we can add thief to your list of character flaws," she said, handing me my table number while eyeing the pilfered slip.

"I could say the same thing about you. What was that all about with my jacket? And where are my shoes?" I had to do this quickly and quietly. People were already starting to look our way.

"I don't know what you're talking about. And stop making a scene. You'd better give me that slip back, Sarah. It was Peter's favorite."

"Peter's talking to you again?"

"Well, no. Not yet. But he will when I tell him I evicted you."

With a Herculean effort that surprised even me, I managed to keep my voice level, "Des, if you drop my shoes off at the office tomorrow, I will have your slip waiting for you. I'll even hand wash it myself, tonight."

She thought for a moment and seemed about to argue when two young, attractive tuxedoed Wall Streeters walked over to get their place cards. Abruptly, she switched gears and moved into hair-tossing mode. As she bantered with the boys, she mouthed, "OK." to me. Thankfully, I could cross one thing off the list. Now I had to get to my table, say hello and thank you, and then start circulating the room to get quotes for our article. As I entered the banquet hall, I ran smack into

Peach Chandler and Keeley McPheters huddled together, no doubt critiquing everyone in the room.

"Hello, ladies." I was tentative but decided to push ahead as I needed a quote from Peach. "You look lovely, as always." And of course, they did. Both smooth-haired blondes, Peach with a sleek bob and Keeley, hair to her waist and stick straight, they'd clearly borrowed dresses for the occasion. Peach held court in a red Carolina Herrera strapless number and Keeley was poured into the damn black Emporio Armani slip dress that I thought Des' cheap imitation could pass as. But now that I was up close and personal with the real version, I could see what I had on wasn't even a poor knockoff. It was a disaster. Both girls also sported skyscraper stilettos and true to Fashion Flamingo form were gracefully shifting from one foot to the other. I couldn't help but wonder when the last time either editor had eaten a sandwich was. Years ago, by the looks of it.

"Oh, hi. Sarah, right? You're with FDG?" Peach murmured, scarcely looking up.

"Yes. Yes, I am. And at some point, I'd like to get a comment from you on your move to digital. Congratulations by the way."

"Oh, that's right. You trade rag reporters have to work tonight. Well, I'll let you get your nose back to the grindstone. You're certainly dressed for it." And without further ado, she resumed her conversation with Keeley. But when I wasn't even out of earshot, Peach administered the *coup de grâce* proclaiming in a voice much louder than the one she used to speak to me, "Oh God, Keeley. What was that all about? How could anyone think of wearing a nylon slip with a pleather jacket to the Gotham Gala? Not to mention Doc Martens and that hair. No wonder she hides in the business end."

"Shh, Peach, she'll hear you." Keeley giggled, negating any humanity I might have attributed to her.

"Well, I'd be doing her a great favor if she did."

Michael's pep talk wasn't even a distant memory. I tried to calm myself down because I was about to throw up all over the Met's marble floors. *Come on, Sarah, breathe. And smile for God's sake. You're here for work and you're okay. Nowhere to go but up.* These were conversations I'd been having with myself since I was a kid but, to be honest, they never helped. I couldn't believe how far I'd miscalculated. At least my black lace cocktail dress was unobtrusive. But then I still would've had the damn shoe problem. While I never thought it could be possible, this fashion emergency was even more humiliating than the first day of the eighth grade when I showed up at school in the dark wash Bonjour jeans that I'd babysat all summer to save up for, and everyone had been wearing the last two years, only to find they'd been replaced secretly by pin-striped, ankle-zipped Guess peg legs over the summer. the Terror Trio had a field day. It was just one of the countless terminal fashion goofs I made throughout my adolescence. If there were a radio station that played all my wardrobe choices over its airways, its slogan would be, "WNEW Sarah Mandelbaum Fashion FM: All Wrong All the Time."

Damn Des. And damn Nils for making me take a crowded, sweaty subway and then forcing me to run across town. Without even looking in a mirror I knew my hair had to have expanded beyond the realm of all possibility. I wondered what Saffron Meadows would do on a night like tonight. Sure, she was Ollie's mythological creature, but somehow, I knew that if she existed, she would be rocking these very same threads and throwing down with Plant and Page, shaking her crazy hair for all she was worth. She certainly wouldn't have put up with any of this. Still, a girl's gotta eat and pay her bills, so I pushed onward as bravely as I could and tried to find my table amidst all the shimmer and shine of the glitterati.

When I finally located Lancôme's area of the banquet hall, Nils was already seated, grinning and guffawing away with its president. He raised an eyebrow at me as if to say, "Where have you been? I've been holding down the fort all this time by myself." It took every ounce of self-restraint I possessed not to roll my eyes at him, or worse. Instead, I said hello and thanked my hosts, then flipped open my notebook, uncapped my pen, and got down to business, which meant working the room to get scintillating quotes from beauty execs on trends and sales.

About midway through the evening, I remembered that I was supposed to find Fiona. And even though I looked and felt about as low as I ever had, I certainly didn't want to blow off a reliable source, which she was becoming. I scanned the room and saw her in a smashing Marni saffron-colored silk gown, her wavy sable hair side-swept, standing next to Henri-François who was wearing his trademark tight white Levi 501s along with a sapphire blue velvet Saint-Laurent Le Smoking jacket with an open well-past the neck white ruffled shirt and Vuitton off-white snakeskin embossed shoes. It was fairly obvious he'd selected the jacket to bring out the color of his eyes. I could almost hear him say as much, dragging out all his vowels and over-emphasizing his consonants. His salt and pepper wavy hair was still thick, though receding a bit at the temples, and he was embarrassingly tan for October. Rumor had it he'd persuaded *Sophistiquée*'s top brass to buy a villa in St. Barts where he spent most of his time shooting for the magazine. Nice life. Considering the night I was having, I wasn't particularly overjoyed to see him. But I couldn't back out now as Fiona already was waving me over.

"Hello, Sarah, lovely to see you. Have you met Henri-François?" Before I could reply, Henri-François took my hand, kissed it, and bent over slightly (he wasn't very tall) to lock me in his gaze.

"Sarraah, I am very happy to meet you in person. Fiona says you are an exciting writer and very well-connected with potential advertisers since you interview them all time. We love both these things." And despite his smarmy reputation, all the sexual harassment suits against him, and the fact that it made me sick to even think this for a split second, I could see why Henri-François had bedded practically every supermodel he photographed and even married a couple of them. Yes, he was well-connected and could make you a superstar, but he was also pretty magnetic and even handsome in his way.

I was intrigued by what he said about me being an exciting writer and my ability to generate revenue. I'd never actually thought about myself in those terms. Maybe I was a "catch" for a high-fashion magazine, after all. My beauty industry Rolodex was crammed with the private lines of all the captains of industry, marketing bigwigs and grand poohbahs who made the decisions on where to spend their advertising dollars. The three of us chatted for a few more minutes until I spied Nils gesticulating for me like a maniac across the room. Clearly, he'd realized it was time to stop enjoying himself with the industry executives who wined and dined him, hoping to get good press, and was in a panic to flesh out our story. What he didn't know was that I already had a notebook full of quotes and comments.

As I said my goodbyes and turned to go, Henri-François put his hand on my arm and said in his Frenchified fashion, "Sarraah, you will speak more with Fiona, yes? We are seeing people this week for our new beauty director."

And even though I wasn't sure I meant it, for some strange reason I said, "Yes," and then joined Nils across the room. After about another two hours or so, we were pretty much fried and ready to call it a night, except Nils wanted to catch up with the president of Clinique and I needed to use the restroom. So we made plans to meet at the front entrance to briefly discuss story angles and to give me the petty cash I needed to take a cab back to my new apartment in the Bronx. But when I got there, he was nowhere to be found. This was not particularly unusual as Nils was a chatterer. His goodbyes were about the longest on record. So I waited. And waited. And waited. For a brief moment, I thought about climbing back up those red-carpeted stairs to see if I could find him and drag him out of the hall. But as more and more people started gliding down those very same stairs and out the exit, I realized that somehow Nils and I had gotten our signals crossed.

I reflexively checked my wallet, even though I knew there was nothing in it. My search did yield a single subway token, so at least I could get home. But now that I lived off West 238th street, that journey involved walking the three avenue blocks back to the 6 train, taking it downtown to 42nd Grand Central Terminal, hopping the shuttle across to Times Square, and then jumping on the 1/9 train up to 238th and Broadway. If I made it home by one, it would be astounding.

As my train crawled along, I couldn't help but wonder how Peach Chandler and Keeley McPheters got home that night, likely by car service. And then there were the perfect dresses they'd scored and the professional hair and makeup they had done. I bet they got paid a hell of a lot more than I did too. Maybe, just maybe, I would call Fiona tomorrow and hear her out.

Nearly two hours later, I climbed down the 1's elevated platform and started my short walk home. As I took in my new neighborhood, which seemed surprisingly clean and quiet, I saw an all-night bodega that had one bouquet of roses left for sale. They were coral. Penny would love that. Impulsively, I put them on my just-for-drop-dead-emergencies-credit card for her as a thank you for moving me in. I checked my watch and realized that even though it was late, she likely was en route from the restaurant, which was in Tribeca. Still, I had to pick up my key from her apartment so I could leave the flowers for her to find when she got home.

That felt like the best plan I'd had in ages. I climbed the five flights up to her one-bedroom and let myself in. She'd left the key for me and one perfect cupcake—yellow with chocolate frosting and ornate blue and yellow flowers, my favorite—along with the note. "Welcome home, kitten." I couldn't have been happier that I'd picked up those flowers.

But now, all I wanted to do was peel off my now incredibly sweaty clothes. My leather jacket felt like a scuba suit, and Des' slip was clinging to me in places I'd rather not mention. People must have gotten quite an eyeful of me on the subway. I walked out of Penny's building and into mine. It was four flights up to my new place. I was glad to be home. And this was *my* home. Not Des'. I hadn't been in the apartment for five minutes when my phone rang portentously. There were only two people in the world that made the phone ring that way, Des, and my mother, Anna Elias Mandelbaum. And since Des was probably rolling around in bed with or shrieking at some guy she picked up tonight, it had to be Anna.

"Hi, Mom," I said, not waiting to hear who the other person was on the line.

"For God's sake, Sarah, I have been calling you all night. Where have you been? It's one-thirty in the morning. And when did you plan on telling me you had moved and changed your phone number?"

"How do you know I moved?" I sighed.

"I'm not an idiot, Sarah. You used to have a 212 number and when I called you on that tonight a recording said it had been disconnected and gave me a 718 number for you, instead. That is not a Manhattan exchange. Where are you?"

"I'm in the Bronx."

"The Bronx! What in the world are you doing up there? "

"It's a long story, Mom."

"Are you still living with that crazy roommate?"

"I am not. Being able to afford to live without her is one of the reasons I'm up here."

"It can't be safe."

"It's perfectly safe, Mom. It's a family neighborhood. Penny's lived here for years." I'd said the magic words. My mom, like everyone else, loved Penny.

"Well, if Penny thinks it's safe, it's fine, then. I still don't know why you won't ask your sister for help with your loans and living situation. She's doing so well. And honestly, you wouldn't even have these loans to repay if you had listened to me and your father and had become a lawyer or a teacher like respectable girls do. And here you are, all this money to pay back and not even using your fancy conservatory degree. I just don't understand you."

There were so many different things to unpack here I didn't even know where to begin. And I just couldn't seem to come to my defense and say that if my parents had let me go to CCM where the professors, at least to my mind, were more supportive than the ones at the conservatory. I might not have been terrorized out of trying to go pro by the scalding hot flood of criticism they doused me with daily. CCM, I'd decided, wouldn't have cared about the size of my guitar.

But no matter how much my mother goaded me, I never could bring myself to say this out loud. Because deep down inside—in places I'd rather not mention—I was petrified that size *didn't* matter, at least in this case, and that the real reason I hadn't gone pro was that I just didn't have what it takes.

But there *was* the undeniable truth that Morrisa wasn't going to help anyone—ever—and that, I could and would say out loud. "Mom, Morrisa wouldn't help me or anyone else for that matter if you held a gun to her head."

"Why would you say such a thing?"

"Because, Mom, Morrisa is a witch. She was born a witch, is still a witch, and will likely die a witch."

"Sarah, don't talk about your sister that way, and you know I don't tolerate language like that."

"Language like witch? Whatever you say, Mom. Was there something specific you were calling me about?" I hugged the receiver between my ear and neck as I tried mostly unsuccessfully to kick off my Doc Martens and wriggle out of Des' damn slip.

"I'm your mother. Do I need a reason to call?" It was getting so late I could practically hear the second hand on my exceedingly quiet watch ticking.

"Have you talked to Morrisa lately?"

"Morrisa's very busy with her movie mogul clients."

"Morrisa is always busy sucking up to some superstar somebody or other."

"Well, that's why she's so successful. You could take a page or two from her work ethic book."

Funny, I didn't think the book Morrisa read, much less took a page from, had anything to do with a strong work ethic. Named for my wonderful grandfather Morris, my older sister Morrisa had dropped out of Skidmore college when my father Seymour Mandelbaum left us when I was fifteen for Caroline, a junior partner at his firm with whom he shortly thereafter if not before fathered my half-brothers—

twins, named Jared and Jason. And since my dad specialized in matrimonial law, he managed quite the settlement for himself and his new family, leaving very little leftover for my mother.

Instead of sticking around to help us move out of our childhood house in Teaneck, NJ into an apartment off Queen Anne Road, Morrisa followed the Grateful Dead around the world selling tie-dye T's in parking lots, leaving me to take care of my mom by myself, who was beyond devastated and barely functioning. And the entire time my mother praised Morrisa for being so adventurous and independent, even though she was wearing herself out teaching 10th-grade history at a not-so-nice high school in Englewood and spending evenings and Saturdays as a salesperson at Hit or Miss on Cedar Lane.

I picked up work at Igor's Records, where I'd always hung out anyway and Igor, a truly decent guy, gave me as many shifts as I wanted. It was heaven for me to talk about music for hours on end, and the guys who worked in the store were great. We even started a band together. My mom and I did all right, even though it was a big comedown for her, and she was pretty damn tired all the time.

Yet, somehow, Morrisa was always a hero. And now that she'd traded her overalls and Wallaby shoes for chic, black Donna Karan suits and was a top banana Hollywood agent, I never heard the end of it, even though she seldom spoke to, much less saw, either one of us.

"The last time I spoke to Morrisa she said that when I retire, she'll get me a house next door to her in Santa Monica and a car with a driver, and I will be just like driving Miss Daisy." I didn't point out to her how racist that dream was since I could say without hesitation that it would never come true. My sister was a talker.

"Mom, was there anything else? It's late and I have to get up early tomorrow for work."

"Sarah, you know I don't like it when you try and rush me off the phone. It's disrespectful. Remember, I'm the mother and you're the child."

"I understand, Mom. What else did you want to talk about?"

"My dentist's son just went into practice with him and he's looking to meet someone, so I told him about you. I'm going to give him your new number. Please be nice to him when he calls. And if he looks anything like his father and is half as successful, this could mean big things for you, Sarah."

I was speechless with terror. No Anna Elias Mandelbaum fix-up could be anything other than utterly horrifying. Now I would have to screen my calls so I wouldn't have to speak to her dentist's son. I resolved to lie and say I never got his message if he left one.

Anna pushed on, annoyed by my silence. "Sarah, are you there?" Can you please pay attention to me? We only speak a few times a week, so the least you can do is focus on what I am telling you when we actually do talk."

"Yes, Mom, I'm here."

"His name is Stuart Felsenfeld."

"Stuart Felsenfeld?"

"There's nothing wrong with Stuart or Felsenfeld for that matter, Monkey Face. To my mind, it's a whole lot better than Mandelbaum. If I hadn't been married to your father for twenty-five years, I would have taken back my maiden name."

I cringed at her "pet name" for me. Anna called Morrisa, "My Beauty."

"Mom, can you not call me that?" I asked, knowing full well her answer.

"There's nothing wrong with Monkey Face. It's affectionate." She sniffed, and then I felt additional waves of tension crackling over the phone lines. "Have you talked to your father?" Her typically high-pitched voice rose even higher as she prepared to start in on my dad.

"Mom, I'm not going to get into this with you. It never turns out well and it's late."

"Well, I certainly don't know why you need to keep secrets from me. I'm the easiest-going person in the world. But you're right, Monkey Face, it's late, and I've got to get today's tests graded. Make sure you're pleasant to Stuart. We all know how you can be. And remember, you can call me once in a while. Don't make me be the one to always have to pick up the phone. It isn't nice."

"Mom, it's two in the morning. Don't you need to get some sleep?"

"Sleep? Who sleeps anymore? Good night."

It wasn't until I hung up that I realized Penny and Holt had outfitted me with a real living room/dining area with an actual coffee table, couch, dining table, and black leather high-backed chairs. It was wonderful. Holt had even set up his old TV and my stereo, and Penny had made my bed. Having such incredible friends made up for my horrible evening and that horrible conversation with my mom. But by this time, I was determined to call Fiona in the morning and interview for that job. I just had to start taking control of my life.

I finally got to shed the rest of my sticky clothes and eat my perfect cupcake. I pulled on my Keith Richards shirt and tumbled into bed, anticipating the best night's sleep I'd had in ages now that Des was out of the picture. But almost as soon as I dissolved into my sheets, an electric guitar started blaring at Madison Square Garden decibels from the apartment above me. I gave it a minute or two because the playing was outstanding, and I figured someone else in the building would put a stop to it. I hated being a narc and doubly hated it since I had just moved in and didn't want to be "that neighbor"—you know the one people hate because she's in everyone's business all the time. Still, it was now almost two-thirty, and it'd been a ridiculously rough night, so a narc I would have to be.

I couldn't find my robe or slippers, so I grabbed my keys and ventured out into my new hallway barefoot in just my Keith shirt and up the stairs to the fifth floor. It was obvious which apartment the music was coming from because its walls were vibrating. There was no way whoever was in there was going to hear me unless I made a statement. So, I began to pound on the door with as much might as I could muster. After what seemed like years, a tall, lanky guy with straight black hair that fell into his large hazel eyes nearly obscured by enormous black plastic-framed glasses opened it and poked his head out. He was wearing large headphones over his ears with the cord dangling around his neck and holding a gorgeous

Gibson Gold Top electric guitar.

"Those work a lot better plugged in," I said, pointing to his headset. He gestured to me to wait a minute and slid the headphones off.

"What did you say?"

"I said that your headphones would work a lot better if you plugged them into your amp."

"Oh no way, was I not plugged in?"

"Couldn't you tell?"

"Not really. I was so into this new tune that just came to me. I wanted to get it down before I forgot it."

"It sounded great. But it's like two-thirty in the morning."

"Oh wow. I'm really sorry."

"Okay, thanks. Good night." I turned to go.

"Nice shirt," he called after me.

"Nice Gold Top," I returned, wondering what this guy's deal was.

Chapter 4

When I woke up the next morning, the first thing I saw was Des' sweaty slip balled up on the floor. Crap. I was supposed to wash it and hang it up to dry last night. If it wasn't in perfect condition, she could use it as an excuse to keep my shoes. I'd have to run to the cleaners to see if they could do a quick steam. Since Des didn't usually emerge from her coffin before noon, I figured I had some leeway. I realized that at the end of all this I would have spent nearly twenty dollars on the care and feeding of an article of clothing that had done nothing but bring me heartache. I wondered if the rumors were true about beauty editors at high fashion magazines getting clothing allowances. Well, I was going to talk to Fiona today and maybe find out.

Since I didn't have any business meetings that day, I went rogue and wore a pair of black pants, a striped shirt, and a short black blazer instead of one of my God-awful suits. My outfit wouldn't be written up on anyone's best-dressed list, but at least I wouldn't embarrass myself if Fiona wanted to meet. Penny had located my work flats from the day before and placed them by my futon, so I was good to go. I found my Walkman, popped in The Black Crowes *Amorica* so I could hear "Wiser Time", which never failed to make me smile, headed down the stairs and out the front door only to find the guy from last night sitting on the front stoop intently smoking a cigarette.

"Hey," he called out to me. "I'm really sorry about last night." He was wearing a white T-shirt, a tweed jacket that revealed his long, bony wrists, black sneakers, and the same white Levi 501 button-fly jeans from the night before. There obviously was a trend in snowy denim that I didn't know about. But this guy wore his jeans loose and roughed up, which I found to be way more appealing than those of Henri-François, which were not only painted on but also pristine and pressed. I took off my headphones, essentially re-creating our meeting from the night before almost to a T.

"What did you say?"

He laughed a little and repeated himself. "I said, 'I'm really sorry about last night.'"

"Oh, it's fine. Ordinarily, I would've loved it. I just haven't gotten much sleep lately."

"Well, still. It won't happen again. Are you new to the building? I haven't seen you around before."

"Yeah, last night was my first night here."

"You must be the one who used the New York Missiles as your moving company. I was outside grabbing a smoke with some of the guys who work in the building when they pulled up and we were all wondering who was moving in." That reminded me that as soon as I got my next paycheck, I had to buy Holt, Richie, and James a really nice dinner. And now that I paid a reasonable rent instead of one that took half my salary, I might even be able to afford it.

"Well, second-string Missiles," I joked, embarrassed that I'd asked such celebrities to do my grunt work. "My best friend is Holt Abernathy's twin sister."

"He lives in the next building, right? One of the guys said he's outstanding and that the real fans are hoping that guy Darius, I think his name is, will retire or get traded so your friend can start." He lit another cigarette with his butt before stubbing it out and inhaled deeply.

"Holt's a great guy. We've been pals for years." It was late and I had to get to work but I liked standing around talking to my new neighbor, as quirky as he seemed. I tried to think of something else to say and couldn't, so I turned to go. But he stopped me.

"I'm Sean. Sean Weiland," he said, holding out his hand. It was impossible not to notice how long, slim, and graceful his fingers were. No wonder he could make his Gold Top sing.

"Weiland? Like Scott Weiland from Stone Temple Pilots? Cool."

"I guess so. I never really thought about it that way. I'm more into punk, classic and alternative rock than grunge, but they're a good band."

"I love STP, Alice in Chains, and Nirvana. But I dig classic rock, too. And some alternative is cool, like The Cure and P. Furs. And then there's Bowie." I just couldn't seem to stop chattering away.

"And then there's Bowie," he repeated quietly.

"I'm Sarah by the way. Sarah Mandelbaum."

"Nice name." He smiled a little, rested his cigarette on the pavement, and then picked up both of my hands to examine them. This guy was so strange but in the most appealing way. "Ah, I guessed from the way you were eyeing my Gold Top last night that you played guitar. Now I have confirmation. And you're a lefty, too."

I couldn't for the life of me figure out how he could tell. My hands were ridiculously stubby and totally un-rock star. But I liked that he was holding them. So much so, I think I might have blushed when I replied, "What gave me away?"

"You have callouses on your fingertips, and the ones on your right are thicker than the ones on your left, which means you finger with them—exactly the opposite of a righty."

"That's very astute of you. I do, indeed, play guitar. And I am left-handed." I paused, waiting yet again for something witty to fly out of my mouth. It didn't. So instead, I said, "Hey, it was nice talking to you, but I need to get to work, so we'll have to gab more about music another time."

"It's a deal, Sarah Mandelbaum. Now go and have a beautiful day." He smiled wider this time, revealing a crooked front tooth, and released my hands. I walked over to the subway, resisting the urge to look back at him, wondering if he had already lit up another cigarette, hoping he hadn't.

When I got off the subway, I dropped off Des' slip at the cleaners for the second day in a row, which earned me a wink from the elderly proprietress, picked up Nils' coffee, and grabbed the latest *Sentinel.* On the front page, a headline screamed out: "Finally! A Facelift for *Sophistiquée"* with the accompanying caption reading: *Sophistiquée top brass hint at new blockbuster edit and ad sales strategy.* I couldn't resist smiling to myself, wondering if this "new blockbuster edit and ad sales strategy" had anything to do with potentially hiring me. But the article was pretty ambiguous since both Henri-François and Fiona had only hinted to the *Sentinel's* Gotham Gala reporters that something "big", "groundbreaking", and "iconoclastic" (Fiona's word) was in the works. I hoped Nils would be so obsessed with writing up last night's coverage that he wouldn't ask me to follow up on this story and would turn it over to the media reporter. I was starting to feel guilty in my role as a double agent. And mercifully, when I got to his cubicle to hand him his coffee, he was thundering away at his keyboard and didn't even mention the article.

"Hey, thanks," he said, accepting the coffee. "What happened to you last night? I waited for you at the side door like we planned, and you never showed up."

"Well, Nils, I wasn't at the side door because we said we'd meet at the front entrance. And I ended up having to take three subways and getting home at one in the morning." My tone was far more strident than I intended. But it was hard to play it cool after the stress, drama, and general misery of last night.

"Really? Are you sure?"

"Yes, Nils, I'm sure."

"Well, you're here now, so, no harm, no foul. Let's tame this beast," he said, turning away from me to his notebook. "Why don't you type up your quotes and jot down any ideas you have about a theme for our Gala Beauty Trends Report, then we can sit down after lunch and write the story together." Nils had flipped on his boss mode switch—the usual indication of his realizing he'd messed up. But I wasn't in a forgiving mood, so I remained firm in my commitment to call Fiona, which I did as soon as I got to my desk.

"Hello, Sarah," Fiona sang when she came on the

line. "Did you have a nice time last night?" Nice was hardly the word. Craptastic was more how I'd put it. But now was definitely the time to keep things pleasant and professional.

"Oh sure," I replied. "I got a lot of great quotes and story ideas."

"I love that you're always working, Sarah, even at the most glamorous event of the year. It says a lot about you. Did you want to have lunch today?"

"I'm not sure I can get away since I'm on deadline for the story. Would there be another time that works for you?"

"I completely understand. Let's meet for a drink tonight around seven. Will you be free by then?"

"I think eight would be better, but I hate to ruin your evening."

"Not at all. There's always a ton for me to do around here. So, let's say eight at Balthazar. We can grab a bite." Balthazar was as fabulous as it got. What a relief that I'd left my navy polyester at home.

"That sounds great," I said. "I'll see you then and there."

"Looking forward, Sarah. Have a lovely day." After we hung up, my message light came on. I prayed it wasn't Des bothering me about something else. But it was Penny.

"Hey, kitten, you're an absolute angel. Those roses were gorgeous and just what I needed after one of my most horrific nights with Rex ever. He was being the Mount Everest of all a-holes yesterday—even more so than usual." She sighed briefly, but then quickly regained her signature upbeat attitude. "Anyhow, Holt and some of the guys are coming over to my place at around eleven tonight when I'm off work for a Thursday-is-Saturday cocktail party. So, I'll see you tonight, and, no, I don't need you to bring anything, but you're sweet to ask."

Penny knew me so well. It would be yet another late night, but it would be a fun one, and maybe we'd even have something to celebrate. I smiled as I started typing up my notes from the night before and shaping a theme.

Around noon, I called the dry cleaner and Des' slip was ready, so I ran out to grab it and then left it with the front desk security guard. Fingers crossed that Des would stick to our agreement so I could be rid of her once and for all. I settled down with Nils amidst the clutter and chaos of his cubicle and we got to work. At six, we sent the story through to the managing editor, answered his queries, and then moved it over to fact-checking and copy editing. By seven-fifteen, it was ready to be "shipped electronically" to the printers so we called it a night. I would have just enough time to try and smooth out my hair in the ladies' room and get down to SoHo to meet Fiona at Balthazar. On my way out, I asked the security guard on our floor if he had a bag for me. Surprisingly, he did—a large drawstring garbage bag that I locked up in my file cabinet before racing down the stairs onto the street to try and make my meeting on time.

Of course, Balthazar was mobbed when I got there, and the maître d' kept avoiding eye contact and seating other patrons first. Finally, after what seemed like thirty minutes and an 8-mile trek, he led me to Fiona's table. She was as perfect as ever in a wine-colored Von Furstenberg wrap dress.

"Well, hello, Sarah. How'd the story go? Will you have a drink?" Really, she was lovely.

"Hi, Fiona. Thanks for asking. I'm pretty happy with the way it turned out," I replied, trying not to knock my silverware off the tiny table. "I think I'll just have a Diet Coke." Now was not the time to get tipsy.

"Are you sure? Will you eat something? I'm famished. The Pommes Frites are exceptional here. The mussels—too. Shall we get some?" I actually loathed mussels, but then again, I was so happy to be sitting with a member of the high fashion community that ate French fries, I decided it didn't matter.

"I'm not big on reading resumes, so why don't you just chat with me for a minute about you and your career? What school did you go to? What other jobs have you had?" She took a sip of her red wine and smiled. I couldn't help but smile back. This didn't seem like it would be as painful as most other job interviews, so I launched in.

"I graduated with a BA Cum Laude in English and French with an art history minor from Robert Lowell University," I said, intentionally leaving out my music degree. It just didn't seem relevant and besides, mentioning it always brought up these condescending and cringeworthy questions, such as, "You have a degree in music? How marvelous. What are you doing with it?"

And since Fiona merely nodded encouragingly and said, "Oh, you speak French. Henri-Francois will love that."

I knew I'd made the right call and just kept on going. "My first job out of school was at *40 Days & 40 Nights* as both a fact-checker and reporter. I've been at

FDG about a year."

"You do a terrific job at FDG," she effused. "And from what I've heard, Nils Petersen and Michael Gallagher are great to work with. Why would you be willing to make a move to *Sophistiquée*—especially when you've repeatedly told me you don't consider yourself high-fashion material?"

"Well, I don't, to be honest with you, but I love your ideas about making the magazine more accessible to the average woman. I'm good at accessibility. I think it's one of my strongest suits." I laughed a little hoping she'd get the joke. She smiled again so I felt like it was okay to continue. "And I'm definitely up for a new challenge. Not to mention the fact that I likely would have a positive impact on your ad sales given all my contacts." I was selling myself for a job that scared the hell out of me. Being beauty director at *Sophistiquée* meant going to daily press events with the Fashion Flamingos. And I'd heard horror stories about the *Sophistiquée* staff members themselves, especially Samara Taylor, the beauty assistant, and Christie Somers, the associate. Did I really want to spend the next phase of my career with girls so mean they made the Terror Trio seem downright friendly in comparison? Then there was the whole Henri-François situation.

Still, maybe I could make it work. It was a big job. A good job. And it could mean greater things for me down the line. I certainly didn't want to end up like some of the reporters at FDG who'd been there for thirty years. I mean, I guess it was fine for them and they would likely receive some decent benefits when they retired, but I didn't want my life to look like that.

"These are good answers," Fiona jumped in before

I could go on. "Let me tell you about the job. As beauty director of *Sophistiquée,* you would be running the department, which means you'd be responsible for the entire content of the beauty section, including both visuals and editing. So, you would concept out every issue, assign and edit all the stories and write a few yourself if you have time. You'll be out in the market quite a bit at industry press events and ad sales calls with our publisher Giancarlo Romano, and you would work out the visuals with Henri-François and our art director Didier Tremblay. You would also manage the beauty team." Fiona took a deep breath and then another sip of her wine.

"I won't sugarcoat this next bit," she said. "You'll be the youngest person running a department on staff, and Samara and Christie are not only pretty close to your age but rather difficult to work with. I'm betting they'll also be highly disappointed about not getting promoted, especially Christie, who's been campaigning heavily for this job." Fiona paused for a moment and sought my eyes as though trying to gauge my reaction. I struggled to keep my face, which I'm pretty sure was twisting up in terror, as impassive as possible, and take several covert deep breaths in the hopes of steadying my suddenly racing pulse.

Mercifully, Fiona didn't seem to notice and went right on listing all the minuses of the job. "Also, I'm sure you've heard about Henri-François," she continued. "Didier is no easier; he just has less power. I will do my best to shield you from their nonsense, but you should go in knowing you'll have to be tough and not take anything they say or do personally. Everyone is always finger-pointing and backstabbing in the hopes of stealing the job of the next person higher up. But I think you'll be terrific in this position, and you and I can do rewarding work together so it'll be a good experience for you."

I took a swallow of my Diet Coke, wishing I'd ordered a cocktail because I was about to lose my nerve, thank Fiona for the evening, and take myself out of the running. A job at *Sophistiquée* seemed like it would be just as agonizing as my adolescence. And only an idiot would willingly repeat that. But instead of bidding Fiona good night, for some strange reason, I said, "I think I can handle all of that. It doesn't really worry me that much." Now I was an idiot *and* a liar.

"Good. I'm glad we got that out of the way. So, here's my next concern. Your job also covers health and fitness, so how are you with physical fitness? I don't mean all that terrible lose five pounds in five hours stuff that women's magazines are famous for. But real health and fitness coverage that makes women's lives better. And please don't tell me you were always the last person picked for a team in gym class. We all were." Fiona sat back waiting for me to respond. But the forecast was gloomy.

Sure, I was a size 2, which in the real world was considered small, even though most fashion designers would expect someone my height to be a 00. But my measurements aside, I was by no means physically fit or remotely interested in becoming that way. In terms of health, well, I guess being a social smoker was better than sucking cigarettes down as fast as my new cute neighbor did, but my diet consisted of whatever was cheapest to eat, which often meant unlimited margarita Sunday brunch for thirteen dollars. Meanwhile, the

President's Council on Physical Fitness's gym class rope-climbing demands and my sniggering classmates had cured me of any desire whatsoever to exercise in any way, shape, or form.

"Sorry to say, but not only was I the last person picked in gym class, but I also got sent to the vice principal's office for refusing to jump over the hurdles," I admitted, looking down at the plate of mussels the waiter had just brought, knowing full well I wouldn't even take one bite.

"Really? That's funny. What happened? You may have to write about that." She dipped a fry in mayonnaise, Belgian style, and waited for me to finish the story.

"Well, in the seventh grade, we had a track and field unit in gym class, and one day the teacher, Ms. Ludwig, who used to call me Mandelcrap, set up these hurdles for us to jump over. Only I was something like four feet eight inches tall and the hurdles came up to my shoulders. Meanwhile, I'd just gotten my braces off, and my Bat Mitzvah was that Saturday. I knew my mother would kill me if I fell on my face and knocked out a tooth. So, I just said that I wouldn't jump. I don't know where I got the nerve. I'd never talked back to a teacher in my entire life. But my mom was even scarier than Ms. Ludwig and Mr. Manfred, the vice principal—still is, in fact. I guess I was in fight-or-flight mode. So, when the teacher said either I jumped or would have to see Mr. Manfred, I walked off the field to his office."

"That's a riot. What happened when you got there?"

"Mr. Manfred thought it was unbelievably stupid to waste his time punishing a kid for being too short to jump over the hurdles, so he made Ms. Ludwig apologize to me in front of my next period typing class. And to her credit, she did, in quite a nice way, actually. And then she asked me if I would come to the field after school and try jumping over the hurdles if she lowered them, which she did. And so, I did. She never called me Mandelcrap again after that."

"That turned out surprisingly well. It seems like it might even have been empowering for you. I think you'll do just fine covering fitness," Fiona nearly enthused, taking another sip of wine.

"Great. But, please, don't make me write things like, 'Instead of eating pepperoni pizza, have a rice cake with fat-free string cheese, sliced tomato, and one teaspoon of bacon bits'," I replied, working myself up into a small fury. "I hate those articles. A rice cake is god-awful in and of itself but topped with cheese that has the taste and consistency of plastic, it's misery incarnate—even with bacon bits."

At this, Fiona let out a real, genuine belly laugh. "I feel the same way," she said. "Now, are you going to eat some of this food or make me finish all of it?"

It was good, really good, sitting there with her, nibbling French fries, not eating mussels, commiserating with each other about how cruel most women's fashion magazines were and how different we would make *Sophistiquée*. Fiona was, as my mother Anna Elias Mandelbaum would say, "good people."

By the end of the evening, we'd made a deal that involved my getting way more than twice my salary at FDG, plus car service to and from all industry appointments and a clothing allowance, which was laughable given that I wouldn't even know how to spend it. I just knew I wouldn't be using it on frumpy pants suits. Fiona and I hugged goodbye with the understanding she wouldn't announce my new position until I gave notice to Nils and Michael, which I would do tomorrow, though I wasn't looking forward to it. Still, I couldn't wait to tell Penny.

I took the N to Times Square and transferred to the 1/9 uptown. Miraculously, there were no delays. On my way home, I stopped at the liquor store near the subway, picked up a bottle of the cheapest sparkling wine I could find, and put it on my credit card. There was no way I could afford champagne until I got my new paycheck, but I felt like celebrating. On my way to Penny's, I passed my building and saw Sean out on the steps smoking away and strumming the most gorgeous Gibson Dove acoustic guitar. How in the world did he afford these fantastic guitars but have to live in a walk-up in the Bronx? I hoped to find out. I waved the bottle at him and called out, "Hey rock star, I just got a new job. Want to come celebrate with me, Penny, Holt, and some other friends?"

"Hi, Sarah, that's great news. What kind of job?"

"You're talking to the new Beauty & Fitness Director of *Sophistiquée* magazine."

Sean looked puzzled for a minute but tried to hide it. "You work for a fashion magazine?"

"Well, not right now. But after I give my notice to the Fashion Daily Gazette, where I'm currently beauty products and features editor, I will." Even as I said it, I couldn't believe it—me, of all people, having a director spot at *Sophistiquée*. The Terror Trio would die. Sean couldn't seem to take it in, either. He studied my face, then his cigarette, brushed back the hair that had fallen over his glasses, and looked like he was about to say something. But instead, he just took a drag and then started strumming his Dove again. The chords were beautiful but not the answer I'd hoped for.

"So, can you come celebrate?" I persisted. Maybe he was just in a bad mood. But I wanted Sean to be happy for me and I wanted him to come with me to Penny's so I could spend more time with him. Sean looked up at me and smiled, revealing that adorable, crooked front tooth of his. But still didn't say anything and kept on strumming.

"I guess that's a no. Have a good night," I said. This moody, tortured artist thing was getting on my nerves, so me and my sparkling wine were going to go where we'd be appreciated. Penny and Holt would be ecstatic for me. I barely even knew this guy. Why should I give a damn what he thought, anyway?

"Hey, wait a minute," he said, finally looking up from his playing. "Sorry, I was just kind of in the middle of working out this tune. I just didn't picture you in fashion. But if you're happy about this new job, that's great. Tell me about it." He patted the step next to him. I reached over and took a cigarette out of his pack of American Spirits and sat.

"Well, there's not that much to tell. I was offered the job tonight. And it's more than double my current salary and has a lot of perks. Plus, the editor-in-chief is this really cool woman who wants to produce a fashion magazine that real women can relate to. It's kind of exciting, actually."

"And this is your dream job?" Sean asked, lighting up another cigarette with the butt of the one he'd been working on.

"Well, no, not really. My dream job didn't work out," I replied, not wanting to wallow in my past failures when I was feeling lighter and brighter than I had in ages.

"Sometimes, things don't work out, even when they should," he said, not pressing me for any details, which I loved. "But let's toast to your new gig." He touched his cigarette against mine and for a second, I thought he might come with me to Penny's. I got to my feet hoping he'd follow. But he seemed pretty well glued to the cement.

"I'd better go," I said, tossing my cigarette into the street just to give me something to do even though I wasn't finished. "My friends are expecting me. Thanks for the smoke."

"Anytime. I'm not much of a partier, especially with a group of people I don't know, but enjoy your success. It sounds like a big deal." He stopped strumming and held out his hand to me. Was I supposed to shake it? Is that what we were doing? I stood there clutching that damn bottle of cheap wine in my left hand, wondering if I should just shake and be on my way. This was my role in life—everyone's sister or buddy. But as I extended my hand for the expected gesture, Sean pulled me down to him and brushed his lovely mouth against my cheek about a millimeter away from my lips.

"Don't be a stranger, Sarah Mandelbaum," he said, as I straightened up, definitely flushing and desperately wishing I weren't. "We should jam sometime." Now I had two thrilling things to tell Penny.

I pretty much bounded up all five flights to her apartment and walked in the slightly open door. The party was in full swing with some of Holt's teammates and Penny's co-workers milling about. Holt caught sight of me first.

"Well, hey, darlin'. We weren't sure you'd make it," he said, ruffling my hair with the hand that wasn't holding his beer. Yup, definitely a move reserved for your kid sister. But for the first time since I could remember, I didn't mind or want more from him. Sean's kiss still warmed my cheek.

"I owe you, Pen, James, and Richie a big fancy dinner to thank you. I can't believe all you've done for me and how great you made the apartment look." I reached up on my tiptoes to ruffle his hair right back. He had to bend down to let me do it but grinned at my attempt. "And now that I have this big news, I'll be able to take you out somewhere great."

"You have big news?" he asked, his already ridiculously big blue eyes widening. "Of course, you do. You're holding a bottle of champagne. Hang on, let me lower the music and get Pen. She's in the kitchen." Holt turned down the stereo and then called out, "Hey, Pen, Sarah's here with champagne. Come on out so she can tell us why she brought it." He was sweet to call it champagne when it so clearly wasn't." Penny poked her head out the kitchen doorway, holding a tray of mini quiches.

"Kitten! Hang on. Don't tell anyone before I get out there." She emerged seconds later and deposited the tray on her dining room table. Instantly, the apartment became filled with the warm toasty aromas of butter, eggs, and cheese. "So, tell me!" she said, giving me one of her signature enormous hugs. "I feel like it's been ages since we had a real chat."

I felt nervous—almost fluttery inside. But I knew she'd be happy for me, so I plunged ahead.

"You are looking at the new Beauty & Fitness Director of *Sophistiquée* magazine," I announced proudly, repeating word for word what I'd told Sean. But rather than overflowing with jubilation and congratulations, Penny was quiet and studied my face, just like Sean did, as she fiddled with the large floppy bow around the neck of her favorite leopard print blouse. Despite my confusion at her lack of enthusiasm, I couldn't help but notice how much better bows looked on tall people's blouses than on petites. But then, suddenly, she burst out laughing, cutting through my fashion musings.

"Oh, wow. You had me going there for a second, kitten! That's really funny. But seriously, tell us your big news." My chest got tight and my skin felt way too small for my body. I mean, I knew I wasn't the prototypical *Sophistiquée* girl but was it that impossible to believe I could land a senior spot at a big-time woman's magazine?

"That *is* my news. I was offered that job tonight. And I took it." I was quiet and unsure of what else to say. The room had hushed, and everyone seemed to be staring at me. It was Holt who tried to thaw the icy silence.

"Well, hey, Sarah, that's amazing! Let's pop open this bad boy so we can toast you and your fantastic new job and then you can tell us all about it. Penny, why don't you get some cups so we can give everyone a taste?" He leaned in for a hug, which was comforting, but couldn't make up for how crappy I was feeling since I wasn't sure it was one hundred percent sincere.

Holt likely was just being a good sport, like always. At least Richie and James were grinning at me from across the room, and I figured I'd score a high five or two from them before the night was over. Meanwhile, Penny, who appeared to have contracted an exotic form of paralysis and wouldn't make eye contact with me, finally stopped fidgeting with her bow and looked happy that she had a task to perform. She regained her typically bustling style and started passing out the plastic champagne flutes that she seemed to have an endless supply of. Penny used any occasion as an excuse for a party—except for my new job, which clearly didn't seem to give her much cause for celebration.

When everyone had a glass, Holt took over once again, putting his arm around my shoulders and raising his glass. "Here's to our Sarah and her brand spanking new job. Congratulations, darlin', and all the best."

"To Sarah, congratulations!" echoed the rest of the room. And as I'd suspected and hoped, James and Richie immediately came over to me and the high-fiving commenced.

"Thanks, you guys. You're the best. And I'm still in your debt for moving me out of that lunatic's lair into my own place." It felt good to be around people who were happy about my news. "I told Holt that I want to take you all out to dinner, once I get my first paycheck from my new gig. So, think about where you want to go. I want to do something big."

We chatted for a few minutes until they spied the very pretty sous and soup/sauce chefs from Penny's restaurant and went off to pursue greener pastures. I scanned the room but didn't see Penny. I needed to know what was going on. I walked down the hall to the bedroom and found her in there quietly talking to Holt. She was winding one of her chestnut waves around her index finger, so I knew it was a serious conversation. When she saw me, she stopped talking.

"Sarah, come on in," Holt said, a little too brightly when he realized I was in the room. "I'm going to let you and Penny chat while I play host for a minute, but don't leave tonight without giving me all the juicy details." His super-sized legs carried him to the door in less than a second. He pulled it shut behind him.

"So?" I stood a little away from Penny, who was sitting on her bed and now toying with her gold "P" pendant instead of twirling her hair.

"So, tell me about this new job. It seems really sudden." She finally looked at me, but it seemed like it was a struggle for her.

"Penny, what's going on?" My stomach was twisting up inside of itself. She didn't say anything for the longest time. I guess she was gathering her thoughts—something that seemed to be fairly common that evening.

"Why don't you tell me about this job, kitten?" And again, I found myself repeating what I'd told Sean.

"Well, earlier this week the new editor-in-chief of *Sophistiquée*, Fiona Doyle, called me and asked me to interview for the beauty director spot that had just opened up and we met tonight and made a deal." For some reason, I was looking down at my feet when I spoke to her. This wasn't how Penny and I were. Ever. Why was it so damn tense? I wondered if there were any magic words I could say to get her to be as excited about the job as I was until I started talking about it to people in the Bronx. Doggedly, I pushed onward. "It has a lot of perks, like car service, a clothing allowance, and seats at the fashion shows, plus, it pays more than twice what I'm making now," I enthused, even though the mere thought of a fashion show gave me a panic attack. "And Fiona wants to produce a fashion magazine that real women can relate to. I think we can do something meaningful. It's kind of exciting, actually." I tore my eyes away from my flats and looked up at her. She still wasn't smiling.

"Are you sure you want to do this?"

"Penny, why wouldn't I want to do this?"

"I honestly can't believe you would. Fashion shows? Clothing allowance? Car service? Those so aren't your things. And you've spent the entire last year at FDG telling me how mean those fashion magazine girls are. Don't you call them the Fashion Flamingos?" Her inflections were full-tilt Southern now and her tone was rising. Penny rarely got this upset, so it was alarming when she did. "And what about that Henri-François jerk? You can't pick up a newspaper without reading what kind of bastard he is. Why would you ever go and work with someone like that? Rex is a malignant piece of garbage, but this Henri-François guy makes him look like a total gentleman." I was starting to get mad. Why wasn't Penny happy for me? Clearly, something else was up with her. So, I choked back my defensiveness, sat on the bed next to her, and squeezed her hand.

"Pen, what's going on? Are things even worse at work than usual?"

"Rex is a pig and makes my life a living, breathing hell. But I don't want to talk about that right now. I want to talk about you." She sniffed a little and a few enormous tears slid down her cheeks. "I think this is a really bad move for you. I don't want you to be in a snake pit like that. These people will flambé you and you won't play dirty enough to burn them right back. That's not who you are." She sniffled again and squeezed back.

"I don't think it'll be that bad, Pen; Fiona's really cool and completely agrees with me that you shouldn't have to pass a groove test to read a magazine. We're going to totally redo its coverage. It'll be okay—maybe even great." But Penny's well-meaning concern had ripped off the bandage that I'd applied to my own fears, and now I wasn't sure whether I was consoling her or myself. And there was no denying she'd reached the crisis point at her job, and we had to get her out of there.

Suddenly, I was really tired. Bone tired. Dog tired. I looked at the clock and it was past midnight. Tomorrow was going to be one of my least favorite days ever; I'd have to give notice to Nils and Michael. I should at least try and get some sleep. But I needed to make sure Penny was all right.

"Pen, you know, you can always leave the Rustic Root. Any restaurant in the city would snap you up. You're the hottest pastry chef going. Why don't you start putting feelers out? I can help you with your resume." She nodded and seemed to brighten a little. I stood up and hugged her.

"Okay. To be continued. But think about what I said. I've got to get some sleep so I can give Nils and Michael notice tomorrow without throwing up."

"Wow. That's going to suck. I'm so sorry." She

looked exhausted herself. "I know you can do this job in your sleep, Sarah; I just hope those horrible people won't make you miserable. And I hope you're not mad at me for bursting your bubble. Sunday Margarita brunch celebration?"

"Who could be mad at you, you sexy skyscraper, you? Sunday's a date. Love you." And trying to make myself as inconspicuous as possible so I wouldn't have to speak to one more person, I walked down the hall and out the door hoping to focus on my futon instead of my future for the next six hours.

Chapter 5

Needless to say, I didn't close my eyes for more than a few minutes at a time the entire night. I was twisted up with guilt for abandoning Nils and Michael, not to mention panicked about leaving the relatively safe ship they'd built for me to help me navigate the industry's shark-infested waters. And then there was that horrible metallic bile that kept rising in the back of my throat, choking me with the idea that I'd made a monumental mistake in accepting Fiona's offer. How in the world was I going to face the Fashion Flamingos and Henri-François every day?

Nobody was supporting me in this venture. Holt, as always, was unfailingly polite but not enthusiastic and Penny downright horrified. Even my new friend Sean seemed bewildered and quietly disapproving of my decision. Perhaps it wasn't too late to change my mind and just stay put. Yes. That's what I'd do. I'd call Fiona as soon as I got to the office and tell her I'd decided it wasn't a good time for me to leave FDG.

I got dressed as quickly as I could and raced down the stairs, out the door, and over to the 1/9 train. But as I passed the corner newsstand and saw the cover of today's *Sentinel*, an even more intense version of the acid reflux I had from the night before rose into my mouth and threatened to gush out all over the sidewalk. There was a photo of me with my worst hair day on record, wearing my much-maligned Doc Martens and Des' cheesy slip, creeping up the Met steps at the Gotham Gala looking like I needed a little black bar across my face to protect my identity in one of those fashion *Dos and Don'ts* pages everyone loves to snicker over and feel superior about.

The headline read: "FDG Frump is new *Sophistiquée* BD." And even though it felt like I couldn't descend into a lower circle of hell, there was one opening below me now and I was plummeting right in. Nils had home delivery of the paper and Michael, another early bird, read the *Sentinel* in his town car on his way to work every morning. It was pretty certain that both of my bosses had seen this an hour before I did. Crap. Crap. And crap again.

There was no chance of reversing my decision now, plus Nils and Michael would likely despise me for not giving them proper notice. And I felt betrayed that Fiona went back on her promise to keep things quiet until I told them. This new turn of events made me even more anxious about working there. If my so-called protector wasn't protecting me, what chance could I possibly have in a place like that? What was it Penny called it? A snake pit. It was feeling like that more and more with every passing minute.

Nothing to do but jump on the subway and get to the office. I would have to "face the music," as my mother, Anna Elias Mandelbaum would say right before she grounded me, withheld my allowance, or administered any other punishment or reprimand when I was growing up, none of which were infrequent occurrences. My mother had a pretty short fuse and held the all-time record in harboring grudges. "When the right amends are made, I may forgive," she would say. "But I never forget." I doubted Nils and Michael would ever forgive me and they certainly wouldn't forget how heartless and unprofessional this revelation of my new job was. And I couldn't blame them.

When I got to the office Nils was pounding away at his keyboard with such brutality that I knew it would have to be replaced by noon.

"Nils, I'm so sorry. It wasn't supposed to happen like this," I pleaded, trying to hand him his coffee. But he kept his back to me and continued to hammer away. "Please, Nils, let me talk to you about this." I saw Michael intently concentrating on the two of us from across the room. But he, too, remained silent. Finally, Nils reached for his coffee and turned to face me.

"How was it supposed to happen, Sarah?" His voice was quiet but his face was red so I knew he was making an effort to control his temper, which, according to Dana and even Ursula, could be terrifying. I'd never seen it in our work together and prayed silently that I wouldn't experience it now.

"Fiona promised me that she wouldn't tell anyone until I talked to you and Michael first. I'm horrified you're both finding out this way. I would never disrespect either one of you."

"Aside from the way we found out about it, Sarah, the news itself shocked the hell out of me. First off, you're a little young and inexperienced to be running a department and, more importantly, this job is totally not your scene. How could you even consider a move like this? *Sophistiquée* is likely one of the worst places imaginable for someone like you." He growled while tugging at his mustache. There it was again, *someone like me*. But what if I wanted to be someone else instead of "someone like me?" Saffron Meadows would've told him to go to hell. But I saw his point because I wasn't Saffron Meadows. I was Sarah Mandelbaum.

"Well, Nils, I'm pretty terrified at the idea myself and don't really understand how I said yes. But here's the thing. It's a big job and a good job. It pays more than twice what I get here, and Fiona says we're going to turn the women's high fashion world upside down by creating a stylish magazine that's accessible to real women."

"Well, I hope for your sake that's true, but my gut instinct is that Fiona isn't going to be able to do any of that. Henri-François seems to be gaining more and more power and that's never been his MO. And there's always the chance that she just fed you a line about what you wanted to hear so she could lure you and your big fat Rolodex over there to help sell ads. They're floundering, as you know, and she's under tremendous pressure from the higher-ups to turn things around."

Oh God, what if he was right? Suppose I'd been completely duped? I had to take a minute to process this concept. But then, I became strangely calm because even if Fiona had manipulated me to go there, I couldn't spend the rest of my life wearing frumpy pants suits and earning just above minimum wage at FDG.

"Nils, I'm really sorry this went down the way it did. I'm not sure what else to say." He took a sip of his coffee and then went back to pulverizing his keyboard. There was nothing for me to do but go to my desk and hope Nils would cool off as the day went on. As I turned to go, the voice I'd been most dreading to hear since walking in, thundered across the newsroom floor.

"Mandelbaum, my God, what a horrible picture," Michael roared. "And what a shit way to tell us you're leaving." I walked over to his desk, trying to steel myself to face more justifiable anger. When I got there, he continued his tirade, only slightly lowering his voice.

"I don't know how you could let something like this happen, Mandelbaum. It's not only incredibly unprofessional but extraordinarily callous, considering how much time and energy we've invested in you and how supportive we've been."

"I know, Michael. And I feel terrible it happened this way. Fiona assured me total discretion until I gave you and Nils proper notice, so I'm truly as surprised and upset as you are."

"Well, there's nothing more to be said here, except, given that it's now a conflict of interest for you to be in this newsroom, today is your last day here."

I wasn't sure if this were a good thing or bad. I'd been thinking I'd have two weeks to get used to the idea of leaving. But maybe it was better not to prolong the agony, especially since Nils and Michael were so pissed. I went back to my desk to call facilities to get some boxes to pack up my stuff. My message light was blinking out of control.

"Hello, Sarah, it's Fiona. I'm sorry about this morning's paper. I told Henri-François last night and urged him to secrecy, but he must have called the late desk. I hope it wasn't too terrible for you with Nils and Michael this morning. And my goodness, where did they get that photo? Why don't we take professional headshots of you after you start and get them out to all the media outlets so we can control this type of thing in the future? We'll send you to Dash Nichols for your hair first. Everyone in the office uses him. He's genius. Phone me when you get this so we can fix your start date."

"Honey!" It was Des. "I just read the news and am so excited for you. Think of all the sample sales you can take me to and all the free beauty products we can share. And of course, I'll go with you to all the fashion shows. It will be good for you to be seen with me. We must take you shopping, get you a facial and have your hair straightened before you start your new job. That picture was beyond heinous. Call me, honey. Bye." Clearly, I'd been a mass murderer in my previous life. It was the only acceptable explanation of why the universe had cursed me with Desiree Dershowitz for what seemed like all of eternity.

"Kitten, I hope you're all right. Call me. Love you." Penny was whispering fast and furiously so I knew Rex was already in the kitchen with her. Friday was their early prep day so they could get things in order before the weekend.

"Hey, darlin', well look at you on the front page of a newspaper. Now I can say I know someone famous." God bless Holt.

"So, when were you going to tell your mother about your fancy new job?" Anna Elias Mandelbaum was not happy. "And how could you let yourself look like that at a formal event? That is not how I raised you. I made a hair appointment for you with Tito at eleven tomorrow morning, so you can just hop on the bus at the George Washington Bridge and go directly to Mason Antoine in Englewood. I'll meet you there and we can have lunch so you can tell me everything. I shouldn't have to read about my daughter in the newspaper."

This latest bit of news was the most terrifying and the most irritating. My mother knew I taught Dana Saturday mornings, at least until today, but never took it seriously because it was just that "waste-of-time-ridiculous music thing I did that distracted me from what was really important." And what was important was being a teacher or lawyer and landing a rich husband that would support her in a lavish lifestyle and give her grandbabies, especially since even she knew the chances of Morrisa doing any of those things were slim to none. But my God, a hair appointment?

My mother also knew that the last time she forced me to go to Tito, her hairdresser of over twenty years, I ended up with a Dorothy Hamill wedge cut—in the Eighties. The cut, while iconic on the champion figure skater, was horrifying on me, especially since Tito gave it to me more than a decade after its run. But to add insult to injury, wedges and wildly curly hair don't mix and I ended up looking like a bonsai tree. I would have to call my mother back and tell her I couldn't make it, which wasn't going to go over well. But the good news was she almost assuredly had been calling me from the faculty lounge at the school where she taught so I could get away with just leaving a message on her machine at home.

"Hi, Sarah, it's Kevin Carson, publicist for Robbie Rose Beauty. Congrats on your new gig! To celebrate, Robbie wants you to come in so she can shape your brows and do your makeup. We'll send you home with day and evening looks. It'll be fabulous. Also, don't know if you know this but I also rep. supermodel Cecil and we may have an exclusive for you. Call me and we can set everything up."

I'd never met Kevin but knew his reputation well. He was rapacious in his pursuit of new clients and would promise them the moon to get them to sign, even when his agency was at full capacity and couldn't service them properly. He also wasn't above bending the truth to get editors to cover these clients. And if he got caught in a lie, he'd gift the journalist a Prada bag to compensate. He also regularly sent the Fashion Flamingos Manolo Blahniks in their size, "just to say hello." This system seemed to work well because every magazine constantly wrote big stories on his clients, even after he screwed over the editor involved. I wasn't in any hurry to call him back.

"Congratulations, Sarah. It's Dash Nichols. I'd love for you to come to my salon for a cut, straightening treatment, and color. I think you'd look fabulous with smooth hair and highlights. Just call my assistant Rory and he'll set it up for you. *Ciao*, darling, see you soon."

Hmm. I wondered if Fiona had put him up to this. Handsome, charming, and wonderfully English, Dash did, indeed, do all the A-Listers and even had his own upscale hair care line called "Rich Girl Hair." But I couldn't get excited about getting my hair done by someone who wanted me to look like everyone else. Still, I had to do something about this mop, as it seemed like everyone and their mother was talking about it. I'd watched Des straighten her waves a million times with a blow dryer, round brush, and copious amounts of Frizz-Be-Gone. How hard could it be? I made a mental note to hit the drugstore on my way home.

I spent the rest of the day finishing up the dot.com

story, packing up my stuff, carrying boxes to the mailroom and fielding "congratulatory" calls from nearly every beauty publicist on the planet. What was astounding was just the day before, few, if any of these people would've given me the time of day. While the big business executives would stop at nothing to get favorable press in FDG since the retailers read us and stocked their shelves based on our reviews, the public relations peeps were more apt to court the fashion press and the splashier coverage it gave in their glossy magazines. In fact, at all the press events, we lowly trade publications were seated at the worst tables hidden in the back of the room. The only journalists who had it half as bad as we did were the ones who edited the bridal magazines and the workhorse women's service books—the ones that feature cakes and casseroles on the covers and give tips on how to clean your house more efficiently while staying on a budget. I liked those editors. They stood firmly on both feet.

Fiona and I agreed that since Michael didn't want two weeks' notice, I would start at *Sophistiquée* first thing Monday morning—just a weekend away. She apologized again for the leak in the press, once again attributing it to Henri-François, but to be honest, I wasn't sure if I believed her. The bloom, as my mother Anna Elias Mandelbaum would say, was off the rose and I couldn't help but wonder if we were really going to make all the changes to *Sophistiquée*'s editorial coverage that she had wooed me with. I guessed I would find out Monday. I couldn't help but wish that Sunday unlimited Margarita brunch with Penny was happening right now.

At six, I slid my Rolodex into my tote, grabbed my trash bag of shoes from my file cabinet, hoisted it over my shoulder, and walked over to Michael's desk for the last time.

"I just wanted to thank you for all the opportunities you gave me here, and for everything you've taught me, Michael. I'm really grateful to you. And again, I'm truly sorry things turned out the way they did." I tentatively held out my hand. Thank God, he took it and shook it almost warmly, as he eyed my large green plastic accessory with amusement.

"You're welcome, Mandelbaum. I hope this gig goes well for you after all this drama and heartache. Just don't let me catch you flapping around on one foot." He allowed himself a small chuckle, so I allowed myself to exhale. One down; one to go. Next up was Nils, who was scribbling furiously in his reporter's notebook, giving his keyboard a well-deserved break.

"Nils, I don't know what else to say except to tell you again how sorry I am this happened, and to thank you for all you've done for me, here." He kept right on scribbling for a minute or two and then finally looked up.

"Well, Sarah, I have to tell you, this really sucks. I expected better from you. But the industry is what it is, and I realize there's a distinct possibility this isn't entirely your fault." He paused briefly and stroked his mustache, which was a good sign he was coming around since he yanked it when he was agitated and smoothed its white bushiness when he was thoughtful.

"Well, let's just try and put this behind us and move ahead. I'm assuming we'll see you tomorrow at eleven for Dana's lesson, yes?"

"Yes, of course." I exhaled for the second time in ten minutes.

"All righty, then. Soup's on. I gotta finish this story tonight. It's a dog-eat-dog world out there and I'm wearing dog biscuit underwear. See you tomorrow."

Despite my heavy bags and misgivings about leaving FDG, I felt a little lighter as I walked out of the building toward the 1/9 train than when I'd walked in this morning. At least Nils and Michael didn't hate me, and I'd made amends as best I could. My relief, however, was short-lived as I squeezed my way into the packed rush-hour subway car, which barely had any room for me, much less my damn garbage bag of shoes. Despite my best efforts at contorting myself to take up as little room as possible, I kept whacking innocent bystanders, who not only shot me vicious looks but also cursed me not entirely under their breath.

But sadly, this was not the worst part of the ride. It seemed that at least half the train was intently reading today's *Sentinel*, the one with that horrifying picture of me on the cover. And now, people were starting to stare at me and make snide comments to each other about my hair and Des' tacky slip. How on earth did I think wearing it was a good idea? Christ on a cracker. Why was it taking so long to get home?

This nonsense was going to stop as soon as I reached 238th street. That is *if* I ever got there. But when I finally did, I would head straight to the corner drugstore for a damn blow dryer, round brush, the hair clips I'd seen Des use, and a bottle of Frizz-Be-Gone. And while I was at it, I would stop at the liquor store. I figured I'd earned a drink or two or three. What were a few more expenses on my credit card since, as of my next paycheck, I'd be able to pay my bills? And considering the state of things, these were, in fact, emergency expenditures. How much ridicule could one girl take?

This particular drugstore was cavernous and chock full of everything you didn't need on the planet and not much of what you did. The hair care aisle stretched out for what seemed like a mile. I briefly thought about asking someone for help locating my weapons of tress destruction, but there didn't seem to be any clerk patrolling the aisles. In fact, by the looks of it, there was only one clerk in the entire store, up at the cash register and seemingly intent on making the twenty or so customers in line wait even longer than they had to by working extra-slooowly. People were starting to eat the candy they were there to buy, snap at each other, and yell at the indifferent sales associate. If this establishment didn't open at least one more register, it seemed entirely possible that a riot would ensue. Welcome to my Friday night.

When it was finally my turn, I dropped my items on the counter and smiled as pleasantly as I could.

"What's that?" the clerk asked, eying my trash bag with suspicion.

"Those are my shoes. I just moved them out of my old apartment." I picked up the bag and opened it to reveal its contents so she could see for herself I wasn't stealing anything from the store. She nodded and then turned her attention to my purchases and my hair.

"This stuff will be good for you," she approved. "You really need it." She finally started ringing up my hair supplies when she abruptly stopped and stared at me.

"Hey, wait a minute. Is this you?" she asked, gesturing to the rows of today's *Sentinel* with my damn picture on the cover behind the counter.

"Sadly, yes. Why do you think I'm buying all this stuff?"

"You should get some deep conditioner, too," she advised. "And a moisturizing shampoo." These may have been very good points but given that I'd been waiting in line for twenty minutes and there were at least sixteen people queued up behind me now, there was no way I was going to brave that enormous haircare aisle again only to have to get back onto that crazy line.

"Thanks, but I'm all set," I replied as politely as I could since my throat was starting to tighten up and the tears were about to free fall.

"Hey,"—It was the clerk again.— "it'll be okay. Why don't you just take these? These versions are supposed to be even better than the originals and should help." She motioned to the jars on the counter that held samples of New and Improved Miracle Conditioner and So Much Moisture Shampoo. Her compassion about did me in, and now the tears were really flowing. Christ, I had to get a hold of myself. It was just hair. I thanked her probably more profusely than necessary and made a beeline to Kingsbridge Liquors, which wasn't easy considering I was dragging around my shoes, Rolodex, and the biggest blow dryer the store sold. Bigger must be better in this instance, I reasoned since I couldn't for the life of me figure out why one model would be superior to another.

Thank God the guy in the liquor store was engrossed in a horror movie when I came in and so scarcely looked up at me when I plunked bottles of tequila and margarita mix on the counter. Margarita brunch would come early—as in five or ten minutes from now, though I didn't see much food in my future. Hopefully, I wouldn't run into Sean on my way home, and I could just get down to business.

Mercifully, the front stoop was empty as I rounded the corner and somehow made it up the four flights of stairs without falling to my death trying to balance my gargantuan bags. When I finally opened my apartment door, my answering machine was beeping like crazy, and that annoying digital woman who lived inside of it kept repeating in her disinterested monotone, "You have six messages. You have six messages." Jesus H. Christ. Who was calling me now?

I dropped everything on the floor and made myself a drink. The question of the night was whether to get this mane-taming out of the way first so I could try and relax, or put it off till I was good and drunk? One thing for certain was all those messages could wait. They were likely just a repeat of the criticisms and slimy sucking up to's I'd gotten all day long. I gulped down my drink, made another, and headed over to my ancient answering machine, a hand-me-down from my stepmother, Caroline, and tried to turn down the volume on digi-girl's voice. Apparently, this was as low as it got. You have six messages. You have six messages. You have six messages. Wow. Maxine Headroom was getting on my nerves. But sadly, the on/off switch was stuck. Piece of shit. Okay. Time to focus. Pretty soon I'd be in the shower and wouldn't hear Miss Thing then, much less over the roar of the blow dryer as I embarked on my quest. It would be all right.

I took a sip of my second drink and perused the hair-straightening instructions on the back of the Frizz-Be-Gone bottle.

"Dispense a dime-sized drop (nickel size for extra coarse or frizzy hair) into palms and rub together to emulsify, then comb through damp hair. Pull up the top sections of hair and clip them, then, starting at the back, wind small sections of hair from the ends up to the scalp around a round brush. Slowly unravel the brush, rotating your wrist to maintain maximum smoothness. Repeat until the whole head is done. Lightly comb through any remaining kinks with your fingers."

Piece of cake. I hit the shower with my cocktail, sudsed up with my brand-new shampoo, and slathered on the new conditioner. I thought about shaving my legs while I waited the prescribed three minutes for the "miracle" to kick in, but it seemed like much too much exertion, considering all the clipping, blow-drying, and brushing I had ahead of me. I emerged from the shower, toweled off, and slipped on my ratty yellow terry cloth robe from college, determined to have smooth, straight hair in thirty minutes or less. But first, another drink.

Things were starting to look up. On Monday I was going to start a big job with a big salary and big perks. I would even be able to afford a new bathrobe. And so what if the people weren't nice? If I had survived the Terror Trio and conservatory, I could survive anyone. Who did these Fashion Flamingos think they were, anyway?

I opened the bottle of Frizz-Be-Gone and metered out what looked like a "nickel-size drop" into my palm. But it seemed surprisingly puny. How was that little slick of serum going to ease all my insane frizz? I squeezed out another dropper-full and rubbed my hands together, as directed, and smoothed the whole slippery mess onto my hair, ponytail style. Instantly, I knew I'd made a huge mistake. Sure, my wet hair wasn't drying out in all directions, but it was now sticky and matted to my head. Okay. Don't panic. Maybe it will be less greasy when it's dry. Nothing to do but start clipping. I took another big swallow of my drink as answering machine-woman monotonously called out over and over and over again, "You have six messages. You have six messages. You have six messages." If I didn't listen to those messages soon, I was going to throw that damn machine out the window. But first, I had to finish my freakin' hair.

I put the clips in as instructed and wound the brush around a small section of hair in the back of my head. Next, I fired up the blow dryer and prepared to slowly unravel said brush as I aimed the blow dryer down the length of the section as it unfurled. I flicked my wrist all set to start gliding, but there was no unraveling. The brush and all the hair in it remained inexorably fixed to the top of my scalp.

"You have six messages. You have six messages. You have six messages." What the hell was I going to do? "You have six messages. You have six messages." I walked over to that God-forsaken machine and yanked the plug out of the wall. I had to think. How was I going to get this damn brush out of my hair without creating a bald spot in the process? You'd think with all this slippery, goopy stuff in my hair the brush would slide right out. But that just wasn't the type of day I was having. I took another swig of my drink and tried once again to loosen the brush's tenacious grasp on my hair.

If anything, this maneuver caused it to grip even more tightly. Crap. Crap. And crap again.

I checked the clock. It was eight-thirty, which meant Penny was still at the restaurant. And since Friday night was a late one for her and Saturday an early start, she was pretty well out of commission until brunch on Sunday, though I could turn up at her door around midnight tonight if I didn't get things figured out by then. And, God, I hope I didn't have to keep this brush in my head for another four hours. Time for another drink. After a few sips, I decided I'd call Holt. Yes. Dear Holt. Lovely Holt. Handsome Holt. Holt who only liked me like a sister. Yes. I'd call Holt and he'd come to my rescue. It was the brotherly thing to do.

I lurched out into the living room, banging into a stack of boxes in the process, and over to the phone. While I punched in Holt's numbers, I tried to rub my knee with my other hand, but it was holding my cocktail, which I didn't want to put down. After several rings, the machine picked up,

"Hey y'all, it's Holt. Thanks for calling. You know what to do. Just do it after the beep." Now that was odd. Why was Holt's new message virtually identical to Desiree's? I doubted it was a coincidence.

"Fucking Des! Fucking Holt," I yelled, slamming down the receiver as hard as I could. I wondered if Penny knew about this. She had to. "Fuck. Fuck. Fuck," I yelled louder still, kicking the little table the phone and the machine sat on, which promptly sent them both crashing to the floor, awakening that infernal robo-girl who immediately started intoning, "Battery low. Battery low. Battery low." I was pretty sure I'd broken my big toe.

"Can you just shut up?" I shouted even louder than before. So loud that I barely heard the knocking. But there it was. Someone was knocking, well, pounding on my door. I felt myself brighten a little. Maybe Penny got off work early. Maybe Holt had telepathically heard my cry for help. I was completely pissed at him, but if he could help me get this blasted brush out of my hair, all would be forgiven. I hopped over to the door since I couldn't seem to put any weight on the foot I'd kicked the table with, and opened it. It was Sean. Fuck.

"Hey, neighbor. Everything all right?" He peeked around me and seemed surprised that I was alone in the apartment. I guess I'd been making quite the racket.

"Sure, everything's just wonderful," I replied as airily as I could, but I wasn't entirely certain the words came out that way. My head was whirling, and my tongue felt furry. How much tequila had I had? Meanwhile, answering machine girl was droning her tuneless, "Battery low" mantra over and over again, and the recently tipped-over phone was buzzing like mad to try and get me to hang up the receiver.

"What happened here?" he asked, first gesturing to the clips and the brush lodged on the top of my head, and then to my knee, which I just realized was bleeding.

"Occupational hazard." I tried to joke without throwing up all over his white Levi 501s and brown suede cowboy boots. They were nice.

"Do you want some help?"

"Thank you," I gave in, knowing full well this was the end of anything romantic that might've started between us. I mean, this was crazy town, and after tonight he would likely never speak to me again. But clearly, I had no choice.

"Let's first get you some peace and quiet. May I?" He motioned with his hand asking my permission if he could come into my apartment. When I nodded, he strode across the living room, hung up the phone, placed it back on the table, and popped out the batteries of my crazy answering machine to finally silence that woman once and for all before returning it to the table, as well. He slid the batteries into his pocket and seemed to think a minute.

"That's better. Moving on to the next issue. I'm pretty sure I can take care of your hair situation. My eight-year-old frequently has run-ins with his bubble gum, and we manage to win the fight without using scissors. It'll be easier if we can get you upstairs to my place where I keep all of my tricks and tools since I'm not exactly sure what will get this job done best." I could see him mentally gathering the instruments he would need to accomplish this insane task. "But first you may want to put on some clothes," he continued. "I mean, you look great and all, but given how much tequila seems to be missing from that bottle on the table, we may not want to leave things to chance." He smiled somewhat wryly.

I looked down and suddenly realized that my robe was wide open. Great. Now I was pulling a full-on Des as well as standing on one leg like a friggin' Fashion Flamingo. There was no graceful way to do this. So, half hugging the wall, I slowly hopped down the hall to my room and even more slowly put on the work clothes I'd peeled off just a little while ago.

"All right in there?" Sean called out when I guess I'd been taking too long.

"Oh sure, I'm great." I somehow made my way

back to the front hall where Sean stood, waiting patiently.

"Do you have your keys?" God, he was so nice—paternal to the bitter end. Luckily, they were on my dining room table. I scooped them up and jammed them into my back pocket. I reached for the bottle of tequila to bring with me.

"Why don't we leave that here?" His tone was gentle, but even as snookered as I was, I realized that wasn't a suggestion. I hobbled out into the hall wondering how the hell I was going to get up those damn steps. But luckily, Sean's fatherly instincts kicked in again; he draped his arm around my waist and half-carried me up the flight. Terrific. I'd somehow forced both of the best-looking men I knew to treat me like either a sibling or progeny. But given my dire circumstances, there was absolutely nothing I could do about that right now. So, I just closed my eyes and rested against Sean's long, lean body. He was so warm and smelled really good—like lime, spice, and autumn leaves. I felt myself drifting off.

"Thank you," I murmured. "I'm really sorry."

"Let's just get you fixed up," he said kindly, as we finally made it up to the landing and into his apartment.

Chapter 6

I woke up the next morning with a blistering headache, sour stomach, and the most rancid taste in my mouth that I couldn't have made up if I tried. I was in what I assumed was Sean's bed, fully dressed and by myself, which hopefully was a good sign I hadn't had sex with him. The events of the night before were a little fuzzy, but they were still sharp enough for me to realize I'd put on quite the show. This was not how I'd planned for things to go with us.

My keys, as well as the offending round brush, cleaned out from all my hair that must've been embedded in it, and all those stupid hair clips lay on the bedside table next to me, along with replacement batteries for my answering machine, plus a glass of water and two aspirin, which I gulped down as quickly as I could. I gingerly touched the part of my scalp that was pounding more than the rest of it to see if I had a bald spot from last night's entanglement. Mercifully, I felt nothing but hair and a generalized throbbing. Things were better than I expected. But despite my best intentions of getting up and out of Sean's hair, so to speak, I involuntarily slid back down onto his pillows and pulled the covers over my head to shut out the sadistic sunlight streaming through his open white curtains. It was crazy bright out there; how could anyone expect a girl to function under such conditions?

I must have dozed off again because I felt a hand on my shoulder shaking me gently and heard Sean's voice in the very back of my brain.

"Hey, I have to get moving to pick up my son from downtown."

I struggled to sit up even though that was the last thing on earth I felt capable of doing. I knew I must've reeked and looked like death warmed over, as my mother Anna Elias Mandelbaum would say. Yup, that was me, sowing the seeds of romance wherever I went.

"Okay. I'll get up now. I'm sorry. What time is it?"

"It's eight. You've been out for something like ten hours. That was some night you and that bottle of tequila had, not to mention that hairbrush." I felt a sickening shame creep into every bone in my body, which somehow made me defensive.

"Well, if it's any consolation, I feel about as bad as I've ever felt in my whole life—maybe even worse than the morning I woke up in college after throwing up Melon Balls the entire night before."

"If you feel worse than that, that's pretty bad." I could tell he was trying to be nice but was pretty much over me by now. I couldn't blame him. I was sick of myself. Last night had to be ghastly. I silently prayed that I hadn't thrown up anywhere other than in his toilet. There was no question in my mind and mouth that vomiting played a starring role in what had to be my most horrifying performance ever.

I decided to change the subject while I attempted to swing my legs out from under the covers and onto the side of the bed. The floor would have to come a little later as I didn't feel like standing was a great option. My knee and toe were hammering almost as hotly as my head.

"How do *you* feel?" I asked tentatively, hoping he'd at least had a drink or two himself.

"I'm great. My back's a little tweaked from sleeping on the couch all night, but other than that, I'm fine. But I'm going to be late if I don't get out of here in the next few minutes. So, we need to get going."

"You're not hungover at all?"

"Nope—one of the benefits of not having a drink for seven years." Crap. On top of it all, I'd gotten rip-snorting drunk in the presence of a teetotaler, or worse yet, a recovering alcoholic. Weren't they always telling you exactly how long it was since they had their last drink? Those hits just kept right on coming. Nothing to do but gather my clips and that damn brush and then slink downstairs to my apartment and crawl into bed. I looked around for my shoes but couldn't find them anywhere. God, this was mortifying.

"Have you seen my shoes?"

"We brought you up here without them. So, you're good to go." He was polite but insistent as he bustled around the room collecting his keys, wallet, and American Spirits from the top of his peeling white dresser and stuffing the former into the back pockets of his white Levi's and the latter into the front pocket of his white denim jacket. What was with him and white? Now didn't seem to be a good time to ask. I finally hoisted myself onto my feet and, limping slightly, started walking toward his front door with him and then out into the hall. We slowly made our way down the stairs to my floor together, though I could feel that he was itching to sprint away from me or to his son or both as fast as his long, lean legs would carry him. When we got to my landing, I turned to him and tried to smile.

"Hey. Thank you for coming to my rescue last night. I don't know what I would've done without you."

"Well, I can't say it was a pleasure. But I'm glad it turned out all right." He continued to walk briskly down the stairs as I walked to my door, fumbling for my keys. There was a piece of folded peach notepaper taped to it that had to be from Penny.

"Kitten, I left you a message at work and at home, and now your machine isn't picking up. Are you all right? Seems like yesterday was one helluva day. Call me when you can. If I'm not home, I'll be at the restaurant. Xo, Pen."

I suddenly remembered the torments my answering machine had put me through last night causing me to unplug it. Now, what was that horrible woman inside of it blathering on about? Five messages? Six messages? I decided I'd better listen to them sooner rather than later so I wouldn't have to think about any of them beyond the next few minutes. Then I would disconnect my phone and the damn machine until I felt better. I plugged in the machine and hit play.

"You have six new messages," she sang tunelessly. I know. I know. Get on with it.

"Hey, Saffie, I know you probably won't come—you never do—but we're playing today at my studio on Hudson St. You gotta get back on that horse." It was Ollie. "So why don't you and Dana pop by after your lesson? One dude even brings his eight-year-old son—so it's all good clean fun and totally fine for her. It'd be great if you'd come and throw down. And what's with the seven-one-eight number? Are you in a borough now?"

Crap. I completely forgot it was Saturday, and I was due to give Dana her lesson at eleven. I walked into the kitchen and checked the clock. It was eight-forty-five. I had just enough time to shower, brush my teeth, and get down there. The machine beeped again.

"Kitten, it's Pen. Call me. I want to make sure you're all right."

"Good evening, Sarah, this is Stuart Felsenfeld. I got your number from your mother who is, um, a patient of my father's. She thinks we would have a great time going out together. So, I, um, thought I'd give it a shot. My number is 212-752-6653." Good evening? Um? Stuart Felsenfeld was clearly not going to be the man of my dreams. And there was no way I was going to call him or any other son of my mother's dentist back—especially after the night I'd just had. "Message deleted," Machine girl droned.

"Sarah, it's your mother. I'm not pleased you refused my offer of an appointment with Tito when you obviously need it and that you aren't coming out to see me tomorrow. I really can't understand how you would choose this silly hobby of yours over your own mother. I'm expecting to hear from you this weekend. And by the way, Stuart Felsenfeld just called and told me he left you a message, so I'm also expecting you to call him back. It's the polite thing to do. Please do not humiliate me."

"Wow, little sister, that was some picture. What the hell's going on with you? I'm thinking you need a publicist to manage your image and control your press now that you have this big, new job—by the way, what's with that? You at *Sophistiquée*? I don't see it. But if you're going there, you need to straighten your hair and get some decent clothes. Call me and I'll hook you up with names and digits of some top-notch NYC folks who specialize in damage control." So much for big sisterly love. I hit delete.

"Message deleted." Yes, I know. Thanks.

"Sarah, it's Dad. We haven't heard from you in a while and the twins have been asking to see you. Why don't you take the train out to Scarsdale Sunday morning, and we can have brunch? You can tell us about this new job of yours, and I think Caroline has some ideas for you about your hair."

My God, it was just fucking hair. I was sure other things in this universe were more important than my tangled mass of matted-down frizz, which now I had just a few minutes to wash and tend to or I would be late for Dana. But first, I had to at least leave Penny a message on her machine to beg her to change venues for Sunday, as an unlimited margarita brunch was out of the question, and to let her know I was all right. I mean, I think I was.

The subway gods, at least, were smiling down on me that morning because somehow, I made it down to the Village with enough time to hit the deli near the Petersen's to score a ham, egg, and cheese on a roll and an orange soda—the best hangover helpers I knew. I was starting to feel like I could at least pull off today's lesson with Dana, which was good because I was pretty anxious about seeing Nils. I mean, it seemed like he'd forgiven me, but I couldn't be one hundred percent sure. And then there was Ursula and Dana I'd have to get into all of this with. I wish someone, anyone, would be happy for me about my decision to defect to *Sophistiquée,* but it didn't seem likely. Apparently, I had the worst judgment on the planet.

Ursula answered the door, tall, willowy, and as serene as ever, in a gold floor-grazing Indian print dress with her ginger hair flowing to her waist. Her feet were bare, as always, and her silver and turquoise bangles jingled on her wrists and left ankle as she let me into their fantastic loft.

"Hey now, Sarah, I hear you have some big news." She was as warm and breezy as ever as she discreetly eyed my enormous sunglasses, rumpled not-quite-clean boy's jeans, and tattered black Joe Perry T—all I could find since I hadn't had the chance to unpack yet what with last night's hairmageddon and all. I hoped against hope that I still didn't stink of tequila. I'd scrubbed myself as hard as I could with the orange blossom body wash Ursula had given me last Christmas, shampooed and conditioned repeatedly with those damn new hair products, and rinsed out my mouth several times with mouthwash after brushing my teeth, not once, but twice.

"Yeah, I guess I do. It didn't quite go down how I wanted it to, though." I figured it was better to just get it all out in the open than to dance around the issue. My head hurt too much for pretenses.

"It will be all right, Sarah," she said, turning to me and enfolding me in her long, slender arms. She smelled like magnolia and sunlight. I thought I might cry. "If you have a minute or two extra today, I thought we could sit down and have a coffee together before you went into Dana," she said, releasing me. "I just put on another pot. Do want some?"

Of course, I did. There was nothing in the universe that I wanted more than a cup of Ursula's famous strong, aromatic Indonesian coffee, which she blended with turmeric and coconut milk.

"That would be heaven," I replied, feeling eternally grateful to Laurel Canyon, Woodstock, and various Eastern spiritual practices for creating this divine woman.

Ursula led me into the amazing Petersen living room, which she had decorated with Oriental carpets, embroidered floor cushions made from orange, gold, and violet sari silk, and gauzy magenta curtains floating around the open floor-to-ceiling windows. The most extraordinary black and white photos of rock stars hung on every wall—all taken by Ursula, which was how she and Nils met. She'd been assigned the photo shoot for the story he was writing. Nils and Ursula were about the loveliest couple I knew. They'd been married by Ursula's guru in India in 1975 with rock's best and brightest in attendance and had been inseparable ever since. And their kids, Dana and her older brother Lucas, who was a sophomore at Bowdoin and played killer bass, were terrific.

"Have a seat. I'll just be a minute," she said, motioning for me to sit on one of the floor cushions. Now that would be a good trick. I seriously doubted I could balance on one of those things without tipping over, much less spilling my coffee. All I could do was hope for the best. So, I pulled off my Puma California kicks and tried to fold my legs yogi style on a deep purple glass beaded number. But between my rootin' tootin' hangover, along with the lovely breeze and toasty sunshine streaming in the windows, I must've fallen asleep because for the second time that morning, someone was gently shaking my shoulder and calling my name. I snapped awake with such a start that my sunglasses flew off. Would the indignities never stop?

"Oh my," Ursula said, laughing a little. "Here, drink this. It always helps." I gratefully accepted the ceramic mug with one hand as I felt around for my sunglasses with the other.

"So, listen, hon, Nils had to run out for a minute, but he'll be back to congratulate you on your new journey." She seemed so certain that I knew she must've had one of her calm but insistent "talks" with him last night. Ursula was the quietest reprimander on record. "I know he was pretty tough on you yesterday but, well, I'm sure you also know that's how Nils is." Indeed, I did. You don't work with someone closely for a year without getting to know how they handle stress. But then again, given how my news broke, I really couldn't blame him.

"You know, when Nils first took this job so we could move to New York, I was worried it wouldn't be enough for him. He was so passionate about music; I didn't see how he possibly could be satisfied writing about the beauty industry. What we've both realized, though, is he grooves on breaking news and getting "the story"— any story. He saw you as his equal in that, plus you have that same music thing going on. It was a blow for him to lose you. But to everything, there is a season."

"I've always wondered why you guys left LA and Nils switched from music reporting to beauty." I could feel myself starting to wheedle. "It just seems so out of character, even for a total pit-bull of a reporter that just cares about breaking a story—any story." Maybe I'd finally find out Nils' big secret.

125

"Well, Sarah, that's just not my story to tell," she replied gently but firmly. Oh well. Can't blame a girl for trying. "Okay. I don't want to keep you. Let's go tell Dana you're here. She's been locked in her room all morning with her headphones on, so she probably has no idea," Ursula continued, gracefully unwinding her lithesome legs and getting to her feet while extending a hand to help me do the same. Suffice it to say, I was not as elegant in achieving that goal.

"She recently discovered Led Zeppelin," I confided. "No wonder she's got her headphones practically glued to her head."

"Now that *is* a life-changing discovery," Ursula smiled.

"Hey, did you ever hang with those guys?" I was wistful. I would've given anything to have been working at *40 Days* back in Zep's heyday. If I'd been there then, I might have scored tickets to see their awesome 1969 Whiskey a Go Go show.

"I'll never tell," she answered cryptically, before knocking loudly on Dana's door.

"Whaddaya say Cheese Danish?" I asked when Dana finally opened the door to Ursula's repeated knocking.

"I say, 'P.U.,' you smell like the living room after one of Mom and Dad's New Year's Day recovery parties." Wow. Was I that bad? Ursula, as wonderful as ever, had been too polite to say anything and hadn't even remarked that I was limping as I followed her through the loft. It was absolutely astonishing she let me near her kid. But I guess, given her history, she'd seen far worse.

"Those are some pretty wild times," I agreed,

reaching up to ruffle Dana's short, spiky, bleached platinum hair. And I knew from personal experience. You didn't go to Nils and Ursula's on New Year's Day to detox, make resolutions or confess transgressions from the night before. You went to get in one last day of serious partying before January's puritanical get-back-to-work/the gym/ a strict diet/doom and gloom set in. It was the winter Mardi Gras before the cold-weather Lent.

After about ninety minutes of jamming with Dana and another cup of Ursula's ambrosial coffee, plus the two extra aspirins she fed me, not to mention her compassion, I was starting to feel almost human again. Nils knocked on the door just as we were wrapping up.

"Hey, ladies, that was excellent." He stood in the doorway, hesitating.

"It's all right, Dad. Mom smoothed the way for you, as usual," Dana said, putting down her gorgeous full-scale Gretsch electric. At fourteen, Dana already had fabulous hands with exquisitely long fingers. I felt a pang of envy as I packed up my black short-scale electric.

"Can you give us a minute, Punk?" he asked, motioning for her to step out of the room.

"I will, but make sure you're nice. Sarah had a rough night." Dana grinned and grabbed her guitar case. She was beyond excited when, against my better judgment, I told her about Ollie's invitation. It was the only way I could think of to try and get her to stop begging me to take her to an open mic at Sidewalk, which she'd been doing for months now. And frankly, I did not see that ever happening again in my lifetime, and I certainly wasn't going to tell her the reason why.

Nils came into the room and sat on the chair opposite Dana's bed.

"So, hey, about yesterday…'' he started.

"It's okay," I blurted out. It would be too agonizing to rehash all of yesterday's events and this whole painful *Sophistiquée* mistake thing. I'd made my bed, as my mother Anna Elias Mandelbaum would say, and would have to lie in it. I was just grateful that Nils wasn't mad at me or worse, still hurt and disappointed.

"I was just, well, frankly, shocked. But I talked it out with Ursula last night and we agreed that this is a good opportunity for you, and you had nothing to do with how the news broke."

"Thank you, Nils. I know it must've sucked for you. And I'm sorry. Really sorry."

"Okay. Let's not say another word about it. Onward and upward. So, what's this about you and Dana jamming with some pro-musicians? Do I need to worry?" Ursula must've told him about Ollie's invite.

"You absolutely do not need to worry. We'll be with my teacher Ollie, who's a great guy, and some of his cleaner-cut buddies."

"Clean-cut rockers? Now that's an oxymoron."

"No, seriously. Ollie says one of the regulars even brings his eight-year-old son. I want Dana to play the Rickie Lee Jones tune with a band backing her. She'll totally groove on it."

"You're a good man, Charlie Brown," Nils said, extending his hand for one of his hearty shakes. I was glad he thought so.

When Dana and I got to Ollie's rehearsal space, I recognized Mayumi, the bass player, and Charisse, the drummer, right away; both women were in One-Eyed

Snake and were fantastic. I only hoped I could keep up since I hadn't played in a band for over a year. As we were chatting and setting up, Ollie tossed me Glenn the gorilla's, or should I say Saffron Meadows' top hat that had mysteriously made its way into the studio. Given what happened to me at Sidewalk the last time I refused to wear it, I donned it immediately. Better to be safe than sorry and I could certainly use all the help I could get playing with pros like these.

As I lowered the mike stand so I could reach it and unpacked my guitar, the door opened and a little boy ran in, though I use the term "little" loosely because while clearly, he was still a young child, this kid was as tall as I was. And his hands were unreal.

"Hey, Wyatt! Come on in. We're just setting up. I've got all your stuff right here," Ollie said, holding one hand up for a high five and gesturing to a bench that held a tambourine, triangle, and cowbell. Wyatt, dark-haired and hazel-eyed with enormous, black, plastic-framed glasses, immediately picked up the cowbell and began to beat an impressive rhythm with a drumstick.

"Wow, buddy! You've been practicing. That's awesome," Charisse, Ollie's longtime girlfriend, called out, echoing the same time on her bass drum. Ollie was about to introduce us when the door opened again and in walked a lanky, dark-haired guy in white Levi 501s and a white denim jacket, holding an electric Gibson case in one hand and a pair of boy's skates in the other. It was Sean. How was this possible?

"Hey, everyone, this is Dana, a mad amazing guitarist, and an all-around cool girl," Ollie called out, causing Dana to blush as she gave the band a little wave. "And this," he continued, "is the rock icon, Saffron Meadows." Charisse looked up from her drum kit and twirled her sticks at me, while Mayumi threw me a mega-watt smile. These girls knew I was Sarah Mandelbaum but seemed totally cool with my new alter-ego. Dana looked a little puzzled but was so thrilled to be there that she didn't comment. But Sean, who'd been eying me cautiously, perhaps waiting to see if I would spew green vomit or my head would spin around, didn't do the same.

"Saffron Meadows? You mean like the porn star?" he muttered not quite under his breath, glancing over at Wyatt to make sure he wasn't listening.

"Saffron Meadows is a porn star?" I felt myself heat up with embarrassment. I'd been so certain she was just Ollie's completely made-up goof. But maybe there was a porn star out there with that name. And if so, how would Sean know, and Ollie wouldn't? Was Sean big into porn?

"Well, if she's not, she should be," Sean retorted, glaring at me and then looking over again at Wyatt. I probably shouldn't have shouted out the words, "porn star" in front of an eight-year-old. But wow. Sean was cranky. I guess he was still mad at me. Why oh why did I buy that damn brush and all that crazy tequila?

"I beg to differ," Ollie chimed in. "Saffron Meadows was a famous rock muse from the Sixties that inspired all three Jims—Paige, Hendrix, *and* Morrison. Donovan wrote that *I'm just Mad about Saffron* "Mellow Yellow" tune about her because she played wicked guitar and outsang Janis." Chloe and Charisse grinned full-well knowing Ollie was spinning one of his tales. And it wasn't exactly hard to catch on since he was clutching one of his ubiquitous cans of fluorescent soda. Sean, however, didn't notice and clearly wasn't in the mood for joking around.

"Well, I prefer Sarah. Sarah Mandelbaum."

"Wait, you guys know each other?" Ollie put down his soda to tune his Guild.

"We live in the same building," I replied as off-handedly as I could, wondering if Sean would rat me out about last night.

"Oh. I guess you moved. That explains your new seven-one-eight number," Ollie said, clearly understanding something was going on between us but not wanting to get into it. Ollie was the best.

"Okay, boys and girls. Let's warm up. Saffie, why don't you start us out with something phat? We'll follow your lead."

My heart hammering in my chest, I hesitated for a minute or two before I plugged in my guitar. "Okay, here goes," I said to myself as I started strumming and singing one of my favorite most rocking Guns N' Rose songs.

"Righteous," Ollie enthused, as Charisse and Mayumi both laughed out loud, and everyone started playing along. I snuck a look at Sean who was jamming away on his Gold Top. Wow. He was good. He actually caught my eye and smiled a little. It was going to be all right. Even if nothing ever happened between us again.

After the closing chords, Ollie put down his guitar and switched to keyboards. I don't think there was any instrument this guy couldn't play.

"Rickie Lee's in the house," Ollie chanted as Dana took my place at the mike and everyone joined in.

The afternoon just whizzed by with some Stones,

Zep, Ramones, Elvis Costello, Iggy Pop, and a few One-Eyed Snake numbers. Ollie had me play lead on a couple of tunes and it felt really, *really* good.

At around four, Ollie called out, "Okay, guys, time to blow it out. Wyatt, you're up."

Charisse clicked her sticks and Ollie and Sean dove into Bowie's "Rebel Rebel." Wyatt charged up to my mike stand to sing the opening "Doo doo doo's", beating excellent time with his cowbell. Dana grabbed the tambourine, Sean played and sang lead, and I followed on rhythm guitar. When it came time for the chorus, we all sang as loudly as we could.

As we were all packing up to go, Sean came over to me, gestured to my T-shirt, and said, "Hmm, Slash? Joe Perry? I'm sensing a pattern here."

And I don't know whether it was because I was actually beginning to feel like Saffron Meadows, or the fact that I'd had a fantastic throw-down with a group of amazing musicians, but somewhere, somehow, I managed to reply, "George Harrison, Jimmy Page, and David Gilmour too. Guess I have kind of a thing for dark-haired guitar players with mystique, especially when they wear glasses." Sean flushed slightly and smiled just a little. Maybe, just maybe, I could get us back on track.

"Hey, Saffie," Ollie yelled across the room. "I'm going over to Matt Umanov. Want to come?" Matt Umanov was like the most amazing candy store for guitar players. Since '65, it'd been selling and repairing some of the coolest and rarest guitars in the world. There was no other place on earth like it.

"Dunno," I replied. "It always makes me sad when I'm there to see all those amazing guitars I can't play.

It's not like they have a ton of lefties, much less lefty short scales."

"Aw, come one. He gets new stuff in every day. You won't know unless you check it out." Dana looked at me imploringly. She loved it there. I mean, of course, she did, she could play real-sized guitars. But then again, what did I have to go home to other than obnoxious messages on my machine and a whole lot of unpacking?

"Okay. I'm in."

"Saffie, Dana, and I are going to Matt Umanov. Anyone else want to come with?"

"That sounds fun, bunny, but May and I are on set up for the meeting and want to grab a bite to eat beforehand," Charisse replied. Oh, that's right. One-Eyed Snake had all met at an East Village 12-Step meeting five years ago or so and had been sober and together in various bands ever since. I wondered how long Sean'd been playing with them.

"Bunny?" Dana was giggling like a madwoman. I mean, calling Ollie bunny was pretty funny.

"Yes, bunny," Charisse said firmly, kissing Ollie on the top of his bald head and then turning to me and saying, "Sarah, that was outstanding. I'm so glad you finally came. Let's do it again soon."

"Yeah," Mayumi echoed. "Come jam with us any time."

"See you later, pumpkin," Ollie called out to Charisse, blossoming under her attention and sweeping us all from the studio so he could lock up.

"Pumpkin? You guys are cracking me up." Dana was having a great day.

Sean decided he and Wyatt would come with us to

Matt Umanov and then we'd all head uptown—me to my apartment and them to Van Cortland Park for a skating play date. As we walked into the Bleecker Street store, Nick, a longtime sales associate, immediately greeted us. Ollie was kind of royalty there. They even sent him guitars to work on when they were backed up.

"Hey, guys, what's happening?" he asked, slapping Ollie on the back.

"Hey, Nick, good to see you, man," Ollie answered, pulling Nick in for a brief hug. "Did that ax come in that you were telling me about?"

"It did indeed," Nick replied. "I'll get it from the back." He disappeared for a few minutes and then reappeared with something I'd never seen before in my life, a lefty version of the Gold Top Sean, not to mention Slash and Duane Allman played. Sure. I'd heard about them. But because they were in so little demand since most lefties played righty guitar, you typically had to get Gibson to custom make one or, at the very least, get one on special order and they often cost well over two thousand dollars. But before I could even try to tally up how much I had left on my credit card for a possible layaway arrangement, I realized since it was full-scale, I wouldn't even be able to play it. In fact, my heart started thudding like a ticking time bomb at the mere thought of attempting to play it.

"Hey, that's magnificent, Nick. Thanks for bringing it out. But I only play short scale." God, that was so embarrassing, but I felt calmer now that I'd decided not to take her for a spin in the middle of a pro-music shop filled with pro-musicians.

"That's definitely not too much guitar for Saffron

Meadows. Give her a whirl," said Ollie, forever (and now maddeningly so) my champion and cheerleader.

"Well, I don't know about Saffron Meadows, but I can say that from what I heard and saw today, Sarah Mandelbaum can totally take this baby on." It was Sean.

"Come on, Sarah, try it. It's amazing." Dana was practically jumping up and down. It *was* a beautiful guitar. But I knew from personal experience that I needed to stick to my short scales. I just didn't have the hands or reach for anything bigger.

"Hey, Ollie, Nick, that's so great of you to get this in for me, but I just don't have the Benjamin's for this now. What is she like, two thousand?" That wasn't exactly a lie since there was no way in hell I could afford her, even if I could play her.

"Well, this one's actually closer to three," Nick replied.

Before I could plead poverty again, Sean interrupted, "Hey, didn't you just get that big fancy new job with the big fancy new salary?"

It took every ounce of self-restraint I had to extinguish the laser beams that started shooting out of my eyes at him.

"You got a new job?" Ollie asked, raising an eyebrow. "Wow. I'm the last to know everything these days. First, you move to the Bronx without telling me and now I find out you have a new job. Don't mind me. I'm just the lowly guitar teacher."

That was funny. I'd almost totally forgotten about starting *Sophistiquée* on Monday. But Sean was right, with the new salary I'd be making plus my lower rent I would be able to afford her and the idea of owning a

Gold Top was electrifying. Except there was that little matter of my not being able to play her.

"Well, yes, I'll be making more money," —I started to hedge— "But I still have all of these horrific student loans to pay off, so I'm afraid I just can't shell out that cash right now."

"Woah, enough with the pressure here," said Nick, probably the best salesperson on the planet. "Sarah or Saffie, or both women need some time and space to see if this is a fit. So, I have an idea. Why don't you put two hundred fifty down today, and I'll hold it for you for a little while and you can come back and play it when the store is less busy? If you decide you don't want it, I'll refund your deposit. She'll be snapped up in a minute if you don't take her. We hardly ever get lefty Gold Tops in."

"I can lend you the cash until your first paycheck, if you don't have it," Ollie offered up, oh so helpfully. "It'd be sweet for you to play a Gold Top. It's the perfect guitar for you." Nick glared at him, which eliminated my need to do the same.

"Okay. All right. Sorry. But that's such a cool deal. If you don't like it, no harm, no foul."

"Come on, Sarah." Dana could barely contain herself. "Just do it!"

And somehow, someway, against my better judgment, once again I found myself pulling my emergency credit card out of my wallet, which was now dangerously close to its limit—Penny's flowers, those crazy hair products, and all that damn tequila were adding up. I figured when I got home, I would just call Nick and cancel the transaction. Maybe Saffron

Meadows could play a full-sized Gold Top, but I was pretty damn sure Sarah Mandelbaum couldn't.

Chapter 7

When I got home, I had all sorts of good intentions to unpack in earnest and return those irritating phone calls. Instead, I ended up ordering cheap Chinese food and crashing early, which was no surprise given that I hadn't had a decent night's sleep in forever coupled with the battle I'd lost with that bottle of tequila last night.

I woke up the next morning feeling pretty good for a change and excited to see Penny. I wanted to hear everything. It'd been ages since we had a proper chat and I felt like our sit-down Thursday night at her apartment barely scratched the surface. I hoped against hope that Rex had suddenly morphed into a decent human being, though I seriously doubted it. Some people were born jackholes, stayed jackholes, and died jackholes. Rex, it seemed to me, was just that type of jackhole.

I guess we would also talk about this *Sophistiquée* business, though I didn't want to. I was dreading my first day there enough as it was. And I was pretty sure her apprehensions would make me feel worse about it. I *would* tell her about Sean, though I hoped I could leave out the whole hairbrush fiasco—which didn't seem likely since she was already suspicious of my switching our typical Sunday Caliente Cab Unlimited Margarita Brunch to Isabella's on the Upper Westside, where brunch came with only one screwdriver or mimosa. Frankly, I didn't think I could stomach it either.

I was also dying to get the skinny on Holt and Des—maybe I'd hallucinated the idea in a tequila-induced haze and that whole similar answering machine message thing was just a coincidence. I totally accepted the fact, well, almost totally accepted the fact, that Holt and I were never going to be anything other than family, but the idea of him being with Des just killed me. Still, all in all, I was just tickled pink about seeing my girl Penny and spending some QT with her.

So, I was a little perplexed when she met me in front of my building with a hug and the words, "Kitten, this may sound crazy, but I called Esme and she's meeting us at Isabella's."

"You called Esme? Why in the world would you call Esme? You can't stand her." Wow. Esme was going to be so pissed that she wasn't the first person I called when I got the *Sophistiquée* job. I'd just been crazed with the move, the Gala, leaving FDG, and well, my hair. I was amazed she hadn't seen that damn picture and called me herself, but, mercifully, I guess a few people in NYC didn't read the paper that day.

"It's not that I can't stand Esme, it's just that sometimes she's a little much." There was Penny, forever tactful. Esme'd been my best friend since we met in ballet class when we were four, back before we read Salinger's *Nine* in middle school, and she insisted on everyone calling her Esme instead of Esther. She was graceful and lithesome; I was klutzy and typically the target of the other tutu-wearing tots. Esther, who was even shorter than I was, would race to my rescue, her miniature fists and strawberry blonde hair flying.

Esther wasn't small. She was concentrated. In fact, she'd kicked the crap out of those hurdles in Ms. Ludwig's gym class, clearing each and every one.

I hadn't been hanging out much with her lately because since she got promoted to analyst at her investment bank, she was spending most of her evenings wining and dining financial bigwigs and partying with the frat boys in her department. While I wasn't sure what happened when she went out with them, when we did spend time together, she almost always was, as Penny said, just a little much, which often meant my pouring her into a cab and escorting her home personally to make sure she got into bed all right. Esme was irresistible in her own indomitable way, not to mention my oldest friend and fiercest protector.

I wasn't sure why Penny had called her, though; there were probably no two people in the world more opposite than them. So, as we walked over to the 1/9 train heading downtown, I looped my arm through Penny's and asked her point-blank.

"Well, kitten, you and I are completely clueless about this whole *Sophistiquée* thing. We're not super fashionable, and let's face it, you've never been one of those popular girls who stood up to the Queen Bees. And you're about to dive headfirst into a nest of high-fashion yellow jackets."

"Wait a minute," I said more defensively than I intended. "I was totally popular at camp." And mysteriously enough, I was, too. I sang the lead in most of the musicals, had a large circle of friends, a few boyfriends over the course of five summers, and sometimes even got picked third or fourth for softball.

"I don't want to hurt your feelings but being

popular at camp is like being big in Japan," Penny said kindly enough so I couldn't get mad. Besides, she was right. "I thought Esme may have some strategies," Penny continued. "I'm pretty sure you told me that she was the only one who stood up to the Terror Trio."

"Yeah, Esme was the bomb; after a few scrapes with her, they never bothered her again."

Penny squeezed my arm as we walked up the stairs to the subway platform and waited for the train.

"I also thought she could help you with the clothes thing." Penny's voice grew quiet, so I knew she realized she had to tread carefully. I waited a moment or two before I replied because I could feel myself getting fired up. It seemed to me I'd heard more about my rotten fashion sense and horrible hair in the last few days than I'd heard in all twelve years of school combined, which certainly wasn't true, but didn't make any of those comments from the Gotham Gala reporters, subway riders and Peach Chandler and Keeley McPheters, who I'd privately started calling the Toxic Twins, any less devastating.

"Pen, you know I don't care about clothes," I said, wishing we could just end this conversation before it went any further.

Penny nodded and pointed to the black Hendrix T I was wearing with the same not-pristine boy's jeans from the day before. Crap. I had to unpack. "Seems to me you're going to have to start," she continued. "That's your job now—just like you had to wear those God-awful suits at FDG so you'd be taken seriously by those middle-aged beauty moguls. Now, you're going to have to be a fashionista if you want to be taken seriously as an editor of a high fashion magazine."

Me? A fashionista? What a horrible thought.

"Most unlikely fashionista ever," I joked, trying to lighten the mood.

"I wouldn't say unlikely," Penny said. "You clean up nice when you want to. Let's just say you're a reluctant one. I'm betting Esme will have all sorts of ideas."

"Esme always has all sorts of ideas."

"Yes, she does, doesn't she? And she has fabulous clothes." Penny bent way down to briefly rest her head on my shoulder as we rode the train to 79th Street. When we got to Isabella's, Esme was sitting at the bar drinking a screwdriver and smoking a Camel.

"Baumie, you bitch. I can't believe you didn't call me with your big news," Esme shrieked, calling me the nickname she gave me in kindergarten as she jumped off the barstool and practically leaped into my arms. As always, she looked flawless—wearing black Celine flair pants and a ribbed cream and black Missoni top. Esme spent a fortune on alterations to get even 00s to fit her tiny frame. The Fashion Flamingos would've killed for her super svelteness—the result of hyperactivity and genetics, not starvation and exercise mania. She also sported towering canvas Stuart Weitzman wedge sandals. Esme was a serious animal rights activist/vegetarian and would wear no leather or eat any meat.

"Es, it's been crazy. Really crazy. I'll tell you all about it when we sit down. I thought about calling you every minute. I just didn't have the chance." Okay, so that was an exaggeration, but why hurt her feelings? Here she was on the Upper West Side at Penny's request on a Sunday at noon when, typically, she'd still be asleep in her Upper East Side apartment.

"And you," she said, turning to Penny and craning her head, "how's it going up there?"

"Oh, it's going," Penny replied, clearly trying to keep her voice level as she tightened her large pearl earrings. This brunch was going to be torture for all of us if I didn't rein Esme in. She was already off and running. Esme snapped her fingers at the maître d' signaling him we were ready for our table, causing me and Penny to wince with embarrassment. This was how Esme rolled. I knew we'd all end up over tipping—even Esme—to compensate. Before the maître d' could beat a hasty retreat, Esme ordered champagne—Dom Perignon, to be exact. Her investment firm must've handed out extra-big bonuses this year, or she got another raise. Even though she was a "she," Esme was a superstar there. Then again, raises and bonuses likely didn't matter to her all that much—except to stick it to the Biffs and Brads she worked with who called her "Short Stuff and Blondie." Esme came from an insanely wealthy family.

"This is on the bank, ladies," she said, waving her Platinum card. "So, now that we're sitting down and about to celebrate, I want to hear everything," she continued, slipping her card back into her Gucci canvas wallet before lighting another Camel. Instantly, the maître d' dashed back to our table.

"I'm sorry, Miss, but there's no smoking in the dining room," he said, seeming resolute that he and Esme were about to get into it.

"Call a cop," she retorted, wrinkling her freckled nose and narrowing her grey-green eyes.

"Es, come on. Let's not do this today. You just

finished one and you can go smoke in the bar if you want another."

"It's your day," she said brightly, stubbing her cigarette out in her bread-and-butter dish. The maître d' motioned for the busboy, who was hovering at his station, to whisk it away and bring over the champagne and three flutes.

"All right," she continued, wrapping her tiny hand around the glass so her six rings clinked against it. "Let's first toast Baumie and her fab new job and then I want all the juicy details." She raised her glass and said, "To Baumie."

"To Kitten," Penny echoed, clinking her glass with mine and Esme's.

After we ordered and Esme got herself another screwdriver, she turned to me. "Okay, showtime." So, I launched into the same story I'd been telling everyone else. I left out the parts about the horrible picture and headline, and my tussle with the round brush.

"Well, this Fiona broad sounds like she's full of shit," Esme cut in before I'd even finished. "I wouldn't be surprised if you end up having to write the usual crap articles like *Thinner Thighs in 30 Days* and *Seven Sexy Scents to Snag a Hottie*. You're a catch. We all know that. Seems to me she lured you over to that rag by telling you she was all peace, love, and granola. But I'm not buying it."

Why was everyone trashing Fiona? I honestly believed she was one of the good guys. Or at least I needed to. God, I hoped she was. Esme's voice was starting to rise partially in habitual indignation for me —after all, she'd been defending me against bullies since we were kids—and partially due to the two and a half screwdrivers and two glasses of champagne she'd downed in about an hour. I had to get some food in her fast but her plate of pasta primavera lay untouched. I surreptitiously buttered a mini-croissant and put it on her plate. Esme never could resist a good piece of bread and butter.

"That's not the main issue here," she continued, draining her champagne flute and motioning for the busboy to refill her glass as she picked up the croissant and nibbled at it. "We've got to get you ready to go into battle." Penny nodded her assent as she ate her quiche Lorraine and mixed greens.

"First off, you have to dress the part, and we have to manage this mane of yours. I think you're gorgeous and so does everyone who knows you, but these high-fashion bitches are going to be all over your shit all the time if we don't chic you up a bit."

Oh God, again with the hair and the clothes. I took another sip of champagne and debated getting good and drunk. This was exactly what I didn't want to think about, much less talk about. My stomach had other ideas, however, as just that little sip of bubbly started it burning and churning all over again making it just a little bit hard to keep down my eggs, so I ordered a peppermint tea instead. "Es, let's not worry about this. You know I'm not into clothes, and I've resigned myself that my hair has a life of its own," I replied as I slid a buttered baby brioche onto her plate.

"Can you not fight me on this? You're out of your league here and, trust me, the right clothes and hair will be like a suit of armor for you. Without it, these barracudas will eat you alive and I'm not sure they won't even if you have great clothes. Remember, everyone in that industry is going for the gold in the a-hole Olympics."

"Sarah calls them the Fashion Flamingos," Penny chimed in, getting upset all over again that I'd thrown myself into the depths of hell with Satan's minions. Esme eyed me quizzically. So, I explained their zeitgeist.

"That's perfect," Es snorted, "except you need to insert the word vampire, as in Vampire Fashion Flamingos." Despite my intense anxiety, I laughed. So did Pen. "And the look is only part of it. You have to stop caring what they think and trying to make them like you. They will never like you. They don't like anyone—not themselves and not each other. This has been your downfall since ballet class, and it totally fucked you with the Terror Trio. So, repeat after me, I do not give a shit what the Vampire Fashion Flamingos think, and I double do not give a shit if they like me." Penny laughed again, adjusting her stack of enamel bracelets that we bought her at Fortunoff's last week to celebrate her successful stint on the Cuisine Channel's "Piece of Cake" show.

"Baumie, I'm waiting." I knew better than to make Esme wait any longer. Waiting was not her strong suit.

"Okay. Okay. I do not give a shit what the Vampire Fashion Flamingos think of me, and I double do not give a shit if they like me."

"I'm not one hundred percent convinced, but it's a start," Esme said, liberating a Camel from her gold case and a gold lighter from her Valentino studded canvas bag. Penny and I both gave her the hairy eyeball. "Seriously, you are such narcs. I was going to go to the bar to smoke this. Cool your jets. And when I get back, we can discuss your new uniform. I raided Irma's Goodwill pile."

"Irma?" Penny asked, raising an eyebrow.

"Esme's mom," I replied, feeling a little relieved despite my reluctance to enter the fashion fray. Irma Levine was the most glamorous person I knew. And oddly enough, she was exactly my size and had wild curly hair that she wore in the most magnificent and expensively tended afro in the seventies and now in smooth, romantic ringlets down her back. Esme was always griping that she was too small for Irma's hand-me-downs and had fine, pin-straight hair. Not to say people wouldn't kill for Esme's clothes and strawberry blonde silky tresses. But I guess no one wants what they have. And in all honesty, Irma's wardrobe was astonishing—even to someone like me who didn't care about clothes.

"Explain this to me ladies, how can Esme's mom's cast-offs help Sarah?" Penny was understandably puzzled, never having met Irma, total club queen and fixture in the underground art scene even after she and her oral surgeon husband Mel moved to Teaneck to raise Esme. She was also a member of the staggeringly wealthy Rothman family who'd made their fortune in suburban supermarkets.

Most of all, I remember Irma taking us shopping in the city when we were nine or ten. Her driver would first drop us off at Fiorucci on Lexington where she would lie on the floor of the dressing room as the sales associate used a pair of pliers to zip up Fiorucci's signature body-hugging-within-an-inch-of-your-life jeans that she would pair with gold Lurex cowboy boots. Meanwhile, the store's roller-skating personnel loaded us down with Fiorucci Angel T-shirts, cropped sweatshirts, and heart-shaped sunglasses. Next, we went across the street to Bloomingdales for iridescent Stagelight and Madeline Mono makeup, Guerlain L'Heure Bleu perfume, and lunch.

I reminisced with Penny while we waited for Esme to come back. But she was in no hurry. I figured she was having another drink and flirting with the bartender. So, I decided to use this alone time to our advantage.

"So, Pen, what's happening? We've been so ridiculously obsessed with my stupid job we haven't talked about you."

"This is important stuff for you. And things are the same for me. Work is still a beast, and Rex gets more horrible by the minute."

"Come on, Pen, you can't keep this up forever. It's just too goddamn miserable. No one should have to take this kind of crap and especially not you. I mean, you're amazing," I squeezed her hand. "Let's get your resume out."

"Well, I may have some good news. I was waiting to see what happened before I told you." She hesitated a moment, but when I nodded encouragingly, she continued. "The Cuisine Channel contacted me about the possibility of having my own show. Our working title is *Savannah Sweets*."

"That's amazing. I love it. You so deserve this. When do you find out?"

"I really don't know. It's all super preliminary."

"I would pay money to be in the room when you tell Rex." I couldn't help giggling, thinking of how red-faced and irate he would become. What a dick.

"Well, let's not count our chickens. Do you think Esme is coming back?" As if on cue, we spied Esme teetering on her wedges trying to walk the straight line back into the dining room without much success.

"Let's go, girls, I called my driver so he can pick us up and take us down to Baumie's place in the Village to go through all of Irma's things. I hope your whack job of a roommate isn't home." I realized I hadn't told Esme about my impromptu move. So, I hastily filled her in, while asking her about her driver. This was a new thing for her. And it caused me no end of relief since she'd no longer have to rely on the kindness of cab drivers.

"Oh, yeah, Vladimir is great—he's like family to me now. And it's so much easier than taking a cab. It may even be cheaper," she said, not very convincingly.

"I think it's terrific," I cut in, not needing any further info. We all knew why she shouldn't take cabs—everyone was better off when she didn't.

"Well, it's about time you cut that crazy bitch loose, but you in the Bronx?"

"There's nothing wrong with the Bronx," Penny immediately interjected. "Holt and I love it up there."

"Holt? How is that babelicious brother of yours?" This reminded me of what I'd been dying to find out, so I took a chance.

"Holt is apparently seeing that crazy bitch I used to live with," I said, looking Penny square in the eye to gauge her very first reaction.

"Oh, Kitten. I've been meaning to tell you. I just wanted to make sure it was for real and not a moment of temporary insanity. How'd you find out?"

"I called him the other night because I needed

some help around the apartment and his answering machine message is now exactly the same as Desiree's." I was crestfallen.

"Wow. You're an amazing journalist. I can't believe you figured it out just from that." I could tell she was trying to butter me up because she felt bad that she didn't have the stones to tell me. "What did you need Holt to do?" She continued contritely. As if I'd ever tell the real reason I called him that nightmare of a Friday night. "We can call him again when we get back home, and he'll take care of it. I feel terrible I didn't tell you sooner. I was just hoping he would come to his senses."

"It's fine. I'm over it." I thought briefly about bringing up Sean until Esme cut in.

"Holt's with Des? That's a rough gig. I wouldn't wish her on my worst enemy. Well, maybe some of those douchebags I work with. But I think she's already boned those guys." Esme waved her credit card at the waiter. "Come on, ladies. Let's blow this Popsicle stand. We have a fashion show to get to." After she paid, she led us out of the restaurant as best she could in her current condition, ushered us into the waiting town car, and promptly fell asleep in the back seat.

She was still snoring away when we arrived in front of my building. I did my best to wake her as gently as possible, but she wasn't having it. Vladimir came to our rescue, clearly accustomed to this part of his job.

"Ms. Levine, we're at your destination now. Do you need me to go to a deli and get you your provisions?" It must have been a tempting offer because Es woke right up, though she certainly wasn't peppy—

no surprise considering all that vodka and champagne she had downed.

"Vlad, you're the best. Let's do a super-sized bag of Nacho Cheese Doritos, a six of Corona, three limes, a pack of Camel's, and two Ben & Jerry's Chunky Monkeys. And please get the bags from the trunk." She fumbled in her purse for her wallet and handed him a one-hundred-dollar bill. "Keep the change. I don't think you've had lunch yet and we're going to crash here for a while. There must be someplace to eat in this hood." Esme struggled to sit up and get out of the car.

"Really, Es, I can just run to the corner deli and pick this all up. You don't have to send Vladimir," I cut in. "There's a Cuban place up the street and a Chinese restaurant around the corner," I continued, turning to the man himself. Penny had popped the trunk and started pulling out two Vuitton duffle bags and a large tote. I could tell she felt just as uncomfortable as I did having someone wait on us. Vladimir, however, was smooth and professional and didn't seem put out at all, likely because as whacky as she was, Esme was phenomenally generous and an overall decent human being. Or maybe he was just a really great guy.

"No problem, ladies. I'll be back in a few minutes and then I can help you with these bags." True to his word, it was like he was never gone. When he returned, Vladimir picked up all three bags and followed me into my building. When she saw the stairs, Esme stopped short.

"What floor are you on?" she asked suspiciously.

"Four," I replied as nonchalantly as I could.

"You hike up and down four flights of stairs every day?" She was not happy. Even though she was naturally athletic, Esme loathed any form of exercise. In fact, I was positive that if she ever felt the urge to engage in physical fitness, she would lie down and take a nap until it passed.

"It's not so bad. It goes fast," I replied. Esme grunted a little and fumbled for a cigarette and her lighter.

"Come on, Es, that's not going to help, and you'll stink up the stairwell."

"Jesus Christ, you're killing me." After what felt like twenty minutes and two rest stops for Esme, we finally all made it up the stairs to my apartment. Vladimir left the bags on my new dining room table, courtesy of Holt, and excused himself. Esme promptly tore into the bag of Doritos, opened a Corona, and lay on the couch. She handed me a lime to cut up for her so she could put it in her beer. Now if only I could find a knife. After I located the knife, cut the lime, and pushed it into Esme's beer, Penny and I started to unpack those Vuitton bags.

They were stuffed with barely-worn tops, black pants, cashmere sweaters from hip brands I'd learned about at FDG—brands like Scoop, Anik, and Theory, a gorgeous black one-shouldered de la Renta cocktail dress, and three pairs of fabulous Earl Jeans—all perfectly tailored to fit my and Irma's 4 feet 11-inch selves. And then there were the shoes: Assorted impossibly glamorous ballet flats, low-heeled boots, pumps, and sparkly not-too-towering sandals from Chanel, Très Cher and Ferragamo, Sergio Rossi, and Jimmy Choo. Esme remembered that I couldn't wear heels. She really was an amazing friend. There even a spectacular rock star black leather jacket from

Barney's Co-op and this unbelievably studded, tasseled Balenciaga bag. Maybe I was more into clothes than I thought.

"Es, this is crazy. Your mom's going to freak you took all this stuff. I can't accept any of it."

"This was all in her giveaway pile. And let's face it, these clothes are all her second and third-string brands except for the de la Renta and the accessories, which are all from a couple of seasons ago which makes them not old enough to be vintage but not new enough to be happening now," Es said sleepily from the couch. "What I can't believe is that I never thought of this sooner. The Terror Trio would've been out of their minds if you'd showed up at prom in one of Irma's Versace's or Armani's." Not to mention the Gotham Gala, I couldn't help but think. Still, this was way too over the top.

"What about this Balenciaga bag?"

"Oh my God, that's so '97. She's not even carrying this year's version since she pre-ordered 1999."

"Es? Are you sure? You'd better take back these Vuitton duffels, at least. I mean they're classics."

"Baumie," she said very slowly and deliberately, "those bags are '96. Irma hasn't thought about them since '95 when she preview-ordered them." I looked at Penny helplessly and she looked back at me totally perplexed. While the Abernathy's were comfortable, this extravagance was mind-blowing for both of us. It seemed utterly batty that Irma would simply just give this all away. But then I thought for a moment about all the years of wearing my sister's hopelessly out-of-date hand-me-downs that my mother had to alter for me, and how they gave yet another excuse for the Terror Trio to torture me. And then I thought about how I would have to face the Fashion Flamingos and Toxic Twins in my own serviceable but completely unfashionable clothes. It couldn't possibly go well. So, I did what almost any girl in my situation would do. I said, "Thank you," and went into the kitchen to unpack my spoons and bowls so we could eat the Chunky Monkey.

I settled on the couch next to Es, and Penny curled up in the enormous chair that Holt had left. Man, I still owed them all dinner. And now I owed Es something wonderful, as well. Still, I felt pretty content for the moment until Es said in between bites of ice cream, "What're we going to do with your hair? I know you aren't going to straighten it. You've never been gifted with hair appliances." If she only knew. But for the love of God, why was it that there didn't seem to be one single second of the day when someone wasn't talking about my damn hair?

"I know. I'm going to ask Irma to get you an appointment with Mossimo," Esme was suddenly wide awake.

"Who is Mossimo?" Penny asked, leaning in for an answer.

"Mossimo? He's the Queen of Curl."

"There's a Queen of Curl?"

"Yes. And he's fabulous. Mossimo's the only person my mom lets near her hair, and she swears by his products," Es enthused, back to her usual commanding self now that she was making plans. "You're going to have to wing it tomorrow but Irma's a pretty influential client, so maybe she can get you in Tuesday or Wednesday. Mossimo will probably give you a freebie or an editorial discount since you're with

Sophistiquée now. Gotta work those perks." She handed me her empty bowl, my cue to refill it, and turned her attention to Penny.

"So, Georgia Peach, you've been awfully quiet. What's cooking with you?" I could picture Esme cracking herself up at her own bad chef's joke as I stood dishing out ice cream from the kitchen. The two started chatting amiably enough with Penny describing the new desserts she'd created—Esme just loved her desserts—and Es recounting some of the particularly jerky things some of her male colleagues said to her. They certainly had that in common. But Penny kept quiet about Rex. We'd already talked about him once that day and I guess she didn't want to discuss it anymore. I plunked myself back on the couch and handed Es her ice cream, which she devoured as though she'd never eaten ice cream in her life.

"I'm gonna head out soon so let's do something first," she said after a few more minutes of chatting with Pen. I knew just what she meant and walked across the room to unpack my acoustic guitar from its case. I tuned up and started playing Heart's "Dog & Butterfly", a song we'd been singing together since we were kids. Esme had a shockingly sweet and pure soprano voice. In fact, her pain-of-death secret was that when we went to Robert Lowell together, she was a member of Mix it Up, our school's co-ed acapella group. And if there'd been a group at the Ivy League school where she got her MBA, she would've signed on, though she never in her life would admit to it. Penny joined in, with a beautiful mezzo voice that I didn't even know she had.

"You're both such rock stars," I said when we

finished. I was about to launch into Fleetwood Mac's "The Chain"—another childhood favorite —when there was a knock at the door. It was Sean and Wyatt.

"Hey, that sounded wonderful," Sean said, lurking in the hallway, clearly embarrassed that he was making an unannounced visit. "Sorry to barge in on you but Wyatt wanted to say goodbye before we took him back downtown to his mother's."

"Hey, Wyatt," I said, motioning for them to come in. "Glad you stopped by. How was the rest of your weekend?"

"Cool. We skated a lot."

"That's great. Do you guys want to have some ice cream with me and my best friends, Esme and Penny?"

Sean cut in before he could reply. "Thanks, Sarah. We'd love to but his mother will kill me if I spoil his dinner."

"Sorry, pal, next time for sure," I said, remembering how much it sucked to be a kid when you were told you couldn't eat ice cream when you wanted it most.

"Hey, Saffie, are you coming to jam with us next week?" Wyatt asked as Sean maneuvered him back toward the door.

"You jam every week? That's awesome," I replied.

"Yeah, we're thinking of going back in the studio and it looks like we're close to lining up a couple of gigs, so we've been hitting it hard," Sean answered. "Ollie and Charisse have written some great new tunes that we've been working on."

"That's amazing. Where are you playing?"

"Oh, you know. We'll start with the usual suspects like Otto's, Sidewalk and Max's Kansas City, and

Ollie's working on Mercury Lounge and Brownie's," he listed, getting excited despite his shyness. "And CBGBs said to invite them if we get the Mercury Lounge or Brownie's gig. It's all a little loose right now, which is why Ollie probably hasn't told you about it yet."

"Hey, Sean, that's great." I had so many questions to ask him, like how long he'd been playing with One-Eyed Snake, and we still hadn't covered why he always wore white or smoked American Spirits like they were going out of style. But now didn't seem to be the time.

"You should come by and play again. Next week even." Sean looked down at his brown suede cowboy boots when he said this last part and then forged ahead with the wrangling of his son. "Come on, Wyatt, time to get going. Say goodbye to Sarah."

"I thought your name was Saffie." Wyatt pouted.

"Well, it sort of is. I'm also Sarah."

"I like Saffie better."

"That's fine, Wyatt. Call me whatever you want." This kid just knocked me out.

"Well, I like Sarah, Sarah Mandelbaum," Sean said quietly, finally looking at me, which gave me hope that he might kiss me goodbye, even a peck on the cheek since Wyatt was there, but they were out of my doorway and down the steps before I knew it. When I walked back into the living room, Esme and Penny stared at me expectantly.

"So, who was that scrawny old guy with the kid?" Esme blurted out even before the door closed behind them. Old? Sean wasn't old. And he certainly wasn't scrawny—just beautifully lean, at least as far as I was concerned.

"That's my neighbor, Sean, and his son, Wyatt. It's the wildest thing—he plays in One-Eyed Snake with Ollie. I don't think he's old. You think he's old?"

"He's pushing forty, if he hasn't seen the other side of it for sure. But it's fine, Sarah. He clearly likes you and maybe if you see him, you can finally work out your daddy issues. Sean and Sarah sitting in a tree, k-i-s-s-i-n-g," she sang, as she grabbed her bag and fished out her cell phone to call Vladimir.

"And what's with that kid calling you Saffie?"

"It's a long story," I replied, wondering if, I did indeed, have daddy issues. But I mean, didn't everyone?

"Okay, chickens. I'm off. Remember, Baumie, don't take no shit from nobody never." She hugged me goodbye and even gave Pen a little squeeze.

As I saw her minute figure retreat down the stairs, I called out, "Es, I love you madly and can't thank you enough, but no smoking in the stairwell."

"Girl, you are killing me," she called back. "Just killing me."

Chapter 8

I woke up the next morning well before my alarm, which I'd set for six, because crap, it was my very first day at *Sophistiquée*. And after all of Nils's admonishments that the best stories came in before sunrise, I certainly wasn't going to mess up today of all days by missing out on breaking news. I figured if I got there by eight-thirty, I'd be in decent shape. But because I'd been up since five, staring at the ceiling trying not to hyperventilate, now I could get there by eight or even earlier, but that would be pathetic. So, I stuck with eight, which would give me time to settle in and figure out what the hell I was going to do with myself over there. Hopefully, Fiona was an early riser like Nils and Michael and would help me navigate. I was sure my friends were just being overprotective of me and that she and I would be a united front. I even thought about how I'd write up my story of Ms. Ludwig and those damn hurdles, as Fiona had suggested when we met at Balthazar.

I jumped in the shower, dumped more conditioner on my hair, and hoped for the best. I hadn't washed it since Saturday morning, so it wasn't at its craziest— maybe all I needed was an extra dose of it to achieve its so-called miraculous results. Ignoring the Terror Trio's sneering jeers about how I "looked like I'd stuck my finger in a socket" going full-force in my head, I pulled on the Irma outfit that Penny had helped me choose last night after Esme left. Black Theory fitted stretch-wool pants, Ferragamo ballet flats, Cheap and Chic by Moschino black and purple floral silk blouse, and that fantastic Barney's leather jacket. My hair wasn't great, but it wasn't as horrible as it was the night of the Gotham Gala, so I considered that a small victory. And I told the Terror Trio as much as they laughed at me in the mirror. I loaded my Rolodex and work stuff in the Vuitton tote and transferred my wallet and keys into that jaw-dropping Balenciaga bag. I briefly thought about putting on makeup, but considering how terrible I was at applying it, I didn't think it would do me any favors. Kevin Carson's offer of a makeup lesson with Robbie Rose was looking better and better—even if it was from him.

As I scurried around my apartment looking for my *The Rise and Fall of Ziggy Stardust and the Spiders from Mars* tape, my phone rang in that awful Anna Elias Mandelbaum/Desiree Dershowitz way. Crap. It was only six-thirty, which meant it had to be my mom since Des was probably in a post-coital tranquilizer-induced coma. I thought about letting the machine pick up but decided to answer since I had the excuse of having to get to work so I could jump off the phone before things got too painful.

"Hi, Mom," I said quickly, without waiting to hear the voice on the line.

"How did you know it was me?"

"Mom, it's six-thirty in the morning. No one else would call me now."

"Well, Sarah, I wouldn't have to call you this early when I'm trying to get ready for school if you had called me back over the weekend like I'd asked you to. We've talked about this before. It's unkind and disrespectful of you to make me chase after you like this."

"Mom, I'm sorry. I have to leave for work in a few minutes."

"Why do you think I'm calling you? To wish you well. Can't a mother wish her daughter well on the first day of her new job?"

I knew this wasn't the only reason for the crack-of-dawn call. But in the interest of saving time and aggravation, I replied, "Thanks, Mom. That's really thoughtful of you."

"Also, why haven't you called back Stuart Felsenfeld? I just can't understand this stubborn streak of yours. It must be from your father's side of the family since you certainly don't get it from me. Morrisa is far more flexible and practical—an Elias through and through."

No one in their right mind would call Morrisa, my mother, or any of the Eliases either flexible or practical, though at least now Anna had given me an opening to get her off the phone quickly.

"How *is* Morrisa, Mom? Have you guys spoken lately? Is she coming in for your birthday?" I knew I was being mean since there was no way on earth my sister was coming in for my mom's birthday or anyone else's, for that matter. Still, I had to end this call, get to work, and nip this Stuart Felsenfeld thing in the bud.

"Morrisa is very busy with work and most likely hasn't had a chance to make plans for my birthday, which is still a few weeks away, so I'm sure she'll do something nice. She always does." Her voice got low and sad. I started to feel bad and didn't point out that I called Morrisa's assistant, Sookie, every year to remind her to send flowers on Morrisa's behalf.

"I'm sure she will, Mom. Everyone wants you to have a nice birthday."

"Birthday, schmirthday. Get off your high horse and call Stuart Felsenfeld back. I don't want to have to discuss this with you again. And good luck today. Did you do something with your hair?"

"My hair is fine, Mom. Everything is fine. Today will be fine." But as we hung up the phone, I knew I was really trying to convince myself.

As I passed the newsstand en route to the 1/9 train, I picked up a copy of the day's *Sentinel*. Sadly, the front-page headline read: "Supermodel Kiki Slams *Sophistiquée* CD." The article went on to detail Creative Director Henri-François Bernard's horrifyingly bad behavior on and off set and how Kiki and several other top mannequins refused to work for *Sophistiquée* until "has-been," "sexist-pig" Henri-François stepped down or was fired. This did not bode well for my first day in the office. Crap. Crap. And crap again. Nothing to do but crank up Bowie as loud as he'd go on my Walkman and try to think happy thoughts. When I got to the lobby of the building, it was deserted except for a lone security guard. I gave him my driver's license and told him it was my first day.

"No one usually rolls in there until around ten-ten-thirty," he explained, completely shattering Nils's "early bird catches the worm" ethos. "But someone from HR just came in so you can head up there. If your supervisor put in your paperwork, they can get you started. Who's your supervisor?"

"Fiona Doyle," I replied, wishing I'd stopped to pick up a coffee on my way in and wondering what Nils and Michael were up to. I knew the FDG newsroom was already humming and buzzing away.

"Ms. Doyle? She's great. You're probably all set," he said, much to my relief. Finally, someone agreed with me that Fiona was a good egg. And she had, indeed, set me up with HR. Still, it felt eerie that no one was there yet. After filling out the requisite paperwork, I took my key, pass, voicemail instructions, computer password, and benefits package folder down to the *Sophistiquée* offices on the 22nd floor. By this time, it was nine-thirty and there were still no signs of life. I wandered around the maze of the editorial floor until I found 2214—my designated office—and let myself in. There were at least twenty floral arrangements, mostly dead, and rows and rows of shopping bags festooned with ribbons and colored tissue paper laid out across every available surface.

And then there were the mountains of press releases, newspapers, and unedited manuscripts— towers so high and teetering, they made the heaps in Nils' cubicle look positively neat and tidy. There were also the September, October, and November issues of *Sophistiquée*, *Fashion Chic*, and *Simply Finesse*, which were all the size of telephone books. Someone had the good grace to pull out invitations to Très Cher and Back to Basics luncheons—both happening today—and place them on my keyboard. Well, this was an interesting development. Two lunches in one day—my first day? What I wanted more than anything was to skip Très Cher and hit the Back to Basics event, where I'd be less likely to run into the senior Fashion Flamingos since they'd send their assistants so they could go to the more exclusive Très Cher lunch. Sadly, though, I'd likely have to go to Très Cher since it was about the most important high fashion brand the magazine covered, even though the mass market Back to Basics was a bigger advertiser. Meanwhile, what the hell was I going to do about this crazy office?

I started sifting through the stacks of stuff. All the flowers had cards from publicists and beauty luminaries loaded with exclamation points, congratulating me on my new post and saying how excited they were to work with me. Pretty funny considering most of these people didn't give me the time of day last week when I was at FDG. Still, it was amazing how they'd just read the news on Friday and immediately tied up the phone lines of every New York City florist. I figured I could drop off the still-blooming bouquets with Esme's doorman tonight after work. Next, I turned to the festive shopping bags, which were full of swag that even Irma might have drooled over, accompanied by identical enthusiastic notes. Some people even dotted their "I's" with hearts or smiley faces. Wow!

YSL had sent over a gorgeous Rive Gauche chocolate brown suede bag, along with all its fall and holiday makeup shades; Très Cher had delivered an actual 24K gold chain link belt with not only its new makeup shades but all of its skincare products. Hermès had packaged its hefty signature sterling silver bracelet with its latest fragrance. Gucci sent a wallet and key case with its new scent, and Guerlain had gift-wrapped each and every one of its fragrances. And the embarrassment of riches went on and on. There was even a pair of black Manolo Blahnik pumps in exactly my size from Kevin Carson. How in the world did he know I was a 6? The heels were too high for my terrible feet, but perhaps I could exchange them for a lower-heeled version. Did they even make a lower-heeled version?

Wait a minute. I had to get a grip. I wasn't even into this stuff, and I wasn't supposed to take any of it, anyway. FDG had a strict policy against accepting gifts for fear it would compromise our journalistic integrity. And it seemed virtually impossible to have any kind of integrity whatsoever if I kept this loot. Still, I didn't want to be the lone gift-refusing editor—it would make me stand out even more than I did already, and it could cause hurt feelings and resentment, which I couldn't afford since my position in the high-fashion world was already tenuous at best. Plus, that Rive Gauche bag had Penny written all over it, and the Guerlain L'Heure Bleu was a no-brainer for Irma. As I worked my way through the mounds making a mental note of who to send thank you notes to, a tall, reedy platinum blonde with eyebrows tweezed to the point of no return, and wearing head-to-toe black Très Cher, peeked into my office.

She looked me up and down not once but twice before she made her way across the threshold and said, "Hi. You must be Sarah. I'm Christie Somers, associate beauty editor."

"Hey, I'm glad you're here. I was wondering if I'd shown up on the wrong day or something." I tried to laugh a little and extended my hand, which she didn't shake. I couldn't tell if it was just because she was preoccupied with the chaos that was my office, somewhat rude, or completely loathed human contact of any kind.

"We don't start till around ten - ten-thirty, and Fiona doesn't get in till eleven. They'd have a lot of nerve expecting us to come in any earlier since we're out so late most nights at events," she said, eyeing all of the piles with disdain.

"Samara was supposed to take care of all of this on Friday before she went home for the weekend. She's the department assistant." Christie paused for a minute, and then looked me up and down yet again. "You're not wearing any Très Cher and we have that lunch today." Aside from the Très Cher faux pas, I couldn't tell if she approved of my outfit or not, but at least she didn't look at me with the overt disgust of the Toxic Twins at the Gotham Gala. I was making progress, I guess. But wow. You had to wear the label of the designer whose event you were attending? I silently cursed myself for choosing Irma's Ferragamo flats over the Très Cher ones that morning.

"What about Back to Basics?" I asked hopefully, even though I knew there was no chance in hell I was going to get out of Très Cher.

"Très Cher is much more important to us than Back to Basics. Samara can go to Back to Basics, and don't let her tell you she can't. She's all about booking her own appointments and doing her own thing instead of the administrative work she's supposed to do. She's just an assistant, no matter what she thinks. And you shouldn't hesitate to send her out on any personal business you may have. Your time is more valuable than hers." Christie looked around for a place to sit without finding one. So, instead, she crossed her skinny arms over her bony chest and went on, "I don't know what you've heard about me, but I'm glad you're here. I think you'll be a brilliant breath of fresh air," she said, nearly knocking me over with a feather. Maybe, just, maybe. She was all right. "You probably feel like you're an outsider since you're coming from the business world. I'm kind of an outsider too. In high school, everyone picked on me because my mother made me wear Comme des Garçons to the prom when everyone else wore Laura Ashley ruffled prairie dresses."

I took a deep breath so I wouldn't burst out laughing at that absurdity. "Trust me. She made the right choice. I wore a ruffled prairie dress to my prom, and it was not well-received."

Suddenly, a breezy voice out in the hall interrupted our exchange.

"Oh God, Christie, are you telling that ridiculous 'pity-me because I had to wear Comme des Garçons to prom' story again? I keep telling you that people will hate you if you do." The voice was musical, tinkling even, and it echoed my exact thoughts, though it made me nervous. Esme was right. These women didn't like anyone. Not themselves and not each other—although, the one who just spoke seemed to like herself tremendously. Was that worse than her not liking herself? Before I could fully decide, another tall, super svelte woman, this time with long, straight mahogany hair and dark skin, bounded into my office. She wore hot pink leather pants, a pink and orange Très Cher logo blouse, a matching Très Cher scarf like a headband, dangling interlocking TC earrings, and 4-inch Très Cher boots. Apparently, these girls took their Très Cher very seriously and either had trust funds, or someone even more fabulous than Irma Levine giving them hand-me-downs.

"You must be our new fearless leader. Welcome. I'm Samara, lowly beauty assistant," she said, extending her hand and giving me a hearty shake, making it crystal clear she didn't believe there was anything lowly about her. "Sorry about this mess, Chief. I'll get to it as soon as I can, maybe after that Très Cher lunch and the few other appointments I have today."

Christie glared at me. I knew that was my cue to be a boss.

"About that, Christie and I have Très Cher covered. It'd be great if you'd go to Back to Basics," I said, doing my best to sound firm and friendly simultaneously.

"You're not even wearing Très Cher. And besides, our readers don't care about Back to Basics." Samara pouted. Clearly, she was going to persist until she got her way. But Christie took over before she could wear me down.

"First off, Sarah just got that Très Cher belt that's sitting right there so she can wear that. And secondly, you know that Giancarlo will completely freak out if one of us doesn't go to Back to Basics. They're huge advertisers," she said, her eyes practically boring holes into Samara's pretty face. Giancarlo Romano was *Sophistiquée*'s publisher, and obviously someone we didn't want to piss off.

"It's Sarah's decision," Samara cut in, waiting for me to come to her rescue, which I wanted to do because I felt much safer at Back to Basics. Unfortunately, though, this was apparently some kind of test that I had to pass or be screwed forever. So, I worked up all my courage and said, "Samara, it would be super if you could go to Back to Basics this afternoon. And we'll be sure to fill you in on Très Cher." God, I hoped that would put a pin in this. I was exhausted already, and the day had barely started.

"Hey, that's a great bag," Samara said, changing the subject as she picked up the chocolate brown suede Rive Gauche I planned to give Penny. "Can I have it? Brown is definitely not your color."

"Stop being such a vulture, Samara. Can't you see that she needs it more than you? That Balenciaga she has is so last year," Christie retorted as she eyed all my loot just as covetously.

And even though she said exactly what Esme'd jokingly said last night, the fact that Christie wasn't even addressing me directly anymore showed me that I'd committed a terrible sin. Clearly, it was a felony in the fashion community to carry a year-old bag, even if it was a former "it" bag costing over a grand.

"Actually, I was thinking of sending all this stuff back. You know, for journalistic integrity and all."

"Send it back? This is how the companies let us experience their brands so we can write about them more accurately. It makes us better journalists, not worse," Samara lectured as she rolled her eyes about me to Christie. While I wasn't convinced, at this point I was pretty much speechless, so I waited for Christie to chime in. I didn't have to wait long.

"The lunch starts at twelve-thirty, so we'll need you to call a car for twelve. Pick-up time from the event is two," she instructed Samara, ignoring the last exchange, her preternaturally pale skin flushing prettily with her victory as she flounced out of my office. As Samara made her equally dramatic exit, Henri-François and another man squeezed past her in my tiny doorway.

"Sarraah! Welcome," Henri-François said, glaring at the towering piles of newspapers, magazines, press releases, beauty products, and dead flowers littering my office. "What happened here?" he asked, assuming his legendary stance of pelvis-thrust-forward-with-hands-on-hips, crushing my hopes that all the stories surrounding his desire to showcase his private parts at all costs were gross exaggerations.

I kept my eyes averted from him and his white, body-suffocating crotch-emphasizing Levi 501s as I replied, "Hello, Henri-François. Thank you. I'm glad to be here. Samara and I are working together to get all this organized."

"Sarraah, you cannot let these girls in your department run wild," he retorted, rolling his Rs and stretching his vowels for all he was worth. "I do not know why Peach hired them, but now it is up to you to train them to be more, how you say, professional." I murmured something that I hoped sounded polite and business-like. "Sarraah, he continued interrupting me. "You are not wearing Très Cher?" And even though his voice rose as if it was, this was not a question.

"Actually, I have this belt," I said, hurrying over to the pile of gifts, and picking it up to show to him.

"This is not good," he replied darkly. "Samara was supposed to call you and alert you of this event and get you something to wear. But since you are bigger than the sample size and cannot fit into anything from our fashion closet, the belt will have to do." Those hits just kept on coming. But he wasn't finished with me yet.

"Sarraah, you read the *Sentinel*?" He narrowed his blue eyes, daring me to answer in the affirmative. Instinctively, I knew now was not the time to tell the truth.

"Sometimes, Henri-François—not often. It's kind of a rag," I replied as convincingly as I could.

"Ah, *bon*, I agree. It has no journalistic integrity," he said empathetically, and then gestured to the bald, plump, pasty, freckle-faced man standing next to him, who nodded at me without so much as a greeting. "This is Didier Tremblay, our very good art director." I nodded back, hoping I wouldn't have to spend too much time with him.

"Sarraah, I have a *fantastique* idea for a story you need to start immediately," Henri-François continued breathlessly at the idea of his brilliance.

"Of course. That sounds great." I searched in vain for a pad and pen. As if reading my mind, Didier curled his virtually non-existent upper lip into a sneer and silently handed me the pad and pen he was holding.

"We are going to do a phenomenal piece on butts. It will be at least four spreads on everything about the butt. I want you to cover creams, scrubs, lingerie, exercises, plastic surgery, and diets especially good for creating a beautiful butt. And I will shoot an iconic story."

It seemed odd to me that after the latest article in the *Sentinel,* he would choose to go in that direction, but I was pretty sure he'd find other models to do that shoot. Has-been and sexist pig or not, he still had the power to make or break a career. And all those class-action lawsuits against him never seemed to go anywhere. Henri-François seemed completely untouchable.

"What a unique idea," I replied, fighting to keep the mounting panic from my voice. A butt story was certainly worse than "Seven Sexy Scents to Snag a Hottie." "What was Fiona's take?" I asked, hopefully.

"Do not worry about Fiona, Sarraah. This is not her concern," he scolded, leaning dangerously close to my face, causing my eyes to tear and clogging up my nose and throat with his cologne. Funny, I didn't remember his scent being this noxious the night of the gala. Today, however, it was positively radioactive. And what was this about the butt story not being Fiona's concern? Wasn't she the editor-in-chief of the magazine?

"Get your team together and brainstorm for me an outline. You will have it for me first thing tomorrow morning. And call Kevin Carson. He has an exclusive for us about Cecil and her first fragrance." He turned to go so abruptly that the pile of papers closest to him went flying. Thank goodness he was almost gone. But just as I thought I'd have a few moments of peace to process all of this, Henri-François stopped at my door, causing Didier, who was following right behind His Majesty's heels, to almost trip up the pair of them. "Sarraah, you are Jewish?" he asked. Great, now it was coming to this?

"I am, Henri-François. Why?"

"I love Jewish people. But you will do something about your hair, yes? You are the beauty director of *Sophistiquée* now. We are counting on you." The two were almost out the door when he poked his head back in, once again nearly bumping into Didier, and asked, "Sarraah? You speak French?" And I don't know why, but for the third time that morning, I found myself telling a lie, despite what Fiona had said the other night.

"No, I'm sorry, I don't."

"Ah, *bon*. Bye, Sarraah."

When everyone was finally gone, I sank on top of the mountain of papers covering my desk chair. I thought about calling Penny or even Esme but couldn't bring myself to. It was too humiliating that they'd been so right about everything. Righter than right, if there was such a thing. For a split second, I tried to channel Saffron Meadows. But her image was fleeting and not in the least comforting. While I was still discovering who she was, I knew without a doubt she never would've signed on to a freak show like this. I needed to hear a friendly voice, so I picked up the phone and prayed I wouldn't get a voicemail on the other end.

"Petersen," came the voice on the other line after just one ring, answering my prayers.

"Nils, it's Sarah. I just wanted to make sure you have everything you need for that dot.com story I left you on Friday." Was that just Friday? I felt like two years had passed since I'd been at FDG.

"Hey, Sarah, the flood is swirling all around me and I'm treading water like mad just to keep my finger in the dike." I almost laughed. It never ceased to amaze me how he was such a gloomy Gus when he did his job perfectly and was so highly regarded. "The story was fine, Sarah, good even," he continued. "But you didn't have to call me about that on your first day there. Anything up?" I couldn't tell whether he was looking for a scoop or genuinely concerned. Maybe it was a little bit of both.

"Sure, it's fine. I just didn't want to leave you hanging if you needed anything else," I lied for the fourth time that day. "Everything is great. Are you going to the Très Cher lunch today?" I really needed him there. Otherwise, I'd have to face the Fashion Flamingos with no one except Christie by my side, and it was an easy bet that she'd ditch me as soon as we got to the event to schmooze with the popular girls. She was probably one of their stars.

"You know I never go to these things," he said, now sounding distracted. I could hear him pummeling his keyboard. "I interviewed the powers that be this morning, so I don't have to waste my time and subject myself to those pampered princesses known as beauty editors. What is it you call them again?"

"Fashion Flamingos," I sighed. This conversation wasn't making me feel any better.

"Yes. That's it. Perfect." I could barely make him out through all his pounding. "Hey, gotta go. Other line is ringing, and I've got to haul this ship onto shore."

That was so not helpful. I wondered where Fiona was and if I dared to go look for her. I had to get this butt story thing straightened out. But the idea of leaving my office, even as chaotic as it was, petrified me. So, I started sorting through the first pile of press releases—many of them were over six months old—past the three-month lead time of the magazine—so mercifully I could just throw them out, though I couldn't find a trash can or recycling bin. I decided to start a list of all the things I'd need to clean up this mess and then I'd get cracking on editing the 4-5 unread manuscripts waiting for me. I figured even if Samara wouldn't do any of the grunt work, at the very least she could tell me where to find supplies. Didier's pen and pad were coming in handy.

At noon, Christie stuck her head in my office to tell me the car was waiting downstairs and it was time to go. I hadn't even had a chance to go to the bathroom and check my hair, much less put the Très Cher belt on. She waited none-too-patiently for me to thread the gold chain links through my belt loops, put on my leather jacket, and sling my now much-maligned beloved Balenciaga bag over my shoulder.

As we walked past Samara's cubicle on the way out, she said, "Samara, when you get back from Back to Basics, we want a full report. And then you need to get started on Sarah's office." Samara didn't even look up at her when she spoke but as I passed by, she smiled probably one of the most engaging smiles I'd ever seen and winked at me, making it about as clear as day that she would be doing neither one of these things.

When we got to the Très Cher offices on West 57th Street, members of its PR team—all tall, thin, blondes wearing Très Cher—ushered us to a conference room decked out with flowers, tables set with expensive china, photos of Très Cher models, products and the latest fashion collection, and waiters serving wine and champagne. I would've killed for either of those, but immediately decided against it. All I needed was to get drunk in a room full of people who already looked down on me on my very first day of work at a magazine everyone thought I had no business being at. So, I accepted a glass of sparkling water as Christie selected a champagne flute from the same tray before she made a beeline for the sea of blondes in black Très Cher that was the Flamingos, who were standing with the Toxic Twins in front of the room.

I looked around for the president to say hello—

something Nils had taught me was a priority at any event. He was MIA and likely planning a grand entrance. So, I searched the room until I found the friendly bridal and women's service book editors who stood in its furthest recesses. I started to walk over, but Très Cher's VP of beauty publicity stopped me.

"Sarah, so glad you're here and you got our belt," she said, her eyes giving me the once over like everyone else had that day. "I'm just dying to set you up with a few more things so you can get a better feel for the brand."

"Thanks, Lisa, this belt is great. I don't need anything else," I replied, clutching my water glass in one hand and my bag in the other.

"We insist. It's our pleasure." She said, staring at me like I'd just spilled red wine on her white carpet. I guess it was hard to fathom someone not wanting free Très Cher stuff. "Also," she continued, "We're having a little raffle and the winner gets something very exciting. You'll want to put your business card in this bowl to enter." She passed a crystal bowl practically overflowing with cards so close to my nose I thought it would brush against it.

"I don't have a new business card," I said, finding it hard to be excited about anything that day. But maybe I could win something for my mom's birthday. I still felt guilty for throwing Morrisa's inattentiveness in her face. And if I won whatever it was by chance, maybe it technically wasn't a bribe.

"That's fine. We all know what masthead you're on now. Congrats by the way. We're just thrilled to be working with you."

Searching unsuccessfully for a place to put down

my water glass, I finally had to ask Lisa to hold it, which she did somewhat unsteadily against the bowl so I could find one of my old FDG business cards in my bag and drop one in.

"Great, you're all set. The presentation and lunch are about to start. I've seated you over there with your colleagues so you can be front and center for the presentation. This is a very important launch for us," she said, pointing to that damn corner of the room dominated by the Flamingos.

And with that, she gave me my seating card and a little shove toward my table. As I trudged over to what I presumed would be certain death, I looked behind me to seek out Linda Donohue from *Your Beautiful Home* and Bonnie Chen from *Your Big Day*—my two favorite editors. Clearly, they hadn't gotten the "wear Très Cher today or else" memo either. Linda looked incredibly chic in a black pants suit from Banana Republic while Bonnie rocked a pink tweed skirt and jacket from Ann Taylor. When I caught their eyes, I gave them a sad little wave. They both smiled compassionately at me and then took their places with the other nice girls.

Of course, I was seated dead in between the Toxic Twins, neither one of whom acknowledged me as I settled in. As the lights dimmed, I caught a flash of hot pink and orange slipping into the room. I was pretty sure it was Samara, even though I prayed it wasn't. This being a department manager thing was tougher than I thought. At least we were about to eat lunch, which would have to improve things. It was already 1:30 and I was famished. But when the presentation ended, and the waiters brought out the plates, my hopes were dashed. In front of me was a sliver of salmon, two asparagus spears, and a thimbleful of squash or sweet potato puree. Sadly, I loathed salmon and asparagus as much as I loathed mussels. So, I was almost grateful that the portion sizes were insane, which brought me right back to my philosophy that part of the reason the Flamingos were so mean was that they were half-starved, whether by choice or dictate.

I looked around for the sourdough roll and butter that'd been at my place when I sat down, but some sadistic or well-meaning waiter had already cleared it. I fared better with "dessert": two strawberries, one slice of mango, and a thin drizzle of raspberry "coulis." Still, I made a mental note to stop in at the Au Bon Pain in our building before I went upstairs to tackle the butt story issue and now this Samara problem. Sample size or not, a girl had to eat, especially if she were going to stand up to one of her bosses and her assistant in the same afternoon.

As coffee was being served, Lisa went up to the podium with her crystal bowl of business cards and asked the president of Très Cher to "do the honors." Smiling, he reached into the bowl and said, "Drumroll, please," —as he withdrew a card. — "And the winner is Sarah. Sarah Mandelbaum from FDG, I mean, *Sophistiquée*. Sarah, come up here and claim your prize."

As I walked over to him to receive the very large, very pink Très Cher bag Lisa handed him, I couldn't help but hear Peach Chandler stage whisper to Keeley McPheters, "Figures it's her. She wouldn't know what to do with a Très Cher Bag if she had one in every color. I mean, can you believe she thought it was in good taste to bring a Balenciaga to this event and a last year's one, at that? And where does she shop? The kiddie department?"

"Shh, Peach, she'll hear you." Keeley giggled, true to form.

"Well, she should. I can't believe Fiona chose her to replace me. This girl's a walking nightmare. She's probably one of the reasons Fiona's on the way out."

"I do not care what Peach Chandler and Keeley McPheters think of me," I said over and over in my head as I thanked the president of Très Cher as graciously as I could. Fiona on her way out? Peach wasn't as smart as she seemed to think. Irma didn't shop in the kid's department, even though I frequently did, and Fiona certainly wasn't going anywhere. Or was she? And good lord, what would anyone do with a bag that big and that pink? It would be over-the-top even for my mother, a woman who put the "f" in flamboyant with her fuchsia lipstick, plum eyeshadow, jewel-toned Talbots petite skirt suits, and contrasting silk blouses. Ironically, the bag matched Samara's outfit perfectly, so we'd probably have to get into that when we got back to the office. Say, where was she, anyway? I looked around but she'd wisely fled the scene of the crime before the lights came back on.

As I headed to the door, planning to walk the eight or so blocks back to work to clear my head from the Toxic Twins' latest slam fest, Lisa handed me a Très Cher shopping bag with a press kit along with a few Très Cher boxes inside and Christie darted over to my side.

"The car should be waiting for us downstairs. Samara's in big trouble if it isn't," she threatened and then brightened. "How amazing is it that you won that fabulous bag? You should wear it instead of that old Balenciaga. I wonder what Lisa gave us today?" The last thing I wanted on earth was to be trapped in a car stuck in traffic, rehashing the event with Christie. But she wasn't leaving me much choice. And right now, she seemed like the closest thing I had to an ally at *Sophistiquée,* so maybe I could use the drive time to try and bond with her a little. However, once again, she had other plans; one split second after we got into the car, Christie started opening the boxes in the Très Cher bag.

"I can't believe how cheap they were today. All we got was a scarf and a pair of sunglasses," she said with equal parts disappointment and disdain. I personally was over the moon about both gifts. The scarf would make a great birthday present for my mom, and I'd try the sunglasses. I'd never had a pair that cost more than ten dollars at the drugstore, and these looked super glam in a vintage Brigitte Bardot/Mia Farrow/Audrey Hepburn kind of way. Saffron Meadows might even approve.

"Hey, I'm pretty sure I saw Samara sneak into the event," Christie tattled, her voice rising in indignation as she cut into my thoughts.

"Yeah," I admitted hesitantly since it meant I'd have to do something about it. "I think I did too. I'll ask her when we get back to the office." Christie seemed intent on saying more but suddenly held her tongue, which made me more nervous than when she spoke. I didn't know her that well yet, but silence from people like her typically meant they were up to something.

A few minutes later, however, she perked up again and said almost contritely, "I'm sorry about all those freelance manuscripts waiting for you on your desk. It's been a little crazy without Peach. But you're here now so I'm sure things will settle down." She paused for a moment and looked like she might even pat my arm, though, of course, she didn't. "Anyhow, I'd be happy to look at them and do a first edit if you want. I can get them back to you this week so we can get the ball rolling. That's how Peach and I used to work."

"Hey, that'd be great. It may take me a day or two to get situated, and I'd hate for them to sit around any longer than they have to. That's so unfair to the writers."

"No problem. That's what I'm here for," she replied and then started to gripe about the unspeakable traffic and how inconsiderate Très Cher was to take up so much of our time before I could be too excited about our budding relationship. I didn't point out to her it would have taken us only fifteen minutes to walk back to the office rather than the forty-five by car since her ridiculously high heels precluded her from doing much more than climbing in and out of a car. As we were walking into the building, I excused myself to hit the Au Bon Pain.

"Didn't you eat at Très Cher? I'm positively stuffed," she asked, looking me up and down yet again.

"No. I didn't. I don't like salmon or asparagus. And besides, that was barely a snack, much less a meal."

"But they're so healthy. And besides, if you want to fit into sample sizes so you can borrow clothes for events, you'll need to eat less. You get used to it after a while. Nothing tastes as good as being thin feels," she intoned, leaving me to wonder if she'd paid good money for those words of wisdom from some Madison Avenue diet doctor and went to sleep with headphones on repeating that mantra over and over again throughout the night. It made me a little sad for her.

Despite her admonishments, I picked up a chicken salad sandwich and a jumbo iced coffee with half-and-half and made my way back upstairs. Samara was not in her cubicle. I put my food down and decided it was time I found Fiona. I wandered around until I came to a very large office with an impressive view and an assistant's cubicle out in front. Like Samara's, it was empty, so I poked my head into Fiona's office. She was there cradling the phone between her chin and neck as she shrugged into a black Burberry trench. Clearly, she was on her way out.

"Sarah," she said warmly, as she hung up the phone and picked up her breath-taking blue ostrich Hermès bag. "Good to see you. How's your first day going? Splendid, I hope. I have to dash out so let's try and touch base tomorrow before lunch."

"Fiona, has Henri-François told you about the butt story?" I asked, scurrying to keep up with her as she hurried down the hall.

"Butt story? No, he hasn't. But don't worry about it. I'll talk to him tomorrow. There's no way we'd run anything like that."

"He wants an outline for it first thing in the morning."

"Oh." She stopped for a second, as though considering something really important, and then much to my crushing disappointment said, "Well, why don't you get him something just to humor him? No need to poke the hornet's nest. But I'll take care of it." She turned to squeeze my shoulder before she practically ran onto the elevator. As the doors closed, she called out, "It'll be fine, Sarah, you'll see." But she sounded a lot like I did this morning when I was trying to convince myself and my mother that everything would be okay when I was pretty damn sure it wouldn't be.

As soon as I got back to my office, the phone rang. I was almost certain Samara was supposed to pick it up, but after the third ring, I realized Samara's main job was completely avoiding her required responsibilities. So, I answered.

"Sarah, Giancarlo Romano here. I know it's your first day, but I just got a disturbing call from Back to Basics. It seems that no one from your department attended their event."

"No one attended at all?" I couldn't believe that even Samara would be a total no-show. For anyone else that would be a career killer, but she seemed to have superpowers.

"Well, someone swung by and picked up a gift bag and press kit, but no one talked to the executives or stayed for the presentation."

"I'm sorry, Mr. Romano. The department did send someone to the event. I'm not sure what the mix-up was but I will find out and call Back to Basics to apologize."

"Giancarlo, please. Let's do one better than that. I've arranged a lunch for us with their president and vice-president of marketing at La Grenouille on Wednesday so we can express our appreciation to them for being such great business partners. Why don't you come up with a few story ideas that feature some of their products, particularly the new ones? It will go far in restoring goodwill."

"But, Giancarlo, don't I need to get the story ideas approved by Fiona before we make promises to advertisers?"

"Sarah, if a publisher decides it's good business to write a certain kind of story, the editor-in-chief will clearly agree." Now, this was news to me. At FDG, the publisher and ad sales team were on a completely different floor from the editors and couldn't talk to us without Michael's permission; he insisted on a no-exceptions separation of church and state—editorial being the church and advertising being the state.

"I had the publicist messenger over some of the press releases of their latest products and the bag from the event. Take a look and write up a few ideas for me for tomorrow so we can present them at lunch. And, Sarah, please don't let this happen again." As soon as I hung up, Samara breezed into my office carrying more shopping bags of floral arrangements and more swag.

"Wow, boss, you're so popular," she said, looking around for a place to put them. There wasn't any.

"Samara, what happened with Back to Basics today?"

"I went to the event just like you told me to," she replied easily.

"Actually, Back to Basics called Giancarlo and said you didn't stay for lunch."

"Well, I didn't waste our time for the whole three hours or whatever, but I was totally there for the important parts. As soon as I put these things down, I'll bring you the gift bag and press kit. They're doing some pretty cool stuff."

"Samara, were you at Très Cher today?"

"Chief, you told me not to go to Très Cher today,

so I didn't go." She was positively angelic. "I know. How would you feel about my tossing the dead floral arrangements and old press releases? I can work on your office the rest of this afternoon after I pick up Christie's dry cleaning." This was about the biggest admission of guilt I'd ever heard. But still, I needed this chaos organized, even if it meant taking a back seat to Christie's dry cleaning, and decided I had to pick my battles.

"Listen, that's great, but while you're doing that, I need you and Christie to help me brainstorm a line-up for Henri-François for this butt story he wants to do and one for this Back to Basics lunch I have to go to with Giancarlo on Wednesday."

"Christie stepped out, and I'd love to help you with those two things, but I think you really might want me to concentrate on your office."

"Where is she?"

"She has Gyrotonics every Monday at three-thirty and then Pilates at four-thirty."

"Does she come back to the office after?"

"Not usually. In fact, she had me book a car to pick her up at the studio at five forty-five and take her home. But show me this Très Cher bag you won. Lucky you."

Chapter 9

Somehow, I woke up the next morning and three months had flown by. It was winter and things were pretty damn nuts. Reporting and writing the butt story was followed by an exclusive interview with supermodel Cecil about her return to the runway post-pregnancy at 38 and her first fragrance. Then Henri-François had me finish the butt story, research, and write "Give it a Shot", a piece on the wrinkle-preventative benefits of Botox for women in their 20s, which killed me, and "Blonde Ambitions", a pictorial with short interviews of dark brunette models who "transformed their lives and careers" when they went blonde, which killed me even more. The topper? "The Next Breast Thing", Henri-François' magnum opus on mammary glands. Then there were the endless press events and ad sales lunches with Giancarlo, which thankfully had gone well. I wondered if these meetings would continue to be so lucrative after Henri-François' stories came out. To my mind, they were as low as low could be, even by women's magazine standards.

On the plus side, my new paycheck was giving me breathing room for the first time in my life. I was chipping away at my student loans and had enough cash left over to afford crazy little luxuries, like cable TV. I'd had my makeup lesson with Robbie Rose, who'd beaten my bushy brows into submission and taught me the art of applying eye and lip liner. Meanwhile, Esme and Vladimir had dropped off two Vuitton duffels and a garment bag packed with Irma's cold weather castoffs.

I was appreciative of the delivery, though a little alarmed at the circumstances surrounding it since Esme brought my new wardrobe to my office in the middle of the workday smelling like vodka on top of her cool, green, signature scent, Gucci Envy. Of course, she became defensive when I asked her about it and why she wasn't at the office or a client lunch.

"Can't a girl take a mental health day and just see her best friend once in a while?" She griped and then grew sullen.

"Es, while I'm over the moon to see you, it feels like something's going on. Are you okay?"

"I'm fine. I mean as fine as I can be working in that hellhole."

"Do you want to talk about it?" I asked, hoping she wouldn't, which might've been terrible of me, but I was swamped with work and expected at a press event in ten minutes. Still, Es was obviously in trouble or at the very least troubled. So, I motioned for her to sit down.

"No. There's nothing to talk about. It's fine. I'm fine," she murmured, first eying, then picking up and coveting some of the wallets, belts, and handbags I'd received as thank you's for beauty product mentions in articles I'd written that I'd piled up on the small table by the window. Even though I'd already given a bunch of this stuff to my mom and Penny, there was still a ton that I didn't need or want. I mean, really, how many small leather goods could a girl possibly possess? And besides, I loved Irma's Balenciaga despite the criticism it drew.

"Es, talk to me. Seriously, I'm worried about you."

"No really, Baumie. Everything is A-OK. Can I have this?" she asked, threading a too-big Versace canvas belt through the loops of her black Narciso Rodriguez pants.

"Of course, you can have anything you want," I said, hugging her and handing her a navy Kate Spade nylon tote to put everything in. She scooped up a bunch of items and seemed poised to scoop up several more when her cell phone started to ring up a storm. When she finally looked at it to see who was calling, her eyes widened, and she hurried out of my office with the tote without so much as a backward glance or goodbye. After she left, I had to race to the press event, which forced me to push the incident to the back of my mind.

And so, things kept rolling along. Thanks to Irma's generosity, I hadn't even touched my clothing allowance, except to buy Christmas presents for Christie and Samara, even though the latter didn't seem to serve any other purpose than to make my life a living, breathing hell, and I was still on the fence about Christie. But to quote my mother, Anna Elias Mandelbaum, "You have to keep greasing the wheels." At least my office was no longer drowning in papers, press kits, and shopping bags. From what I could gather from Samara's furtive phone conversations, Henri-François had given her a stern, heavily accented talking-to. And to her credit, Christie kept chastising Samara to stay on top of it.

Most days I didn't even recognize myself since my life was now far more about lipstick and far less about music than ever—not a ratio I was proud of, much less happy about. Because of beauty industry evening events, I hadn't been able to make any of One-Eyed Snake's gigs, or even play with them in the studio despite the band's (and more importantly Sean's) repeated invitations. Saffron Meadows was becoming increasingly elusive to me, though I channeled her whenever I could—especially when facing the Flamingos and my supposed staff.

I'd even had to cancel several lessons with Ollie— something I'd never done before—because of last-minute late nights trying to get an issue out the door to the printer or Giancarlo insisting I join him and clients for drinks. Ollie would graciously let me make them up on Sunday mornings before margarita brunch, which was now lunch, so I could have my lesson and Penny could sleep in. We held onto this ritual even more tightly since both of our schedules were so crazy that it was our only opportunity to connect. She hadn't received an offer from the Cuisine Channel, though they seemed serious enough to call her every few weeks to let her know they were "working on it." And she still frequently guested on other Cuisine Channel shows.

In the meantime, I begged her every chance I got to switch restaurants or open her own place—I knew she'd be able to get backers in a minute. Rex had gotten so aggressively nasty to her, I was certain someone had filled him in on her talks with the Cuisine Channel. And all her recent raves in the *Sentinel*, *Village Voice,* and *Time Out,* didn't help. Yet every time I brought up the idea of her leaving, she said, "Kitten, are you the pot or the kettle? Henri-François isn't any better. And at least Rex doesn't make me write about behinds, breasts, and Botox for twenty-somethings." And that would be that.

Most mornings I looked away when I passed a

newsstand because I couldn't bear to see the *Sentinel,* which always seemed to have some kind of shame-on-you cover story about Henri-François, the sexual harassment suits against him, the models panning him, and how Fiona was going to be shipped back to London at any minute—a story that may have had some truth to it since in the few months I'd been at *Sophistiquée,* I'd seen her just a handful of times and she was frantic at every one of them. The only time she'd stopped and chatted with me was when we ran into each other in the lobby of our building as I was finally coming back from the Mossimo appointment, which I'd had to keep rescheduling since things were so insane.

Six feet six and almost as wide, Mossimo was marvelous. When he saw me, he started singing an outstanding rendition of Cher's "Dark Lady," and then said, "Oh my gawd, we're so cute together. We're like Sonny and Cher." He proceeded to flip an imaginary hank of long, straight hair off each shoulder and introduce me to everyone in the salon as "Son," which everyone, including me, found hilarious. The problem was that Mossimo worshiped not only at the altar of Cher (and Streisand) but also at the altar of rubber-cement-like hair products. And while his religious fervor may have kept my frizz from flying out in all directions, it also shellacked my curls flat against my head and left a dusting of white flakes on my clothes. So, I was feeling even less confident than usual about my hair—if such a thing was possible—when I came face to face with Fiona that afternoon.

"Sarah! Hello, you had your hair done." I could tell Fiona was fighting to keep her voice neutral.

"Yes, I went to see Mossimo during lunch." I felt

guilty about having a beauty appointment in the middle of the day even though every *Sophistiquée* staffer got her grooming on during the workweek with multiple rounds of manicures, pedicures, facials, waxing, salt scrubs, and brow shapings. Most of the masthead's schedules were so jam-packed with primp sessions (and industry events) the office was practically empty from noon to three every afternoon. And if you were like Christie (and most of the fashion department) with at least one or more daily exercise classes you were basically in the office for just an hour or so a day. And God only knows where Samara was when she wasn't at her desk, which was more often than not.

"I can see," Fiona replied, looking for all the world like she was trying to restrain herself from brushing off the small snowdrifts accumulating on the shoulders of Irma's black Neiman Marcus Collection leather-trimmed alpaca coat. "Mossimo definitely left his signature stamp on you. How do you like it?"

"You know, I'm not quite sure," I lied through my teeth since I damn well knew I looked better before he got his hands and almost two full bottles of his "Twist the Night Away" gel on me.

"Everyone here goes to Dash, and we just love him. I think I mentioned that to you before you came on board. I know he'd be delighted to see you." While she was warm as ever, this felt like more of a command than a suggestion. And frankly, it stung that Fiona, who had previously reassured me that my hair was fine, was jumping on that set-Sarah-straight-about-her-horrible-hair bandwagon.

Honestly, the idea of going to another hair appointment—especially one that would involve hours of pulling, tugging, and noxious chemicals to straighten and lighten it within an inch of its life— after sitting in Mossimo's chair for two hours, was about the least appealing thing I could think of. Plus, I had absolutely no intention of becoming another sheep in fashion's flock of smooth-haired blondes—which was no doubt Dash's plan for me—he'd even said as much in the message he left me right after that horrible *Sentinel* Gotham Gala picture. Since it was likely bad politics for me to say so, I just thanked Fiona for her help, said I would give Dash a call, and tried to move our conversation into the realm of more positive story ideas than the ones Henri-François had been assigning me.

I didn't get a chance to mention my story ideas or the fact Samara mostly did her own thing because, just as I was about to move into these topics, Fiona cut me off. "Listen, Sarah, I don't know what you've been hearing about me, so I want to reassure you that everything is fine and I'm not going anywhere." She was quietly emphatic, which helped assuage some of my fears of being left alone with Henri-François and Didier. "The reason I've been rather hard to pin down is that I've had to turn my attention away from the U.S. edition to work on the special international issues Giancarlo has sold ads against. We're producing each one with just three or so people." She paused for a moment and again made a gesture as if to brush away those damn white flecks from my shoulders and again restrained herself. "Also, I've wanted to talk to you about what happened with your first batch of freelance manuscripts. I was a little surprised that you let Christie be the final word on edits and whether those stories would run in the first place. I've gotten all sorts of calls from disgruntled writers."

I felt my heart beating in my eyelids and struggled to remember what'd ever happened to that pile of manuscripts sitting on my desk the first day I got there. Sadly, I'd lost track of them after Christie took them off my hands. Since I realized there was no way in hell this was a valid excuse, I did my best to reassure Fiona that it wouldn't happen again. I also made a mental note to check in with Christie about why she never kicked them back to me.

"All right, Sarah. I'm sure you'll stay more on top of these types of things in the future. So, we can just move on," she said in her usual we're-in-this-together way. "I also wanted to have a quick chat with you about the latest Henri-François stories. I know they're not what you and I talked about doing together, but if you can just hang in there a little while longer, I'm working out a plan that will hopefully get us back on the track we mapped out. Can you do this for me?"

I shook my head in the affirmative, even though the thought of what else he might have in store for me and our readers made my stomach churn.

"All right then, keep fighting the good fight and do phone Dash. You'll be so happy you did," she called over her shoulder as she swept through the revolving doors, a blur of cognac-colored Dolce & Gabbana shearling. I couldn't help but wonder if somehow Henri-François hadn't cooked up this "special" international issue scheme to keep Fiona out of his hair (and by God, I wish I could keep everyone out of mine) so he could do his butt stories. And Giancarlo, the consummate salesman that he was, couldn't resist the idea of all the additional revenue these issues would generate. And more to the point, I knew in my heart of hearts that whatever strategy Fiona was working on to turn things around would never come to fruition. She clearly had very little if any power at *Sophistiquée.* Henri-François had made certain of that. I was starting to feel like a colossal fool. Everyone in the universe had me dead to rights about this job, and I'd ignored them all. *So stupide*, I actually heard Henri-François' voice in my head, which worried me.

When I got back to my office Christie was nowhere in sight, which wasn't surprising given it was close to three—the usual witching hour for one or more of her exercise classes, so I couldn't broach the manuscript subject with her. In the end, to avoid what was likely going to be the mother of all confrontations, I decided to just drop it and make sure to be more take-charge from now on.

At least I'd gotten Stuart Felsenfeld out of my life after sixty torturous minutes at I Tre Merli in SoHo. Sadly, it was even more painful than I'd imagined. He showed up wearing a fur coat which was always horrifying to me. And on a man? Unforgivable. And it only got more wretched from there. As soon as he sat down, he started complaining about how cold and drafty the restaurant was and made us move tables twice. He also sent back each appetizer we ordered. When the waiter suggested a third round of drinks, I hurriedly pulled out my credit card, which was no longer just for emergencies, thank God, and explained I had a press event to attend that had slipped my mind until that very second. It was a dick move, but since the evening was going nowhere fast and I had enough on my plate with Henri-François and Didier, I didn't need another hypercritical man in my life. To Stuart's credit, he offered to pay and help hail a cab. Not being able to stand another minute, I just thanked him and sped out the door as quickly as my legs would carry me.

While my mother wasn't thrilled that I wouldn't be seeing him again, she didn't reprimand me too much because she was tickled pink with the Très Cher scarf and her birthday brunch at Isabella's. In fact, she was so happy with her celebration that she didn't even mention Morrisa once the whole afternoon, though that kind of made me a little sad for her. While I knew her assistant Sookie had sent the birthday flowers, Morrisa hadn't called this year.

Meanwhile, my little crew and I were finally going to have our long-awaited dinner so I could thank them for moving me up to the Bronx in my hour of need. I figured that large steaks and even larger martinis were in order for a dinner party comprised of three New York Missiles. So, after checking their travel and game schedules, I booked Angelo and Maxi's on Park Avenue South. Maddeningly enough, Holt had asked if he could bring Des, who'd mercifully vanished from my life these last few months. I knew, though, that once Fashion Week hit, she would leave me no peace about getting into shows and sample sales. So, I was in no hurry to rekindle our relationship. Saying no to Holt with his chestnut waves and freckles, however, wasn't an option. And considering he was hanging my bookshelves and mounting my guitar racks on my living room walls when he asked, I *really* couldn't turn him down.

"Truly, Sarah Sugar, she's a doll. You just have to get to know her better," he said, momentarily turning

195

his enormous blue eyes away from a shelf and fixing them on me.

"Holt, I'm intimate with Des in ways that I don't care to discuss, so there's no way on earth that I'd want to get to know her better." I put down the Tecate Light he'd brought over for me in addition to the Guinness for himself and got up off the couch to walk over to him. "I don't see it. I don't understand it. And I don't want you to explain it to me. But if you want to bring her to our dinner party, then you go ahead and bring her. You come to my rescue like every day." He smiled that ridiculously engaging smile of his and pinched my cheek. Yup. Brother and sister, we were and would always remain. What the hell did Des have that I didn't? Those 36DDs to start.

"Thank you, darlin'. Who is awesomer than you? Now let's get these shelves up so you can finally finish unpacking."

Still, as I was brushing my teeth that morning, it was all I could do to not fixate on all the trouble Des would cause at the dinner party, especially now that I'd invited Esme. Those two together were about as bad as bad could be. And as I got dressed for work—Irma's black suede Philosophy pants and a TSE violet cashmere turtleneck—I suddenly realized that I had something even scarier to worry about; the butt story was coming out in the issue that was hitting the stands today. If the *Sentinel* had seen it, the reporters there were going to rip it to shreds. The only saving grace of this whole mess was that I didn't have a byline on it, so no one would know that I wrote the whole damn thing myself since Samara and Christie had made themselves unavailable at every turn. I wrapped myself up in

Irma's coat and scarf, and without even taking the time to pop *Led Zeppelin IV* into my Walkman, even though "When the Levee Breaks" was practically screaming my name, and then dashed down the stairs and the few blocks to the newsstand. Suddenly, I had to see the *Sentinel* that very second.

And there it was, front and center, right next to one of our issues. "No Ifs, Ands, or Butts." *Sophistiquée CD scales new lows,* ran the headline and caption accompanying a scathing story panning Kick Butt, our eight-page-ode to butt lifts, butt implants, butt exercises, butt creams, butt scrubs, micro-thongs, and the endless photos of perky posteriors that Henri-François photographed throughout a six-day jaunt to St. Barts. Crap. Crap. And crap again.

When I got to the office, my message light was blazing, and my office was already swimming in thank you flowers and trinkets from the companies whose products I'd mentioned. Some publicist or other even called the story a "Tour de Force," which made me feel like throwing up. As I took off my coat and scarf, Henri-François and Didier poked their heads into my office before slithering all the way in.

"Sarraah, did you see? This is stupendous!" Henri-François was holding the *Sentinel,* which made me think he didn't understand the article. Was his English that bad? Didier nodded and almost split his face in half by emitting what could be considered a slight smile. I was dumbfounded. So, I merely repeated, "Stupendous?"

"*Oui*, Sarraah. Stupendous. We are provocative now. We are not the same old, tired women's magazine. This is what the American woman wants."

It was all I could do to not reply, "Eet ees?" Because it was a stone-cold fact this story was the last thing on earth any woman anywhere wanted. Instead, I just waited for him to continue. He was so irritated with my lack of enthusiasm that he couldn't address me directly and, instead, turned his back to me and started speaking rapidly to Didier in French, a habit they'd adopted ever since the day I lied to Henri-François about my fluency in his native tongue.

"*Vraiment, Didier, elle est assez stupide. C'est presque triste n'est-ce pas?*" Didier concurred, allowing himself to smile somewhat more broadly though his face was truly about to crack with the effort. "*Mais, Giancarlo dit qu'elle était bonne avec les annonceurs et nous faisons de l'argent.*"

They had just agreed that I was quite stupid, which they thought was sad. However, since Giancarlo told them I was good with the advertisers and making money for the magazine, I would have to be their cross to bear. Once he got that off his chest, Henri-François turned his attention and his pelvis back to me.

"Sarraah, you bite your nails?"

"No, Henri-François. I do not."

"Then, why do they look so terrible?"

"I play guitar, so I have to keep them short."

"You will fix them, yes? This is no way for the beauty director of *Sophistiquée* to be," he scolded. "And please start thinking along our new direction. Your story ideas are so sad and tedious. No one wants to read foolishness like, 'Love the Skin You're In.' *C'est stupide.*" And with that last zinger, he finally swept out with Didier, as always, nearly treading on his heels.

Somewhat numb, I picked up my phone to replay the rest of the messages, even though I dreaded hearing them.

"And another slam dunk for Sophisticrap magazine—scaling the lofty heights of intellect. Glad you're putting that conservatory degree to good use. Really, Baumie, this sucks. Do you even play guitar anymore?" It was Esme, and if I weren't mistaken, she was a little bit drunk, already.

"Oh gosh, Kitten. I just saw the butt story and the *Sentinel* article. Are you all right? Call me when you can, if not, I'll see you tonight. Thank you for this. Should be fun." Penny's voice was barely a whisper, a dead giveaway Rex was standing by.

"Sarah, Sugar what a great story. It made me want to get a subscription to *Sophistiquée.* Keep up the good work." Maybe it was good Holt was with Des.

I had a few other messages of congratulations for a "sensational story," a message from my father, inviting me a bit more insistently this time to have brunch with them in Scarsdale over the weekend, and one from Kevin Carson confirming the issue date for our Cecil exclusive—it had already gone to press and was due out next month. I would have to tell him later as I just didn't have the heart to call him or anyone else for the foreseeable future. I had to find Fiona today and get things on track. Henri-François only might want to cover legs next, but I had this nagging suspicion that after butts and breasts there was only one other body part that he was itching to photograph and I wasn't going to write about it.

True, she had told me I had to suck it up. That Henri-François was my boss. But how could she, an editor-in-chief of a woman's magazine, allow these shenanigans to continue? And she was above Henri-François on the masthead, which made her his boss. Fortified by the facts of the situation seeming to be in my favor, I headed over to Fiona's office, where I found her assistant crying in her cubicle and packing up a box.

"Delia, what's wrong? Are you all right?" I wondered if I had a tissue on me, though it seemed unlikely since there wasn't much room in Irma's suede pants to fit anything in the pockets.

"I was fired, that's what. I have to leave the building immediately or be escorted out by security," she half sniffled, half snarled as she threw some knickknacks and keepsakes into the box.

"What? Are you sure? Did Fiona tell you that?"

"Fiona? Fiona's gone. She or someone else packed up her office last night after I went home, and she isn't picking up her phone," Delia continued as she sorted through her things while glancing furtively around the office. Someone had put the fear of God into her.

"Fiona's gone?"

"You can look into her office and see for yourself." I walked the few steps across the hall to Fiona's office and peered in. There wasn't a trace of her. No clothes swinging on satin hangers from the door, no papers on the desk, no magazines or books on the shelves, no shoes under the desk, and none of her art hanging on the walls. And for the first time, I can remember, Fiona's computer was off, so there were no humming or buzzing sounds. She was gone, all right.

"Does Henri-François know?"

"Of course, he knows. He's been gunning for this

for months. He's upstairs now with the president and CEO crowing over it. What do you think I should do?" Delia had her hand on my arm now and was waiting for me to say something brilliant. Sadly, I had nothing brilliant to say. I had no idea what she should do. I had no idea what *I* was going to do. The full weight of being left completely alone with Henri-François and Didier hit me like a cannonball. Not that Fiona was much help while she was here, but I somehow felt like a feminine presence at the top of the masthead kept me safe, even though we'd produced some pretty deplorable stuff under her watch. It was becoming clearer and clearer to me, however, that Giancarlo and Henri-Francois had tied both of her hands, if not all her appendages, behind her back in terms of her actually running the magazine.

So maybe, just maybe, it wouldn't be much different with her gone. Or maybe we'd get another editor-in-chief, one who could stand up to Henri-François. None of these scenarios seemed likely, though—especially the one about having a new EIC that would put Henri-François in his place. He clearly had some kind of hold over our company president and editorial board. So, I knew things would only get worse. And in the meantime, what to tell Delia?

"You should call HR at other magazines, you know, like *Simply Finesse* and *Fashion Chic,* and let them know that since Fiona has left *Sophistiquée,* you're available. Make it sound like it would be a huge coup to land you. I'll give you a reference." A reference? I barely knew the girl, though it seemed like the right thing to do, except, to be honest, I wasn't quite sure what I could say. "Chin up," I continued as I turned to slink back to my office with my tail between my legs. "It will all work out for the best." She stared after me like I was the liar I was. Who was I kidding, anyway? There was likely no best in this situation. At least for her and me.

When I got back to my office, Samara and Christie were perched on my two chairs whispering and giggling, which stopped abruptly when I walked in.

"Did you hear? Fiona's gone and Henri-François is now the Editor-in-Chief *and* Creative Director." Samara was nearly bursting at the seams. Unlike me, she and Christie seemed to know from the get-go that Fiona wasn't in charge and despite her title, had been completely dismissive if not downright rude to their boss. In fact, Fiona had scolded both girls several times for insubordination and reported them to HR. No doubt it was great news to them that she was gone. I, on the other hand, was pretty damn certain now that Henri-François was EIC *and* CD, my premonition of things getting even worse was about to become a reality. And their chirping away about how great things were about to get pretty much sealed the deal.

By six o'clock, I'd returned Kevin's call and assured him Cecil's exclusive was running in our very next issue, wrote thank you notes for all the damn flowers sent to me for the butt story, messengered the flowers to the children's wing at Sloan Kettering, had two desk-side new product presentations from cosmetics companies, and finished what I believed to be the least offensive line-up of breast story ideas I could manage that would still make Henri-François happy. In all honesty, it seemed pretty futile because to fully understand what made Henri-François happy, I'd have to descend to a very deep and dark place, and I wasn't going there. There was just enough time to fix my hair (as best I could) and makeup and get down to Angelo's and Maxi's.

I was almost out the door when I remembered something I'd decided I wanted to wear that night. So, I reached into my bottom desk drawer and pulled out the 2.5-inch black Manolo Blahnik pumps I'd had Samara exchange for the 4-inch ones Kevin Carson had sent me. Maybe, just maybe, they'd help me stand up to Des and intervene between her and Es should things get real.

Chapter 10

The traffic downtown was at a standstill, so I had the driver drop me off a few blocks from the restaurant, figuring I could walk there faster than he'd get there. It only took me one block to realize why the FFs never walked anywhere. My feet were on fire. When I finally got to the restaurant, I was sweaty, limping, and about as miserable as miserable could be. Esme was at the bar in a black Alexander Wang sweater and burgundy wool Helmut Lang side-zipped flair pants clutching a martini the size of her head in one hand and a Camel in the other. And judging from her ramrod-straight posture, it likely wasn't her first or even her second cocktail. Before Esme went to the point of no return drinking-wise, she was a master at holding her body upright. It was her way of giving gravity the finger. She appeared to be having a heated discussion with the bartender.

"How's it going, Es?" I asked cautiously.

"Fine, except they're all bastards. Each and every one of them."

"Who, Esme? Who are you talking about?"

"Those banker douche nozzles who threw me out like a bag of dog shit after all the money I made for them. Fucking assholes." She lit another Camel.

"You're not working at the bank anymore? Since when? Why didn't you tell me?" I dropped Irma's Vuitton tote and Balenciaga on the floor and climbed up onto the stool next to her, resisting my insane urge to kick off my shoes and rub my feet.

"I was waiting till I won my wrongful termination suit. I was going to call your dad to get on that for me." She took a deep swallow of her drink. "He'd do that for me, right? I mean, even though you and I aren't friends anymore."

"Not friends anymore? Why would you say that?" I felt sick inside.

"Because all we do is give each other things. I give you Irma's hand-me-downs and you give me all of your swag, so you don't have to feel like you're being bribed to write shitty stories, which you are, by the way, writing shitty stories and taking bribes." She pulled on her Camel and drained her glass. "We don't see each other or hang out anymore. You spend all your time with the Georgia Peach Sequoia. Bartender, let's have another."

"Aw, Es. I spend all my time at work. God, I feel terrible you feel that way. I'm glad you told me. We'll see each other more. I promise. I want to. And of course, you can call Seymour if you think you have a lawsuit. Do you?"

"Who the fuck knows? Regardless, I'm not going down without a fight. Bartender, I said I wanted another drink."

"Hey, I know. Do you want to go to the table with me and have some dinner? There'll be some very cute boys there, in addition to Holt. It might be fun." I was hoping that if we got a little food and espresso into her, she wouldn't make a scene. Or would it be better to just call Vladimir and get her home? Frankly, scene or no scene, I didn't think she should be alone. Just as we were both weighing our options and Esme was paying for her drinks with the enormous wad of cash she pulled from her canvas Gucci wallet, Penny came into the bar looking for us.

"Kitten, everyone's here and waiting for you. What do you want me to tell them?" She glanced worriedly at Esme, who was glaring at her.

"Oh look. It's the Georgia Peach Sequoia friend stealer. How's it going up there?"

Penny, amazing woman that she was, realized we were in crisis mode and merely tucked a chestnut wave behind each ear and adjusted the cuffs of her grey-sequined cardigan that she wore with gray wool trousers.

"It's going great, Esme, thanks. It's good to see you. Come join us for dinner."

"What the fuck am I going to eat at a steakhouse?" Esme muttered to herself, trying to pick up her cash and tuck her wallet, lighter, and cigarette case back into her Birkin cotton bag.

"You're going to eat the pasta the chef said he would make specially for you. Dining with three promising second-string New York Missiles and the beauty director of *Sophistiquée* magazine has its privileges."

"You mean Sophisticrap magazine," she retorted, wobbling off her stool as Penny caught her elbow.

"Yeah, I guess I do," I said, and we all laughed, but only a little. As we walked over to our table, I saw and heard Desiree holding court. Clad in the same ridiculously low-cut black strapless micro-mini dress she wore to the Gala, Des' laugh was so throaty I was pretty certain she would start hacking up a lung, or maybe even a furball, at any minute. James, Richie, and Holt, however, were transfixed. They did, at least, have the good grace to wave cheerily at me as we walked in, and Holt extricated himself from Des' death grip and stood up.

"If it isn't the blow-up doll and her consort," Esme hissed as she stumbled past the two of them.

"Knock it off, Es," I cautioned as Holt, true to form, graciously overlooked Esme's outburst and gave me a huge hug.

"Hey, Sarah Sugar. This is great. Thank you. We need to toast to your amazing story." Oh wow. Were we going to talk about the butt story?

"Well, I didn't like it," Des said, standing up. "I mean, none of those girls had anywhere near my derriere." She turned around and wiggled her back end at us. "It's pretty perfect, isn't it?"

"Sure is, darlin'. Sure is," Holt responded as though on cue, though he mercifully didn't give her the playful slap I was fearing he would, and she appeared to be waiting for.

"You're not perfect. You're a grotesque caricature of an oversexed sex toy," Esme growled from the seat that Penny had settled her in—the one between James and Richie. It was a good plan. I knew Penny had reasoned that the two handsome men would distract Esme enough that she would drink less, eat something, and ignore Desiree. Sadly, Esme was too far gone for this "jingling keys" strategy to work.

"Es, come on. This is supposed to be a dinner party to thank everyone for being so wonderful to me. Can you please try not to ruin it for everybody?" I could see where this was going and it was about to take a nosedive straight to hell. And because Des was Des, she just couldn't resist adding fuel to Esme's fire.

"Ooh, I see someone's got their drink on already and is jealous on top of it. So tacky," Desiree cooed, snuggling into Holt as they both sat back down.

I'd known Esme long enough to realize that in about ten seconds or less, she was going to fly across the table and cause bodily harm to Des, which actually would have appealed to me if we weren't in a public place.

"Tacky? *I'm* tacky? You're a filthy whore," Esme was practically yelling now and reaching for her water glass clearly about to splash Desiree in the face. As always, Penny came to the rescue and quietly covered Esme's hand with hers and whispered, "Come on, Esme, this is Sarah's dinner party." Esme relaxed her grip and sat back in her chair.

Penny continued. "You know, we only put up with Miss Thing because of my crazy brother. Let's not let her ruin our evening."

I limped around to Esme's side of the table about to insist that she calm down until I saw her face start to crumple, so I pulled her into a hug instead. She pretty much dissolved into my arms, though she didn't cry. Esme never cried. Lord only knew what she'd been going through these last few months while I'd been at *Sophistiquée.* Well, I was going to find out. And frankly, I felt pretty crappy that I had let things get to this point.

"I'm so tired, Baumie," she sighed into my shoulder, and then sat upright as though electrified. "What the actual fuck. Are you standing on one foot?" she demanded.

I looked down at my feet and realized to my horror that I did, indeed, have one leg folded up under me like a damn FF, and this time I wasn't moronically drunk and idiotically injured. Well, I couldn't think about that now. I had bigger fish to fry.

"That's not important right now," I soothed, patting her back. "Let's get some food in you. I think it'll make you feel better."

"It's important to me," she murmured, but without her usual fire and then suddenly obedient, she nodded and picked up her fork to dig into the fettuccini Alfredo the waiter had somehow unobtrusively managed to place in front of her despite the drama. Unfortunately, just as I thought things were settling down and we might be able to start eating the ribeyes, prime rib, and filet mignons now crowding the table along with the mashed potatoes, home fries, and creamed spinach I'd ordered in advance, Des stood up and shrieked,

"I will not be talked to this way." Her enormous chest heaved up and down as her voice became shriller and shriller. And then she turned on Holt. "And you, just sitting here like a big fat slob. Aren't you man enough to defend your woman?" And with that, she pushed herself back from the table and jumped to her feet so quickly, she knocked her chair over as she fled from the dining room.

Holt looked at us apologetically, clearly weighing the pros and cons of going after her or not: sex if he did, steak if he didn't. Not surprisingly, he chose the former. "I'm sorry, guys, but you know how it is," he said as he got up from the table and crossed the room in three long strides as pretty much everyone in the restaurant turned around to watch him go. "Thank you, Sarah Sugar, for a lovely dinner," he called back over his shoulder, gracious till the bitter end.

This was turning out to be the mother of all nights. And what was the *Sentinel* headline going to say? I hoped James, Richie, and Holt wouldn't get into any trouble with their coach. Maybe it would be all right since they were in coat and tie and not making a scene, though we clearly had overstayed our welcome as the manager was already at our table asking us how he could "help" us. He invited James and Richie to eat their meal at a smaller table or in the bar where he'd happily bring the food. There would be no charge for the evening, and they were welcome back anytime with quieter escorts. For the life of me, I didn't know what to say to them. James, however, came to my rescue, asking the manager to box up our food so we could take it with us.

"How about we take this party uptown?" he asked, smiling at Penny who smiled right back.

Hmm. Maybe something good would come out of this evening after all. But first, there was Esme to look after, and I was pretty pissed at myself for ignoring all the signs that things were this bad for her. I took her phone out of her purse and called Vladimir. James and Richie said they'd give me and Pen a lift uptown in Richie's Bronco. Pro that he was, Vladimir was only a few minutes away. We wrapped Esme up in her gold Joseph coat and helped her into the back seat, where she immediately fell asleep.

"I'll call you tomorrow," I promised as I kissed her forehead.

"Great party," Penny deadpanned, keeping her voice low enough so that Richie and James wouldn't hear as we settled into the back of the Bronco.

"Yup, totally killer," I replied, resting my head on her shoulder.

"What are we going to do about Esme, kitten?"

"I'm not sure. It's not like we can just force her to go to rehab." The mere thought of staging one of those interventions like you saw on those sordid TV shows made me feel sick inside. How in the world did I let it get so bad?

"Do you think Irma knows? Can you start with her?"

"I guess I'll have to. I'll call her first thing tomorrow. Pen, thanks for tonight. I know Esme isn't your favorite."

"You know you're my girl, and besides, ever since our brunch and how she's stepped up your line of defense against those Flamingos, that little critter's been growing on me." I squeezed her arm. Penny was as good as it got. We spent the rest of the drive engrossed in our own thoughts. As we rounded the corner to our apartment buildings, I saw a tall, lanky figure bundled up in white on the front stoop.

"I think that's Sean," I said, surprising even myself at how high-pitched my voice sounded.

Penny squeezed my hand and said, "Go get him, kitten."

"What about James and Richie and steak? I'm not going to just abandon you."

"Trust me. There are far worse things than being alone with two handsome men and several pounds of porterhouse." She laughed and gave me a little shove out of the car.

"Hey, you guys, something's come up, but I really

hope you'll enjoy your dinner and look after my girl here," I said as I hurried down the sidewalk to my building carrying my shoes, trying to look as casual as I could. On the way, I passed a garbage can and, without hesitation, tossed in those damn stilettos. They were clearly not for girls like me, and if I were completely honest with myself, there's no way Saffron Meadows would've been caught dead wearing them.

"Good night, Sarah, and thanks a lot for this," James said, giving me a friendly wave as he and Penny walked over to her building and Richie drove away to look for parking.

"I'll phone you tomorrow," I called after her retreating figure.

"You better," she replied, turning to look over her shoulder and waving me on.

I took a deep breath and walked over to Sean. "Can I bum one of those off of you?"

"Rough night?" he asked, offering me his pack while staring down wordlessly at my bare feet now turning blue from the cold.

"I don't even know where to start."

"Start at the beginning," he said, holding his lighter to my cigarette.

"It's a little cold for that," I replied because, damn, it was cold. *Really* cold.

"Well, we can finish these out here and then go inside if you want. I never smoke in my apartment. Wyatt's got asthma and even if he didn't, I wouldn't want him to associate that stink with me," he explained, searching my face to see if I was going to go inside with him. Or at least that's what I think he was searching my face for. He seemed as nervous as I was and kept chatting away. I took this as a good sign. "I don't even smoke in front of Wyatt. Don't want him to pick up my bad habit." He laughed a little and lit another before he finished the one he was already working on.

Oh, that explained why he was outside on even the most frigid days smoking away. Or at least that was one explanation. Maybe he was just crazy. It seemed like everyone I knew, myself included, was teetering on the brink of lunacy.

But I didn't want to think about any of that right now. So instead, before I could stop myself, I found myself saying, "Hey, why do you wear white all the time? Are you an angel?" Was I flirting? God, I was terrible at this.

"Lord no," he snorted. "My acupuncturist says white is healing for your lungs, and I need all the help I can get," he said before taking another deep drag.

"You know what's good for your lungs? This," I said, tossing away my cigarette.

"Ha! One day at a time, as we say," he replied, stamping it out with a toe of his brown suede cowboy boot before picking it up and putting it in a plastic sandwich bag full of dead soldiers. This guy was too much. He didn't even litter.

"So tell me what happened tonight," he said, stamping out his cigarette and bagging its remains.

"It was a disaster from beginning to end, and the upshot is that my oldest friend Esme has a drinking problem and needs help."

"Esme? The small strawberry-blonde woman who was drinking beer on your couch when I came by that time with Wyatt?"

"The very same," I sighed, taking out my key to unlock the front door. As happy as I was to be hanging out with Sean, I was freezing my butt off (there was that damn word again) and wanted to be in our overheated apartment building.

"What are you going to do?"

"I'm not sure. I think I'll start by calling her mother tomorrow morning. Irma's pretty cool, and I think she's had some experience with this kind of thing."

"How so?" Sean lifted an eyebrow, obviously intrigued.

"Well, I can't say for sure except I know she was a big club queen back in her day and was really into the underground art scene."

"My guess, then, is you are correct in your assumption," he replied, holding the door open for me before continuing. "And hey, let me know if I can help. I've got more experience with this stuff than I care to admit, and here I am still standing."

"I don't know what kind of help she needs. I just know she needs help." Wow, I was tired. So tired I didn't know how I was going to make it up those four damn flights, especially with my throbbing now frost-bitten feet.

Once we got that out of the way, Sean seemed ready to bound up the stairs but slowed his pace to match mine while sliding my tote and Balenciaga off my shoulders and onto his. Maybe he was an angel.

When we got to my apartment door, we both stood there so beyond awkwardly that I thought I might scream. Instead, I said as quickly as I could so I couldn't change my mind, "You're coming in, right?"

"Only for a minute. Early day tomorrow." He was definitely as self-conscious as I was, which was comforting. When we got inside, he put my bags down on the table, pulled off his white wool hat, unwound his long, cream-colored scarf, then unzipped his off-white fleece, then a white hoody sweatshirt, and lastly, pulled his white Irish fisherman's sweater over his head to reveal a white long-sleeved thermal shirt. This guy clearly took his white seriously.

"No coat?"

"When you have an eight-year-old who likes to skate, it's best to dress in layers. You never know when things are going to heat up." He smiled and looked down at his brown suede cowboy boots for a second, so I realized despite his expensive guitars he probably didn't own a coat, which made sense given he was a divorced (separated?) father, lived up in the Bronx and likely had zero extra cash. I walked over to where he was standing in front of the milk crates holding my records.

"I love that you still have vinyl and not any CDs. They're completely soulless," he said, transfixed by every album. Finally, he extracted *The Kinks Are The Village Green Preservation Society*. Not exactly romantic mood music, but a great record all the same. "This is one of my favorites," he said, passing it over to me to do the honors. As the opening strains filled my apartment, he walked around examining my books and looking at my guitars mounted on the wall.

"There's an empty space," he noted approvingly. "Is it for the Gold Top?" That's funny. I hadn't realized that I'd asked Holt to hang an extra holder.

"I don't know," I answered truthfully.

"You should get it if you can. You'll love it."

"Not everyone can afford those two glorious Gibsons of yours," I teased, not wanting to get into the real reason I hadn't been back to Matt Umanov's and wishing he would kiss me or something.

"Those were twice-in-a-lifetime gifts to myself. First when I had one year sober and then again when I had five."

"Seems like they were well earned, then," I said, putting my hand on his arm. He moved in a little closer and I was about to close my eyes and move in myself when I realized instead of kissing me he was picking up my empty bottle of Diet Arizona Iced Tea from the coffee table. Crap, this was awkward.

"Do you want one? I think I have some non-diet ones," I offered, grateful that getting him one from the fridge would give me something to do.

"No. I was just making sure it was empty."

"Why?"

He strode across the floor to my couch but instead of sitting on it, he lowered himself to the floor and stretched his beautifully long legs out in front of him, and motioned me to sit opposite him. He put the bottle down and spun it. It didn't quite land on me. So he spun it again and then again until it did. And then he kissed me. Really kissed me.

"That's why," he said, polishing the steam off his glasses with his thermal shirt when we finally stopped. "Now it's your turn." So I spun, and we kissed. And then he spun again, and we kissed again.

After about thirty minutes of making out, I was pretty sure I was ready to take it to the next level. Sean was wonderful.

"Do you want to go into the other room?" I'd never done that before.

"I do. Just not tonight. I haven't even taken you out to dinner or a show or played "Wild Horses" with you," he said, getting up off the floor and sitting on the couch, pulling me up next to him. He eased off his white thermal shirt revealing the black sleeveless T that was his last layer. It was striking to see him in black for a change. His arms were beautifully lean and sinewy, and he put one of them around me.

"Hey, how old are you?" I blurted out before I could stop myself.

"Are you asking me that because I want to take you out to dinner and a show and play "Wild Horses" with you before we, um, go into the other room together?"

"Well, um, yes, partially. Most guys I know do everything they can to go, um, into the other room without having to buy dinner and don't even know what "Wild Horses" is, much less how to play it on guitar." Crazy how we were both saying, "um" like Stuart Felsenfeld. "Also, I was also just wondering. Esme thinks you're forty."

"Esme doesn't know everything, poor thing." He pulled me closer to him. "I'm thirty-eight. Is that okay?"

"It's perfect," I said, just before he kissed me again.

Chapter 11

I woke up the next morning on the couch with Sean's lean lovely limbs wrapped around me and covered with the pink and green afghan my granny Sarah had crocheted for me for my Sweet 16. His glasses and watch were on the coffee table, our shoes on the floor next to us, and the buttons from his white Levi 501s were digging into the small of my back. He was also snoring none too softly. I didn't mind. He was so warm. Sadly, though, I would have to get up and pretty soon too. I needed to call Irma and then the office to say that I'd be late since I wanted to get over to Esme's to see how she was doing.

As carefully as I could, I slid out from under Sean's arm to check his watch. It was six-thirty and likely he was already late for work, but he seemed to be having such a good sleep I didn't want to disturb him. We had slept for what felt like a long time, though it couldn't have been really since after our make-out session we'd talked ourselves hoarse. I learned that he was separated for two years, was about to finalize his divorce, and that Wyatt was pretty broken up about the whole thing. His soon-to-be-ex was frustrated by and not supportive of Sean's desire to pursue a music career while being a husband and father and working full-time. I also learned that Sean was the head chef at a private Hebrew day school on the Upper West Side, and although he wasn't Jewish by birth, he considered himself an "honorary member of the tribe," which I found ridiculously cute.

"Hey, don't go." Sean pulled me close to him again. I let myself nestle back into his shirt until I felt my eyes closing, and then jolted up with a start.

"I don't want to. I'm sorry. We have to get up. You're already late for work and I've got to get over to Esme's," I said as I gently tried to untangle my arms and legs from his.

"What time is it?" he asked, half-sitting up and feeling around for his glasses.

"It's probably close to seven." I had succeeded in putting my feet down on the floor. Progress.

"Oh yeah, I'm late. I don't mind," he said. "Can I use your phone? I'll call my sous-chef who should be at the school by now. It's fine. What about you? Do you want me to make some coffee?"

"I have to jump in the shower and then call Esme's mom and my office to tell them I'll be late," I replied, mentally calculating how many minutes everything would take. "And then I'll go over to Esme's and see what kind of help I can give her. Coffee sounds great." I reached my face up to kiss him, and he bent down and brushed his lips against mine.

"Okay. Shower for you. Phone for me. Coffee for both of us," he said, cutting the kiss short. He was brisk now, probably trying to get us up and on our feet before we started making out again, which seemed likely if we kept sitting close to each other on the couch.

I peeled off last night's clothes, showered quickly, and threw on Irma's navy and beige striped Scoop V-neck sweater and her navy wool Chaiken pants. As I was pulling on her beige Stuart Weitzman boots, Sean came into my bedroom with coffee.

"Your milk was bad, so I hope you take it black," he said, handing me my AC/DC mug. "Nice mug, by the way."

"Oh wow. Sorry. I rarely have time to drink coffee at home." Even though black coffee wasn't my favorite I figured with the day I had ahead of me I'd better fuel up.

"Listen, Sarah, I should get going. I just want to make sure you realize something. You can't help Esme if she doesn't want help. And you can always talk to Charisse or Mayumi about this, and even Ollie or me." He looked around my room until he found a pen and a piece of paper and scrawled two phone numbers down. "This one's the school and this one's home. Call me if you need a rescue...or want to play "Wild Horses" together." He winked at me and put the piece of paper in my free hand and closed my fingers around it.

When he left, I picked up the phone and dialed the Levine's number, which I'd memorized since Esme and I were five and allowed to make phone calls for ourselves. A voice picked up on the first ring and said, "Good morning, Levine residence." It was Sonia, the housekeeper, and Esme's nanny, who always had a sympathetic ear and the most wonderful advice when Irma and my mother Anna Elias Mandelbaum were otherwise engaged, which was more often than not.

"Hi, Sonia. It's Sarah, Sarah Mandelbaum. It's wonderful to hear your voice. How are you?"

"Sarah, it's so good to hear from you! It's been such a long time. How are you? We are doing just fine over here."

"Oh, I'm pretty good, I guess. I hope I can come out to see you one of these days soon. I miss you and our teas with your amazing coffee cake," I said, realizing that I really and truly did, especially now when things were so crazy. Still, there was work to be done. "Do you think I could talk to Mrs. Levine?" I asked.

"I don't think she's awake yet. Is it important?"

I hesitated a second and then said, "I'm sorry. It *is* important." I'd waited long enough to help Esme, and it seemed crazy to prolong things even another minute.

"All right, Sarah. I'll go wake her."

After a few minutes, a very sleepy and concerned Irma came on the line. "Sarah? Is Esther all right?"

I decided the only way I could see this through was to be direct. And so I quickly blurted out, "Mrs. Levine, we need to help Esme. I'm pretty sure she has a drinking problem." There was a pause on the other line and a deep inhale. Irma had lit up one of her Benson & Hedges.

"Of course Esther has a drinking problem. I've been trying to get her to go to Silver Sequoia for months. She just keeps swearing to me she has it under control, and you know there's no forcing Esther to do anything she doesn't want to do."

Ah, that explained it. No wonder Esme had that Sequoia bee in her bonnet when she was mocking poor Penny last night.

"Silver Sequoia?" I asked.

"You know, the rehab in Connecticut. It's on the beach. It's nice. I went there myself back in the day," Irma replied as she exhaled.

"You did?" I had no recollection of Irma being

drunk despite hearing about all those wild parties they had in the 70s and early 80s. She always seemed perfectly together to me.

"Oh, sure. Remember those couple of times I went to that weight loss spa?"

"Yeah, I always thought that was weird considering how small you are," I answered, still racking my brain to come up with a time I'd seen her drunk. I wondered if any other of her glamorous buddies had gone with her. Obviously, now was not a great time to ask her, though it would've made one hell of a story if I were still at *40 Days & 40 Nights*.

"After two stays, I got it. Haven't had a drink or Quaalude or anything else in twenty years. Who would've ever thought I'd be the president of the Teaneck chapter of Hadassah?" Her words spilled out in anxious, rapid succession. "Sarah, has something happened to Esther?"

I took a deep breath and recounted some of Esme's wilder moments of the last few months, how she showed up drunk at my office and the events of last evening. I finished by telling her they had fired her from the investment bank.

"They did? Since when?" Irma was now close to panicking. I heard her calling out to Sonia to ask her driver, Dmitri, to bring the car around. Then she got back on the line. "When we hang up, I'm calling Silver Sequoia to let them know we're coming. It shouldn't be a problem since I just donated to its new fitness center. Can you meet me at Esther's? If I know our girl, this won't be easy."

"Of course. I'm on my way," I said, thanking God once again for *Sophistiqée's* car service, which would help me avoid having to take three different trains during rush hour over to Esme's apartment on East 75th. I left word on Henri-François' assistant's voice mail I was at a breakfast presentation that had somehow not made it onto my schedule. While I was pretty sure Samara wouldn't back me up about this unaccounted-for event if he asked, I would have to cross that bridge when I came to it. I wrapped myself in Irma's Saks Private Label charcoal and black tweed coat and maroon cashmere scarf, popped *Abbey Road*—my favorite Beatles album—into my Walkman and dashed down the four flights of stairs into the waiting town car.

When I got to Esme's, somehow Irma was already out front, leaning against her silver Rolls Royce, smoking.

"Sarah, dear, thank you for coming. I figured I'd better get one in now since Esther won't let anyone smoke in her apartment." That was funny. I'd forgotten. As much as Esme loved her Camel's, she kept her apartment smoke-free because of her two Maine Coon cats Dow and Jones, and her teacup Chihuahua, Nasdaq. Irma offered me the pack. I shook my head. It was too early for me, and besides, I'd just decided to quit if only so I could help Sean do the same. He'd been coughing this morning and no matter what his acupuncturist said, wearing all the white in the world wasn't going to help. As we stood shivering a little in the cold, I saw Vladimir out of the corner of my eye, talking to a man who could've been his twin. We waved at each other.

"Of course, you must know Vladimir. He's Dmitri's brother and has been a godsend in helping us look after Esther," Irma said, tossing her cigarette to the curb and stubbing it out with a toe of her boots. I briefly thought of Sean and his sandwich baggie of used cigarette butts and wished I had one as Irma hooked her arm through mine and we started to walk into Esme's building, with Dmitri and Vladimir following at a discreet distance.

"Hey, that's a great bag," she said, patting her cast-off Balenciaga that I was carrying without a trace of recognition. "It's from a couple of years ago, right? That was one of the best versions. Good for you for hanging onto it. I never keep things more than a season or two." Irma didn't recognize her coat or scarf either, and I doubted she would realize the rest of my outfit was something she'd worn and maybe even loved just a few winters ago. Fashion was so funny.

Despite our rather dire circumstances, I couldn't help but notice how terrific her hair looked without so much as a sliver of white gel residue on her red Anne Fontaine coat. I was dying to ask her how she managed to escape Mossimo's two bottles of Twist the Night Away gel though, of course, now wasn't a good time. So I made a mental note to call her once we knew Esme was safe and sound. As if reading my mind, she turned to me as we got on the elevator and asked, "By the way, did you ever make it to Mossimo?" Clearly, my hair was not looking as terrific as hers.

"It's a long story," I sighed.

"I know what you mean," she said, laughing a little. "You have to rein him in sometimes. You should give him another try." Between our bag discussion and now this hair repartee, I realized we were starting in on that false banter and fake jocularity that always indicated acute anxiety.

"Esme will be all right," I said, squeezing Irma's arm, trying to convince the both of us.

When we got to Esme's sprawling two-bedroom apartment, Irma let us in with her key and motioned for me to go find her. I was pretty sure she'd still be in bed and expected Nasdaq to start barking at any minute, which he did, as he raced around the apartment, jumping up on everyone's legs. Irma scooped him up absently and settled herself on the couch, nervously jingling one crossed leg over the other. I walked back to Esme's room, which looked like a tsunami had hit. Dirty clothes were piled up on every available surface, while stacks of shoes, CDs, books, used cocktail glasses, and empty vodka bottles littered the floor. There were also a few half-eaten bowls of cereal that emitted a sour milk smell. As I suspected, she was in bed with her sage green and white quilt pulled over her head and an enormous Maine Coon cat pinioning each of her legs.

"Es, Es. It's me, Sarah. Are you all right?" I walked over to the head of the bed and gently tried to free her face from her quilt and top sheet, which she screwed up as soon as the sunlight streaming through her windows hit it.

"Baumie? What are you doing here? You woke me up." She yanked the covers back over her head.

"Es, I'm here with Irma. We're worried about you."

"You brought Irma? Why the hell would you bring Irma?"

"Come on, Es. We just want to help. Why don't you shower and get dressed, and I'll make us breakfast?" I drew the covers away from her tiny frame,

225

which still wore last night's clothes.

"Go. Fuck. Yourself," she said, as if each word was a complete sentence, snatching the covers away from me to pull them back over her head. She turned over onto her side to face the wall, which caused both cats to scramble to find a new resting place.

Clearly, this was a job for Irma. I went back to the living room and announced, "Esme won't get up and she's pissed. I'm not sure what to do."

"Well, Esther damn well better get up," Irma declared, putting Nasdaq down and jumping to her feet. She pulled all 4 feet 11 inches of her up tall and strode down the hall, her boots clicking on the freshly varnished hardwood floors. When she got to Esme's doorway, she called out sternly, "Esther Ariella Levine, you get up this instant." Esme played possum for a minute or two, causing Irma to march over to the bed, yank down those damn covers and stand over her.

"Esther, this has gone on long enough. And I blame myself for believing you when you told me you had this under control," Irma spoke rapidly as if afraid she would lose her nerve. "That was crazy of me. No one can control problems like these by themselves. So no more excuses. We're taking care of you and this today."

"Ha. It takes an old drunk to know a new one. I learned from the best."

"Oh, I see it's blame the parents o'clock now," Irma replied glancing down at her breathtaking bejeweled Piaget watch and then pausing to take ten deep breaths before she continued. "It was a horrible shame, and I am beyond sorry for what our house was like when you were a small child. But your father and I cleaned up our acts by the time you were five, so we've had many good, healthy years together as a family. You're an adult now and responsible for your own choices. And you have been making very bad ones for the last several years."

"I bet you called Silver Sequoia to reserve a bed for me, didn't you? Well, maybe you can't buy your way out of things for a change," Esme muttered into the pillow. I could tell she wanted to shout her retort but her thundering hangover stood in the way. I mean, she couldn't even open her eyes, much less lift her head.

"Yes, Esther I did," Irma said, clearly stung by Esme's endless stream of accusations, yet forging onward. "We don't have a lot of other options right now. When were you going to tell me about losing your job?"

"Oh my God, Sarah, you told her? You're such a narc. You always have been. How would you feel if I tattled on you to Anna Elias Mandelbaum?" Rage and fear that she was getting shipped off to Silver Sequoia gave her the adrenaline rush she needed to finally sit up and fight back. "And I'd have plenty to tell her. You're on the fast train to shit town with that Sophisticrap magazine job," she said, quoting the song we'd written together in ninth-grade detention after we got caught cutting biology class. "You're writing nothing but crap and you're not even playing guitar or singing anymore."

"Es. I didn't tell your mom to hurt you. I told her to help you," I answered, about to cross the room to the bed and try to soothe her. Irma motioned for me to stay put, which I did, as I pondered Esme's words. She was spot on about my job, of course. But it felt like too enormous a thing to think about on top of everything that was going on right now.

"For the love of fuck, Sarah. Don't piss on my leg and tell me it's raining," Esme retorted.

"Sarah, why don't you leave us for a minute and ask Vladimir to put on some coffee?" Irma jumped in before the conversation could escalate. I nodded and left the room, looking forward to more coffee and hoping Vladimir had kept an eye on Esme's milk so I could have a cup the way I liked it. A few minutes later, I returned to Esme's room with two mugs of coffee.

"None for me, sweetie, I'm off caffeine," Irma said, waving one cup away as she accepted the other for Esme. Esme took it without looking at me and gulped at it greedily.

"What the hell am I going to do at Silver Sequoia with all of those nut jobs and drunks?" she said when she came up for air.

"You're going to get well," Irma said, relaxing her face just a little as she realized Esme might be willing to go.

"How's the food there? It better not suck."

"Well, honey. It's somewhere in between Le Bernadin and Camp Skowhegan," Irma replied, referring to the Maine sleepaway camp with the worst food on the planet that Esme and I went to for six straight summers.

"What about my babies?" she said, looking lovingly at Dow and Jones, who once again were lying on top of her feet.

"I'll take them, honey. The only thing you need to worry about right now is getting better."

Esme said nothing for a few moments, swallowed some more coffee, and then finally let out a sigh.

"They'd better let me get some goddamn sleep there."

"Good. That's my girl," Irma breathed with obvious relief. "Let's get you showered and dressed, and Sarah will pack some of your things," she continued as she somehow managed to get Esme out of bed and move unsteadily toward the master bathroom.

As I surveyed Esme's room, I wondered if she even had any clean clothes left. And then I remembered she had a whole other walk-in closet and at least two chests of drawers in the second bedroom down the hall, which mercifully was pristine. It didn't take me too long to find two of those Levine-family-signature Vuitton duffle bags and I started filling them with what I thought people would wear in rehab. Esme didn't have any sweats or fitness clothes, so I settled on jeans, cords, and some of her more casual sweaters. I threw in a couple of pairs of pajamas, a robe, her flatter shoes, and some underthings. I figured she and Irma could take care of her toiletries as they were in the bathroom together. As I zipped up one of the duffels, Esme came into the room wearing a sunglasses and cobalt terry robe with her hair wrapped in a matching towel. Her head must've been on fire.

"So what's the latest at Sophisticrap magazine?" she asked as if the last hour hadn't happened and we were about to go have brunch together. One of the greatest or perhaps most terrifying things about Esme is that once she blew up, she was done and never held onto anything. It was a little tougher for me to recalibrate although given the circumstances I figured I had to give her a free pass.

"Breasts," I replied as off-handedly as I could.

"Are you serious?"

"As a heart attack," I said with forced cheerfulness. She walked over to her ridiculously enormous custom-built closet and pulled out something shocking from the back—a black and white nylon tracksuit, complete with the brand's enormous logo. "When did you get that?" I asked, barely suppressing a giggle. "And more importantly, why did you get that?"

"Oh, you know me, full of surprises. Of course, I've never worn it and never thought I would, yet it does seem to have rehab written all over it, doesn't it?" She laughed darkly and then continued, "Listen, Baumie, I meant what I said about you at Sophisticrap magazine. Butts? Breasts? Botox? It's complete and utter shit that's sucking out your soul. You need to get out of there and get out fast."

Since I'd decided to Scarlett O'Hara the topic of my crappy job and think about it another time, I decided not to answer and busied myself instead with finding her a T-shirt to wear with that wild warm up suit. After she got dressed, Esme reached even further into the back of that crazy closet and pulled out a pair of white canvas Pumas—the only sneakers I'd seen her own since high school gym class.

"Betcha didn't know I had these either," she said, grinning despite everything that was going on.

"Esther Ariella Levine, you are truly full of surprises," I said, pulling her in for a long, teary hug. I was pretty sure from what I knew about rehabs, at least the ones on TV, it would be a week or longer until we'd be allowed to talk on the phone.

As we finally released each other, she sang, "*I'm on the fast train to shit town. Heading toward insanity.*"

"*I'm on the fast train to shit town afraid of where*

it's taking me," I sang back, completing the line from our song that we always sang together when things really hit the fan. Only this time, it finally looked like Esme was finally riding the fast train *out* of shit town.

We chanted several verses together until we were laughing too hard to continue.

As soon as we stopped, Irma poked her head in and said, "You girls doing all right? Esther, are you almost ready to go?"

"I need to say goodbye to my babies," Esme said, shaking her hair free of its towel and walking out into the living room where she first scooped up one cat, then the other, and lastly lifted Nasdaq for an extra-long cuddle. "Okay. I'm ready. I want Vladimir to take us. Dmitri, no offense."

"None taken, Miss. I'll transport your pets over to Mrs. Levine's house," he replied.

"Thank you, Dmitri, and will you please bring Sonia and Natasha back here this afternoon to straighten this place out? Please tell them since this is extra work they'll be compensated. And of course, you two will be, as well." She nodded at both men as Vladimir picked up the two duffels. "Really, Esther, this is the last time I'm having your apartment cleaned for you," Irma scolded, helping Es into her plum Max Mara cashmere coat and pulling the hood over her wet hair.

As they left the apartment, Esme called over her shoulder, "Hey, Baumie, did you ever nail that scrawny old guy?" Irma shot me a concerned look, which I ignored as I waved goodbye to the whole crazy crew. I wondered if Esme would be disappointed if she knew that Sean and I hadn't sealed the deal. I know I wasn't.

To me, it was a wonderful night.

After I helped Dmitri stuff the cats in their carriers and Nasdaq into his satchel, he offered me a lift to work by way of a thank you. It was no easy task getting two 18-lb cats and a tiny jumpy dog settled into confined spaces. I gratefully accepted as it was now almost eleven. When I got to *Sophistiquée,* Henri-François and Didier were waiting for me in my office. Henri-François was standing with one hand on his hip in his habitual "worship my privates" pose, while Didier was settled comfortably in a chair with his beefy arms folded across his chest. This morning's *Sentinel* lay across his lap and both he and Henri-François were sniping away in rapid, angry French that I couldn't quite make out. As I walked into the room, they stopped abruptly and Didier leaped to his feet, nearly dropping the *Sentinel* onto the floor.

"Sarraah, you've seen this?" Henri-François growled grabbing the paper from Didier and thrusting it under my nose so forcefully I had to take a step back to read the headline, which declared in big bold type, "CeCe's Back", and accompanied an article about supermodel Cecil's resumption of her career, her new fragrance and the exclusive interview she'd given to *Chic & Now* magazine's Keeley McPheters. This was not good. *Chic & Now* came out two weeks ahead of us so our story would be outdated by the time it ran— hardly the breaking news Kevin Carson had promised me. Figures he'd screwed me over with one of the Toxic Twins.

"Sarraah, you told me this was an exclusive. This is a disaster for us. How could you let this happen?" Kevin Carson's treachery was going to cost me dearly.

"Kevin swore up and down that we had the exclusive—we even confirmed several times," I found myself blathering away, wishing I had even an ounce of Penny's composure or Esme's take-no-shit attitude. I mean, I just sounded guilty even though it was all Kevin's fault. And everyone seemed to have forgotten that Henri-François had pushed me to do the story—his enormous ego (and white jeans) bursting at the seams to be the first to photograph the sensational Cecil after she gave birth.

"Sarraah, this is not good for you. And it will mean very bad things for you if you let it happen again." He was inches away from my face now. So close I almost started to choke on his cologne. "You must fix this, Sarraah, and let this little shit know he cannot do this again. I hold you responsible." He turned to look at Didier and fired out in French, "*Combine de temps devons-nous la garder? Elle est tellement idiote.*"

He had just asked Didier how much longer they would have to keep me because I was such an idiot. And I was starting to agree. I was an idiot for taking this job, writing about all sorts of nonsense, and enduring all of Henri-François' insults and indignities. For a second, I almost started to laugh. Esme was right. I was on the fast train to shit town and it was gathering speed at every turn.

As Henri-François turned on the heels of his Tod's loafers to go, he stopped in my doorway with Didier in his favorite position at his boss' backside and tossed out his signature last zinger, "Sarraah, why is your skin so terrible? I can see your every pore," he scolded. "Please take care of this. You are the beauty director of *Sophistiquée*. Can you try to be at least a little beautiful?"

As soon as they were gone and I'd sunk into my chair, the phone rang. I picked it up on the first ring even though I didn't want to, hoping whoever it was would distract me from Henri-François' tirade and Kevin Carson's duplicity.

"Mandelbaum," I answered wearily.

"Oh, my mistake. I was hoping to speak with Saffron Meadows." It was Ollie, of course. No one other than Wyatt and Dana called me that, and that familiar voice didn't belong to either one of them. In spite of myself, I smiled.

"Oh, hey, you. What's happening?"

"We're jamming at Mercury Lounge tonight. You coming?"

"Mercury Lounge? That's amazing." I was so happy for them. That was a great gig. But then I remembered what my evening plans were. "Crap. I have this damn Sakura makeup event. What time do you guys go on?"

"Oh, you know. It's loose. Maybe around eight. You should come. Sean asked me to ask you and then told me not to tell you he did. You guys are cute," Ollie teased, prompting me to picture his movie star smile as he gripped his can of Mello-Yello.

"Yeah. I guess we are. It's nice though, right?"

"I hope it's however you want it to be," Ollie answered shifting into Zen master mode. "Sean or not, you should come tonight. You haven't seen us in ages, and we've got some new tunes I want you to hear. And the guys from CBGBs are coming tonight."

"That's amazing! I'm in." If Sean wanted me there, I was going. And Ollie was right; I hadn't supported him or the band in months. It was time—especially at an important gig like this.

"Hey, do you happen to have your ax with you today by any chance?"

"Nah, I don't get to play much music here at Sophisticrap magazine," I answered, feeling sorry for myself.

"Damn. I was hoping you'd jam with us for a tune or two. You could go and pick up that Gold Top after work."

"I won't have time. And you know I'm not sold on it yet. But count me in for tonight. Promise."

"Going to hold you to it this time. And I think you need, no, have to have that Gold Top. So go and get it, Saffie, and I'll catch your act later." I couldn't help feeling just a little bit happy despite the misery that'd been my morning. Sean wanted me to come to his gig. And Ollie? Ollie was the best. The phone rang again rousing me from my reverie.

"Mandelbaum," I sighed.

"Sarah, Kevin Carson here. How are you? Hope you're having a lovely day so far. Just calling to give you your car number for today's Sakura event. Pick-up time is four-thirty and it's Industry Car Service No. 52."

Was he kidding me? I was so mad I was practically spitting. "Did you just ask me how I am and say you hoped I was having a lovely day?" I demanded. "How do you think I am? And what kind of day could you possibly think I'm having? I just got my ass chewed off and handed back to me thanks to your lies and deceit."

"Sarah, what on earth are you talking about? Why are you so upset? How can I help?" This guy's sleaziness knew no bounds.

"You can help by explaining to me how you promised me an exclusive that is now appearing two weeks earlier in another magazine." I fought with myself to keep from shouting and only half succeeded.

"Exclusive? First off, I don't give exclusives. It's my job as a publicist to get as much coverage for my clients as I possibly can. And secondly, I got a call from someone at your magazine telling me the story was being bumped a couple of months so, of course, I wasn't going to just sit on this major news and wait for you to get around to it."

"Are you kidding me? You promised me an exclusive and we confirmed the run date several times. And there's no way someone called you from here and told you we weren't running it."

"Sarah, this is business. It's nothing personal."

"This absolutely is *not* business," I fired back and then momentarily collected myself to try and get to the bottom of all of this. "Well, tell me one thing then, if you say someone from the magazine told you we were holding the story, the least you can do is reveal their identity."

"I'm not at liberty to say. But no worries, even though Cecil and I were disappointed that the story isn't running when you said it would, we're so appreciative you're covering it at all. We've sent you a little gift to thank you for your professionalism and what we know will be a great article whenever you decide to run it," Carson forged ahead as if on autopilot. This was all in a day's work for him.

"I don't want a gift, Kevin. What I want to know is why you wouldn't call me to double-check the run date? You and I've been working together on this for months and I assured you repeatedly it would run in this issue. Why would you take someone else's word over mine?"

"I have to dash," he continued, brightly ignoring my questions. "Sakura and I are looking very much forward to seeing you at today's tea ceremony. We have a special surprise planned afterward to celebrate Keeley's new gig at beautifulyou.com that I think you'll enjoy."

"Keeley's going to beautifulyou.com?"

"Yes. Haven't you heard?" Kevin was ecstatic. "We were lucky enough to get that Cecil article in as her grand finale with *Chic & Now*. Great timing, don't you think?"

Before I could help myself, I found myself shouting into the phone, "Great timing, Kevin? Screw you and screw Sakura." This was just too much. "We're not working with you or covering any of your clients again. And when they ask me why I'll tell them it's because you're a liar and a cheat."

"So long, Sarah. Have a great day and I'll see you later this afternoon," he sang into the phone and hung up. As I tried to gather my thoughts and calm down, Samara sailed in carrying a Fendi shopping bag.

"Ooh. Look what you got. Let's see." She set the bag down in front of my desk and began to untie the ribbons decorating the handles. She pulled out a card and read it out loud, 'Many thanks for a wonderful collaboration and what we know will be a terrific story. Love always, Cecil and Kevin.' And there was Samara oohing and aahing and opening the damn box to pull out a purple sequined Fendi Baguette, which had to run at least two thousand dollars. "That's beyond gorgeous. Aren't you thrilled?" Samara cooed, slinging it over her long, graceful hot pink and orange Pucci-clad arm.

"Send it back. Wrap it up and send it back this very second," I stormed. When she looked at me as though I was insane, I continued even more forcefully. "I mean it, Samara. I want you to messenger this back right now and call the store and Kevin to let them know it's coming. I want to see the confirmation of receipt on my desk this afternoon. And I want you to eat lunch in the office today so you can take care of this mess." I gestured to the mounds of press kits and magazines that had once again started piling up.

Startled by this new tone of voice I was trying on for size, Samara stared at me for a minute, and then asked almost plaintively, "What about Sakura this afternoon?"

"We're not going to Sakura this afternoon and make sure Christie knows that. And we're not covering any of Kevin Carson's clients anymore, so take out any mentions of them from your upcoming columns." I paused briefly and then remembered another thing that pissed me off about the way Samara did, or rather didn't do her job. "And starting now, I want to see your column two weeks before it ships, not the night before. Understand?"

Wordlessly, she packed up the bag and tiptoed out of my office on the tops of her Christian Louboutin pink suede boots. Things were going to change around here. As Ollie would say, "Saffron Meadows was in the house."

Just as I was reveling in my small victories, my phone rang again. I waited to see if Samara would answer it now that I'd laid down the law. Apparently, we'd have to have another chat, and so after the fourth ring, I picked up.

"Sarah, Giancarlo here. What's this I hear about you not attending the Sakura event this afternoon?" Fucking Kevin Carson—he just couldn't wait to fuck me over again. Or did that little sneak Samara rat me out? The timing seemed a little off, but I wouldn't put it past her.

"Giancarlo, I don't know if you read the *Sentinel* this morning and saw how Kevin completely screwed us over by promising us the Cecil exclusive and then actually giving it to *Chic & Now*."

"That *is* unfortunate. Almost unforgivable. Still, I find it puzzling that you would then turn around and let him screw us over twice." Giancarlo spoke very slowly and deliberately, which likely meant he was really pissed, thought I was really stupid, or both.

"I'm not sure I understand, Giancarlo."

"First you let him double-cross you about Cecil and now you're giving him a very good reason to tell Sakura to pull their advertising from our magazine because you're not supporting them at their event." His voice rose slightly and then, with what seemed like a huge effort, he lowered it again before saying, "From now on, Sarah, you need to run these things by me first. I'm having serious doubts about your judgment. I'll let Kevin know you'll be delighted to see everyone at this afternoon's event."

Before I could even hang up the phone, Samara glided back into my office scarcely suppressing her glee. Evidently, she'd been listening in on the other line, a fact she didn't even try to conceal. "So, Chief,"

239

she purred, "I guess we're back on for Sakura and Kevin Carson. Good thing we didn't send this gorgeous Baguette back." She set the Fendi shopping bag on the chair facing my desk and looked me dead in the eye as if daring me to scold her for not carrying out my orders. When I remained silent, she didn't even have the good grace to look relieved. Instead, she scrutinized my face and chirped, "How about I book you a facial for tomorrow? A few extractions will work wonders on those pores."

Chapter 12

As I was sitting at my desk cursing Kevin, Samara, Giancarlo, and my wretched existence, Christie, who was over three hours late and hadn't phoned or put her appointments on our schedule, popped her head into my doorway and said, "Tough break about the Cecil story. I hope you told Kevin Carson where he could stick it."

"Yeah, I did—not that it did any good. And you know, on top of screwing us over, he had the nerve to lie and say that someone from our office told him the story was being held. Can you believe the gall?"

"He said that?" she asked, crossing her arms even tighter around her boniness than I thought possible. "What a sleaze. Too bad we can't punish him by not going to his Sakura event this afternoon and not covering his clients until he's out of business. I could've probably gotten some of the other editors on board. Everyone's sick to death of Kevin Carson's sliminess. But I heard Giancarlo doesn't agree with us." Wow. Word traveled fast. She'd probably been in the office for all of three seconds when someone, likely Samara, had spilled the beans—probably gleeful at the crap I'd taken from Henri-François and Giancarlo.

"Well, I'm hoping there's some way we can make him realize he can't keep screwing people over like this without any consequences," I replied. "So if you have any ideas, I'm all ears."

"Sure thing," she said, settling into one of the chairs facing my desk—something she rarely, if ever, did, considering her propensity for scolding me from my doorway. She crossed one leg across the other and hell must have frozen over because she kicked off a shoe to reveal one of the most enormous bunions I'd ever seen, several bruised and bloody toenails, and a completely crooked second toe.

"Are you all right?" I couldn't help but ask, even though I knew it would do me no good. "Have you had that looked out?"

"Of course, I've had it looked at," she said, quickly stuffing her misshapen foot back into her Saint Laurent pumps and immediately silencing the wince that flew out of her mouth before it could become a howl. "Repeatedly. But everyone just wants to do surgery after surgery, which means first using one of those horrible scooters and then wearing one of those humiliating boots afterward and then doing it all over again on the other foot. And they keep telling me to wear sensible shoes like those awful ones you wear. Thanks, but no thanks."

She jumped up faster than I thought anyone with her injuries ever could and made her way to the door but instead of hobbling on out, she stopped and turned around and said, "Hey, I was so upset at all these personal questions you've been asking and incensed about Kevin for us that I almost forgot. There's this rather large woman with a Southern accent here to see you. Do you want me to get rid of her?" Southern? Had to be Penny, though I took issue with the "rather large" description; my girl was statuesque. Still, what was she doing here in the middle of the afternoon when typically, she'd be closing out lunch and prepping for dinner?

Before I could answer, Penny pushed past Christie and filled my office with her luminous Elizabeth Arden Sunflowers scent. She was carrying a Sherry Lehman shopping bag and her cheeks were pink from the cold and maybe something else—we didn't typically shop at Sherry Lehman; it probably was the most expensive wine store in the city maybe in the entire world. Christie exaggeratedly jumped out of her way, looking injured.

"You must be Christie." Her voice was confident and cheerful. "Why don't you skedaddle like a good little girl and have a sandwich? The grownups need to talk." God, she was smooth. I wished like hell she'd been on the phone with Kevin instead of me.

At the mention of food, her least favorite thing under the sun, Christie shot Penny a haughty look and replied, "I think you have that covered. Sarah, remember the Sakura car is coming at four-thirty, which is soon." She looked at her watch and then pointed at the Sherry Lehman bag as if to say we'd have to cut our illicit afternoon happy hour short. After she left, Penny closed the door.

"So that's Christie, huh?" she mused, shrugging out of her emerald green wool coat and plaid scarf. "She's a pip."

"Oh, she's not so bad, really," I sighed, needing to believe it. Despite her snootiness, sense of self-entitlement, and the fact that she appeared to work only a 3-hour day, I was starting to feel a little sorry for her. And besides, Christie seemed to be the sole person in this industry who wasn't intent on getting me fired.

"I wouldn't be too sure of that, kitten. From everything you've told me and from what I've seen today, she seems like a bad apple to me. A really bad apple. I don't want to see you get hurt."

"Thanks, pal. You're the best. But I think she's okay," I said, squeezing her arm. "Hey, wait a minute. What are you doing here in the middle of the lunch rush and with a Sherry Lehman shopping bag, no less? What's going on?"

Without answering she reached into the bag and pulled out a box holding two fancy floral Perrier Jouet champagne flutes and a frosty bottle of the champagne itself—a far cry from the cheaper-than-cheap sparkling wine I'd brought up to her place to "celebrate" my new job at *Sophistiquée*, which now was even more fitting, crap wine for a crap job at a crap magazine.

Quickly, quietly and efficiently, Penny popped the cork as only a chef can and filled both glasses. She handed me one and then lifted hers. "I got the TV show. We go into production for *Savannah Sweets* this month."

"What? That's the greatest news I've ever heard." I clinked my glass against hers and closed in for a hug. "Did you tell Rex? What did he say? He must've totally freaked out. So devastated I wasn't there. Tell me everything."

"Oh, it was good. Really good. He started cussing and swearing and bad-mouthing me. And I just walked out," she explained, glowing with pleasure as she pushed her tortoise-shell glasses further back onto her nose. "I called Bobby, the restaurant owner, from the street, and he was nice about it. He even said he was about to open another place and invited me to come over depending on my Cuisine Channel shooting schedule."

"We need to go out and celebrate and not just our regular brunch," I said, the wheels turning in my head as I tried to think of a special enough place. Unfortunately, my grand plans were interrupted by the memories of last night's botched affair flooding my brain. "I probably shouldn't throw you a dinner party given how last night's turned out," I said, feeling sorry for myself again, which made me mad. This was Penny's moment and I needed to suck it up and not ruin it for her. "Let's go somewhere great," I continued before she felt obligated to join my pity party. "Anywhere you want."

"Wait, here I am running off at the mouth and you must have a ton to tell me. What's going on with Esme? And what happened last night with Sean?" She scrunched herself into one of my chairs and crossed one leg over the other, indicating she was in full-on listening mode. Her Fortunoff enamel bracelets jingled as she took another sip of champagne. "And by the way, Holt, that pussy-whipped brother of mine, is going to call you to apologize for running out last night. So pathetic. I'd be so tickled if that boy cut that tramp loose."

"Aw, Pen. I don't want to talk about all that. I want to talk about you. Where's the show shooting? What's the premise? You're going to be amazing. They're so lucky to have you."

"We're meeting this week to flesh it all out," she explained. "But I want to hear about you. Tell me everything." And so I did.

She let me go on and on and on without saying a

word, nodding sympathetically until I asked, "Penny, do you think I have terrible skin?"

"What? You have beautiful skin." She patted my hand, obviously baffled.

"Henri-François said he could see every pore on my face, and Samara said I needed to get extractions." I could feel myself almost starting to whimper. When did I become such a whiner? And more importantly, why was I being such an ass and complaining to Penny when she came over to my office to celebrate her spectacular news with spectacular champagne?

"Kitten, you can't take nasty little sneaks like Samara and rat bastards like Henri-François seriously." Her accent was full-blown Savannah now, so I knew things were about to get deep. "If you're going to stay here, and I can't understand why you'd want to, you have to remember what Esme said and not give a shit about these people. None of them are worth it. But honestly, don't you think it's time to cut your losses and get out of here?" I didn't remind her that she continued working with Rex way after the party was over.

My go-to for quickly and cleanly ending these conversations, which seemed to happen more and more frequently these days, was to make excuses for staying here—excuses that sounded lame even to me. You know, like rent, student loans, food and the Gold Top I might purchase one day when I got up the nerve to try it. But if I was being painfully honest, I knew it was because I was petrified of what I'd do or where I could go if this didn't work out. There just didn't seem to be a place for me in any world I tried to inhabit. And that was way too scary to say out loud.

Luckily, and I can't believe I thought this, Samara and Christie appeared in my doorway wearing fuchsia and white Michael Kors wool coats, respectively, and expressions that somehow managed to look bored and harried at the same time. It was probably the first time in our acquaintance I was happy to see either one of them. At least now they served the purpose of ending this squirm-worthy conversation.

"Come on, Captain. Car's downstairs," Samara sang, and then turned to Penny. "And who are you? You're so tall. That's nice. I'm Samara."

"Funny, I knew that without you even telling me," Penny answered, as she collected our glasses and re-corked the leftover champagne.

"That's so sweet," she gushed, her face lighting up. "Does Sarah talk about me?"

"Doesn't everyone?" Penny breezed. Man, I loved that woman.

"Did she show you the fabulous Fendi bag that came for her today?" Now that she believed them to be best buds, Samara was prattling away to Penny without so much as coming up for air.

Despite her mindless babble, Samara had given me a brilliant idea.

"It's for you," I said to Penny, picking up the Fendi shopping bag and handing it to her. "I want to give you something really special to celebrate your fantastic news. Even Irma doesn't have this yet."

As Samara saw the Baguette bag move from my hand to Penny's, her face dropped down to her ankles—a dead giveaway that she'd planned on browbeating me (in her own relentlessly bubbly way) into giving it to her. Christie stood by the window in her habitual stance

247

of scrawny arms folded across her concave chest and feet splayed in fifth position. Knowing what I knew about her now, I was certain that in a minute or two she'd start shifting from one leg to the other, as I'd come to realize that her perpetually pinched expression wasn't just from annoyance with all of us but from the excruciating pain she experienced all the time.

"We have to go," she scolded, wincing and limping slightly as she turned to walk out of my office.

"Are you sure?" Penny asked, a note of awe creeping into her voice as she pulled the Baguette bag out of the Fendi pouch that housed it. It was dazzling.

"I've never been surer about anything," I replied, hugging her goodbye and slipping on Irma's coat. If we didn't get moving soon, we were going to be late and frankly, the last thing I needed was that bastard Kevin Carson tattling on me to Giancarlo that I was tardy to the Sakura event. The four of us headed down the hall and onto the elevator.

As we walked through the lobby, Penny suddenly turned to me and said, "What do you think of James?"

"James? He's nice. Cute. Hot, even," I said, realizing we had a whole lot more ground to cover than that, which we couldn't do on the fly in the lobby of my building with Samara and Christie hovering.

"I think so too," she said, smiling as wide as I'd ever seen her. "Phone me later, kitten. We're not done talking," she continued as she disappeared through the revolving doors. "You didn't tell me one single solitary thing about Sean."

"Sean? Who's Sean? Ooh, do you have a boyfriend?" Samara clapped one hand across her mouth and giggled as we settled into the sedan sent by Sakura parked at the curb. While I was grateful Samara overlooked the fact Penny called me kitten, I knew the car ride to the Sakura event would be even more torturous than our usual trips. I prayed there wouldn't be traffic. Of course, there was. How was it that we always took a car to these events when they were only a few blocks or a subway ride away?

After sitting for over an hour in bumper-to-bumper traffic, we finally pulled up to the Sakura offices at 900 Third Avenue. Kevin, who was wearing a kimono, stood in the lobby. He bowed in faux obsequiousness to each of us as we passed him inside and were ushered to the elevator banks by his frantic fellow kimono-clad assistants.

"Hello, Sarah. Good to see you." His voice was so oily I almost slipped in it. "Hope you loved the bag. We're so happy you're here. This is going to be wonderful. You'll be so glad you didn't miss it. We've built an authentic ceremonial tea house in our offices."

When we got upstairs, Japanese musicians and the glow of swinging lanterns from makeshift stands greeted us. Shoji screens and fans decorated the walls and not a conference room table, desk, chair, phone, or computer was in sight. It seemed Kevin had hauled it all out of the Sakura offices so he could execute his vision. There was even a Japanese footbridge modeled after Monet's painting covering a small pond teeming with koi. Once we crossed the bridge, we were led to a bamboo-matted room decorated with Japanese orchids and shoji screens draped with ornate silks. A woman wearing a beautiful pale pink floral kimono and pastel peach sash was waiting for us there and asked us in Japanese, as Kevin translated, to take off our shoes and place them in the cubbies lining the wall. This did not go over well with the Fashion Flamingos, who communally felt and voiced no small amount of indignation at the idea of letting their Jimmy Choos and Manolo Blahniks out of their sights for even a second.

The next request met with even more resistance since it involved asking the FFs to remove all their jewelry and place it in the little red velvet bags she was handing around. This was to ensure that nothing would scratch any part of the delicate antique tea sets, the woman explained in Japanese with Kevin dutifully interpreting every syllable, a fake pious expression plastered to his face. The FFs were about to kick up quite the rumpus at the mere mention that they'd have to unhinge and unhook all their David Yurman and Bulgari baubles until they saw the pouches were from Cartier and that each one held one of the slimmer Love Bracelets. Then the hallway became filled with oohs and ahs. I figured I'd send mine to Esme at Silver Sequoia. Temper tantrums averted, Kevin ushered us down a hallway to a small opening in a wall and instructed us to crawl through it one at a time.

"This way everyone comes into the tea ceremony the same size," Kevin said, a mock reverence worming its way into his voice.

Again, the FFs looked like they were about to blow a gasket. Especially Peach Chandler who tossed her blonde bob and muttered not quite under her breath, "Don't these people realize how much of our time they're taking up and how much they're inconveniencing us? This is beyond inconsiderate." But since she held a Cartier Love bracelet in her hot little hands, she left it at that.

"Sarah, why don't you scamper on through and show us how it's done," Kevin suggested oh-so-helpfully. Scamper? What a dick. Still, for a change, I was happy to oblige. I could walk through the opening practically upright. I couldn't help but smile as I watched the Toxic Twins and other Flamingos having to contort their impossibly long limbs to fit through when I got to the other side. I wished I had a camera.

As I made my way into the serene ceremonial room decorated with more shoji screens and gorgeous, spare floral arrangements, I was astounded and beyond thrilled to see Nils sitting uncomfortably cross-legged in his khakis on the tatami mat next to the Sakura executives in suits and ties who were hosting the event. Nils never went to these things since he typically had enough pull to schedule private interviews with the company bigwigs.

"Nils, what're you doing here?" I exclaimed, practically running over to him. And without waiting for him to reply I chattered away, trying to relieve my nervousness at facing the Flamingos and Kevin. And I was just so damn glad to see him. "Can you believe this is all just for the launch of a new green tea-infused line of lipsticks?" I doubted Sakura would recoup in a year of international sales all the money it shelled out for this press event alone. And who knew what other shindigs it was hosting globally?

"I know. This is insane," he muttered gloomily and then continued. "I'm here because Rome is burning, and it's time to stop fiddling."

"Nils, what does that even mean?" I asked barely able to contain a laugh. He was such a Chicken Little.

"It means that with all these new beauty dot-coms

springing up we lowly paper publications are going to have to fight even harder for every speck of advertising," he lamented. "That's why I'm here. Michael wants me to get out even more than I do already and press the flesh and you know when Michael thinks about advertising, we're in trouble. They're saying that these dot-coms will be the death of print media—no matter how shitty their writing and reporting are."

"Nils, who's saying that?"

"You know, *they*. Everyone who counts."

The death of print media? Wow. That fast train to shit town I was riding was careening out of control.

"Who's the latest defector? Kerry McGinley?"

"Keeley McPheters," I replied softly, conscious of more Sakura execs and the Flamingos filing into the room and arranging themselves as prettily as they could on the mats. "She left *Chic & Now* to go to beautifulyou.com right after Kevin screwed me by promising me the Cecil exclusive, only to give it to Keeley and *Chic & Now* two weeks before we hit the stands." I was irate all over again.

"I never liked that guy. How'd Henri-François take it?"

"Not well." While I wanted to say more, Kevin, who was kneeling in the front of the room, signaled us all to pipe down and pay attention as the lovely Japanese lady graciously began to prepare the green powdered tea in an exquisite bowl with a bamboo brush. Kevin started passing out small plates of pretty little cakes. As they reached us one at a time, he lectured us on the custom of eating a traditional sweet before drinking the matcha tea to enhance its flavor. It all would've been charming and interesting if Tamiko San, our hostess, had delivered the same speech. Since it was Kevin, it was neither.

A collective shudder of terror went through the FFs at the idea of having to eat cake—even one that was no bigger than a strawberry. They stared at each other, waiting to see if anyone of them would be the first to take the plunge. Nils and I, as well as the super nice and professional women's service book ladies, dug right in. I'd skipped breakfast and come to think of it, even lunch. So I quickly polished mine off and was looking around for seconds.

When it became apparent that we and the Sakura executives were the only ones eating, Kevin finally took the bull by the horns. "Ladies, let's not offend our hostess by neglecting our sweets." Peach nudged Keeley, whose eyes widened in panic. But since no one crossed Peach, she picked up her pretty pink confection and nibbled off the tiniest crumb one could possibly eat. The rest of the FFs looked over to Peach, awaiting instructions.

"Yes, ladies, let's finish our sweets so we can continue with this wonderful tea ceremony," she crooned, picking up her cake like she was about to eat it only to stealthily slide it underneath the tatami mat behind her when she thought none of the important people were watching. I could see each Flamingo mentally struggling with how they would execute the same move; however, it turned out they didn't have to. Kevin had lost interest in this part of the ceremony and started to distribute the tea informing us that a bowl of it was "the universe held between the palms," a beautiful sentiment if Kevin weren't simpering his way through it. He then instructed us to, "Forgive the things that were in our hearts and take a sip," while looking pointedly at me.

He was seriously mistaken if he thought all I needed was a Fendi bag and a beautiful tea ceremony to forgive his treachery and his ratting me out to Giancarlo. The tea ceremony also didn't help me not to be crestfallen when Peach hissed to Keeley, "Figures she would eat the whole cake. That girl is dead set on wearing size four her whole life."

There was, of course, no correcting her, and I wish I didn't want to. Saffron Meadows wouldn't give a shit about the Toxic Twins and would likely just hop on the tour bus to her next gig. That is if she'd even bothered to show up here in the first place. But sadly, there was nothing I wanted to do more than inform them that I wore a size two, not a four, which by the way, happened to be a perfectly respectable size—small even, though all sizes as far as I was concerned were perfectly respectable. Needless to say, I said none of these things and just stewed silently.

The good news was that it seemed like we were finally wrapping up and I'd have plenty of time to get downtown to the Mercury Lounge on East Houston for the One-Eyed Snake gig and maybe even grab a bite at the Kiev Diner beforehand; its Challah French Toast Reuben was calling my name. As I was turning to Nils to invite him to come with, it became clear that once again my plans were being thwarted by that douche nozzle—as Esme would say—Kevin Carson.

"We have a special surprise for you now," he said, finally rising from his knees. "I know you'll be thrilled to celebrate Keeley's fabulous new job and get to know our Sakura hosts a bit better with some traditional Japanese entertainment. Please follow me into the next room, which we've transformed into an authentic karaoke bar."

Karaoke? Christ on a cracker. There was no greater hell on earth than karaoke. And with the FFs? That was entirely too much to bear. I looked over at Nils, who was struggling to his feet looking so glum it seemed possible we'd have to scrape his face off the floor. I hoped against hope he was thinking up a way to gracefully get out of it, which would make me feel like I could too. I mean, Giancarlo couldn't freak out that I skipped karaoke. Or could he? Crap. Crap. And crap again. In the meantime, consummate schmoozer that he was, Nils had rebounded from the terrible news, moved over to another group of Sakura execs, and was chatting enthusiastically. I guess he'd decided to make the most of this torturous time and press the flesh, to quote Michael. As miserable as I was, I realized this was a good plan and so joined their coffee klatch as best I could. The talk centered around all of those upstart beauty dot-coms popping up like pimples on adolescent cheeks and how terrific it was that Keeley and Peach were right there in the thick of it. They wondered who and what would be next. Personally, I did not, though I was pretty sure it was eating away at Nils.

When we got inside the make-shift karaoke club complete with a stage, cabaret tables chairs, and red candles, I could tell Nils was relieved to see waiters taking cocktail orders. He and the Sakura execs asked for Hibiki whiskey neat. When I looked up to see who delivered their drinks, I felt my blood almost freeze in my veins. It was Des, in a teeny tiny cocktail waitress outfit, tossing her hair and laughing with her usual throatiness. Somehow, she even managed to put a hand on every man's arm in the group while still holding her cocktail tray aloft. I guess that could be considered a talent. Still, it was unfathomable to me that I just couldn't seem to get rid of her.

When she realized I'd spotted her, Des excused herself from her now captive audience and sauntered on over to me, her 36DDs leading the way. I could see Nils trying to meet my eyes. He was clearly as perplexed as I was, though he couldn't seem to keep an amused little smile from playing about his lips that even his big, bushy mustache couldn't completely hide.

"Well, look at you, honey, all dolled up in almost-designer duds. You've come so far. And we can take care of any remaining little blips before Fashion Week. This way, we can kill it when we go to the shows together." She was all breathy banter and faux concern. I decided to ignore her oh-so-helpful hints and her preposterous idea of my taking her to any fashion show and get straight to the point.

"Des, what in God's name are you doing here?"

"I'm auditioning to play a cocktail waitress in an Off-Off-Off Broadway play and my agent thought it would be a fabulous idea for me to experience what that's like. So they got me a gig with the catering company doing this event."

I was pretty sure that Off-Off-Off Broadway was code for Staten Island, yet this realization didn't stop me from engaging with her. Somehow, I was falling back into our old patterns.

"Des, serving cocktails to beauty magazine editors and cosmetics executives at a makeshift nightclub in a corporate office is hardly the same thing as being a bonafide cocktail waitress."

"Says you." She pouted. "Anyway, I have to get back to work on my craft. I'll look forward to hearing from you about our upcoming dates." And with that, she wriggled off without even so much as taking my drink order. As soon as she left, I noticed Samara and Christie walking over to her. I guess they needed a drink too. I mean, who really liked karaoke, anyway?

I started to wander around in search of another waiter, but I couldn't help overhearing Des' husky voice crowing, "Do you guys know Sarah? Sarah Mandelbaum? We used to be roomies, so she's going to take me to all the shows. Maybe I'll see you there."

"That would be great," Samara giggled, prompting Christie to shush her and then respond in a voice so low and measured, I couldn't make it out over the din of the beauty editors and Sakura execs already getting tipsy. I assumed Christie was setting Des straight on the fact that since even fashion editors had to fight tooth and nail to get a seat, there was no way in hell Des would be attending any of the shows—with me or without me.

What I wanted was a Grey Goose on the rocks, but if I was going to maintain the slightest bit of composure throughout what was sure to be a horrible evening, I would have to be as dry as toast. Besides, I wanted to be in decent shape when I got to the Mercury Lounge and saw Sean. The Flamingos gathered around the song directory, squealing for more champagne and giggling over their selections as they signed up for their turns. I walked over to the women's service book ladies, who were sipping sparkling water or white wine and seeming unconcerned by the whole affair.

"Are you going up?" I asked Bonnie Chen and Linda Donohue, motioning to the stage.

"Sure," Linda replied with a shrug. "Bonnie and I are going to do "Enough is Enough", you know, the Donna Summer and Barbara Streisand duet. Should be fun."

Fun was not the word that came to mind. All I could think about was how the Terror Trio had taunted me during auditions for Grease our senior year. Bevin Feldshue and I were going head-to-head for Rizzo and so when I got up for my turn, the three girls gave me such the hairy eyeball and started to cough so loudly and repeatedly drop their binders on the floor, that my voice cracked about four bars into "There Are Worst Things I Could," Rizzo's power ballad. I barely made a spot in the chorus, which I had to take or risk Esme's wrath for the rest of the semester. With her sweet lilting soprano, she'd landed Sandy with barely any competition and wanted me around to root her on. Unfortunately, the chances of performing tonight in front of the Toxic Twins, the other FF's, and now, Des, going any better than those damn auditions were slim to none.

My doom and gloom were interrupted when Will Smith's "Gettin' Jiggy Wit It" started to play through the speakers and Kevin leaped up on stage. This was going to be some night. I looked around for Nils only to find him knee-deep in Sakura executives and drinking what appeared to be his second whiskey. I was on my own.

"Hello everyone," Kevin breathed into the mike after he'd finished his tune. "Welcome to Sakura Karaoke night. And please join me in congratulating

Keeley on her fantastic new job. Keeley, why don't you come on up?"

As Keeley dashed over to the microphone as fast as she could in her sky-high Prada heels, Peach and three other Flamingos shrieked with delight and joined her. The intro to "Wannabe" filled the room and the ladies went full-on Spice Girls, shaking their cans, wagging their fingers, and shimmying their shoulders. Seems like Kevin had given them advance notice and they'd been rehearsing. I had to admit, they had all the moves down and even sounded pretty good.

Next up was *Fashion Chic's* Darci Vogel, who giggled her way through Madonna's "Deeper and Deeper", followed by *Simply Finesse's* Serena Matthews, who did a damn good Toni Braxton "Unbreak My Heart".

I checked my watch. It was 7:30, so I had to leave in a minute or two if I wanted to get to Mercury Lounge by eight. Kevin had said cars were waiting downstairs for us, which meant I had a decent shot of making it downtown in time for One-Eyed Snake's opening number. It was highly unlikely anyone would miss me here—it was turning into quite the raucous night. I walked as inconspicuously as I could to the door, only to find Nils standing there waiting for me.

"Hey, you can't leave now. I signed you up. After all this Top 40 pop, it's time to rock out." He raised his whiskey glass in a cheery toast, clearly proud of himself.

"What? Nils, you're kidding me. I'm not going up there." We were now entering complete and utter nightmare territory. "Anyhow, I have to leave. I promised Ollie I'd get to Mercury Lounge for his gig tonight." All of a sudden, I was dripping wet in Irma's sweater, even though the room was almost chilly. I tried making a beeline for the exit but clearly, the universe was hell-bent on thwarting me at every turn. I heard the opening riffs of Guns 'N Roses' "Sweet Child O'Mine" over the speakers and Kevin back on the mike.

"And now, we have something retro and rockin' from Sarah Mandelbaum. Sarah, come on up," he commanded. I guess I should've been thankful that Nils didn't sign me up for a Janis, Grace, or even a Steven Tyler number. Not that trying to sing Axel would be a picnic. I mean, he was epic. And GNR? In front of this crowd? And just me up there in general? As Keith Moon said when he first found out about Robert Plant and Jimmy Page's new band, I was going to go over like a lead zeppelin. I'm pretty sure I was never more pissed at anyone in my entire life than I was at Nils right now. Until he said the magic words.

"What is it that Dana calls you now? Saffron? Saffron Meadows? Well, Saffie, get up there and show 'em how it's done." And so, even though my heart was hammering so crazy loud that I could barely hear the music and I could imagine the Toxic Twins making snarky remarks, I did. Somehow, I walked onto the stage, closed my eyes, and did my damndest to channel Saffron Meadows. When I got to the middle of the song, I opened my eyes and was astounded to see some people grooving on the dance floor and several even singing along.

When the song ended, the room practically shouted at me with its silence. And then the Sakura executives started clapping like mad. Nils and the lovely service book ladies, too. A few Flamingos forgot themselves for a minute and even Kevin joined in the applause. And for once, the Toxic Twins seemed to have run out of disparaging remarks and kept quiet.

Okay. It was never going to get any better than this, and it was time to go. If One-Eyed Snake started on time (and I prayed they wouldn't) I was going to miss at least two to three tunes. Once again, though, the gods had other plans for me.

The opening bars of "It's Raining Men" came flooding through the speakers, and Samara sashayed up on stage. "Come on, boss, let's boogie." And so, what else could I do? I joined her. And you know what? It was fun. *Really* fun. Then I did En Vogue's "Free Your Mind" with Bonnie and Linda and performed several more tunes. Nils even jumped up on stage with me so we could do the Bowie/ Jagger version of "Dancing in the Streets", which brought everyone back onto the dance floor.

By the time Kevin announced, "Last Call" into the mike, I was having such a good time that it pretty much slipped my mind that I was supposed to be somewhere else. It was only after I buttoned up Irma's coat and said my goodbyes that I looked at my watch again and realized it was nine o'clock and I'd basically blown it. There was no question that by the time I got down there, One-Eyed Snake would be getting off stage; Mercury Lounge typically featured multiple acts, so it kept to a pretty tight schedule. I flew into a waiting Sakura sedan and for the second time that day prayed there wouldn't be any traffic. Sadly, for the second time that day, there was.

When I got there, I dashed into the room only to find Ollie, Sean, Charisse, and Mayumi packing up their gear and leaving the stage. Ollie smiled at me when he saw me come in and walked over to the edge of the stage. Sean nodded but busied himself with snapping closed his Gold Top case and winding up his power chords. I walked over to Ollie and started apologizing profusely.

"It's all good, Saffie. Just sorry you missed us." Ollie squeezed my arm and seemed about to pat my head. I guess I looked that miserable. "The good news is that you can catch us at CBGBs next month. They just gave us a show."

"Really? That's amazing. I promise. Nothing will keep me from that gig."

"Maybe you shouldn't make promises you may not be able to keep," he said gently. I guess I couldn't blame him. I'd been missing their gigs for months. Meanwhile, Sean was packed up and ready to go and didn't seem in the mood for my excuses. But you really can't blame a girl for trying.

"Hey, heard you scored CBs; that's fantastic," I said, approaching him as cheerfully as I could, knowing full well it wouldn't help. I could tell from Sean's face that he was pissed. Or hurt. Or both.

"Yeah, we're pretty stoked," he replied as he strode through the club toward the door, making me practically run to keep up with him.

"I'm so sorry I didn't make it tonight. Work ran late. I had this big Sakura thing." I was chattering a mile a minute for the third time that day. This time, I was both nervous *and* guilty. Clearly, Sean wasn't going to see my conquest at Fashion Flamingo karaoke as a valid excuse.

"Yeah, well, I had the band practice "Wild

Horses". We were going to play it tonight, and then I thought we could go out to dinner." He stopped abruptly and looked down at his brown suede cowboy boots.

"You did?" I couldn't help smiling despite how shitty this evening was turning out to be. Sean had made plans to carry out two of the three things he said he wanted to do before we got together. Maybe I could turn things around.

"Thank you. I love that." I moved in closer to him, partly because people were starting to dance to the next act, and partly, well, just so I could be closer to him. His warm, sexy scent enveloped me. "Listen," I continued. "We can still get dinner. My treat. How about the Kiev? I've been dying for a Challah French Toast Reuben all day. Sakura gave us car service for the evening, so I have a driver out front. He can give us a lift, so you don't have to lug your gear over there." He seemed about to soften until he heard the "My treat" and "car service" parts.

"Sarah, I don't want you to buy me dinner or chauffeur me around. I want you to show up when you say you will," he said so softly I barely heard him above the music. There was no mistaking the look on his face; there would be no Challah French Toast Reuben tonight. Frankly, that seemed a little harsh and unfair. I mean, it wasn't like we'd made a definite date, or he'd invited me. So I pressed on.

"You know, Sean, with Ollie asking me and all, I figured tonight was pretty casual." My words came out rapid-fire again because Sean had picked up the pace and was nearly out the door. "If you'd told me about all of this, there's no way I wouldn't have been here on time."

"Yeah, well, it was a surprise," he replied, clearly not willing to give an inch.

We were standing on the sidewalk now, in front of the Sakura sedan.

"Listen, I'm sorry," I said as calmly as I could. "But I don't think this is entirely my fault. I didn't know."

I figured he would get in the car with me so we could move past all of this on the way home, and then I'd fix us some grilled cheeses and we'd make out. Instead, he merely opened the door, waited until I was settled on the seat, and then closed it behind me.

As the car sped away, I looked out the rear window and could see Sean's lankiness hunched against the cold, his white Levi 501s, and lit American Spirit glowing in the dark as he walked to the 1/9 train. There was no getting around the fact that he preferred taking the subway while hauling his guitar and amp rather than riding with me.

Over the next week or so I must have thought about knocking on Sean's door a million times, but in the end, I always chickened out because he seemed so mad at me. And then I got sucked into the utter insanity that is Fashion Week and I could barely remember my name, much less his.

Chapter 13

What people will tell you about Fashion Week is how thrilling it is. When the lights went down, the music came up and the supermodels strode down the catwalk at my very first show, it was every bit as exciting as some of the rock concerts I've seen. There's also amazing people-watching with A-list actresses and socialites filling in the front row. And then there's the occasional rocker who shows up to support his supermodel girlfriend, which sends me to the moon and back. The shows also give you the scoop on the latest hair, makeup, and fashion trends but that intel doesn't blow my skirts up quite as high as those of the fashionista editors scribbling furiously in their Moleskine leather-bound notebooks, specially bought and expensed for the occasion. Still, since trying to shape these mostly repetitive and to my mind somewhat bland observations into full-blown news stories is far less painful than writing about butts, Botox, and breasts, I took notes dutifully at every show. This season, apparently, jade was the new navy and gold was the new platinum blonde.

What people won't tell you about Fashion Week, which I discovered about two days in, is that it's also complete and utter hell. I can think of only about five or so other major lifetime events, including getting my braces tightened every month when I was a kid, that are worse. I'm not talking about what goes on backstage or on the runways with the models, photographers, hair and makeup people, and designers; for the most part, they all keep it together and are professional. I'm talking about the audience.

For reasons I can't fathom, before each show, all the Flamingos, Fashionistas, retailers, and members of the press are forced to line up in the foyer of one of the Bryant Park tents for nearly an hour. And not one of those ladies or gents waits patiently. There is pushing, there is shoving, there is shouting, and an overall aggressive hysteria that likely rivals any general admission audience waiting to get into a monster truck show. This bedlam is even more ridiculous given that everyone has an assigned seat and that the show only starts when everyone is seated. I can only chalk it up to all the attendees being half-starved and hobbled. Frankly, I'm surprised that no one's ever thought to pass out low-cal snacks and comfy slippers before each show. It would be an incredible kindness to us all.

The only way I knew I'd get through the week was to crank up my "Take No Prisoners" mixed tape in my Walkman and not care if the FFs and Toxic Twins gave me the hairy eyeball or made bitchy remarks because I was singing along to Zep's "Immigrant Song", Alice in Chain's "Would", or Ozzy Osborne's "Crazy Train". Saffron Meadows wouldn't have thought twice about it.

On Valentine's Day, there were at least seven shows, and since a few rogue designers hosted theirs in the Meatpacking district and Hell's Kitchen, there were hours of line-standing, plus a lot of racing to and from Bryant Park in the wind, sleet, and misery that is February. So I was beyond dog-tired and pretty damn defeated as I dragged myself up the four flights of stairs to my apartment at the end of the day. I'd even practically forgotten that Penny would be waiting for me for our Valentine's Day ritual.

Penny must've heard my key in the lock because she called out, "Welcome home, kitten. Happy Valentine's Day," before I was even halfway through the door. This had the instantaneous effect of making my shoulders melt away from my ears where they'd been permanently stuck since things went south with Sean after the Mercury Lounge show last week—not to mention the humiliations galore Henri-François hurled at me daily. A night with my girl and her pastries along with a full line-up of teen angst flix—*The Sure Thing* for her, *Valley Girl* for me (I just loved the Plimsouls, the band in that movie), and *Heathers* if we both didn't fall asleep, was, as my mother Anna Elias Mandelbaum would say, "Just what the doctor ordered."

As we settled on the couch under Granny Sarah's afghan with a sublime tray of mini cakes and tarts in front of us, there was a knock at my door. I had no idea who it could possibly be other than the Bible-thumping guys who'd been making the rounds with a feverish regularity. So I decided to ignore it and turn up the volume on my TV. When the knocking continued and grew even louder, we both got up and cautiously stood in front of the door trying to peer through the peephole at the same time. After a few seconds of jockeying for a clear view, we saw it was Holt with James behind him.

Penny opened the door and chided, "Holt Beauregard Abernathy, what on earth are you doing here kicking up such a ruckus?" She barely moved aside to let him in. James followed somewhat sheepishly, looking like he was trying to make himself as small as possible—no easy feat for a New York Missiles running back carrying two dozen long-stemmed pink roses.

"She dumped me," Holt practically sobbed, which I found utterly amazing. How could anyone dump Holt Beauregard Abernathy, and how could anyone be sad that Desiree Dershowitz did the dumping?

"You mean that insane, vicious little tramp did for you what you couldn't do for yourself and released you from your bondage?" Penny was not sympathetic.

"She said I was just using her for sex." Holt moved into my living room, shuffled over to the couch, and pulled Granny Sarah's afghan up toward his neck over his coat. It barely covered him, of course. All of this was comical, though I didn't dare laugh. Des being angry over someone "using her for sex" was like a fisherman being mad that a trout was wriggling on his worm-baited hook.

"Weren't you? Please say you were." Penny was sitting next to him now and had lowered her voice to a more compassionate tone, though she was genuinely perplexed as we all were. "It's not that I approve of using people for sex; I just can't wrap my brain around why you'd be with her for any other reason."

"It started that way and then I think I really fell for her." Holt sighed with more wistfulness in his voice than I ever thought possible. "Y'all just don't know her the way I do. She really can be a sweetheart."

Penny and I looked at each other. In all the time I'd known Des, I'd never used her name and the word sweetheart in the same sentence and could say with great certainty that I didn't plan to.

Without hesitation, I shoved aside my feelings. I sat on Holt's other side and patted his gigantic shoulder. "Holt, you and I both know Des would've needed a real humdinger of an excuse to dump you or any other red-blooded male on Valentine's Day, and being used for sex is practically her favorite thing," I said gently. "What's really going on?"

"Turns out she's been seeing Richie," he growled.

"Blonde Richie?" Penny and I asked in unison.

"Yeah. Blonde Richie. My supposed pal," he replied, puffing up with anger. "I'm pretty sure they hooked up once he told her he's starting next season."

"Richie's starting next season?" Penny was irate. "What about you?"

"Well, I will once Darius officially announces his retirement. It's kind of up in the air until then. I guess Richie was the surer thing." He looked down at the dessert tray in front of him, clearly agonizing over which sweet he would attack first. Penny moved it closer to him and pointed to the Napoleon, one of his favorites.

"Listen, little brother, we all know you're going to start next season, so let's not even worry about that," Penny said, using her pet name for him—after all, she was a full five minutes older than he was. "And truly, I think you should see Desiree's departure as opening the door for better things. What are you going to be single for, like two minutes? That's your all-time record, right? And, anyway, screw them both. They're not worth it."

Holt seemed to consider what she said for a moment and then slowly nodded his head. While he wasn't one to be so easily soothed, he certainly wasn't one to wallow in despair. So regardless of what he may have been thinking or feeling, instead of responding, he tore into the pastry and pulled out a Blockbuster bag from his inside coat pocket.

"How about letting a couple of roosters into this hen party?" he asked as he showed us the video he'd brought; it was *Everybody's All American*, which was surprisingly emotionally complex and even downright romantic for a football film and Holt, in general, so without any further discussion I popped *Say Anything* out of the VCR and slid in Holt's pick. Frankly, it sort of shocked me that I wasn't more excited about Holt being single again. I guess his going after Des and digging the butt story finally cured me of my crush. Still, he *was* Holt and so damn endearing.

"It'll be all right, Holt," I said. "And just think how much better you'll feel not having small electronic devices hurled at you on a daily basis or having your back clawed within an inch of its life." I patted his shoulder once more. And, thankfully, my last bit of consolation did the trick because his face broke out into an almost smile and he pinched my cheek the way he often did.

"You're a sweet kid, Sarah Sugar," he said, and then busied himself with the remote. Good thing my crush was over and done with.

I headed into the kitchen to see what kind of beer I had for him—probably just Corona Light, which likely meant hitting the bodega to get something else. I hoped James wouldn't mind making the trip since it was freezing, and I just couldn't bear the thought of going back out there. What was he doing here, anyway? If he was just Holt's wingman, he wouldn't have the roses.

So I did what any other girl would do in my situation, I snooped. "James! It's great to see you. Those are some lovely roses. Your Valentine is going to be thrilled."

"I hope so," he said, looking for all the world like he wished I hadn't brought that up. And then he walked over to Penny, who was sitting next to Holt on the couch, and handed them to her. "I guess this is kind of a roundabout way to wish you a Happy Valentine's Day. Holt told me you'd be here tonight, so I thought I'd bring them to you."

This was a bold move on James' part. He and Pen had only been on one date after the whole take-out steak incident. But you had to like his style and he'd clearly lit the candles on Penny's cake. Her enormous blue eyes—identical to Holt's—glowed with pleasure.

"Well look at you tracking me down on Valentine's Day and bringing me these gorgeous roses," she said, smiling as wide as I'd ever seen her and tucking a chestnut wave behind each ear. She patted the couch next to her.

With Holt sprawled out there wasn't much room left, so James had to snuggle in close to her, which they both seemed happy about. Not loving being the third wheel—or fourth counting Holt—I decided to make myself busy playing hostess, putting the flowers in water, figuring that Penny could take them home, vase and all, later. When I got back to the living room with a Tecate Light for me and Pen and the two Guinness's Holt had left behind when he was hanging my shelves, the boys had removed their coats and all three of my friends were huddled together under the blanket with Penny in the middle. I decided I'd take the quilt off my bed since it would have a better chance of covering everyone and also give me something else to do.

As I walked down the hall to my bedroom, there was another knock on the door. This time it had to be the Bible thumpers. There was no way anyone else I knew was trekking up to the Bronx on such a miserable night, especially on Valentine's Day. Penny must've thought so too because she sent Holt to the door.

"We all have religion, boys, just not the kind you're selling," Holt boomed as he swung open the door.

"Oh. Hi. I'm looking for Sarah? Sarah Mandelbaum? Is she home?"

"And who might you be, son?" Holt had flipped on his big brother switch. Curious, I came to the door. It was Sean, in his white Levi 501s and an ivory V-neck sweater carrying what looked like a rolled-up piece of black cloth with a red ribbon around it.

"It's all right, Holt, I know him," I said, quickly inserting myself between the two of them before Holt could get his good old boy on.

"Who is it, Holt?" Penny called from the couch, also leaping into protective mode.

"Don't know. Some guy for Sarah."

This pronouncement brought Penny to her feet and over to the door, where she looked Sean up and down about three times and then said none-too-politely, "We're in the middle of watching a movie. Can we help you?" She still was pissed at him for what she decided was a ridiculous over-reaction the night I came late to the Mercury lounge gig, and he wouldn't talk it out with me. I couldn't decide if I was pissed or not because honestly, I was pretty damn happy to see him, though I was somewhat peeved he assumed I'd be home on Valentine's Day, and lo and behold, here I was.

"I got this, guys. Thank you," I said, signaling for Sean to come out into the hall and pulling the door closed behind me.

"I'm not sure how to start," Sean said, as usual looking down at his brown suede cowboy boots. "I think I was a little intense the other night, and I'm sorry. I haven't dated anyone in thirteen years, and I was never very good at it. I think I'm even worse at it now." He looked up from his boots and handed me the gift he'd brought. It was a vintage XS T-shirt from the 1988 Guns 'N Roses *Appetite for Destruction* tour— probably one of the most monumental events in rock history. I was fourteen when it started, beyond dying to see them, and my mother wouldn't let me go.

"My house, my rules," she said, laying down the law in that no-chance-in-hell-you-could-argue-with-her way. "And my rules are no consorting with thugs on drugs and going deaf because of criminally loud and bad music." I'd debated saying I was staying at Esme's and going anyway, but I knew she'd somehow find out. Anna Elias Mandelbaum always found out. Sean would've had to move heaven and earth to get this shirt—especially in an XS. I'd been searching for it for years.

"Oh, my God. Thank you. This is probably the best gift anyone's ever given me. I had to miss this tour and it practically killed me. My mother wouldn't let me go." Sean smiled and seemed a little taken aback.

"Oh wow, I was twenty-seven then," he said, and then pressed on like our thirteen-year age difference wasn't all that important, which by the way, it wasn't.

"I thought we could get dinner sometime and maybe go to a show. The Stones are touring again, and I heard Soul Asylum is coming around." Get dinner sometime? Maybe go to a show? Wow. He really did suck at this, though I had to admit I wasn't any better.

"Dinner and a show sound great. Do you want to come in?"

"Would you mind if I took a raincheck? It seems like a pretty rough crowd in there." I was disappointed, yet I completely understood. Separately, Pen and Holt were forces to be reckoned with; together, they were invincible.

"Rainchecks are good, especially when they're soon," I said, surprising myself with my boldness by standing on tiptoe for the second time that night. It was time he kissed me already. And thank God, he was starting to bend down and move in. Then all of a sudden, he straightened up.

"Hey, I almost forgot. Sorry." There was no question that Sean was excited about something other than our kiss. "The band that was going to play the Très Cher after party this week dropped out because somebody or other had to go to rehab. And Mayumi knew someone who knew someone, so we're in."

"That's great! First Mercury Lounge and CBGBs, and now this." I lowered myself back onto flat feet since apparently there would be no kiss, though at least now I had something to look forward to. Seeing One-Eyed Snake play at an after-show party would definitely ease the pain of Fashion Week and probably even make my year.

"We want you to play with us."

"What?"

"I said, 'We want you to play with us.' The theme of the party is Heaven or Las Vegas," he continued.

"Oh, like the Cocteau Twins song." I loved that tune but wasn't quite processing that he'd just invited me to play with a pro-caliber band at a major gig.

"Exactly." Sean smiled. "Ollie says you do this killer electric guitar version of it and that you can sing it in the original Scottish."

"Elizabeth Fraser doesn't sing "Heaven or Las Vegas" in Scottish." I smiled back. "She's actually singing in English." It was an easy mistake to make because Fraser had this amazing airy, floaty voice and pronunciation that made her sound like she was singing in some mythological language, which to the casual listener may very well have been Scottish, Fraser's native tongue.

"Really? Here I've spent years thinking she was singing in Scottish." Sean paused for a second, perhaps trying to work out the lyrics in his head, and then continued. "Anyway, of course, Très Cher wants dance music for the party, which means covers, which aren't exactly our thing, but we can still rock out with them. Besides, the money's awesome and hopefully, we'll sneak in some of our own stuff and make some good contacts." He took the T-shirt out of my hands and held it up against me. "That's going to look good," he said, nodding his approval. "Really good." I was starting to wish I didn't have an apartment full of people, because I wanted to take him inside. "What do you think? Can you do it?" He folded the T-shirt up neatly and then handed it back to me while waiting for my response.

My gut instinct was to say no. I mean, performing for all those socialites and Flamingos? Truly the stuff of horror movies. And then I remembered my Karaoke Conquest (or KC as I'd started to call it) and realized that playing in front of those people had to be better than being mauled by them as I waited in line to get into a show and having to endure their endless critiques and criticisms before, during, and after it—not to mention trying to mix and mingle with them at a party. I did have to admit, though, that ever since my KC, most of the FFs, except the Toxic Twins, had been just a little bit nicer to me. Maybe it would be all right.

"I'll do it," I said, leaning in for that kiss, which thankfully lasted a good long time.

"Good." He grinned, revealing his beyond adorable crooked front tooth. "Now go inside. Ollie's calling you any minute with the details."

"You told him you were coming here tonight?"

"I did."

"So I guess you'll be telling him that you and I are having dinner together after the party," I said before I kissed him again. One of us would have to take charge of this relationship or we'd just keep limping along in the lamest possible way. And I had enough lame in my life.

"Nope. Don't think I will. That'll be our secret," he replied, pulling me close and wrapping my arms around his waist even though I was still holding the T-shirt, and kissing me one last time before he disappeared up the stairs. As promised, my phone rang.

"Kitten, it's Ollie," Penny called from inside. "Do you want to take it?"

The party was just two days away, and between everyone's schedules and the short notice for the gig, we could only have one rehearsal the night before—not the way we all liked to roll. I knew, though, that since these guys were such amazing musicians that if I could keep up with them, it would be a killer night. Each of us would also have to squeeze in a fitting at the Très Cher showroom. Its creative director Christophe Christophe was taking his Heaven or Las Vegas theme seriously and wanted us to dress accordingly. Mayumi, Charisse, and I were to be devils/casino dealers in red suede pants with matching vests and black silk shirts, while Ollie and Sean would be angels/Rat Pack lounge singers in white dinner jackets. And all of us were to wear these wild, enormous sunglasses from the new collection. Thank God, Ollie had talked the marketing director out of the halos and wings for the guys and devil ears and tails for us girls, which Christophe Christophe had originally wanted. Even with the amazing money we were making, that could've been a deal-breaker.

While I wasn't sure why Christophe Christophe wanted us to wear shades, I was all for it. If I could just keep my hair under control (no easy feat with the wet February we were having) it would make it harder for the FFs and Henri-François—who would assuredly be there—to recognize me. And hopefully, between the supermodels that walked the show and the celebs who watched them do it in attendance, no one would even notice the band. The only person I'd told about the gig was Nils. I wanted to make sure I had a friendly face standing front and center when we played.

On the day of our gig I had eight different shows to go to, and the weather was beyond horrific, with heavy sheets of sleet shooting out of the sky diagonally. Thankfully, I'd deep conditioned my hair the night before so it seemed to hold its own despite the extra hardships imposed on it by the elements. Through a whole lot of trial and even more error, I figured out that this so-called miracle conditioner was almost miraculous if I left it on my hair a full fifteen minutes.

"Take that, ladies," I said to the Terror Trio who had visited me that morning and were staring me down in the mirror as I got ready to leave the house.

The Très Cher show was at 7 p.m. and the last one of the day. It was being held in one part of Milk Studios on West 15th, with the party directly following it in another. The idea was that we were supposed to start playing "Heaven or Las Vegas" in the party area of the studio when Christophe Christophe took his bow at the end of the show. This meant that somehow I'd have to be in my seat during the show so Samara and Christie wouldn't tell Giancarlo I wasn't there *and* on stage in costume at the same time. I figured I could pack my devil/dealer clothes into one of Irma's duffels, change in the bathroom at the second to last show, and then keep her coat on over it during Très Cher. Then, I'd have to make a mad dash out of my seat and over to the stage before the final few outfits came down the runway.

As stressful as the timing was, it was all doable as long as I didn't run into my so-called team, which frustratingly enough seemed to be happening at every turn that day. For some strange reason, they were like gum on my shoe—sticking to me in virtually every line before and seated near me at each and every show. It was almost like they knew what was going on, though I was probably just being paranoid. I mean, how could they? I thought I finally caught a break at Très Cher because as I stood with Irma's black Barney's Co-op mohair maxi coat buttoned up to my neck getting jostled beforehand, they were nowhere to be seen, even as I scanned the room repeatedly searching for them. My heart, which had been bumping around like a tennis ball in a dryer, temporarily slowed down to a less manic pace. I even felt calm enough to lower the volume a little on my Walkman, which was blaring Aerosmith's "Back in the Saddle" full blast in an attempt to soothe my anxiety. It seemed like everything was going to work out all right for a change and it continued to look that way as the FFs shoved me out of the waiting area into the room where the show was being held—still no Samara or Christie. Without a moment's thought, I handed my ticket to the woman seating people in my row. For God's sake, it was Des clutching a clipboard hip rather than chest height, so her ginormous boobs (as Penny would say) were on full display in the plunging turquoise and gold Très Cher blouse she sported.

"Hi, honey, I thought I might see you today," she said with a superior sniff.

"Christ on a cracker Des, can you not leave me alone for one single second of my life? What is it with you?"

"With me? How about with you? You said you'd take me to the shows and here we are at one of the last ones of the season and I had to get here on my own steam." I didn't bother to remind her that I'd made no such promise. My mother, Anna Elias Mandelbaum, had taught me to never engage in a battle of wits with someone who is only half-armed. Besides, I had more important things to worry about than Des' delusions of grandeur.

"How'd you swing that?" I asked, anxiously

scanning the room for Christie and Samara and starting to walk up the stairs to my seat.

"I got a temp job with the PR company handling this show. It was staffing up during Fashion Week to handle the extra work. I'll be working the after-party too. We should have a drink together."

Des working for a PR company? For the life of me, I couldn't fathom how anyone anywhere would hire her to do anything. But that was not my problem. Still, I had to credit her ingenuity. She wanted to go to a show, and here she was.

"You better hustle on up to your seat because the show's about to start," she said, her innate bossiness negating any positive feelings I might've had for her. "But before you go, look at this gorgeous blouse. Isn't Kevin the greatest? He gave one to all the girls working the show. Even us temp girls."

"Kevin?"

"Yes. Kevin Carson of Carson & Associates. Très Cher's publicity department hired him to do the heavy lifting for the show. And he hired me. Now scoot along, honey."

Kevin Carson. Was she fucking kidding me? I honestly didn't know who was a bigger thorn in my side these days: Kevin Carson or Desiree Dershowitz, because they were both giving me huge pains in my you-know-what on an almost daily basis. Still, despite my annoyance with the pair of them, this latest Des encounter was better than bumping into my staff and having them prevent me from getting to my gig on time. I allowed myself a sigh of relief, which unfortunately lasted only until I got to my second-row seat and found Samara bouncing up and down in it with enough excitement to fuel a rocket ship. She was wearing head-to-toe Très Cher—somehow she managed to change clothes for every show. Clearly, she thought she'd scored the coup of the century.

"Hi, boss," she said with a cheery wave. "You told me you were skipping this one, so I thought I'd make sure your seat wasn't empty because that would've looked really bad for us." This wasn't the first time she'd tried to steal my seat this season with the same fake excuse, and we both knew that it wouldn't be the last. Yet I couldn't entirely blame her for this attempt since Très Cher was considered *the* event of the week and all the poor assistants were relegated to standing behind the back row.

"Hey, what'd you do to your hair?" she asked, obviously trying to distract me so I wouldn't kick her out of my seat. "It looks like you made an effort. Good for you." With every fiber of my being, I summoned Saffron Meadows and so merely narrowed my eyes in response. Never one for subtleties, Samara continued to chatter away. "Wow, you're carrying a lot of stuff and wearing your coat inside. Are you like homeless now?" I was all set to continue staring at Samara in stony silence, except at the sound of our voices, Christie, who was sitting in the front row, turned to nod at me and glare at Samara, spindly arms and legs crossed and tapping one toe of her Très Cher boots on the floor.

"Shh!" she hissed as the lights started to lower and the music came up.

I was about to insist Samara vacate my seat when I suddenly realized it was better for me if she stayed put and I stood in the back—it would mean fewer people to disturb and climb over to get out in time for our gig.

While this seeming victory might seem strange to her, Samara would be so delighted not to have to stand in the back in her 4-inch heels and to achieve the status that comes with a second-row spot, she'd likely just let it slide. And then there was this seat-stealing business. Even Samara, in her zeal to get me in trouble with Giancarlo, wouldn't rat herself out to him as a thief.

"Everything's fine," I replied quickly and quietly since the show was starting and Des, goddamn her, had summoned a security guy who was moving toward me and Samara to throw one of us out. "I'm just tired of sitting. Why don't you stay here, and I'll just stand for this one?"

"That sounds like a great idea, chief," she said, lighting up practically neon as if the thought was just occurring to her and not something she'd been plotting and scheming for days. "I'll take amazing notes so you don't have to." And with that, she bent over her Moleskine, which was filled with hearts, flowers, and curlicues rather than trend descriptions. Clearly, I was dismissed and clearly, I would have to rely on Christie's notes for this show's write-up. Still, I was grateful for this amazing stroke of luck.

As I stood in the back fending off disdainful looks from the Flamingos and quizzical ones from their assistants (Fashion Flamingos in Training or FFITs), I scanned the program. Ah, that explained it. The whole show, not just the after-party, was themed Heaven or Las Vegas, with its sub-collections of daywear, sportswear, and weekend wear assigned names like, "Limbo or Love," and "Pride or Paradise." It looked like the program would end with "Gluttony or Glamour," which was another lucky break since it was evening wear and would be easy enough for me to spot as the sign the show was wrapping up. When the first gown, backless mini-dress, or slightest hint of silver lamé sauntered down the catwalk, it would be my signal to skedaddle, as Penny would say.

While I was on pins and needles the whole time, I have to say the show was spectacular. The models had charisma to burn and the clothes, even to me, were gorgeous. So gorgeous I planned to ask Lisa if I could bring Esme to the showroom to order a few things when she got out of Silver Sequoia, which according to Irma should be in fifty-five days. Sure, Lisa was just the beauty publicist, but it seemed highly likely that she could pull a few strings. I certainly wasn't going to ask that rat bastard Kevin Carson for any favors, or Des, God help me.

Suddenly, the music slowed and a slinky sequined number shimmied down the runway. Time to go. I picked up my tote, duffle, and Irma's Balenciaga and tried to move as stealthily as I could down the aisle and out of the room—no easy feat carrying so much and wearing Irma's floor-sweeping coat that could easily trip me at any minute. How in the world did she ever manage in this thing? Naturally, everyone I passed shot me a dirty look and "shushed" me Christie-style. Nothing to do but get to the stage and get there fast. Since I had no idea where I was and where we were performing, I decided to follow the strains of the band tuning up, which wasn't as simple as you might think because the music from the show was still playing. I figured I was reasonably close when I heard Ollie strumming one of his tunes at a low volume to check the sound. So I kept moving in that direction until I walked straight into a mountain of a security guard standing in front of a red velvet rope blocking off the area, where I was pretty sure I had to be. Crap. Crap. And crap again.

"Hey, you need to turn around and leave the building," he said, forming a barricade between me and the rope. "This event is invitation only."

"I *was* invited. I'm the beauty director of *Sophistiquée*," I said, feeling that tennis ball bang around in the dryer again. One-Eyed Snake was starting to warm up.

"Do you have your invite?" I did not. I'd given it to Samara so she could stay in my seat.

"I don't. I'm sorry. Let me show you my business card." Hurriedly, I dug around first in the Balenciaga, then her tote, and then her duffle until I found one. It was crumpled up and had Nick's direct dial at Matt Umanov written on it, but would have to do. I handed it to him telepathically, urging him to get a move on and let me by.

"Okay," he said, studying the card intently and, of course, taking his time. "Wait here on the side for me to radio Kevin to make sure you're on the list for the party. Right now, no one can go back there except the band."

"I'm *in* the band," I said, fighting to keep my voice level as I contemplated the homicide of Kevin Carson.

"You're in the band?" he asked, eying Irma's coat and all my bags. Maybe Samara was right, and I did look like the world's best-dressed homeless person. Quickly, I unbuttoned the coat to reveal my devil/dealer outfit.

"I guess you are," he admitted with a faint smile of

either incredulity or approval, and unhooked the rope.

"You made it," Ollie said, exhaling with relief when I got to the stage. "I knew Saffron Meadows wouldn't let us down." I had to wonder for a sec. if he'd thought that Sarah Mandelbaum would've let them down. My track record had been pretty craptastic these last few months. Sean, too, it seemed, had been holding his breath. As he took my coat and bags from me and put them behind an amp, I watched his face, which had been wound up with worry, untwist. Charisse twirled her sticks at me in her trademark greeting, and Mayumi stopped noodling around on her bass to give me the thumbs up.

"Okay, rock stars. Time to kick some ass," Ollie said, slipping behind his keyboard and counting us off.

It was easy enough to play and sing in the beginning since no one was in the room with us yet. But as people started crowding in, the Terror Trio appeared in my head again, then the Toxic Twins, and then for some crazy reason my panel of criticizing conservatory professors along with that disgusting weasel Astro Jensen, and none of them seemed to be leaving any time soon.

"*Vous suckez,* Sarah Mandelmerde," Bevin's voice jeered just like it did in seventh-grade French class every time Madame Silverman called on me.

"You'll never be a professional musician as long as you play that ridiculous baby guitar."

"You just blew your chance to be somebody. Pun intended, babe," Rat Boy sneered to me again just like he did on that fateful day in his sleazy motel room.

"My God, Keeley. Can you believe that Mandelbaum girl? What a hopeless disaster." This.

Was. Insane.

I could tell my inner struggle was outwardly obvious when my playing and singing started to falter as we eased into "Running up that Hill" by Kate Bush, and Ollie walked over to me and whispered, "Come on, Saffie, you got this."

It was all I needed to summon up the nerve I'd been lacking since grade school, which despite her tireless efforts, even Esme hadn't been able to impart. I closed my eyes and focused on the song lyrics until I felt steadier. When I finally opened my eyes, I expected to find a sea of hostile faces swimming in front of me.

"Fuck you," I said out loud and almost into the mike until I looked out into the audience and saw Nils and Dana boogying together on a crowded dance floor. The FFs and co. were having a blast, and Dana was chanting, "Go, Saffie. Hey, Saffie. Yeah, Saffie," as she moved and grooved with her dad. "Running up that Hill" faded into Patti Smith's "Dancing Barefoot" into a slew of other songs. And yes, we did squeeze in some One-Eyed Snake tunes, which everyone seemed to dig since they completely jammed up the already-packed dance floor when we played them. The only people not dancing appeared to be the Toxic Twins and Christie, who Des seemed to have taken as her emotional hostage along with Samara, who was bopping around in place. Des was yakking their ears off. I almost felt sorry for the two of them. Regardless, it was a great, great night. And then I had dinner with Sean afterward to look forward to. I thought we could hit Florent on Gansevoort, which stayed open practically twenty-four hours.

At the end of the evening, some underground

documentary guy took Ollie's card, saying he was interested in One-Eyed Snake scoring his next film. And then an indie bigwig dropped by saying he wanted to book the band at one of the festivals he was producing. I hoped they'd let me, or at least Saffron Meadows, play with them again. As we started packing up our gear, a guy from Milk Studios came over to the stage with an enormous cell phone.

"Is one of you Sean Weiland? You have a call from Stephanie." It was Sean's ex-wife. Instantly, his face assumed the same look of anxiety it had when he thought I was a no-show for the gig. He took the phone and strode to the back of the stage. When he returned, I could tell from his expression we wouldn't be having dinner.

"Wyatt had an asthma attack and is in the emergency room at St. Vincent's," he said, handing the phone back to the Milk Studios guy, and then bending down to pick up his guitar and amp.

"Do you want me to go with you?" I allowed myself to brush back the black shock of hair that always fell into his glasses.

"I think it's better if I go myself. Thank you, though." He took my hand that'd smoothed his hair and squeezed it. "I'm sorry about dinner. It'll have to be another one of our rainchecks. You were wonderful tonight, Sarah. Really wonderful."

"Hey, man, we're with you in spirit. I'll call you tomorrow to check in," Ollie said as Sean hot-footed it out the door. When he'd gone, Ollie turned to me and said, "So, you guys are a thing?"

"I think we're trying to be," I admitted. "It just seems to be super slow-going."

"You know what they say about slow and steady," he said, putting on his Zen master hat.

"Yeah, I guess." I sighed.

"Come on, grasshopper, let's load this gear into the van and drive over to Silver Spurs and get some Disco Fries," he said, slinging one arm around my shoulder, wrapping his other around Charisse's waist, and motioning with his head for Mayumi to come with. "We can talk about what a slammin' show we put on, the mad cash we made, and the insane contacts we scored wearing heinous threads playing mostly covers for a room full of people that can't remember the last time they ate. You might even finally be able to snag that Gold Top with your cut."

Chapter 14

I woke up the next morning to a very loud knocking at my door, which was good and bad. Good because, as I glanced at my clock/radio, I realized I'd slept through my alarm and was well on my way to missing the first fashion show of the day at 9 a.m. And bad because who the hell was knocking on my door at 8:00 a.m.? It was early, even for the Bible thumpers. And since the heat was barely working in my apartment, late or not, I was in no hurry to get up and find out. I pulled the covers over my head and willed whoever it was to give up and go away. They kept right on knocking. And then my neighbor started banging on our shared wall to prod me into answering the door. Time to brave the cold since I wouldn't get a moment's peace until I answered.

"Hang on," I yelled, as I pulled on the orange fuzzy, likely flammable, bathrobe my mother had bought me for Chanukah (on sale) and shuffled into the matching god-awful slippers. I stole a glance through the peephole and saw Sean standing there. I considered peeling off my robe and kicking off the slippers before letting him in, but there was no point to it since the gray sweats and red plaid flannel shirt I'd been sleeping in weren't exactly great shakes, either. As I opened the door, he handed me a mug (likely made by Wyatt) of coffee and a bag from the Ecuadorian bakery down the street.

"I figured we should finally have at least some sort of meal together even if it's not dinner, especially since you were so amazing last night," he said, bending down to kiss me. God, my breath must have been God-awful. Mercifully, Sean didn't seem to mind and walked into my apartment.

"You're turning this into a habit, this knocking on my door unexpectedly thing, and, you know, you weren't so bad yourself," I said, flirting just a little, and then taking a good long gulp of coffee before I asked, "How's Wyatt?"

"Much better. Unfortunately, this happens a lot, so we're taking him to a specialist this afternoon."

"Hey, don't you have school?" I asked, suddenly remembering that it was, in fact, now 8:15 on a Friday morning.

"I took a personal day. Can you?" He arched an eyebrow, possibly flirting right back at me.

"I don't think I can take the whole day, but I can be a little late. The shows this morning are pretty unimportant," I replied, moving closer to him.

"How late?" he asked before he kissed me again.

"Pretty late," I said, taking his hand and leading him down the hall to my room, where funny enough, neither one of us minded in the least that the heat wasn't working.

I ended up getting to work around 1:00, only to find that since the morning shows were indeed not very important, most everyone had skipped them and were all at their desks.

"Hey, chief, you didn't go to the shows this morning, did you? Everyone who's anyone didn't,"

Samara chirped as I rounded her cubicle and headed toward my office. "Wow, that new Très Cher serum they gave us in last night's gift bag must really work. You're glowing," she called after me, causing me to smile inwardly. Why, yes. Yes, I was glowing. Sean was wonderful.

When I got to my desk, I found the *Sentinel* open to a spread with a circle drawn around the headline in purple calligraphy pen: Python Charms Paradise. And there was a picture of us playing last night with the caption: *One-Eyed Snake's Ollie Led, Charisse Foye, Mayumi Mori, Sean Weiland, and Saffron Meadows bring Eden to earth at Très Cher after party*. And the story was even better, citing Heaven or Las Vegas as one of Très Cher's best collections to date and its move to have us play at the party "inspired."

This was fantastic, of course, except for the turquoise sticky note attached to the spread with Henri-François' overblown flowery cursive reading, "Sarah, you are late. Call me as soon as you get in. We need to discuss this."

Nothing like that kind of note to suck the glow right out of a girl. I scrutinized the photo repeatedly. How could I've been so stupid? Of course, you could recognize me, shades or not. And it was likely some kind of punishable-by-firing conflict of interest offense that I'd worked for one of our advertisers, even if they had no idea who I was, and it had nothing to do with the beauty industry. Crap. Crap. And crap again.

Well, as my mother Anna Elias Mandelbaum would say, "It's better to take your medicine in one gulp than to drag it out and sugarcoat it." So I picked up the phone and punched in Henri-François' extension.

His assistant Marlene answered on the first ring, as Henri-François insisted his assistants do.

"Hello, Sarah, he's been expecting your call," she lilted in her lovely Trinidadian accent.

"Sarraah, why are you so late?" he scolded as soon as he came on the line letting me know there was no acceptable answer. "You were not at this morning's shows, yes?"

"No, Henri-François, I was not. There were some issues with the heat in my apartment and I had to wait for the super," I replied as contritely as I could. I mean, I *was* having problems with my heat even if that wasn't the reason I was late.

"In your tenement in the Bronx?" he sneered. I figured now wasn't exactly the time to defend my apartment since I was likely about to be terminated.

"Yes. In the Bronx," I answered, waiting for him to drop the bomb.

"Sarraah, I did not see you at Très Cher last night. You were not there?"

"I was. You were wearing that fabulous Très Cher midnight blue suede jacket, right?" I allowed myself a small exhale. Maybe it would be all right.

"Yes. Christophe Christophe gave it to me to thank me for that sensational photoshoot I did with his clothes in St. Barts." I could see him puffing up with pride as he sat on his couch in his enormous office admiring the view of the Statue of Liberty from his floor-to-ceiling windows. As I was struggling to come up with an appropriate response (the story had gotten panned by the *Sentinel* as being stale and hackneyed) he forged ahead, thankfully relieving me of that task. "Sarraah, I want you to write something on that band. Those girls

292

are superb and you should get their beauty tips. Did you see that Saffron Meadows? She should be your inspiration. She is Jewish like you, no? Yet so much thinner, and her hair is fantastique."

"Sure, Henri-François. I'll get right on it," I murmured, wondering if Mercury was in retrograde and wishing I could call Esme to find out. However, since Esme didn't have phone privileges yet and Penny was filming her show today, there was no one I knew who could help me make sense of all of this. So as soon as I hung up with Henri-François I decided to order in a cheeseburger and fries. I was famished from my beautiful morning, which was sadly fading fast and furiously, and would need fuel to figure out what the hell was going on in the universe—that is if I could get the words out because I was pretty damn near speechless. I was just about to pick up the phone again to place my order when it started ringing.

"Mandelbaum," I croaked. Yup. I'd lost my voice.

"I'm sorry I can't hear you. Can you speak up?" an incredibly charming English accent sang in response somehow rousing me from the insanity that was my life.

"Sure. Sorry. This is Sarah Mandelbaum. How can I help you?"

"Darling, it's Dash. Dash Nichols. I'm so glad I caught you." I was about to reply when Christie marched into my office wielding the *Sentinel*. If there was anyone on earth who realized that I was Saffron Meadows it would be Christie. Or maybe Des had figured it out and spilled the proverbial beans. They all seemed awfully chummy last night. And as Twilight Zoney as it was that Henri-François had decided my alter ego was a fashion icon, I knew it'd be worse for both Saffie and me if the truth came out.

"Not now," I warned, waving her away. Christie held her ground in her customary fifth position, looking even more irritated than usual—if that were possible. I kept my head down and stayed quiet. After several minutes of my refusing to look at her or utter another syllable, she stormed out.

"I beg your pardon?" Once again, Dash broke into my swirling thoughts.

"Oh, Dash, I'm sorry. I was speaking to someone else. How are you?"

"Darling, I'm opening my first salon in LA, and to celebrate I'm taking a small group of editors there next week for four days. And since Rich Girl Hair is one of the sponsors of the GDI awards, we'll have terrific seats for it on our last night. Can you come?"

While I can't say that I was keen on spending a few days in LA or anywhere else with *any* FFs, the mere idea of seeing The GDIs (God Damn Independent awards show) was thrilling. It honored all the small, indie musicians who hadn't traded their souls for recording deals with major music labels. Some of the award winners didn't even have records out; they just played local club scenes. Dash was way cooler than I'd thought. And it would be pretty damn wonderful to escape this crappy New York February and get some West Coast sun.

"Hey, that sounds great. Thanks so much for thinking of me."

"I'm so glad you can join us. Kevin will ring you with the details."

"Kevin Carson reps you now?" Christ, that

Jackwad was everywhere.

"Of course. He's fabulous, isn't he?" And without waiting for me to reply, continued, "Darling, were you at the Très Cher party last night with that fabulous band? Their singer Saffron Meadows reminded me of you a bit, and I think you'd look fabulous with her cut and color. All we have to do is relax your curls a little and give you a few face-framing highlights. Let's have you come into the salon before our trip. Tell Kevin what works with your schedule. *Ciao*, darling. Can't wait."

Now, that was perhaps the craziest thing I'd heard all day—chemical treatments that would make my hair look like my actual hair, which all of a sudden was considered "fabulous"? Of course, it was likely a horrible idea to put my head in Dash's hands—maybe even my worst idea ever. So even though I said, "Yes," because that's what he wanted to hear and he was going to host me on a ridiculously expensive trip, I figured I'd tell Kevin I was too swamped with work to make it.

As I hung up the phone, I noticed Giancarlo in one of his trademark black Xenia suits standing in my doorway. Despite being nicely tanned from a recent trip to his native Sicily, he had a pretty intense frown marring his handsome face. I stood up as soon as I saw him and started to walk around my desk to greet him.

"No, no, Sarah. It's fine. You can sit and I will, too," he said as he folded his tall frame into one of the chairs facing my desk. "This isn't going to be an easy conversation. However, it's a necessary one. I'm hoping you can shed some light on a few troubling issues so we can all just get back to work." I felt a wretched-tasting bile rise into my throat and was grateful that I hadn't had a chance to order the cheeseburger I'd been craving. Saffron Meadows and I were clearly going down.

"First off, we need to talk about this business of you taking advantage of your position here and having Samara run all of your personal errands." He paused for a moment and sought my eyes before he continued. "Of course, as an assistant, it's her job to assist but word has gotten back to me she isn't able to take care of her departmental administrative duties because she's tied up with getting your dry cleaning and going to the shoe repair on your behalf."

"Giancarlo, I don't know what you're talking about." Despite my innocence, panic had made my voice take on the high pitch of the guilty. "I've never sent Samara out on a personal errand. Only Christie does that."

"Sarah, I will not have you pointing the finger at other people when there are serious breaches of professionalism in *your* performance. It's also come to my attention that you've been skipping shows and sending Samara in your place, which makes us look completely disrespectful to the fashion community."

"Honestly, except for today, when everyone here told me that the shows weren't important, I've been to every single one of them."

"Please, Sarah. All of the shows are important and, besides, I know for a fact that Samara was sitting in your seat at Très Cher," he interrupted before I could utter so much as a peep in my defense.

"And then I heard something about your accepting a Fendi Baguette from Kevin Carson after he screwed us over on the Cecil exclusive. I recognize that gifts like these change hands all the time in our industry. But, in this instance, it showed a tremendous lack of honor on your part."

Now I was starting to smell a rat—as in that rat bastard Kevin Carson. Could he and Samara be in cahoots together? And what on earth for? There couldn't be a conspiracy against me. I just wasn't important enough. This all had to be some kind of crazy misunderstanding.

Sadly, though, before I could calm my racing thoughts and respond to Giancarlo rationally, one of Anna Elias Mandelbaum's favorite expressions popped into my head: "Just because you're paranoid, doesn't mean the world isn't out to get you."

"Sarah? Sarah? Are you listening to me? This is important. I can't understand why you're not paying attention," Giancarlo scolded, snapping me back to the here and now, where I didn't want to be.

"Yes, Giancarlo, you have my full attention," I somehow managed to stammer out in reply.

"Good. Let's move on. My gut reaction to all of this was to terminate you immediately—especially given your frequent insubordination to Henri-François," Giancarlo continued, barreling ahead before I could even process the monumental injustice of his last statement. "The thing is, under your watch, our beauty section has become more profitable than it's ever been. Our advertisers feel you have tremendous journalistic integrity, which I find somewhat surprising considering that I recently heard that at one of your last jobs there was some kind of impropriety with one of your sources."

"Impropriety with one of my sources? Giancarlo, I

have never in my career had any kind of impropriety with any of my sources, or anyone else for that matter." What in God's name was he talking about?

"That is not what *I've* heard. But the details are a bit sketchy, so let's not dwell on that particular issue for now."

And then it hit me in the back of the head like a sledgehammer. Could he possibly be referring to that total shit, Astro Jensen? And if so, how could Giancarlo think the impropriety was on my part? What in the hell had Des told Christie and Samara last night? And why in the hell was Samara forever trying to screw me over with the powers that be? Christ on a cracker, what had I ever done to her except give her swag, buy her expensive gifts, and let her run wild at work? My face started to burn and my stomach knotted up—this time with anger, not fear. I honestly thought that I'd leap out of my chair that very moment and storm out that door.

But then another feeling started to course through me, one that nearly froze the blood in my veins. It was that same shame that'd been stalking me since Astro Jensen had made his disgusting demands and *40 Days* had tossed me out because I wouldn't stand for them. It didn't matter that a million people had told me what a miserable excuse for a human being Astro was. Somehow, a finger was always pointing back at me, or I pointed it back at myself. Had my jeans been too tight that day? Was my shirt too low-cut? Did I inadvertently say or do something that led him on? Perhaps it had been all my fault. And this thought was so painful and ever-present that I knew it would keep me from ever confronting Des or Samara about their treachery, much less setting the record straight with Giancarlo.

And here he was staring at me expectantly, waiting for something. An apology? Admission of guilt? Well, at least I wasn't going to give him that much.

"Giancarlo," I said, as slowly and carefully as I could, trying to keep the tears now filling my eyes out of my voice. "It feels like what you've been told has been all mixed up and turned around. There was no impropriety on my part." Unfortunately, my voice sounded weak, even to me.

"Sarah, let's not belabor this. I've already wasted enough time trying to get you to do the job you were hired to do." I looked down at my lap preparing to be fired, that is if I could hear him hurl the words at me given that my ears were now ringing at deafening levels.

"I think I may seriously regret this, but I've decided that since the advertising community seems to trust you and there are fiscal advantages to keeping you here, for now, you will remain in your position. However, you need to take this conversation as a serious warning and not let any of these things happen again. Are we clear?"

Somehow, I managed to nod in the affirmative.

"Good. I'll let you get back to it, then." And with that, he strode out of my office, his Berluti Alessandro shoes gliding across the beige wall-to-wall carpet without making so much as a sound. As I sat there paralyzed, trying to wrap my brain around everything that Giancarlo had falsely accused me of, my phone rang. Mechanically, I picked it up.

"Mandelbaum," I whispered. Of course, it was Kevin Carson. True to Dash's word, he was calling me to set up a hair appointment, which I did, without even ripping him a new one for his duplicity. I was more dead than alive after Giancarlo's tirade, and I just didn't have it in me. And more importantly, now seemed like the perfect time to get the hell out of dodge and go to LA. And Kevin had the power to take that trip away from me. Besides, I figured at this point the world was so topsy-turvy and my place in it so precarious that maybe having the requisite straight, fair hair of a Fashion Flamingo would set it all to rights.

It should come as no surprise, though, that it didn't. One week later, I found myself sitting in Dash's chair with hair that was lank, limp, and decidedly crimson in color—thanks to the three hours he'd spent tugging at and bleaching it. I'm not sure if he was as shocked as I was with the outcome because he maintained his trademark enthusiasm as his assistant wielded a round brush and blow dryer, torturing my already tingling scalp to the point of no return. Of course, he didn't get the brush stuck on the top of my head like I did, and there were no globs of Frizz Be Gone. I can't say, however, that the results were any better than my disastrous hair-straightening attempt or Mossimo's gel-soaked ministrations. In fact, they were a hell of a lot worse.

I pointed to the *Sentinel* picture of One-Eyed Snake that Dash had taped to the mirror for inspiration and actually found myself saying, "Dash, Saffron Meadows has curly dark hair, like me. This is nothing like what you said you'd do."

"Don't be upset, darling. I might have just slightly overestimated how coarse and black your hair is and left the relaxer and lightener on a bit too long. You'll see, it'll settle in and be fabulous," he said, patting my shoulder. Did I detect a trace of sympathy in his voice? There was no way in hell he could think I looked good. Yet he stuck to his guns. "Remember not to shampoo for three or four days to lock in this smoothness," he continued. "Now go home and get some rest. We have an early flight tomorrow and a sensational day planned, including dinner at Mr. Chow. Kevin has a car waiting for you downstairs and one coming for you in the morning."

As I got into the car, I couldn't have been more grateful for its darkness so the driver couldn't see how horrifying I looked. But that didn't stop me from straining to look in the rearview the entire ride up to the Bronx to see if my hair had somehow magically morphed back to its black, curly self.

When we, at last, pulled up in front of my building, I saw Sean sitting on the stoop, a beacon in all-white further illuminated by the glowing tip of his American Spirit. With all the tress trauma I'd experienced, I'd nearly forgotten we had plans that night. And while my heart lifted at the idea of being with him, it sank just as quickly at the idea of him seeing me looking like this. I got out of the car and walked over to him as slowly as I might have to my own execution.

"Hey, slowpoke, why so glum?" he called out into the darkness.

"I'm not sure I want you to know," I responded, dragging my heels until I could no longer put off being in his direct line of vision under a streetlight.

"Oh, I see. Someone had their hair done." He smiled and held out one of his gorgeous, graceful guitar player hands, which I instantly took.

"Yeah, it didn't exactly go as planned," I replied,

letting him pull me down next to him.

"It's not so bad. Besides, it's you. And I think you're pretty amazing no matter what's going on with your hair."

"Really?"

"Really. And if you let me take you upstairs, I'll show you." He stood up, pulled me to my feet, and slung Irma's tote and Balenciaga over his shoulder for the trek upstairs.

True to his word, when we got inside, Sean made me forget all about my hair and pretty much everything else. Though, I very briefly contemplated defying Dash's edict and shampooing my hair before the allotted time, and then decided against it. What if washing it too soon would make it look even worse? It seemed a distinct possibility. And besides, I was in no hurry to get out of bed. At around midnight, I realized I would need to start packing, which gave me no small amount of anxiety. I had no idea in hell what people wore to Mr. Chow or music awards shows, or to any place in LA, for that matter.

When I voiced these concerns to Sean, he wrapped his long, lean limbs around me even more tightly, and murmured into my heinous hair, "Why don't you just be the rock star that you are? Seems to me you're just about perfect the way you are for a trip to the GDIs and the Sunset Marquis hotel. Isn't that the place where all the bands stay because it has that recording studio in the basement?"

"You may be the most brilliant man I know," I whispered in his left ear, noticing two tiny holes in the lobe. "Hey, what kind of earrings did you used to wear?" I asked, and then kissed each one individually.

"Oh, nothing all that interesting—just evidence of a misspent youth," he said about three seconds away from falling asleep.

"Hey, don't conk out yet. Tell me something."

"There's nothing to report, angel. Everything's good, especially now," he said before drifting off, prompting me to at last climb out of bed and start stuffing one of Irma's Vuitton duffels with mostly concert Ts and her most distressed jeans. Even if I were all wrong in all my fashion choices, it would be comforting, as Sean said, not to try and act like someone else.

At the crack of dawn the next day (Kevin had put us all on an 8:00 a.m. flight) I slipped on a black Lenny Kravitz T, Irma's wrecked Lucky jeans with the label "Lucky You" sewn into the button fly, her Barney's leather jacket, and a pair of black Converse Chuck Taylor high top kicks. As Sean and I were rushing out the door to leave, he tossed me the Saffron Meadows top hat I'd swiped from Glenn.

"May the force be with you," he said, his hazel eyes gleaming gold behind his glasses.

I donned the hat immediately. Not only would Saffie help give me the confidence I needed to hang with the Flamingos for the better part of the week, but it would also help hide some of this truly terrifying hair, which in the stone-cold light of morning was even more wretched than it was the night before. While I was pretty sure people would think I looked like a freak, short of a hoody, I could think of no other way to cover up a little. Plus, I needed this suit of armor if I were ever going to walk out my front door and onto that plane. My belief was confirmed when the driver waiting for me downstairs asked me at least two times, "Sarah Mandelbaum, guest of Dash Nichols going to Delta Terminal JFK?"

"She is, indeed, kind sir," Sean answered, winking at me before kissing me goodbye, helping me into the car, and carefully closing the door.

When I got to the Delta Sky Club lounge, *Fashion Chic's* Serena Matthews, *Simply Finesse's* Darci Vogel, and the Toxic Twins were already there, perfectly coiffed and made up, perching prettily on the overstuffed chairs and complaining loudly about the early hour and how inconsiderate Dash was for putting us up at the Sunset Marquis instead of what they perceived to be the fancier Chateau Marmont. For the life of me, I just couldn't understand how you could whine about staying at one of the most glamorous hotels in Los Angeles.

Serena and Darci looked up at me briefly from their gripe session and even smiled slightly. I could tell they wanted to say something about my appearance, yet somehow decided not to, which I greatly appreciated. Instead, they started spritzing their faces with rose water mist, crooning almost in sing-song fashion something about trying to ward off that dreaded airplane dehydration. I took their polite indifference as a sign of progress since just a few short weeks ago—before my KC—they would've thrown a full-on snark fest.

Peach and Keeley, however, didn't possess this same kind of discretion or self-control, much less have any kind of respect for me, KC or no KC. So, I wasn't surprised or even fazed all that much when Peach said, "Sarah, you changed your hair. I know we tell our readers they can, 'do it themselves,' but I can't believe you bought into that marketing ploy. It's only so the companies that make at-home beauty products will advertise with us. We all know that most beauty treatments are best left in the hands of professionals."

And then it occurred to me. Not only were these girls mean to me, themselves, and to each other; they were also mean to the millions of women counting on them for beauty advice. This amounted to a meanness of epic proportions. Still, I decided not to burst her bubble and tell her that it was, in fact, Dash, one of the most celebrated professionals in his field, who did this to me, because in the end, it wouldn't have redeemed me in her eyes, and she would've made sure to say something to Dash as soon as we saw him at the hotel later this afternoon. And honestly, that would make me feel pretty damn ungrateful. Dash had footed the sizeable bill to fly me first class on a trip that was getting me away from Giancarlo, Henri-François, and the hellacious New York February, giving me entrée to the GDIs and letting me stay at a rock star hotel. Seemed to me that, despite my hair, I was coming out on top. Saffron Meadows would approve.

Somehow, I slept most of the flight and managed to feel pretty good when we landed. Cars were waiting to whisk us away to the hotel, and when we got there, it seemed like every A-list celebrity was meeting with their agent at a table by the pool. I decided to go to my room, take a quick shower and then grab lunch out where all the action was. Dash had generously allotted us a chunk of free time before we would meet up in the lobby for a tour of his new salon. And he'd left cars at our disposal in case anyone wanted to lunch at The Ivy and shop on Robertson, which I assumed the FFs would all be doing. So I was pretty surprised to come down to the pool and find them billing and cooing in their bikinis around a small group of men drinking bottles of Windswept Wolf ale.

Dressed in feathers, paisley, and velvet, and wearing a whole lot of eyeliner, there was no way these guys weren't musicians. I was pretty sure they were Heavy Artillery, the hottest indie neo-punk band around. I bet they were in town for the GDI's. Comprised of the four flame-haired Scottish Aiken brothers, Jackson, Magnus, Camden, and Malcolm, Heavy Artillery did have a commercial record label, yet somehow engineered and produced all their work without major corporate interference, so they were regarded as independents and even role models of how to "beat the man." I loved them, especially their lead guitar player, Jax. I figured I could get a little closer to steal a better look at them without seeming like a stalker and maybe even say hello if the FFs would ever move on their merry way.

As I reached their table, I overheard Keeley say, "You guys are in a band, aren't you?"

"Well, yes, we are," Jax replied, clearly amused.

"Which one?" Peach asked, batting her eyelash extensions.

"Why don't you guess?" Camden, the rhythm guitar player and lead singer chimed in, strumming a gorgeous Gibson Hummingbird acoustic.

"I don't think you're U2 or Hootie & the Blowfish," Keeley said, furrows creeping into her lovely, smooth forehead.

"No, darlin', we are neither U2 nor Hootie & the

Blowfish," Magnus, the drummer, said, about to burst out laughing. Still, these were pretty girls in bikinis, so he was ready to play along. Suddenly, Jax spied me in a fresh pair of Irma's black jeans and my Converses standing behind the TTs and called out, "Hey, Red, did you steal that hat from Alice or Marc Bolan?"

It took me a minute to realize that *the* Jax Aiken was talking to me. I mean, no one had ever called me Red before, so it was hard to tell. And I don't know whether it was that I was finally feeling like Saffron Meadows after the Tres Cher gig, the California sunshine, Jax's smile which was, as Penny would say, "Just south of the devil," or his beyond irresistible Scottish brogue, but I felt light, bright, and completely up to his banter. "You choose," I replied as if I was just as famous as they were. "Great to see you guys, by the way. You must be here for the GDIs. I hope you're going to play "Stripped Gears"."

Peach stared at me so intently, I thought my horrible hair would burst into flames. She realized she'd been bested and didn't like it one bit. She did manage to slip her card to Jax and say, "We're here till the end of the week. I may have time for a drink." She, Keeley, and the other FFs fluttered away to chaise lounges where they started slathering on copious amounts of sunscreen—the best insurance against lines, wrinkles, and those pesky brown patches, I could almost hear them repeating to themselves like a mantra from across the pool.

"That's our opening tune. How'd you know?" Magnus asked, holding out his hand before Jax could beat him to it. "And you are?"

"Sarah. Sarah Mandelbaum," I said, giving his

hand a hearty shake.

"Nice name," Jax broke in, his green eyes beaming at me.

"Well, you may know me as Saffron Meadows," I said, looking around to make sure the FFs were out of earshot.

"You're a porn star?" Malcolm the bass player asked, at long last looking up from his book, *The Strange Case of Dr. Jekyll and Mr. Hyde*.

"Saffron Meadows isn't a porn star," Jax admonished. "Is she?"

"Wait. Isn't she the lass who played with One-Eyed Snake at the Très Cher after-party?" Camden broke in, noodling away on his gorgeous guitar. "Everyone's talking about that show. Even though it was mostly covers, the band's original tunes were supposedly bloody brilliant. Are you that Saffron Meadows, then?"

"The very same."

"Prove it," Jax said, motioning for Camden to give me his guitar.

"Sorry, boys. I play lefty," I said, for once relieved and not annoyed by what I usually considered a handicap. There was no way I was playing guitar in front of these rock stars.

"Good thing I do, too," Camden said, passing me his sublime instrument—a lefty Hummingbird. I'd completely forgotten Camden Aiken was one of the rare left-handed guitarists. And even though I was so nervous that I couldn't even imagine strumming one chord, much less singing a single note, I just *had* to play that exquisite guitar—even if it was full scale. I had passed on the divine Gold Top and I decided I just couldn't let this opportunity slip through my stubby little fingers. Jax slapped away Magnus' feet from the chair at the head of the table and motioned for me to sit down. So I did, said a quick and silent prayer to the guitar gods, and tuned up before I could change my mind.

"You can do this, Saffie. Please don't fail me now," I murmured to myself, and started softly playing and singing "Heaven or Las Vegas." No one else around the pool seemed to notice as they were all celebrities themselves and likely signing deals running into the several millions. So I just kept going because I realized I could.

When I finished, Jax let out a low whistle and said, "That was bloody amazing. Where on God's green earth have you been hiding yourself, Sarah Mandelbaum? Or is it Saffron Meadows?"

"It's either or both, I guess," I said, almost laughing out loud now that I'd gotten through my performance, nearly flawlessly playing a full-scale Gibson and in front of Heavy Artillery to boot. "And I guess I've been hiding myself at *Sophistiquée* magazine. Wow, I've been dying to play this guitar. It's gorgeous. I have a Gold Top on hold at Matt Umanov."

"You're at *Sophistiquée*?" Malcolm asked with that same tone of disbelief everyone seemed to have when I told them my place of employment.

"Yeah, well. It's a long story. I was at *40 Days & 40 Nights* until I had an incident with Astro Jensen." I wasn't sure how or why I brought that up but there it was, finally out there because I put it out there—not anyone else. And it felt good to take charge of it, own it and release it out into the universe. Somehow, I felt comfortable with these guys, and they didn't let me down.

"Astro Jensen, that wanker? What the hell happened with him?" Jax took an angry swig of ale.

"You know that tosser's in prison?" Magnus broke in. "For shagging an underage girl. Swore up and down he didn't know. Not likely. He's a right foul git that one." I was simultaneously incredibly sorry for the girl and monumentally relieved Astro finally got what he deserved. The world was a safer place with him behind bars.

"Hey, Sarah Saffron Mandelbaum Meadows, play something else," Jax said, those emerald eyes of his blazing. I thought for a minute and then broke into the Stones' "Can't You Hear Me Knocking". By the time I got to the second verse, Magnus was doing Charlie Watts's drum parts with foot stomps and slapping the table with his hands, and Camden had whipped out his harmonica to play the harmonica parts that Jagger sometimes did live. It was then I noticed that the entire crowd at the pool had joined in clapping and stamping. Mercifully, the FFs seemed to have disappeared—either inside the restaurant to pick at fruit plates or back to their rooms to primp for our trip to Dash's salon. Either way, Saffron Meadows and my secret were safe from Giancarlo and Henri-François for now.

When we finished the song, Jax leaned into me as close as he dared with the Hummingbird in between us and said, "So what's this about you're leaving a Gold Top to languish at Matt Umanov?"

"Oh, well. You wouldn't understand, I guess." I felt shy all of a sudden. "The thing is, I've only ever played short scales up until now because of my ridiculously small hands. And I guess I've been worried I won't be able to handle it."

"Seems to me, you can manage just about anything," he said, taking my picking hand and squeezing it. "You chased those dafty birds away, for one thing." I thought for a split second that someone else used the term Fashion Flamingos and had somehow told him until I realized that "bird" was just British slang for a woman you didn't hold in very high regard.

"Hey, I liked those birds," Magnus interrupted.

"You like any bird," Malcolm muttered into his book.

"As I was saying, before I was so rudely interrupted," Jax continued, glaring at his brothers, "how can you think that you can't handle a full-scale guitar when you just out-Taylored Mick Taylor?"

"Hey, thanks. Really, thank you." Even though I knew he was exaggerating, I felt my cheeks getting pink.

"So, what are you up to tonight? We have to go do a soundcheck for the GDIs and then we'll be in the bar here later on. Come join us for a whiskey," Jax said, squeezing my hand even tighter for emphasis.

"I'm not sure I can make it. I'm here with Dash Nichols and those, um, birds, and we have dinner at Mr. Chow's tonight and then drinks at Sky Bar."

"Do your best, Sarah Saffron Mandelbaum Meadows," Jax said, releasing my hand at last and throwing me a wink. "I've no doubt that you can do whatever you fancy doing."

When I got back to the lobby, I expected to find a flamboyance of impatient Flamingos waiting for me but

I guess they were taking their preening seriously, so I sat down to wait, replaying my encounter with Heavy Artillery in my head and thinking about how I would describe it to Sean. I must've been pretty far gone because all of a sudden, I realized this enormous man was talking to me and likely had been for some time.

"Son, Sonny? Is that you?" It was Mossimo, the Queen of Curl.

"Oh wow, Mossimo. Sorry. I zoned out there for a minute. It's good to see you. What are you doing here?"

"I'm here," he said, flipping an imaginary long hank of Cher hair off each shoulder, "because I'm doing hair for some of the girls getting GDIs. However, I'm the one who should be asking *you* the questions. What the hell happened to those gorgeous ebony curls of yours? I don't know how I even recognized you. And trust me, a Cher always knows her Sonny."

"Oh, it's a long story." I sighed. Funny, I'd never thought of my hair as "ebony," much less .gorgeous before. In comparison to the way I looked now, Mossimo probably had a point.

"I've got time." He parked his giganticness next to me on the couch, crossing one leg over another.

I scanned the lobby. Still no FFs or Dash in sight, so I hurriedly explained to him what had happened at Dash's salon just the night before.

"You mean you haven't washed it yet, Son?" he asked, his dark brown eyes lighting up.

"No. Honestly, I was afraid I'd make it look even worse."

"Then there's hope for us yet." I loved how Mossimo was somehow including himself in the problem. Maybe it meant he had a solution.

"Straightening treatments have to bond with the hair for a few days to last, and we can just fix up your color with a box or two of L'Oreel."

"L'Oreel? Do you mean L'Oréal?"

"Son, let's not split hairs when we're in crisis mode," Mossimo said, examining my eyebrows. "Seems to me your natural color is probably their third darkest black. Not blue/black—a warm golden black. It was so pretty. Oh well, no use crying over cake left out in the rain, even if all the sweet green icing's flowing down," he continued, referencing one of Donna Summer's all-time great tunes. "I've got a festive dinner with my girls tonight, so come to my room around ten and we'll fix this. Stevie Nicks wants her hat back."

This was amazing. Mossimo was amazing. I'd never had a fairy godmother before and here he was, sitting in the lobby of the Sunset Marquis. What were the odds? It did mean that I couldn't meet Heavy Artillery for a drink later that night, but first things had to come first.

Throughout the rest of the day into the evening, Dash pulled out all the stops with chauffeured town cars around LA, customized gift bags of his Rich Girl hair care products when we got to his salon, a five hundred dollar gift certificate to Fred Segal presented to us when our cars pulled up in front of the store, and a terrific dinner at Mr. Chow, where we saw at least six celebrities with stars on Hollywood Boulevard. Even the TTs seemed satisfied, having run out of complaints and criticisms—even ones directed toward me. I did beg off from drinks at Sky Bar, saying I was tired from the trip. I didn't want to keep Mossimo waiting.

True to his word, after three shampoos, two boxes of L'Oreel, a generous though not excessive application of Twist the Night Away gel (I'd requested his restraint as politely as I could) and a stint under Mossimo's blow dryer with a diffuser, I had black curly hair again. And I'd never been happier.

"You are a genius," I said when he was finally done after about three hours or so.

"Any time, Son, it's always a pleasure. And don't be a stranger at the salon. All you had to do was tell me to go easy with elgay," he said, using the Pig Latin Esme and I'd long left behind. He pointed to his cheek. "Now plant one here and say goodnight, Gracie, and don't let me catch you straight and red again."

It wasn't until I got back to my room that I realized it was one o'clock, which meant four o'clock in the morning, New York time. It was all I could do to get undressed and brush my teeth much less undertake all the new skincare ablutions—cleanse, exfoliate, tone, and moisturize with eye cream on top of it all—to correct my "enlarged pores" and "premature lines" that Samara had prescribed. Oh well, skipping one night couldn't hurt. I must've crashed and crashed hard because I kept hearing a phone ringing in my dream and couldn't seem to rouse myself to answer it. And then I realized it was the phone in my hotel room ringing, and it was something like three-thirty in the morning, California time. I'd been asleep a mere two hours or so. And it was ringing in that dreaded Anna Elias Mandelbaum way.

"Hi, Mom," I said, probably sounding as impatient and groggy as I felt.

"How did you know it was me?" came her curt

reply.

"Because no one else would call me at three-thirty in the morning, California time."

"Well, how would I know you were in California since you never tell me anything?" She had a point. I hadn't had the chance to alert her about this trip. "If I hadn't called your office, I would never know my daughter's whereabouts, which is the bare minimum information a mother is entitled to. By the way, the woman who answered your line said it was Christie Somers's office. Did you switch your phone number without telling me?"

Now that was odd. It must've been some kind of slip up or was Samara up to something again? Frankly, it was shocking to me that she'd even bothered to pick up the phone, I'd have to call later that day to get to the bottom of it.

"No, Mom, I didn't switch offices or phone lines without telling you. But I'd love to get some sleep. I'm here on a press trip and we're pretty heavily scheduled."

"It's just like you to take off on a joy ride when I'm worried sick about you."

"Worried sick? About me? Why, Mom? There's nothing to worry about."

"Really? You call that *Kick Butt* story nothing to worry about?"

"It isn't. How did you see that, anyway?"

"There was an issue of *Sophistiquée* at my beauty parlor. And, my God, the shame of it all. Is this why I worked night and day to pay for you to get a bachelor's degree at Robert Lowell University and that swanky conservatory you insisted on?" I didn't remind her that

I had paid for the music degree and had the student loans to prove it because she was off and running and I needed to get some sleep.

"Now you sound like Esme," I said, feeling my eyes closing.

"Esme? Do you mean Esther Levine? Well, if she told you that, then she is making good sense for a change," Anna harrumphed loudly into the phone.

"Mom, she's been Esme since the eighth grade, that's like twelve years ago," I said, fully awake again.

"Well, I prefer Esther. It's a good Jewish name and her God-given one."

"Mom, I don't think God gave her that name. I'm pretty sure Mr. and Mrs. Levine did."

"Sarah, I will not have you take that tone with me, especially when this call is costing me a fortune and I am making it just for your benefit. Never mind, though, it doesn't seem to matter what I think. Now that you have this ridiculous job, you have no time for your mother."

"I'm sorry, Mom. Things have been crazy. When I get back from this trip, we can make a date. Did you get the Calvin Klein coat I mailed you?"

"Yes, Sarah, I did. I'm not sure how or why you don't realize that all the expensive gifts you send me can't make up for the fact that I never see or hear from you anymore. That's not how I raised you. A mother wants some time with her daughter. Now get some sleep. You know how puffy your under-eyes look when you're overtired." And with that, she hung up.

I tried to fall back to sleep but between her ire and this latest Christie news, it was pretty damn difficult. I think I finally drifted off at around six only to have my alarm wrench me awake at eight. And when I staggered into the bathroom to finally perform Samara's grueling skincare ritual, Anna Elias Mandelbaum's under-eye bags greeted me in the mirror.

Chapter 15

Even though I was completely and utterly fried when my red eye from LA landed at JFK, I decided to go straight to work. I knew if I went home and fell asleep there'd be no getting me up in time to make it to the office before Giancarlo, Henri-François, and my so-called "staff," came in, which felt especially crucial right about now. What the hell was Samara doing answering my line and saying it was Christie's office? And why didn't either of them return any of my calls while I was away? None of these lapses boded well for my finding my office—or my career—in decent shape when I returned.

And then there was the fact that Sean wasn't calling me back. I'd left him the best message about my playing with Heavy Artillery and one or two, okay, three others, while I was away. Had something happened to Wyatt? Or was there some kind of hint I was supposed to be getting? I was starting to freak out he wasn't into me anymore, which made me feel so sick inside I was positive I'd barely be able to keep down the tea and toast my mom practically force-fed me when I had the flu.

Still, my trip had gone surprisingly well. The Flamingos seemed to groove on the California sun (once they doused themselves in sunscreen) and even kicked off their stilettos now and again, so they stood with both feet on the ground, which made them far more pleasant to be around. Dash continued to be a gracious, generous host and was also completely cool when he saw I'd restored my hair to its normal state. In fact, he seemed a little relieved and even said, "Darling, you look fabulous. Just like you. We shouldn't have tried to make you look like someone else. You and Saffron Meadows are completely different people." It was all I could do to not burst out laughing. But since he'd proven himself to be one of the rare, good guys in an industry of divas, I managed to contain myself.

Meanwhile, we had amazing seats to the GDIs, and it was beyond thrilling to see Heavy Artillery up there playing. I wanted to tap the shoulders of the people in front of me and say, "I know those guys!"

On my way out of the terminal, I passed a newsstand and was confronted with the *Sentinel's* review of our breast story, "Breast in Show," which had come out the day before, when I was in LA. The headline and caption read: What a Boob: *Sophistiquée* CD has slithered down to the point of no return. Along with the article panning the story was a cartoon that depicted Henri-François as a crotch-hugging, white button-fly jean-wearing snake, wound around a bikini-clad woman with grotesque cleavage diving headlong into an abyss. I guess if I'd slept more on the plane and wasn't so anxious about what I'd find when I got to the office, I'd have thought it was at least mildly amusing. It certainly felt true to life. Knowing Henri-François, however, he'd likely take this as a huge compliment and proof of his "edginess"—something he clearly believed was the antidote to the industry considering him a has-been hack, which is pretty much what the news media called him when they weren't labeling him a misogynist pig. And if he deluded himself into believing this article was good publicity, like he had with the butt story, it would mean he had something even more salacious up his sleeve. And then there was this business with Christie and Samara. It was barely sunrise and already turning into one mother of a day.

When I got to our floor, it was pretty much a graveyard, which was great news for me. I figured I had about two hours or more to get organized and put my fears to rest before the staff started rolling in somewhere after ten. As I passed Samara's empty cubicle en route to my office, I noticed a light on in Christie's office across from it and couldn't help but overhear her talking on the phone behind the closed door.

"No, Mother. This fashion thing is not just a foolish fad like you think ballet was," she said mechanically. There was a pause, and I guess she was listening to her mother's response. "Yes, Mother. I realize how much you spent to send me to the School of American Ballet and The Professional Children's School, and then to Bryn Mawr when it didn't work out." She sounded like she was about to cry if she wasn't crying already. "But it honestly wasn't a whim on my part. If you'd remember, I had to leave because I snapped my Achilles tendon and couldn't dance anymore."

Wow. Failed career in the arts? Overbearing moms? Christie and I had more in common than I ever would've imagined. But Christie's mother certainly made me appreciate Anna Elias Mandelbaum. At least she tried to help when I was sick or injured and meant well, even if it seemed otherwise. This revelation certainly explained a lot about why Christie acted the way she did, even if it didn't excuse it—especially not her and Samara's most recent shenanigans. At least now I understood why she always stood in fifth position and why even her bunions had bunions.

Since it was time for me to get to work, and I was starting to feel guilty about inadvertently eavesdropping, I decided to walk right on without announcing my presence. As I rounded the corner to my office, I started playing out the conversation I would have with my so-called staff about what went down while I was in Cali, rather than steadying myself for a possible ambush. Big mistake.

As soon as I walked into my office dragging my bags, I saw Henri-François perched on the corner of my desk in my shockingly neat and orderly office. I wondered how long he'd been planning on staying there, given how early it was. Somehow, seeing him there in my sparkling clean office was more disconcerting than if I'd found him amidst the towers and piles of newspapers, magazines, press releases, and beauty products I'd anticipated.

I'd barely made it through the door when Henri-François droned as slowly, Frenchly, and pompously as possible, "Sarraah, you are coming from the gym?" He seemed to be adding even more syllables to my name than usual. This wasn't a good sign. "Did you see the newspaper this morning?"

"No, Henri-François, I haven't, and I was not at the gym this morning. I just came straight from the airport to get an early start," I said, trying to sound chipper, enthusiastic, and damn excited to see him and to be the

Beauty and Fitness Director of *Sophistiquée*. I was hoping my small fib about not catching the *Sentinel* would help put him in a better mood. Unfortunately, his face was already twisted up in self-righteous indignation.

"If you are not coming from the gym then why are you wearing those horrible shoes and those terrible clothes?" he scolded, glaring at Irma's ripped jeans, my Lita Ford T, and Puma California's that I'd sported on the plane, figuring I would change at work. I had some decent clothes in my bag, courtesy of Dash and our trip to Fred Segal, and had left a pair of Irma's Chanel ballet flats somewhere in my office for just these types of emergencies.

"I just wore this on the red eye from LA. I'm about to change," I assured him as brightly as I could trying to remember where I'd stashed Irma's shoes.

"You know, Sarraah, you *should* be going to the gym," Henri-François continued. "It would help you be less, how do you say, fat. And you should always dress to represent *Sophistiquée* even on the red eye."

He stood up unexpectedly from the corner of my desk and assumed his favored pelvis thrust forward stance, looking me in the eye as if daring me to take in the view. After months of practice, I knew better than to look down, so I kept my eyes fastened on the cabinet that I hoped housed the damn ballet flats.

"I will try to get to the gym today, Henri-François," I promised, knowing full well there would be no time. And that even if there were, I likely wouldn't go.

"Sarraah, you are the Beauty and Fitness Director of *Sophistiquée*. Can you not at least try to be even a little bit fit and a little bit beautiful?" He practically sneered before he continued. "Listen, I have a *fantastique* idea for a story you need to start immediately. Today's *Sentinel* article proved to me once again that we are on the right track with our provocative coverage. Our newsstand sales have been *sensationelle*."

Obviously, this man was insane; there was no way in hell our sales were up because of that heinous story. Besides, given that he'd used those same words to describe the butt and breasts stories, it wasn't surprising that my heart dropped down to my knees. Taking my silence as a sign that I was waiting with bated breath to hear his brilliant idea, Henri-François leaned in dangerously close to my face so that it almost touched mine, causing my eyes to tear and clogging up my nose and throat with his cologne, which he insisted I get him for free by lying to its publicist that we would write about it, knowing we never would because they didn't advertise with us.

He picked up my phone and punched a few numbers. "Allo, Didier? I am with Sarraah. Come now, please." Oh, great. Didier was in the office already, too? I could hear his feet pounding down the hall and his panting with the exertion of doing Henri-François' bidding with as much alacrity as he could muster with his overweight, out-of-shape physique. His plump, pasty face and shiny bald head fairly glistened with sweat as he slunk into my office, somehow simultaneously obsequious and menacing. I wondered if Henri-François had ever chastised *him* about going to the gym.

"Ah, Didier, *bon*. Do you have the fantastic story from French *Sophistiquée* to show Sarraah?"

"*Mais oui*, Henri-François," he responded, bobbing his head slightly in grotesque deference to his master.

"*Pensez-vous qu'elle peut le retirer?*" Didier asked, stirring up trouble as usual just for the fun of it since he was essentially asking if I'd be able to pull off this latest genius idea.

"*Je n'ai pas beaucoup de foi. Elle n'a pas beaucoup de finesse et est assez stupide,*" Henri-François replied, seeming almost sad. And I guess he was sad considering he'd just said he had little faith that I could execute the story because I didn't have much finesse and was quite stupid.

Didier sucked up to Henri-François more than I ever thought possible by responding that if I were incapable of doing this amazing story—the most genius story ever—Christie could execute it since she was far more elegant and in touch with our readers than I was.

Henri-François and Didier abruptly turned their attention back to me. Didier unfurled a copy of the most recent French *Sophistiquée* and opened it to a spread entitled

Trésor Enfoui (Buried Treasure) and there ensued page after page and picture after picture of bikini-bottomed and sheer panty-clad women's nether regions, along with "beauty tips" on scenting, grooming, hair removal, and bedazzling. It was a vagina story.

"Sarraah, we are going to do a poosey story, it's *fantastique*, yes?" Henri-François practically rubbed his hands together with glee. I imagined he was thinking about the photoshoot he would do for American *Sophistiquée* and all the poor, starved-for-work models he would lure into posing for him with promises of future cover stories and a free trip to St. Barts.

I couldn't find the words to respond. Henri-François pushed onward.

"Call your team together and brainstorm an outline for me. You will need Samara and Christie—they have a much more refined aesthetic than you," he said, causing me to wonder, yet again, how he was able to pronounce Samara's and Christie's names correctly even though they had the same number of Rs as mine. And then he forged ahead. "I will be back this afternoon to check your progress. And Sarraah, it is difficult for me to understand why you, the Beauty and Fitness Director of American *Sophistiquée*, would not think to do a story like this yourself—one that is so provocative yet full of necessary beauty tips. Perhaps it is because you are not French like me, which means you do not know what American women want."

I did not call attention to the fact that since the average American *Sophistiquée* reader was a woman in her late twenties, single, a college grad, and an urban professional, I had far more in common with her than his male sixty-year-old-French-self did. I was just hoping he and Didier would beat a hasty retreat. Mercifully, they did, Henri-François' crotch leading the way, with Didier bowing and scraping so close behind that he nearly trampled on his master's heels.

Too numb to even think of getting started researching this latest Henri-François horror, I decided to busy myself with checking my voicemail and examining the new products that'd come in while I was away. Despite the odds against it, Samara had neatly arranged them on the table near the window. When I finally heard her stirring at her desk out front two hours later, I called her in. "Hey, thank you for gracing us with your presence," I was pretty well passed trying to fake pleasantries with her now that she'd proven beyond a shadow of a doubt what a back-stabbing you know what, she was. Okay. Bitch.

"Please call Christie and ask her to come in and meet with us. We need to sit down ASAP and figure out a plan for Henri-François' story idea. He wants to see an outline this afternoon."

"Christie just left and won't be back till the afternoon," Samara said, barely poking her long, shiny, perfectly chocolate brown head of hair into my door. "She has her Celebrity Body Beautiful Boot Camp class."

"What in the world is that?"

"You got the invitation to join the class a few weeks ago. Remember? We decided Christie should take it because well, we all know you don't exercise, and even if you did, because of your body type—short and stout—this wasn't a good class for you; you'd put on too much muscle weight." Samara made air quotes around the words "short" and "stout," and then walked into my office and picked up the new Dior compact and lip gloss that sat in the center of the new products table. After oohing and aahing over how "heavenly" they were, she began to paint her lips a gleaming shade of tangerine that made her skin glimmer.

Not only did I not recall that invitation coming in, I certainly didn't remember giving it to Christie. Sure, Celebrity Body Beautiful Boot Camp sounded excruciating and tedious but there was no doubt in my mind it would have been preferable to having that conversation with Henri-François and Didier. And given that I seemed to have simultaneously shrunk and expanded overnight—at least in the eyes of Henri-François and Samara—I needed the exercise. However, there wasn't much time to wallow in self-pity, bad body image, or annoyance with my team. I had a "poosey story" to pull together in just a few short hours if I was going to keep my job.

"Whatever. We need to get started on this story for Henri-François right away. So let's sit down and just do it." I searched in vain for a pad and pen somewhere in my disturbingly clean office.

"I'd love to stay and help, and maybe I can later today. Right now, I've got to get to a meeting with Kenzo. Remember? You said I should go in your place so I could get out in the market more." Samara helpfully located a reporter's notebook and a pen next to my Chanel ballet flats in a cabinet and handed everything to me.

No. I didn't remember that, either. And Samara was already out in the market a whole lot more than she was at the magazine tending to her administrative duties, which Giancarlo had blamed me for her not doing. Despite my clean office, or maybe because of it, something even worse than usual was going on with my "staff", but unfortunately, I didn't have the time to suss it all out.

"That's fine. But when you get back, let's sit down with Christie and do this." I kept my voice low and light, no easy feat given that I was about three seconds away from a meltdown.

"I'll try, chief. Probably after my lunch with Clarins would be a more realistic goal, since I may need to go there straight from Kenzo, depending on timing. You asked me to take that appointment for you, too, remember?"

I did not remember. This was getting out of control. As I started to contradict her, Samara slipped the new compact and lip gloss into the Prada bag I'd bought her for Christmas, swung it over her shoulder, and glided gracefully out of the office in her 3.5-inch Valentino pumps, bought with the gift card Valentino had sent me as a thank you for covering its latest fragrance. She'd coaxed me into giving it to her in her usual relentlessly, ruthlessly bubbly way. At least I'd gotten her to organize the beauty product closet in exchange for it.

Too defeated to get started on Henri-François' outline myself, I reached for the phone, which stank of his cologne, to call Penny. She was working at the new restaurant, Feast, where she was head pastry chef when she wasn't shooting Savannah Sweets. Despite the early hour, I figured she'd be there prepping for the lunch rush. The same beyond snobby hostess from the Rustic Root answered the line and informed me Penny was in the kitchen and she would have to transfer the call, making it seem like I'd asked her to poke herself in the eye with a sharp stick rather than put me through to my friend.

"Kitten! Hello! Welcome back. How was LA?" Penny was a new woman on the phone at work now that she didn't have that jackhole Rex breathing down her neck. Even in the middle of all my hell, I was happy for her.

"Do you think I'm short and stout?" I asked, surprising even myself. I couldn't believe this was my main concern after the bomb Henri-François had just dropped, and the mutiny Samara and Christie were plotting.

"Is that a trick question? You're not even five feet tall and you're a size two, which is nowhere near stout, by any normal standards. Have you been talking to that nasty little mosquito Christie?"

"Samara," I sighed.

"I don't like that one, either. She's a sneak and an operator and you give her way too much stuff. She takes advantage of you. Not to mention the fact that she's a liar and a traitor." I could picture Penny wearing her white chef's hat and apron, likely pushing her large, round, tortoiseshell-framed glasses back up onto her nose. I found this reassuring. "How can you believe anything she says after what happened with Giancarlo?"

"Henri-François called me fat today too. And he wants me to write an article about vaginas." I'm pretty sure I'd started to whine.

"What?"

"Henri-François wants me to write a story about vaginas," I repeated, hoping it would help me get used to the idea. It didn't.

"I heard you. I just asked you to say it again because I can't even begin to describe how disturbing that is."

"And Didier told Henri-François that he didn't think I could handle this kind of brilliant story because I'm not elegant and don't understand our readers."

"Like a story on vaginas is elegant, and those old perverts know what the average young American woman wants?" she replied, her voice rising. "Where's Christie in all of this?"

"She's at Celebrity Body Beautiful Boot Camp."

Penny snorted. "Of course, she is."

"And while I was away someone was answering my line, 'Christie Somers's office.'"

"What? That's crazy. You need to get to the bottom of that STAT."

"And Henri-François calls this new opus of his the Poosey Story."

"That has to be against some kind of law." Penny's Savannah accent was going strong.

"Do you think?" I momentarily allowed myself to be soothed with the vision of Henri-François and his white Levis 501-clad pelvis being carted off to prison.

"Surely he can't expect you to write a story about your vagina," she continued, and I could almost hear the wheels turning in her head as she tried to come up with a plan.

"Well, the story isn't about *my* vagina. I think Henri-François meant vaginas in general."

"Tomato, tomahto. Potato, potahto. What's the diff?" Penny asked.

"There's a big difference."

"I don't like this. You should check in with HR. I don't want this to come back to bite you in the ass," Penny continued, as always three steps ahead of me. "I don't trust Samara and Christie as far as I can throw them. And there's no way Christie isn't the brains behind this whole take-down-Sarah special ops. Samara doesn't have enough common sense to close her mouth when it's raining so she doesn't drown, much less stage a coup d'état."

I envisioned Penny flinging size double zero Christie across the room, her blonde hair and Jimmy Choos flying with Samara's long, lithesome hot pink and orange Pucci-draped frame following, and allowed myself another smile.

Later that day, when Samara was back, I called Christie into my office to brainstorm. I'd single-handedly pulled off the Butt and Breast stories, and I'd be damned if I'd take on this Poosey story solo, though I wasn't sure I'd go up to HR. That'd be like flushing my career right down the toilet. I mean, look what'd happened to me at *40 Days* when I spoke up for myself. I'd ended up being exiled to this total freak show of the fashion industry. And besides, all the complaints and class-action suits against Henri-François for sexual harassment and discrimination didn't seem to do a damn thing. Here he was, going strong, thrusting his pelvis and demanding stories about private parts for all he was worth, and that was just the tip of his pervy iceberg. He'd even managed to overthrow Fiona Doyle, and on paper, she had more power than he did.

About thirty minutes after we hung up, Christie walked into my office with Samara in tow. Shockingly, instead of standing in the door with her perpetually sour expression contorting her perfectly made-up face, sinewy arms folded across her non-existent chest, and feet splayed in fifth position, she sat on one of the chairs facing my desk as Samara followed suit.

"What's up?" she asked, almost cheerfully.

"Henri-François wants us to pull together an American version of this story," I said, handing her the copy of the French *Sophistiquée* opened to Le Trésor Enfoui.

"Well, clearly, this is all rather outrageous. Traumatizing, even. So, we have to do this right. Samara, why don't you run AP newswire searches on some of the topics covered in this French article? I'll start talking to some hair removal experts in LA." This was a brand new Christie. And while I likely should've worried about her sudden shift in personality, I was so relieved that my "team" was going to help me tame this so-called Poosey story that I put it out of my mind. I also decided that I could overlook these mysterious appointments I knew nothing about, and this issue of someone answering my line as Christie's. You have to pick your battles, I guess, and it felt like I'd won the important one.

"I know, why doesn't Saffron, oops, I mean, Sarah, talk to the A Sisters?" Samara sang, her face brightening, at perhaps what she thought was a brilliant idea and at her sticking it to me. Her victory, however, was only short-lived as Christie nearly instantaneously shot her a look that would freeze hell over in three seconds flat. But there it was. I'd been completely right in my assumption that they would recognize me at the Très Cher after-party or from that damn *Sentinel* photo. Or did, Des, put that bee in their bonnets? My head was starting to swim. I decided it was best to get back to the matter at hand—even if it was the Poosey story.

"The A sisters?" I asked, not having the faintest idea who they were.

"Yes. Michaela, Martina and Milagros Alvarez. They're from Argentina and have a nail and waxing salon on West 57th Street," Christie explained, as patiently as I'd ever seen her. "They've invented this new kind of bikini waxing style where they pull out all the hair on your you-know-what except for a thin strip at the top and take out any hair that's inside your behind. It's called an Argentine wax. I don't think they even do it in Argentina. Seems to me like it's just marketing hype that's actually working. New York City women are going mad for it, and other salons across the country are starting to offer it too."

"Why would anyone in the world rip out all of their hair down there with hot wax?" I was in pain just thinking about it. And then I remembered more about Des than I cared to. She was likely one of the Alvarez Sisters' biggest clients.

But before I could answer my question, Christie cut in, "Why, for sex, Sarah. For sex. Regardless of what it's for, if we want to impress Henri-François, we need to include the A Sisters in the article. They're the hottest thing happening in lady bits right now. Kevin Carson reps them."

Figures Kevin Carson repped a business that pulled out women's short hairs by the roots. Would the indignities never stop? Once Samara and Christie left my office, I was convinced we had the story under control, and that Samara wasn't going to say anything more publicly about my being Saffron Meadows. I picked up the phone to order breakfast. Sure it was only Anna Elias Mandelbaum's tea and toast, but I needed something to fortify me for the call I'd have to place to that little rat bastard Kevin.

The weeks just sort of flew by. I didn't end up going to HR about the story because magically things seemed to be pulling together. Samara and Christie were submitting remarkably tasteful articles, which seemed to please Henri-François. Besides, I reasoned, Henri-François had now run out of women's intimate body parts, so this story had to be his last hurrah. Still, I was, fairly traumatized by his perpetual "Sarraah, how is your poosey doing?" query every time he passed my office and I absolutely will not go into detail about the pain and humiliation that accompanied my Argentine wax, which included having to get on all fours and spread my cheeks for the final hair pull. Considering I was never supposed to have gotten a wax in the first place since I'd stressed that my meeting with the A sisters was for an interview only, I was doubly pissed. Fucking Kevin Carson.

And it seemed like I wouldn't even be able to show Sean the results of all that torture and torment. It was official. He was blowing me off. Not only had he not returned any of my calls, but when we ran into each other in the laundry room of our building he gave me, as my mother Anna Elias Mandelbaum would say, "The bum's rush."

"Oh, hi. How are you?" That was pretty much all he could manage before he beat a hasty retreat and took the stairs nearly two at a time to make his escape. And even though my mother likely gave the worst relationship advice on record, I couldn't help but make myself feel extra sick inside by wondering if she'd been right all these years trying to indoctrinate me with the old, "Why buy the cow when you can get the milk for free?" adage. After all, I'd hopped into bed with him before we'd even had a proper date. It'd just seemed so right. I'd even almost said, "I love you," the morning of my LA trip as he was putting me and my horrifying hair in the car. Thank God I'd held my tongue for fear of freaking us both out.

On a brighter note, for the first time, I felt I had this job under control and things were starting to look up now that we'd reached rock bottom. Ad sales were soaring, and Giancarlo had even started to smile at me again when we passed each other in the hall. So I was pretty much caught with my pants down, so to speak, when Henri-François stormed into my office about a month out with that day's *Sentinel* and tossed it onto my desk.

"Sarraah, what is the meaning of this?" Cautiously, I smoothed out the crumpled newspaper to reveal an unflattering cartoon of him as a lion clawing a kitten that looked suspiciously like me: "Pervy *She* C.D. in Cat Fight with B. D. over Pussy Story" and the accompanying caption: "This is outrageous and traumatizing," Beauty Director Sarah Mandelbaum is overheard saying.

"Honestly, Henri-François, I have no idea where this came from." My heart was about to jump out of my throat.

"Sarraah, I know you did not do this because while you are many things, you are not sneaky. This does show me, however, that you have been complaining about me which means you are disloyal—something I will not stand for." He turned abruptly and strode out of the office, calling over his shoulder, "This is not good for you."

No. This was not good for me. Not at all. I picked up the phone to call Penny, who thankfully was at the restaurant and could talk for a few minutes. Then I called Esme, who was freshly back from Silver Sequoia. And as selfish as it may have been to whine to her about my problems after everything she'd just been through, I felt like maybe I had some leeway since she appeared to be truly on the road to recovery—going to AA meetings, working with Mayumi as a sponsor, seeing a therapist and not even talking about drinking. In times like these, everyone needed both a Penny and an Esme in their corner.

We decided to meet that night at Arcadia on the Upper East Side, one of our favorite spots since there was little risk of running into any FFs because it was no longer an "it" hangout. These days, the fashion crowd and other A-listers were flocking to clubs in SoHo and Tribeca, so we felt safer up "north" in I guess what people were now calling the nosebleed section of NYC. As I was heading out the door to meet them, my phone rang.

"Mandelbaum," I answered in a rush, intending to get whoever it was off the line as quickly as possible. I had important business to discuss with my girls.

"Is this the famous Sarah Saffron Mandelbaum Meadows?" It had to be Jax. Despite my anxiety and haste, I smiled.

"It is. How are you?"

"I'm brilliant, now that I have you on the phone. I was entirely upset that you never met us in the bar that night at the Sunset Marquis. However, I will recover admirably if you see us tonight."

"Oh, Jax, I'd love to, except I have plans with my friends. I'm having kind of a crisis at work."

"That seems serious, then. I wouldn't want to keep you from that. But maybe we can meet you, too. We've something we'd like to discuss with you."

"You do?"

"We do."

"Sounds mysterious." I felt a little thrill run up and down my spine.

"It isn't mysterious at all. We just have a few

details to sort, out so it'd be better to do it in person. Besides, Sarah Saffron Mandelbaum Meadows, it'd be grand to see you again." Well now, of course, I had to make this work. Maybe I could leave Penny and Esme for a few minutes to have a quick drink with them.

"Well, we're just going to Arcadia on the Upper East Side. It's totally not your scene, but if you can grin and bear it, it'd be grand to see you, too."

"Consider it done, Sarah Saffron Meadows Mandelbaum. See you soon."

When I got to the restaurant, Penny was waiting for me, complete with martinis already on the table—gin for her and vodka for me. When Esme came, we'd switch to sodas. She was going to be a little late since she was meeting with the ASPCA for a coveted spot on its board of directors. In the meantime, before I launched into the latest Henri-François and *Gotham Sentinel* drama or talked about Heavy Artillery, I wanted to catch up with Pen and hear all about Savannah Sweets and what new desserts she'd created for Feast. And of course, get the juicy details about how things were going with James. Once again, I was over the moon to see that without Rex in her life, Penny was in fine form, flipping her pink pashmina over her shoulder and laughing about an oven that caught fire on set and fried her bananas foster beyond recognition.

We'd moved on to discuss her Salted Caramel Glazed Donut holes served warm with Sweet Corn Ice Cream and then onto James, which caused her to blush sweetly, just as Jax and Co. walked in. And I have to say it was pretty funny to see them there with their blazing red buzz cuts, all decked out in their velvet, feathers, and paisley among the restaurant's regulars—

these days mostly Upper East Side parents frantic to get their kids fed quickly and back to their apartments attacking their homework so they'd be accepted to a top-three Ivy League college. Heavy Artillery was of no concern to them even if they'd been obsessed with the Sex Pistols back in their day.

Of course, I was burning with curiosity about what they wanted to discuss with me. So when Penny reached the end of her anecdote, I whispered to her, "Don't look behind you. Jax Aiken and Heavy Artillery are here."

"Who in the world is that?" she exclaimed, flipping her pashmina and then adjusting her trademark enamel bangles as she swiveled around to gawk at them.

"I said, don't look."

"Sorry," she chuckled. "You didn't answer my question."

"They're only the hottest indie neo-punk band going," I explained, unsuccessfully trying to stop my face from flushing scarlet since it was clear the band had realized we were staring at them. "Remember, I told you I met them at the Sunset Marquis when I was in LA with Dash? They were super nice—the lead guitarist Jax, especially."

"I don't even know what indie neo-punk means." She laughed again.

"Do I have lip gloss on my teeth?" I asked suddenly.

"Kitten, are you going to stalk those boys? Jax, especially?" she queried, her blue eyes peering down at me from over the tops of her tortoise-shell glasses.

"I am not stalking them. Jax called me when I was leaving to meet you and said he had business to discuss with me," I answered. "My whole life can't be about butts, breasts, and vaginas, can it?"

"Couldn't have said it any better myself." Penny winked and flipped her pashmina, her signal that it was fine to leave her for the time being.

"If it isn't Sarah Saffron Mandelbaum Meadows." Jax's whole face smiled as he slid over on the banquette so I could sit down next to him. "Where's your hat?"

"Slash needed it back," I replied, amazed at how smoothly that response slid out.

"And this? This is your real hair?" he asked, playfully tugging on one of my black curls.

"Why, yes. Yes, it is."

"Well, it suits you—suits you down to the ground. Doesn't it, lads?" Malcolm, Camden, and Magnus murmured their agreement. "And did you get your Gold Top, then?"

"No. Not yet," I sighed.

"Well, lass, what're you waiting for, then? Seize the day, I always say." Before I could make my usual lame excuses, he picked up my hand, gave it an enthusiastic squeeze, and continued. "We're having a little whiskey," he said. "Funny place, this is, just like you said. Shall we get you a glass, then?" Jax was now facing me on the banquette, all mischief and magic, his ridiculously glimmering green eyes rimmed with violet kohl liner.

"Yeah, it's not quite as hot as it used to be," I admitted. "I'd love to have a drink with you guys except I'm here with a friend and another one is joining us. Jax said you guys have something you wanted to talk about. So tell me. I'm all ears." I pushed ahead, gaining more and more confidence as I spoke.

Somehow, these boys just inspired me.

"Here's the thing. We're going to head back into the studio soon for our next album and we're wondering if you want to come play with us a few times before we do to see how and if you can work with us on it," Jax said, his eyes getting even bigger and brighter. "Your versions of "Heaven or Las Vegas" and "Can't You Hear Me Knocking" were smashing and we have at least two new tracks we think you may be brilliant on."

"And since we just signed a bloody amazing deal with a major label, we can even pay you if it works out," Magnus said, raising his glass and downing his whiskey in one neat gulp.

"Really?" You could have knocked me over with a feather.

"As long as you don't step on my lead," Jax said with a broad grin, using the industry jargon for when one musician tries to steal another's thunder during his or her big solo.

"Or mine," Camden chimed in. A lead singer was never going to be outdone by a mere guitar player.

"Well, we can't pay you a fortune but it should be a fair amount of pocket change," Malcolm, always the Eeyore, interjected.

"There you go again, raining on everyone's parade," Jax said, punching him lightly in the arm.

"What's your timing for this?" I asked all four of them.

"The sooner the better. We've got some studio time booked over the next week or so here for rehearsals, and then we'll likely record at Nightbird Studios at the Sunset Marquis next month," Camden replied.

"I don't think I can get away from work," I answered, not quite sure how I could even think about *Sophistiquée* magazine on such a momentous occasion. This was maybe the coolest thing that'd ever happened to me. "I mean, I guess I could take some vacation days." Everyone got really quiet and avoided making eye contact with me. Magnus even started to drum a little bit on the table with his hands as if I weren't there. I guess they were trying to not show me how shocked and offended they were that I'd even think of turning down the opportunity to play with one of the hottest, solvent bands going. I could've kicked myself.

"Tell you what, you think about it and give me a call tomorrow," Jax said at last, breaking the silence. Reaching into the pocket of his purple velvet pants, he took out a green Sharpie, wrote a phone number on my palm, and gently blew on it to dry it.

When I floated back to the table, Esme was there, wearing her new uniform of wrecked jeans, white canvas Vans, and a PETA T-shirt. She looked fabulous. Penny had thoughtfully asked the waiter to whisk our martinis away, and they were both sipping sodas— Sprite for Penny and ginger ale and OJ for Esme. A Diet Coke with lemon sat waiting for me. Pen was the best. The two of them were in deep conversation with three stocky middle-aged men wearing expensive suits seated at the next table. I could tell it was serious because Penny was twisting one of her chestnut waves around her index finger and only nodded at me rather than asking me how it went with Jax when I slid back into my seat. Of course, I was out of my mind with wanting to tell her and Esme.

One of the men they were conversing with was

sweating profusely and even more crimson-faced than I was. He was also pounding the table with his fist and growling, "Fucking writers. I hate fucking writers. And what's with this place? It's totally dead." It was Stone Stephens from that hotter-than-hot Showtime series. There was no mistaking those big, red, wet lips and bushy, black eyebrows. Clearly, he hadn't realized that Arcadia was over and that he needed to hightail it downtown if he wanted any kind of action at all.

"You'll have to excuse him. He's had some bad write-ups in the tabloids recently and the one today was a doozy," said either Stone's accountant or lawyer. Funny, I'd been so obsessed with the *Sentinel's* poosey story scandal that I hadn't read the rest of the paper. I couldn't help but wonder what dirt it had on Stone— probably that he was on his way to earning a drunk and disorderly charge.

The waiter appeared, bringing another round of soft drinks that we hadn't ordered. "Compliments of Mr. Jax Aiken," he said with a flourish.

"Oh my God! Is Jax Aiken hitting on you? What did you say to him?" Penny exclaimed, temporarily turning her attention away from Stone.

"I mean nothing, really, except we talked about working together, which would be amazing."

"What's that number on your hand?" Esme demanded, also breaking away from Stone.

"I think that's Jax's phone number," I replied, and couldn't help but smile just a little.

"I rest my case," Penny said, patting my shoulder and turning her attention back to Stone Stephens.

"Who the fuck is Jax Aiken?" Stone sneered at her, spitting a little as he tossed his head in my direction.

"Only the lead guitar player in Heavy Artillery, the hottest indie neo-punk band going," Penny replied, as if she was their biggest fan.

"Well, how the fuck does she know him, then?"

"Kitten knows everybody," Penny said.

"Indeed, I do," I said, deciding to play along. I was feeling pretty fluffy for a change. Heavy Artillery wanted me to jam with them, and *the* Jax Aiken had given me his number and bought me and my girls a round of drinks, even if they were just sodas.

"Why the fuck does she know everybody?" Stone snarled, still not addressing me directly.

"Oh, that's easy," I purred slipping into Saffron Meadows mode. "I'm a writer." Stone's wingmen suddenly stopped chatting amongst themselves and stared at me apprehensively as Stone finally directed his full attention toward me.

"You're a fucking writer?" he practically screamed. "Who the fuck do you write for, and why are you here? I better not read about this in *The Sentinel*."

This guy certainly was smooth. I knew Penny was racing to think of a way to come to my rescue, and it took every ounce of self-restraint Esme had to not throw her drink in his face.

"Well, a songwriter and a musician," I said in the soothing tone that I reserved for crying children and blustering blowhards. "Perhaps you've heard some of my music?"

"What's your name? You don't look like a musician to me," he barked, eying Irma's charcoal grey Tahari pants and rose-colored Theory sweater.

"It's Saffron. Saffron Meadows."

"Oh yeah, I've heard of you. Aren't you the one

that played with the band at the Très Cher after-party? And didn't I read in the *Sentinel* that you had an affair with that Australian drummer and wrecked his marriage?" Stone did his signature eyebrow cock and dropped his tone down several octaves to what I think he thought was his seductive voice. And if I'm not mistaken, he also slid closer to me on the banquette our two tables shared. So gross. Stone's cohorts relaxed their pained expressions and gazed at me almost adoringly. Penny was shaking with a silent, self-contained laughter that threatened to explode out of her at any second. This was getting good, so I certainly wasn't going to tell him that I'd never had a relationship with a drummer of any kind, much less a married Australian one. How on earth had he fabricated that story?

"Hey, you guys, do you want to play a game we used to play at Silver Sequoia?" Esme was clearly bored with Stone and taking over the conversation. This was going to be good. Now that Esme wasn't drinking, it was always loads of fun when she slid into the driver's seat.

"You went to Silver Sequoia?" Stone sniggered. "So that's why you girls are teetotalers. I never trust people who don't drink."

"You might want to reconsider that, and consider, at least, a short stay there." Esme sounded serious for a second. "My family has a lot of pull there. I could book you a bed tonight if you want." Stone's friends both looked like they thought that would be a terrific idea. I know I did. Stone, however, had other things in mind.

"What game?" he asked me, instead of Esme, as eager as they come.

"It's the "Who Would You Pay Money to Have Sex with" game," Esme explained to our now captive audience.

The younger of Stone's two companions almost sang as he asked, "How does it work?"

"We go around the restaurant and guess what type of person the people sitting here would hire for sex and then tell on ourselves," she said, leaning into the middle of the table to reel in her already captive audience. "Like, for example, that guy in the plaid pants, red polo, and baseball cap sitting with the two crying kids. Who do you think he'd pay money to do it with?"

Stone's accountant and lawyer put their heads together until they reached a consensus.

"That guy would be all about a dominatrix. There's no way he's not leading a secret underground life," the younger of the two said pensively.

"Nice. What about Jax Aiken?" Esme asked, looking pointedly at me. There was no question she was in this for the long haul and enjoying herself tremendously.

"He's a rock star, so he probably never has to pay for it," one of Stone's cohorts mused. "He's tough, though, with all that eyeliner and femme clothes. Hard to get a read on his type."

"You guys are so lame. That's an insanely easy one. He'd obviously go for Sarah Mandelbaum." I nearly spit my Diet Coke out onto the table.

"Sarah Mandelbaum? Who's that?" they asked in unison.

"You don't know Sarah Mandelbaum?" Penny asked. "Well, you should. She's a great girl and super close pals with our buddy Saffron, here."

Thankfully, before we could talk about me and Jax anymore, Esme moved on. "And you?" she asked the suit sitting closest to her.

"Oh, I don't know. A lingerie model, I guess. If I'm paying for the pleasure, it should be someone with a killer body," he said, nodding his head for emphasis.

"Good choice, even if it's not original and likely out of your league," Esme responded, taking a delicate sip of her OJ and ginger ale. "And you?" She nodded over to Stone's other buddy.

"Hmm." He furrowed his brows, giving this life-or-death question the time and attention he thought it deserved. "It's a tough one. I guess I'd pick a painter. Creativity and artistry are always pluses when it comes to sex."

"That's a good one," Esme allowed, scanning the menu. "I had you pegged for paying for a naughty librarian." I could tell she was searching for something vegetarian. Penny and I stayed quiet, trying not to look at each other for fear we'd burst out laughing. The best was yet to come.

"How about you?" Esme asked Stone, who hadn't seemed to be paying attention and was now practically sitting in my lap.

He raised his eyebrow again and leaned in to whisper in my ear, as though I'd asked the question, "How about me, what?"

"Who would you pay money to have sex with?" Esme asked as I shifted myself as far away from him on the banquette as its tiny size would allow.

"What? Why the fuck are you asking me that? Next thing I know I'm going to read in the tabloids that I fuck prostitutes. Nice try," Stone roared, once again pounding the table with his fist.

Penny, Esme, and I looked at each other and knew, without saying a word, that we'd reached our limit. Penny signaled for the check, which we paid quickly in cash, and stood up without so much as a glance at Stone or his associates. As we got to the door near Jax Aiken's table, Stone lumbered to his feet and shouted at me from across the room. "Hey, Saffron, you never said who *you'd* pay money to have sex with."

Without fully turning around, and with as much swagger as I'd ever had in my life, I tossed over my shoulder, "Saffron Meadows doesn't pay for sex."

"Wrong answer," Stone chided, sitting down quickly, his face so fiery I was pretty sure smoke would start swirling out of his ears. As I reached the door, Jax raised his glass in my direction and smiled.

Chapter 16

Vladimir was waiting for us at the curb. We decided to go to my place, eat Chunky Monkey and Doritos, talk about Esme's fantastic new gig with the ASPCA, recap our crazy time with that jackwad Stone Stephens, and discuss that amazing offer from Heavy Artillery. I also wanted Esme's and Penny's take on how I could sneak away from work to jam with them. Of course, with that poosey story/ Henri-François/*Sentinel* fiasco, as of tomorrow, I may not have any work to sneak away from. With all the drama of the evening, we hadn't even covered any of this, and I was hoping they'd have some sage advice on how I could turn things around at *Sophistiquée*. Once in the car, we all agreed that there was no question that Samara was clearly not just self-involved, self-promoting, and insubordinate and that Christie wasn't just jaded, embittered, and self-entitled. They were out for blood. Mine. And I'd been blind, lazy, stupid, or all three for not realizing it and taking action sooner.

"Kitten, I know you like to give everyone the benefit of the doubt and I don't think we need to restate the obvious but these girls have been up to no good since you started there, and maybe even as soon as they heard you were hired," Penny said as Vladimir sped up the Major Deegan to the Bronx. "Didn't Fiona tell you from the get-go that Christie was gunning for your job?

348

And didn't even Henri-Francois warn you they were liabilities versus assets? Besides, the *Sentinel* article quoted word for word what Christie said to you about that ridiculous vagina story. Christie or Samara or both of them planted that story in the *Sentinel* to cook up even more conflict between you and Henri-Francois."

"What I want to know," Esme cut in, her voice taking on that 'don't push me 'cause I'm close to the edge' tone, "Is why that whore of an ex-roommate of yours keeps showing up, and why she's so buddy-buddy with your so-called staff every time they supposedly just run into each other at industry events. And more importantly, I want to know what she stood to gain from being a lying little bitch about what happened with Astro Jensen." Esme paused for a moment to tear into the bag of Doritos that Vladimir had thoughtfully placed on the backseat and stuff a handful of chips into her mouth. "You have to confront them about this," she said before she'd even finished chewing and swallowing. "And you have to tell that a-hole Henri-François to back the hell off. You can't let people shit all over you the way you did in school. This is real life."

Penny had other ideas. "You know what I think, kitten, because I've told you. You need to go to HR. You'd at least be protecting yourself by telling your side of the story and what a harassing sexist jerk Henri-François is, and that he, Christie, Samara, and Giancarlo are all creating a hostile work environment for you," she said, twisting round to look back at me from her seat up front. "Though, honestly, don't you think it's time to tell them all to go to hell and walk out? Haven't you had enough?"

I didn't remind her that it took ages for her to do that very thing with Rex and that when she did, it was only after she'd already lined up *Savannah Sweets*. I left that sort of look-who's-talking-self-righteous-indignation-stuff up to Anna Elias Mandelbaum and, besides, I knew that Penny was only looking out for me. I also didn't remind her of how badly alerting the higher-ups to a sexual harassment situation had turned out for me with the whole Astro Jensen thing since I didn't feel like thinking about my crappy past when I had more immediate crappy problems in the present. So instead, I just sighed and said, "Well, friends, I thank you for your love, support, and suggestions. I do think we're forgetting, however, that my future at *Sophistiquée* is probably no longer in my hands. Henri-François made it pretty clear that I was likely out of there."

As we pulled up to my building, I saw Sean in his white Levi denim jacket and 501s sitting outside on the stoop. He was smoking, of course, and looked about as glum as I felt. I hoped against hope it wasn't because he was deeply unhappy to see me. Still, maybe, just maybe, there was a valid explanation for his blowing me off. There was only one way to find out.

"I'm going to talk to Sean for a minute," I said to Esme and Penny, ignoring their looks—concerned from Penny and outraged from Esme—as we got out of the car. They were over Sean, even if I wasn't. "You guys go on up. Do either of you have your key?" Penny sought my eyes as she dug around in her robin's egg blue Kate Spade bag and then jingled the Aerosmith mini harmonica keychain with my keys that I'd given her. Even though I knew she was probably right to worry about how things were about to go down, I couldn't bring myself to make eye contact with her because seeing all her apprehension would've made me lose my nerve. Surely there was some reason for the beyond-heinous way Sean'd been acting.

Esme continued to fish Doritos out of the now half-empty bag she was holding with orange-stained fingers, staring pointedly at Sean all the while. It was pretty obvious she was about to let loose with one of her "scrawny old guy" comments, which clearly would not help get this conversation off on the right foot. So I was beyond relieved when Pen walked on ahead to open the front door, calling behind her, "Come on, Es, ice cream's going to melt," which prompted Esme to reluctantly tear herself away before she uttered an insult of any kind.

"Hi, stranger. You've been pretty busy this past month," I said as lightly as I could, walking over to him. I was too anxious to plunk myself down on the stoop next to him, so I stood awkwardly beside him.

"Oh, yeah. Hi, Sarah. It's been a little nutty. How are you?" he responded in that disconcerting, vague, detached way he'd adopted lately, and then abruptly got to his feet. This was not good.

"Um. It's been kind of mixed. But I, um, had some good news tonight," I said, forging ahead despite my gut instinct that I was entering the hopeless zone. "Remember the message I left when I was in LA the other day about playing Camden Aiken's Hummingbird and singing a couple of tunes for Heavy Artillery? Well, it turns out they, um, thought I was pretty good."

"Yeah, sorry I didn't get back to you about that. That sounded pretty cool," Sean replied, lighting up another American Spirit and not looking at me.

"Well, it *is* cool. Really cool. They want me to jam with them this week to see if I can work with them on their next album." This last bit of news finally prompted Sean to look at me, although not with the expression of happiness I'd hoped for; he was scowling.

"What about us? If you play with them, you can't play with us," he snapped. His voice was seething with resentment.

"What?"

"Sarah, we've all been considering you part of One-Eyed Snake. And now here you are, just throwing us under the bus when something brighter and shinier comes along." His voice continued to rise. "We have those two festivals coming up, then we're going to do the soundtrack for that documentary we got from the Très Cher after party, and then we're going back into the studio to record our next album. You're just going to walk away from all of that and leave us hanging?"

"What? I'm not walking away from anything," I said. "I'd make sure there were no conflicts. I'd never screw you guys over. Besides, Ollie's been telling me that these are just plans in the works and that nothing's finalized yet."

"Well, you'd better check with him because to my mind, you're either with us or with them. You can't have it both ways," Sean said, turning away from me and walking toward our building.

"People jam with different bands all the time. Look at all those studio cats like Larry Carlton and Jim Keltner who play on everyone's albums. And what about Flea and Dave Navarro playing for both Jane's Addiction and the Chili Peppers?" I asked, skipping a little to try and keep up with him. I couldn't believe he was so upset.

"Well, you're not exactly any of those musicians, are you?" he retorted, slowing down so the full impact of his words could hit me. And they hit hard, but nowhere near as hard as the next ones. "And besides," he continued, practically snarling, "this is probably more about Jax Aiken wanting to get in your pants than anything else. He's that type of a guy, you know."

I thought I would have to sit down on the front stoop. Sean had completely and utterly knocked the wind out of me.

Somehow, someway, instead, I managed to pick up my pace so I could pass him and make it into the building first, all the while praying he would stop for one last smoke outside so I wouldn't have to see him sprinting up the stairs to get away from me. Yet something inside of me started to stir, and I decided not to let him off the hook so easily. I'd had enough of aggressive and insulting a-holes for the evening, maybe even forever.

"You know, that's a really shitty thing to say, which I guess shouldn't surprise me because you've been really shitty to me for a while now. So maybe you're just a really shitty person." And with that, I turned on my heel and flounced off. When I got inside my apartment, Penny and Esme were kind of hovering around and hadn't even dug into the ice cream yet. Clearly, they'd been talking about me, because they got super quiet as soon as I came in and took Irma's purple Patagonia down puffer off.

"How'd it go, kitten?" Penny asked, even though she could read the answer in my face.

"Not good. You know, he's really kind of a dick."

"I called it the second his scrawny old ass walked into your apartment that night. What's his damage, anyway?" Esme asked as she moved into the kitchen.

"You know, I don't know. I guess I can just add him to the steaming pile of poo that I seem to be standing in these days." I was definitely feeling sorry for myself.

"Do you want to tell us what happened?" Penny asked, taking my jacket off the back of the chair I'd thrown it on and hanging it up on one of the hooks by the front door.

"I don't think I can even talk about it. I feel kind of sick." I flopped onto my couch and pulled Granny Sarah's afghan up to my chin.

"Well, fuck him. Jax Aiken is way hotter, way cooler, and way more appreciative of you," Esme called out over the clattering of spoons and bowls from the kitchen. When she came out of the kitchen, she snuggled under the blanket with me and Penny, making, as she called it, a "Kitten sandwich." It was sweet. They were sweet. Just as we were settling in, there was a knock on my door. I'd be lying if I didn't admit my pulse raced a little, thinking it was Sean coming to apologize.

"That better not be that dirtbag," Esme growled, scrambling to her feet and putting her bowl of Chunky Monkey down on the coffee table with a bang. Penny squeezed my hand under the afghan—her signal that she knew I was hoping it was Sean and she wasn't judging me for it.

But as Esme opened the door, it was Holt's voice that answered her greeting.

"Well, looks like I've died and gone to heaven," he boomed as soon as he saw our bowls of ice cream and bags of Doritos. "Here I am with a bunch of amazing women and my favorite foods. Don't think life can get any better than this." He was all smiles until he realized Penny and I were huddled under the afghan, not looking one bit like we were in heaven. "Wait. What's this? What's wrong?" he asked, his brows furrowing as he shrugged off his jacket.

"Sarah's having a rough time of it at work and in matters of the heart," Penny answered for me. Holt wedged his enormous frame in the teeny space Esme'd inhabited next to me and patted my cheek.

"You just tell me who done you wrong, Sarah sugar, and I'll set them straight." He made a fist with his other hand, shaking it. I smiled as best I could, but it was a pretty feeble attempt.

"So, Holt, to what do we owe this honor? Not that we aren't tickled to see you," Penny asked, changing the subject to spare me any further explanation.

"Well, ladies, despite our needing to rally for our Sarah, we also have something to celebrate," Holt said as he accepted a heaping bowl of Chunky Monkey from Esme. "Darius announced his retirement today. So, guess whose starting next season?"

"Aw, Holt, that's amazing," I said, feeling the excruciating tightness in my stomach loosen a little. I even pondered eating some of the ice cream that was sitting untouched in front of me.

"See, I told you it would happen. So proud of you," Penny said, reaching around me to give him a playful punch in the shoulder and then ducked out of the way before he could retaliate.

Holt hung around another hour or so trying to cheer me up, which almost worked until he got up to leave around midnight and said, "Well, ladies, it's been lovely. But I'm off to meet my sweetheart."

"Your sweetheart? You have a new girlfriend? How did I not know this?" Penny asked, teetering between happiness for her brother and annoyance that he hadn't given her the intel on this crucial development sooner.

"Well, she's not exactly new," Holt said, suddenly sheepish.

"Don't tell me you're back with that horror show of a hooker who cheated on you with Richie when he got promoted and you didn't." Penny was standing up now, clearly restraining herself not to shake her finger in her twin brother's face, the masculine mirror image of her own. "And considering all the trouble she's made for Sarah, it's mind-boggling to me how you could take up with her again."

"Sorry, big sister, but the flesh is weak," Holt replied with that damn infectious grin of his and kissed Penny on the top of her head before turning to me. "Fret not, Sarah Sugar. I will speak to Desiree. I'm sure this is all just a misunderstanding that can be worked out in a jiffy." And even though I wanted to, I didn't believe him.

After Holt left, we stayed up another hour trying to figure out a plan to stem this storm of shit that was raining down on me at *Sophistiquée*. Sadly, we couldn't come up with a single thing that didn't involve my quitting or getting fired, which financially was not in my best interests. We did manage, however, to get all the details on Esme's new post and Penny's upcoming episodes of Savannah Sweets, relive our excitement for Holt while trying to figure out how to knock some sense into him, and laugh ourselves hoarse about Stone Stephens.

I woke up the next morning not feeling my best and brightest. I was emotionally hungover from my run-in with Sean and knew, without question, that whatever Henri-François had in store for me would not be good. After a quick shower, I peered into my closet at all of Irma's lovely things and just pulled out a pair of charcoal jeans and a black V-neck sweater. Without question, they were practically the best damn jeans and black V-neck money could buy, but they were quiet. And that's what I wanted. I popped gorgeous George Harrison's "All Things Must Pass" into my Walkman and headed over to the 1/9.

I wasn't in my office for more than fifteen minutes when Henri-François flew into the room in such a frenzy that his crotch had to catch up with the rest of him before it could assume its customary place center stage. He was clutching the *Sentinel* opened to a picture of me, Stone Stephens, and Jax Aiken at Arcadia. It was taken just as I was striding out the door, while Jax was "toasting" me, and Stone was standing at his table shouting after me. The headline read: "They're Just Mad about Saffron" with the accompanying caption: "Rock star rolls with two celebs in one night." Oddly, the paper seemed to have forgotten that it ran negative press and pictures of me as Sarah Mandelbaum all the time.

"Sarraah, *you* are Saffron Meadows? How is this possible?" He was practically spitting with rage. "How can you be a rock star when you are not even a mediocre beauty and fitness editor? How do you explain this?"

How did I explain this? I thought for just a minute and then replied rapidly in my near-fluent French, "*Oui*, Henri-François. *Je suis Saffron Meadows et elle est moi*." As if on cue, my phone rang. I briefly looked at the incoming number. It was Giancarlo. He would have to wait.

"Sarraah, you speak French?" You could knock Henri-François and his body-constricting white jeans over with a feather, which even in the midst of all of this craziness, made me smile just a little.

"*Bien sur*," I confirmed, sliding my Rolodex and Irma's ballet flats into her Vuitton tote. "*Et je pense que c'est toi pas moi qui dois fair l'exercice. Tu obtiens plutôt un grande panse*." I'd just told him quite calmly that he was the one who needed to exercise because of his paunch, which was getting rather large. And with that, I glided gracefully out the door before he could respond. Saffron Meadows and I were leaving the building. As I passed Samara's desk where my "staff" was hovering over the *Sentinel* article, I stopped briefly and turned to Christie.

"Guess you won," I said as I watched her preternaturally pale complexion turn a less-than-flattering shade of crimson. At least she had the good grace to flush. "Oh yeah, I know all about you and your back-stabbing schemes to steal my job," I continued. "You're not as clever as you imagine. And I can't think of a better person than you for the position, considering what a soulless hell hole this is. We've done butts, breasts, and poosies. I guess penises are up next. So you can have at it."

"And you—don't think I don't see you for who you are." I wheeled around to face Samara, who immediately started to sputter out an excuse, which I waved away with a sweep of my arm.

I saw a brief smile cross Christie's face. I didn't know if it was because she'd won, because she'd been spot on about my being Saffron Meadows when everyone else had somehow missed the boat, or because I'd finally let Samara have it. In the end, I decided I didn't care.

As I walked down the hall, I heard Henri-François bellowing after me in astonishingly perfect English, "Sarah, you cannot quit because I am firing you. And do not kid yourself that you are anything special because of this article. You are nothing and will *always* be nothing."

I just kept right on walking onto the elevator, across the lobby, and through the revolving doors. I started to take the stairs down to the street two at a time but stopped dead in my tracks when I saw Des in a daffodil-yellow Ralph Lauren Collection coat, bounding up.

"Well, hi, you. Beautiful day so far, isn't it?" She wasn't actually chewing gum, but she might as well have been.

"You know, Des, I could ask you what you're doing here and how you got a hold of that coat, except I honestly don't care."

"Honey, you are such a meanie," she said, barreling ahead as usual despite my expressed indifference. "I'm meeting Christie. She's taking me to the Chanel sample sale. She also gave me this coat and got me a full-time job with Kevin Carson. Unlike some people, she knows how to be a good friend. Maybe we'll see you at Chanel later today."

"No, Des. I can assure you that you and Christie will not be seeing me at Chanel later today or hopefully ever again."

"I don't see what you have to be so snippy about. From what I've been told, Christie is in line to become the new beauty director of *Sophistiquée*, and you are exactly what?" Des paused for a moment to look me square in the eyes. When I didn't blink or break away, she shifted her gaze down to her coat. "Okay. Bye now. Have to dash," she murmured, first untying and then retying its already perfectly knotted belt, and then at last starting to move away from me up the stairs, causing me to wonder if she was having a momentary crisis of conscience for her role in my short-lived career at *Sophistiquée* coming to a screeching halt. That is until she suddenly stopped dead in her tracks and called out, "You have a great day now, honey. I'll tell Holt you said hi." What a relief. The world order was slowly being restored. Des was still Des.

Without looking back for even a second, I practically skipped down the stairs and over to the nearest payphone.

Nils picked up on the first ring. "Petersen," he grunted into the phone, not quite above the din of his clattering keyboard.

"Nils, it's Sarah."

"Well, if it isn't the rock star? That was some story in the *Sentinel* this morning. How'd Henri-François and Giancarlo take it?"

"Badly. But that doesn't matter now because I left *Sophistiquée* this morning." Student loans

360

notwithstanding, I felt oddly serene about my departure.

"Well, that was always maybe the worst place on record for you. So good for you for getting the hell out of there. I have every confidence you'll land on your feet."

"Thanks, Nils. Hey, can I pick Dana up from school today? It'd be great to have her with me when I finally snag that Gold Top from Matt Umanov's. Also, I may be jamming after that with Heavy Artillery and I want her to come with."

"You're going to play with Heavy Artillery? That's fantastic. And you know, if you want to get back into music writing, I'd be happy to make some calls for you. No one other than that piece-of-garbage editor who fired you ever thought Astro Jensen was anything other than a no-talent prick. And now the former's been shipped off to *Grocery Store Weekly* and the latter's in jail."

"You know about Jensen?"

"Yes."

"Why didn't you say anything?" This was completely and utterly shocking to me. So much so, I could barely register the little bit of joy I felt over that bastard editor who'd banished me to FDG being exiled to a much lowlier publication.

"Ursula and I wanted to bring it up with you about a thousand times, and I tried to give you an opening to talk about it here and there," he replied. "But we decided we should respect your privacy." The wheels in my head started to turn fast and furiously. If he knew my secret, then it was time he told me his.

"Okay, Nils, since you knew all along about how I landed at FDG, you have to tell me how *you* got there.

One doesn't leave the glamorous life of a rock critic to cover the beauty industry unless there's a really good reason."

"Don't tell me you've been brooding and stewing over that this whole time we've known each other." Nils guffawed so uproariously he started to cough. "There was nothing mysterious about my getting a respectable job," he finally continued after he'd collected himself. "It was time to grow up."

"That's it?"

"That's it. Sorry to disappoint you." He laughed again, more of a chuckle this time, and then shifted back into business mode. "Listen, I'm trapped in a towering inferno, and I only have a squirt gun to extinguish the flames, so I have to motor. I'll leave word for Dana at her school that you're picking her up. Thanks for including her and congrats. This is great news." After we hung up, I slid more quarters into the slot and dialed the next number on my list. Thankfully, Ollie was home.

"Hey, it's me," I said.

"If it isn't the newest member of Heavy Artillery—Ms. Saffron Meadows. To what do I owe the honor?"

"You know?"

"I know everything, grasshopper," he replied. "The universe whispers all of its secrets to me." I could almost see him smiling over the phone. "Well, actually, Jax called me the other day to see if he could poach you away from us for a project."

"He called you?"

"Sure. We go way back. He's a great guy. This is amazing. You're going to kick ass in the studio with them."

"And can I still play with One-Eyed Snake—I mean if you want me to—*and* play with them?"

"Of course. People work on multiple projects all the time. Look at Flea and Dave Navarro and studio guys like Carlton and Keltner."

"That's not what Sean said last night. He was pretty pissed about the whole thing."

"Well, Sean's kinda intense. You know, he has a lot on his plate these days. His ex is moving with Wyatt to South Carolina at the end of the school year to be near her family, so he's going to have to find a job down there and relocate this summer."

"Hmm. Maybe that's why he's been such a dick to me lately." I felt lighter all of a sudden, relieved there was an explanation other than Sean simply not being into me, or that he was just a total jackhole. And then I realized maybe it didn't matter all that much because a jackhole was a jackhole and I shouldn't have to make excuses for him—no matter how hazel his eyes, how sinewy his body, how adorable his crooked front tooth, how great a guitarist he was, or what kind of crisis he was going through.

"Sean's being a dick to you?" Ollie interrupted my thoughts.

"Yeah. Kind of."

"Well, I don't like that. Maybe it's a good thing he's moving to Charleston, then."

"But what does that mean for One-Eyed Snake?"

"It means the band will be me, you, Charisse, and Mayumi."

"You want me in the band?"

"We all want you in the band," Ollie said, forever patient with me.

"You mean One-Eyed Snake is going to be you and three chicks?"

"No. It's going to be me and three rock stars," he corrected. And then I remembered the other reason I called him.

"Hey, are you doing open mic tonight at Sidewalk?"

"You know it."

"If you get there before I do, can you sign me up to play?" There was a stone-cold silence on the other end. Perhaps he'd fainted from shock.

But being the extraordinary human that he was, Ollie rebounded quickly and said, "That's dope. Put you down as Saffron Meadows?"

"Actually," I replied. "It'd be great if you signed me up as Sarah. Sarah Mandelbaum."

"Cool," he said. "I'll see you there, Mandelbaum."

After we hung up, I picked up the phone one last time to call Jax. Luckily, he'd written his number on my hand in indelible ink.

A Note from the Author

Thanks so much for reading *The Rise, Fall, and Return of Sarah Mandelbaum*. I hope you enjoyed it. Sarah started out as a way more talented fictionalized me (she plays guitar a lot better than I do, for example) and with my building her world around fictionalized accounts of some of my more momentous experiences in and out of the fashion industry.

But soon enough, she took on a life of her own. Her independence from me was further cemented when a woman in one of my creative writing classes completely disagreed with me when I said that Sarah was a version of me. "There's no way Sarah is you," she said, as emphatically as I've heard anyone say anything. "She is way cooler than you."

If you enjoyed the book, I'd be so grateful if you would consider leaving a review at your online bookstore, on Goodreads, or Bookbub. And I'd be so happy if you select *The Rise, Fall, and Return of Sarah Mandelbaum* for your book group. If you do, please send me a photo of your group by uploading it to the Contact form on my website www.carakagan.com and I will add it to my photo gallery.

I also send huge thanks to anyone who tags me in their social media posts, shares this book on social media or with friends, asks for it, or for me to do a reading at your local bookstore or library. You liking the book and recommending it means the world to me. And please also let me know what parts resonated with you the most and what you'd like me to write next.

My very best to you,
Cara

Questions for Book Group Discussion

I hope these questions will enhance your book group's discussion of *The Rise, Fall, and Return of Sarah Mandelbaum.* They are meant to stimulate conversation and enjoyment of the book. You can find more information and events related to the book on my website: carakagan.com.

1—Do you think Sarah's excuses for continuing to live with Desiree are valid? Have you ever been in a living situation like this? What did it take for you to leave?

2—Why is Sarah's hair such a magnet for criticism and ridicule? Have you ever experienced someone critiquing you for something so seemingly trivial? What did you do?

3—Morrisa is distant and dismissive of her family and Sarah is involved with it. Why does Anna Elias Mandelbaum seem to favor Morrisa over Sarah? Or does she?

4—Sarah constantly says she is not interested in fashion, yet she is unquestionably excited by Irma's hand-me-downs, especially the Balenciaga handbag. How would you explain this contradiction?

5—Even though Saffron Meadows is just a figment of Ollie's imagination, she seems to inspire Sarah. Why do you think that is?

6—How can so many people continue to work with Henri-François despite his abusive behavior? How does he continue to stay in power with so many lawsuits against him and so much negative press being written about him?

7—How is Sarah different from the rest of the staff at *Sophistiquée* and fashion magazines in general? How is she similar?

8—Why does Sarah find it so difficult to deal with Henri-François' attitude and demands when Christie and Samara seem to handle them and even prefer him to Fiona as their boss?

9—How is it that Sarah and Christie have so much in common but can't seem to find a common ground?

10—How does working at *Sophistiquée* change Sarah? Are these positive or negative changes?

11—Do you think there is a shift in Sarah's attitude when she is out to dinner with her friends and Stone Stevens? If so, how would you describe it and what do you think caused it?

12—What do you think finally helped Sarah take charge of her life and stand up to her bullies?

13—Why do you think Sarah finally agrees to do an open mic with Ollie? How do you think it will go?

14—Were you surprised Sarah chose to use her real name vs. Saffron Meadows on the open mic signup sheet? Why do you think she did?

15—What direction do you think Sarah's career will take post-*Sophistiquée*? What about her relationship with Jax?

A word about the author…

Cara Kagan is a writer and musician who has contributed to many national magazines, including *Self*, *Shape, Fitness, Glamour, Real Simple, InStyle*, *Harper's Bazaar*, and *The New York Post Alexa* section.

She got her start writing style and beauty in the trenches as an editor for the fashion and beauty bible *Women's Wear Daily*, and then went on to become beauty and fitness director for both *YM* and *Mode* magazines.

She is most proud of creating *Girl* magazine, the first multi-cultural and multi-size fashion and beauty magazine for teens. Despite her wild hair, sensible shoes, and decidedly "basic" fashion sense, she also served as the beauty and fitness director of *Elle* magazine for several years.

In 1990, her Grandma Ruth Appelbaum insisted on inviting Andrew Kagan to her 90th birthday party completely against her wishes. They married in 1992. They have two grey and white rescue kitties, Mouse and Clyde, and live in the Bronx.

While she still mainly sings and plays guitar for her cats and guitar teacher, she hopes that one day soon, she will finally get up the nerve to perform at an open mic.

carakagan.com